# THE STEALERS

## CHARLES HALL

Matador
9 Priory Business Park,
Wistow Road, Kibworth Beauchamp,
Leicestershire. LE8 0RX
Tel: 0116 279 2299
Email: books@troubador.co.uk
Web: www.troubador.co.uk/matador
Twitter: @matadorbooks

ISBN 978 1784623 593

British Library Cataloguing in Publication Data.
A catalogue record for this book is available from the British Library.

Printed and bound in the UK by TJ International, Padstow, Cornwall
Typeset in 11pt Garamond by Troubador Publishing Ltd, Leicester, UK

**Matador** is an imprint of Troubador Publishing Ltd

*Dedicated to Jack & William Birch*

*In remembrance of my friend, John Hackling*

# ACKNOWLEDGEMENTS

Special thanks to my wife, Jacqueline, for her patient scrutiny of *The Stealers* prior to publication.

*'All that is necessary for the triumph of evil is when good men do nothing.'*
Edmund Burke

# PART ONE

PART ONE

# CHAPTER ONE

Dusk began to cast its heavy mantle over the Thames Estuary. A frantic voice, carried on the rain-flecked wind, drifted across the open tarmac space as Jack Crane walked briskly across the deserted public car park, adjacent to the promenade at Southend-on-Sea. The sound did not connect, as he strode hurriedly towards his cherished iconic 1966 Ford Mustang convertible. His eyes were focused on the ground, guiding strong, nimble legs around huge puddles that had been formed by a recent heavy downpour. The desperate voice called out again, but now it was much closer and was accompanied by the patter of footsteps slapping hurriedly on the wet surface. This time it caught his attention; it was a desperate plea for help.

Crane tossed the shopping bags that he had been carrying into the boot of his car and turned swiftly towards the urgent sound. A young woman, who looked to be in her twenties, was scurrying towards him in a distressed state; her feet carelessly splashing noisily through the puddles. In the half-light, she appeared bedraggled; her long blonde hair splayed limply across her shoulders, her face contorted with anguish and her eyes wide with fear. As she got nearer, her husky breathless voice called out once more. 'Excuse me... excuse me... I'm sorry to bother you, but please, *please* can you help me?'

Crane immediately looked around for signs of trouble; there was nothing that he could see and all was quiet until, suddenly he heard the raucous drone of an engine as a car headed towards the exit at speed; its tyres slithering wildly on the wet tarmac.

He turned to face the woman again as she tried to regain her composure, 'My car... my car.' She raised her arm wavering frantically towards the exit. 'Look, look over there; they're taking my car. *Please* help me. Can you follow them?'

Crane looked towards the exit as the small Ford Ka left the car park. 'Do you have a mobile phone? I've, erm, left mine at home.'

'It's in the car, so is my little boy; he's in the back seat. *Please* follow them.'

Crane hesitated briefly. He looked towards the disappearing Ford and immediately threw the passenger door open saying, 'Okay, you'd better get in.'

The dim courtesy light briefly revealed the woman's wide nervous eyes as she slid into his car. Crane brought the powerful V8 engine to life, slammed the car into gear and headed for the exit. Her voice quivered as she said, 'Do you think you'll be able to keep up with them?'

Crane was about to say, *"Are you kidding?"* but instead he said reassuringly, 'They are not going to get too far ahead in this kind of traffic. Have you seen these men before?'

'Erm... no. I don't think so.'

Crane drove at a steady pace and trailed the woman's car from the busy main road through to the back streets of Southend. The driver of the stolen car appeared to be in no particular hurry; it seemed as though the thief considered it was now safe and had decided to take his time. After a while the stolen Ford Ka turned into a small empty car park and within a minute, Crane followed suit and stopped at the entrance; blocking the only way in and out.

Leaving the woman seated in the Mustang with its engine running, Crane got out and walked cautiously towards the Ford Ka but as he drew near to the Ka, the sound of his Mustang revving up made him turn. At the same time the Ford Ka's lights came on, flooding the grey duskiness of the car park around it. Realising this was a set up, Crane spun round and started to move speedily towards the red shape of his retreating Mustang. At the same time his right hand delved into his jacket and he thumbed a small button on a tiny hand-held unit that he located in his pocket; the Mustang's engine cut out and the car stopped dead. The Ford Ka's driver reacted and leapt out of the stolen car holding a baseball bat high above his head. He growled deeply as he moved menacingly towards Crane, his scrawny silhouetted frame contrasting sharply with Crane's six-foot well-built body.

'Immobiliser!' he snarled. 'Hand it over, dude.' Then, swinging the bat he added, 'You'd better be quick, dude, unless you wanna get hurt.'

Crane put a hand in his pocket and as he pulled it out said, 'Here; come and get it.'

'No, toss it over.'

'If I do, and it falls on the ground, the remote will get damaged, and then it'll never start.'

The guy from the Ford walked confidently towards Crane; the baseball bat firmly clenched in his right hand. 'You'd better not try anything,' he warned, 'I'm pretty good with this.'

With his free hand, the would-be thief reached out for the immobiliser. In the blink of an eye, Crane grabbed his wrist and spun him round twisting the man's arm up between his shoulder blades. The would-be assailant dropped the bat and let out a painful howl as Crane dislocated his shoulder and threw him to the ground.

An accomplice, seated behind the wheel of the stalled Mustang, immediately leapt out of the car. In the poor light, his features were indistinct, but he was bigger and heavier than his unfortunate cohort. Unlike the man from the Ford, instead of a baseball bat he held a semi-automatic hand-gun. A shot rang out as he waved the gun in the air. Crane remained stock still and the new assailant moved menacingly towards him but he stopped a few metres from Crane and with outstretched arm, pointed the gun at Crane's head.

'I can use this,' he growled in a heavy London accent, and looking down at his accomplice said to Crane, 'What have you done to him?'

Crane shrugged, 'His shoulder is out of joint.'

The injured man, his face twisted with pain, sat on the ground looking up at Crane in disbelief. The man with the gun called out to the woman in the Mustang and she came running over to where the injured man lay. She glanced swiftly at Crane before bending down to examine the injured man. Without taking his eyes off Crane, the gunman said to the woman, 'His shoulder's out of joint; can you fix it?'

'I've only been trained in first aid; I can try.'

She ran her hands gently over the man's back, and then gripping his arm, at the same time pushing on his shoulder, she jerked the joint back into place. There was a yelp of pain, and the gunman snarled at the woman, 'Help him up and take him over to the Ka – and make sure he can drive it.'

Still gesturing with the gun, he said to Crane, '*You*, put the remote on the ground carefully, and back away. Do it now!'

Crane did as he was told. The gunman's eyes were still on Crane as the woman returned, 'He's okay, he can drive,' she mumbled. The gunman nodded and pointed to the remote control lying on the ground.

'Pick it up and go to the Mustang.'

She glanced furtively at Crane as she picked up the remote and then hurried towards the Mustang. The gunman backed off saying, 'I wouldn't move if I were you.'

The Ford Ka followed the Mustang as it left the car park and they both sped off down the road. Crane dashed out of the car park and focused his eyes through the misty drizzle. He watched as his car disappeared at the end of the road with its bright tail lights indicating a left-hand turn into the main road. Within half a minute, a man on an old motorbike rounded the corner and Crane stepped out in front; waving and thrusting his hands skywards. The biker slid to a halt on the wet tarmac. After briefly telling him what had just happened, the biker said, 'I ain't got a spare crash helmet, but if you like, hop on the back and we'll see if we can follow them.'

The traffic on the main road had not eased up. A continuous stream was snaking its way out of town, but before long, Crane spotted the familiar rear tail lights of his car. It was steady going for the old motorbike to keep up in the stream of heavy traffic. After two miles the traffic thinned out and they followed the car as it passed through

Rochford and turned off towards the sparsely populated rural area of Stambridge. The road had cleared and the Mustang, true to its namesake, leapt ahead, but the distinctive rear lamps continued to be like a homing beacon. By the time the bike had caught up and turned into Denisons Lane, Crane was just in time to catch a final glimpse of those tail lamps disappearing behind a rapidly closing automatic garage door. The Ford Ka was nowhere to be seen. Crane noted it was the first property – number one.

Crane tapped the biker on the shoulder and suggested that he should pull up further down the road.

'Whad ya gonna do now?' he said.

'Look for a phone box and call the police.'

'Ain't yuh got a mobile?'

'You wouldn't believe how many I've lost or damaged.'

The man stuffed a hand in his pocket and offered, 'Use my mobile if you like.'

Crane took the handset, dialled the emergency number and explained the situation to the officer in charge. After handing the phone back the man said, 'Look mate, I'd like to stay, but I must get back now, or my other half will wonder what I've been up to.'

Crane thanked him profusely and from a distance, kept his eyes on the garage.

Fifteen minutes later a police armed-response unit turned into the road, met Crane and he filled them in on the details. The officer in charge of the armed unit, Chief Inspector Harris, had met Crane before; he said, 'The Ford Ka was reported stolen from a supermarket car park in Westcliff late this afternoon.'

As they approached the front door, the area was

suddenly lit up with bright security lights. A policeman pressed the doorbell. A child raced eagerly towards the door and as he pressed his face against the glass side-panel a woman came scurrying after him. As the door swung open the looming figures of the police startled the child and he shrank back towards the woman, clutching and tugging anxiously at her skirts. She looked startled and fondly stroked the boy's hair as the officer began, 'We have reason to believe that you have a stolen car in your garage; a car that was taken by an armed person. Would that be yourself, madam?'

The woman looked horrified. 'What? Me? Stolen car? You must be joking. There's nothing in the garage. I'll open it and you can see for yourself.'

She pressed a button near the entrance in the hall and the huge double garage door began to roll up. Crane stared in disbelief; it was empty. He walked into the garage and looked around. It was immaculately kept. The wall-to-wall coarse floor covering was bone dry; no sign of a wet car ever having been there. He looked past the policeman and at the slim dark-haired woman standing before them. Although he had only seen her in the half light, and her accent had sounded different, there was no doubt in his mind – he knew it was the same person. She was the right size, five foot three-ish; her hair was now a different colour, it was cut short and it was dark.

'I followed the car here.' Crane said calmly.

The woman's deep-blue eyes flitted from Crane to the policeman, and she said confidently, 'How embarrassing. I've never seen this man before in my life; he's obviously mistaken me for somebody else. You can see that his car is not in my garage. The only car that you will ever find in there belongs to my husband – and he has not yet arrived home from work.'

Chief Inspector Harris took Crane to one side and said quietly, 'Mr Crane, are you… ' he began.

But before he could continue, Crane, realising the futility of the situation, interrupted him and said, 'Look, I'm sorry to have put you to so much trouble, it would appear that a mistake has been made. I was on the back of someone's motorbike and, well he could have followed the wrong car.'

Police apologies were made to the woman and Harris said to Crane, 'I'll give you a lift back to the police station at Southend where you can give details of your car and they'll give you an incident number for your insurance company.'

With some resignation, Crane accepted the offer; given the circumstances, there was little else he could do. Invariably, he would now have to do things his own way.

# CHAPTER TWO

Crane took a cab from Southend to Canford; which was a small village nestling between Rochford and Canewdon. He lived in a picturesque cottage, Bramble View; a low, red-brick and wood-boarded dwelling with neat white Georgian windows and, at this time of year, September, its fences were covered in small roses and the paths were strewn with their fallen petals. The cottage was situated near the far end of a lane known as Palmers Rise and it was one of only two properties in this rustic setting. The other cottage in the lane was unoccupied for most of the year. The entrance to the lane, off of Alders Hill, could easily be mistaken for a gap in the hedge. It was an unmade road with tufts of weed and grass sprouting through its cinder track. The lane rose steadily for half a mile with high unmanaged swathes of blackthorn, hawthorn and bramble on either side.

Within half an hour, and with a wedge of a hurriedly prepared cheese sandwich rammed between his teeth, Crane was driving his old Ford Transit van from the cottage. He was on the way back to Denisons Lane, beyond the boundary of Stambridge. It was pitch dark when Crane turned the van into the narrow road; the few dim streetlights, that were sparsely scattered, merely denoted the road's existence. The Transit's headlamps shimmered brightly as they stabbed into the dark recesses of the surrounding area.

They revealed a sparsely populated road with no more than half a dozen expensive looking houses, spaced well apart and no doubt each one nestling in a sizable piece of land. Beyond their boundaries lay acres of farmland on either side. The road looped round in a crescent and re-joined the main Southend road after a half mile.

Crane parked the van at the deserted unlit end of the road, but within sight of the house. He checked his watch; it was nine pm, almost two hours since the theft. Leaning over the steering wheel, he adjusted a small pair of infrared night glasses; a legacy from his army days, and waited for signs of movement. There were none.

At around midnight, it was time for action. The sparsely lit road suited Crane's purpose well. Most of the lights in the surrounding properties were switched off and number one was in total darkness. Aware of the automatic floodlights, Crane dropped to the ground and inched his way, crawling across the front lawn, until he reached the front wall of the house. Using a pair of long-reach pruning shears, he snipped the power cable of the security lights. Feeling satisfied, he delved into his pockets and pulled out a pencil-beam torch and a set of skeleton keys. He twisted and turned a suitable probe, until he heard a faint audible click as the tumblers released the latch. Slowly, he pushed the front door forward and aimed the beam of his torch inside until it located the power switch to the garage door. Crane's hand reached out and thumbed the button. Immediately, he heard an imperceptible whirr and the garage door began to rise. Crane quietly closed the front door and entered the garage; a dim pilot light showed it was still empty. Crane's eyes scanned the work benches and array of tools. Nothing seemed to be amiss, and yet he knew his car had entered this place. He bent down by the entrance and rolled up a section of the floor covering. The dim light revealed nothing.

Crane straightened up when he heard footsteps and the creak of a door opening at the far end of the garage and he switched off his torch. A woman's voice called out, 'Is that you, Trevor?'

Crane flattened himself against the wall near the door and grunted an assent hoping it may bring her further into the garage. It worked. She flicked on the lights as she stepped inside. Crane pushed firmly on the door, slamming it shut and pressed his shoulders hard against it. The woman, wearing a dressing gown, stood mouth agape facing Crane. Fear spread across her face as she stammered, 'What… what do you want?' A large black and white cat had followed her into the garage and it sprang up into her arms. She stroked the cat's head and said quietly, 'It's alright, Felix,' at the same time trying to regain her composure.

Crane's steel-blue eyes locked onto her as he replied calmly, 'I want my car; where is it?'

Gaining her composure she said, 'I don't know what you're talking about – you'd better leave now or I'll call the police!'

Crane's face hardened as he replied menacingly, 'They'll never get here in time.'

Her edginess returned; she looked anxious. 'What do you mean?'

'What I say; *you* figure it out.'

The woman bit her lower lip and her eyes wandered around the garage as if they were no longer willing to meet his cold, icy stare. Crane continued in a soft, menacing voice, 'I recognised you, despite your change of hair and manner.

I followed my car here, and I'm a very dangerous man to mess with. And I want to know where I can find the two guys you were with?'

She suddenly looked drained and said with resignation, 'Okay. There was only one man that brought your car here. After garaging it down below, he left. The house is built on a slope. The lift takes a car to the lower level; there's a garage underneath the house. There's also a driveway where my own car is parked. There is room for several vehicles. It's not so apparent in the dark. From the drive at the rear, there is an access to a resident's service road.'

The woman looked down, sighed heavily and said, 'We'd better go in the house.'

Crane moved towards the door and opening it, said, 'You'd better not try anything.'

'I won't. I've seen you in action, remember?'

They stepped into the spacious hallway and, after closing the door, she walked up to a small picture on the wall, pushed it to one side and revealed a switch. She flicked the switch up and a faint whirring noise seemed to emanate from below. After a few moments the noise stopped and she walked back to the door and opened it. It was a whole new room. Together they stepped inside and Crane's Mustang was in full view. The woman looked at Crane and said, 'You'd better take it and go quickly.'

Crane shook his head, 'I think the police will be interested in this little setup.'

The woman looked at him pleadingly, 'Please, please don't inform the police.'

Crane looked at her astounded. 'What! And let you and your friends carry on stealing cars?'

She bit her lower lip and said, 'They are no friends of mine. I think I'd better explain things from the beginning. I wanted no part of this – believe me. Jean, my sister – after her husband died – met a man, who called himself Bradley. He seemed very nice at first. He would take her to places, the cinema, the theatre and buy her flowers and so on, and then after a month or so she introduced him to me. We talked; as you do, and he told me he was in the export business. He seemed genuinely interested when I told him that I belonged to an amateur dramatics repertoire company; it didn't take long to find out why. About three months ago, my sister disappeared. Her new boyfriend, who turned out to be her abductor, said if I ever wanted to see her again, I would have to live in this house and help him in his export business. I was expected to pretend to be in trouble while they stole the cars. He said it would only last for a couple of months and then he would bring her back. I know they are holding my sister against her will because she would never leave her little boy, Andrew; the one you saw when the police called.'

'Is this Bradley the man with the gun?'

'No; I haven't seen him since this whole thing started. He only gets in touch by phone.'

'Why didn't you report all this to the police?'

'Why do you think? I took his threats seriously. I have no idea where my sister is being held. They have what they call, 'A client base'; people actually waiting for the cars they steal to order. They don't always bring the cars back here. I expect your car would have been taken to someone by tomorrow evening. Look, I just want my sister back safe and sound; so, please don't go to the police.'

It was a plausible story, but Crane was uncertain. 'You were expecting someone; Trevor. Who's he, one of your accomplices?'

'No!' she replied with some fervour, 'he's my brother. Apart from you, Trevor is the only person who knows about this.'

'Why is he coming here so late?'

'He's an accountant and works in the city. Sometimes he stays on late to complete a job for his clients. Like me, he is worried sick about my involvement and our missing sister, Jean, ever since this whole thing erupted.'

Crane was still not entirely convinced. He had already experienced her acting abilities in the car park. 'I think I would like to meet your brother, so if you don't mind I'll hang around till he arrives.'

The woman seemed unfazed by this and said, 'Would you care for a coffee while we wait?'

Crane accepted the offer and followed her back into the house. The sound of a car pulling into the drive caught their attention, followed by a key turning in the lock of the front door. Footsteps echoed on the hard wooden flooring before Trevor poked his head around the door of the lounge, and upon seeing his sister with a man said, 'Oh, you've got company, I won't disturb… '

'Come in,' Crane interrupted. 'We were just having a chat about your sister.'

Trevor stepped smartly into the room, looking from one to the other as he entered and stood still for a moment. A bespectacled thirty-year-old, he was about five feet ten inches with a willowy hunched-up frame and sallow complexion. His face brightened as he enquired, 'Any news?'

The woman looked at him and said in a rush, 'I helped steal this man's car. He's tracked it down and he wants to report it to the police. I've told him the whole story.'

Trevor rubbed a hand over the back of his neck, let out a sigh and readily confirmed everything that the woman said. 'It had to happen sooner or later,' he said and as he looked at Crane said, 'Penny and I are at our wits end; if it was you caught up in all this, what would you do Mr erm... '

'Name's Crane, Jack Crane. It seems as though I'm already drawn in, by getting this far.'

A noise interrupted them and a face peered around the open door. It was the little boy. He looked around the room, rubbing his eyes and said sleepily, 'Is Mummy back now Auntie Penny?'

Penny smiled and hurried over to him, 'No, not yet Andrew, it's late, you should try and get some sleep.'

She scooped him up and took him back upstairs to bed. 'The boy's been so good considering he hasn't seen his mother for some weeks; he'll be five years old in a couple of months time.' Trevor sighed and continued. 'We hate having to string him along like this.'

Crane drained his coffee and after a few moments, Penny re-entered the room and they all sat down.

Crane stared long and hard at the pair for a moment and decided to believe their story.

'Okay, I won't go to the police, but I'll try and help get your sister back.'

Trevor and Penny looked at each other and turned to Crane with a mixture of relief and fear showing in their faces. They remained quiet as Crane continued.

'Do you know how many men are involved?'

17

'Not really; I've seen four different men and that doesn't include the one called Bradley; the man that got Jean and me into all of this.' Penny hesitated; her eyes were suddenly wide with fear. 'If they find out that I've involved anyone... '

'They won't,' Crane interrupted, 'and don't worry, I won't show my hand or implicate either of you. How many cars do they steal in say... a week?'

'They are very careful not to overdo things, only two.'

Trevor leant forward in his chair and said, 'Who are you Mr Crane? And what makes you think you can help?'

'I wondered when you would ask; let's just say that I have a wide experience dealing with all kinds of situations.'

'But... but some of them carry guns,' Penny stammered.

Crane frowned and said, 'I haven't forgotten; if they had been unarmed we would not be talking here right now; I would have had the pair of them. You might call it good old army training. By the way, do they know about the police coming here?'

'No, the one that brought your car here left straight away by the back door and into the narrow rear service road; it's unlit.'

'So that's why I didn't see him leave,' Crane remarked.

Some of Crane's confidence seemed to have filtered through to Penny and Trevor, and they enthused with, 'How do you propose to start?'

'I'm working on that. Tell me, how do they usually collect the vehicles that are left here?'

Penny ran her well-manicured hands through her hair as she began, 'I get a phone call half an hour before two men arrive in a large dark-coloured removal van. They park outside; always around dusk, when no one is about, and usually within twenty-four hours of the theft. I press the button and the car rises up from the basement, all ready for them. They spend very little time here. One of them heads straight for the garage whilst the other places a pair of ramps at the back of the van. Within minutes, the car is driven out straight into the back of the van. As I've already mentioned, it's not always the same two men. I expect they will come and collect your car tomorrow.'

Crane leant back in his chair, tented his hands and thought for a moment before saying, 'I'll leave my phone number with you. If anything changes give me a call. In any event the first thing I'm going to do is steal my car back.

# CHAPTER THREE

After Crane had left the house, Penny threw a worried glance at Trevor and said, 'Do you think he can really be of help?'

'I wish I knew. At least he's not involving us with getting his car back.'

Trevor pursed his lips before saying, 'Do you think we can trust him? I mean would he jeopardise our chances of getting our sister, Jean, back?'

Penny shrugged and looked pensive. 'He seems to know what he's about, but if they connect him with us in any way, I suppose we can always say we were threatened.'

The pair sat quietly for a moment until Trevor said, 'It's a wait-and-see scenario then.'

*

The following day, Crane sat in his van as dusk crept over the far end of the unlit area of Denisons Lane. Although the area was steeped in shadows, he had a clear view of Penny's house from his vehicle, as the removal van, an old Bedford with a Luton body, slowly backed around the corner from the main road and settled outside the garage. Within minutes, his Mustang appeared and its driver skilfully manoeuvred the car up a ramp and into the back of the Bedford van. With a stiff rattle, the van's shutter came down and the vehicle lumbered off towards the direction of Southend.

Crane followed the van as it veered onto the A127 Arterial Road towards Basildon. After several miles the van slowed down and pulled into a roadside cafe. He followed it slowly into the dimly-lit parking area; laying up his Transit van on the opposite side and could not believe his luck when the pair leapt out and entered the building. As soon as they disappeared inside, Crane ran across the yard and, standing at the edge of a wash of light from the cafe, looked through the window. The two men were seated and a waitress appeared to be taking an order. Crane surreptitiously made his way to their Luton van, which he unlocked using his skeleton keys. He gingerly pushed up the shutter; gritting his teeth as it grated noisily to the top. He paused, now and again, to look towards the cafe entrance for signs of movement from the two thieves; there were none. He placed the ramps from inside the van into position and, using a spare set of keys to start the engine, he drove his Mustang out of the back of the Luton van. He crossed the yard towards the rear of his Transit van, where he connected the Mustang up to a tow dolly at the back of his van. He glanced again towards the cafe and noted the pair of thieves were still seated, no doubt enjoying their supper. Returning stealthily to the Luton van, Crane replaced the ramps, pulled down the shutter and re-locked it. Then with a great deal of satisfaction, he pulled his Transit van out of the car park with his Mustang in tow and headed for Canford; and home.

*

Penny had spent some time lying awake in bed; her brain whirling around recent events. She took deep breaths – in a fashion remembered from past yoga classes – counting three to slowly inhale and four to slowly exhale. She thought Crane an extraordinary ally, but could he really help? Uncertainty began to creep through her. She had just about made the sleep mode when, at around two am the urgent bleep of the telephone resounded throughout her bedroom. Her weary arm stretched out and groped at the cordless handset. The voice at the other end of the line made her whole body shudder.

'It's me, Bradley.' The gruff introduction was unnecessary and he continued, 'Has anyone been around?'

Penny's heart thumped wildly as she hesitated; has something gone wrong? For her sister's sake, should she tell him about Crane?

Bradley was getting impatient at the lack of response. 'You still there? I asked you a question.'

Penny's brain raced; she seemed to reply automatically, 'I've, erm, just woken up.'

Bradley repeated his question and added, 'The Mustang was taken from the van whilst my two idiots were stuffing their fat faces in a Little Chef on the A127.'

Penny put a hand to her mouth; stifling a nervous grin and thinking about Crane, *'He's done it.'*

A gruff, 'Well?' broke the silence and Penny said haltingly, 'I've seen nobody hanging around hereabouts, if that's what you mean?'

She was about to enquire after her sister when the phone went dead. Penny held on to the phone for some while; expecting it to ring again, before replacing it in its cradle and settling down once more into an uneasy sleep.

*

In the dead of night, Crane drove his van into a quiet side road in Southend where he off-loaded the Mustang from the tow dolly at the rear, and then drove the car back onto the main road. After covering a short distance along Victoria Avenue, he parked it alongside Southend Court House, adjacent to the police station. He quickly deflated a front tyre by unscrewing a tyre valve to make it appear as though it had been abandoned because of a flat tyre, then hurried back to his van and sped off in the direction of his home in Canford. He figured that any suspicion the thieves may have would be allayed by this move. He was right. In the next edition of the *Southend Echo*, a local newspaper, there was a report concerning a stolen car being recovered by the police and then returned to its rightful owner. Penny spotted this article and mentioned it to a disgruntled Bradley the next day, when he contacted her by telephone. This seemed to satisfy him that the house in Denisons Lane had not been under observation of any kind.

Six long days passed by, before Bradley contacted Penny again. Her brief was that she would drive to a supermarket car park at the nearby town of Hadleigh. Her role would be to distract the owner of a new model Mercedes Benz. As soon as she learned of this, Penny phoned Crane and put him in the picture. It was Crane's intention to follow the thieves to their lair and, when he was satisfied that Penny's sister was safely released, he intended to expose the whole affair to the police.

*

At ten am on the appointed day, Crane leant back in the driver's seat of his Transit van, a newspaper, which he appeared to be reading, was splayed across the steering wheel. Earlier, by chance, he had seen a large Luton van which he recognised as the one that had been used to commandeer his Mustang. It had been parked in a side road roughly a quarter of a mile away from where he was now parked. He figured that it would most likely be used again on this occasion.

The car park was quiet at this time of day; it was almost empty. Crane saw Penny arrive in a bright red Mini Cooper; Andrew was strapped in the back seat. She remained in the car waiting for Bradley's pair of thieves to turn up. Crane, peering above the newspaper, continually scanned the car park for signs of action. Nearby, he saw a round-faced man in a dark blue Ford Mondeo eating a sandwich and drinking from a thermos flask.

The thieves' target car; a new model silver Mercedes Benz, swept majestically into the car park and its owner – a balding man in his sixties – walked nonchalantly away, leaving the automatic locking device to secure the vehicle as he departed and made his way towards one of the adjacent offices.

Penny checked her watch, opened the door of her car and flicked a meaningful glance at Crane as she strolled across the car park towards a set of noticeboards. She looked back in the direction of Andrew – who seemed to be fidgeting with his seat belt – and gave him a short wave of her hand. Another movement caught Crane's attention. It was one of Bradley's men. He strolled across the car park towards Penny and fell in line behind her as she headed towards the offices. Penny disappeared into the office entrance hall.

Suddenly, Crane noticed that Andrew had let himself out of Penny's car, then, in no time at all, he began chasing around the car park playing with a toy gun; aiming here and there at imaginary targets. Immediately a new development attracted Crane's attention; the chubby man seated in the Mondeo got out of his car and approached the little boy. Crouching down, he began talking to him. Crane's attention flicked back to the man who had been following Penny; he too had disappeared through the office door.

Crane stared at the office door, then his eyes darted back towards Andrew. It appeared to Crane that the overweight man, whose clothes billowed scruffily around him, and who was talking to young Andrew, was a complete stranger to the boy. He saw the child's eyes widen in nervous anticipation. The stranger had extended his arm, he had something in his hand; a bag, and it was being offered to the boy. Crane's attention went back to the office door and then returned to the boy. The child's eyes were locked onto a bag of sweets. Andrew's hand wavered slightly and inched towards the stranger's hand, but the child's feet remained firm. Suddenly, the stranger grabbed hold of the boy's wrist, pulled him off his feet and cradling him with one arm, hurried a short distance across the car park to his Mondeo. Crane felt tormented – *two crimes at once!* Andrew's toy pistol cluttered to the ground as the stranger tossed the boy, whose face had now begun to show signs of distress, into the back seat of the Mondeo. By the time Crane had leapt out of his van, running towards the scene, the fat man's Mondeo had sped out of the car park and onto the main road. It had all taken place in seconds. Crane made an instant decision; he would go after the boy. At the same time, the car thief ran over to the Mercedes, jumped inside and the car roared off. Crane stood briefly; glancing at the car park exit, then immediately scooped up the toy pistol the boy had dropped. He looked up and shrugged his shoulders to a confused Penny, who had just reappeared from the offices. There was no time for explanation; he jumped back into his Transit van and headed off in hot pursuit of the Mondeo.

# CHAPTER FOUR

In the distance, cumulus clouds piled up ominously in the sky as the traffic on the main London Road wound its way steadily towards a busy junction. Ahead, Crane saw the Mondeo, which held Andrew captive, make a turn towards Rayleigh and then take the road towards Chelmsford.

*

Penny scanned the car parking area looking for Andrew. Her only task that day, had been to delay a man in the entrance foyer to the offices, which she did by asking him about employment. Panic began to set in when she could not find Andrew and she dashed into the supermarket, looked swiftly along the packed aisles and then rushed out again. The unfortunate man whose car had been stolen spotted her and called out.

'I've had my car stolen.'

'My child is missing,' she replied hastily and reached for her mobile phone.

*

Crane's mobile phone buzzed two or three times and then it stopped. He glanced at it lying on the passenger seat; flat battery. It was one of the few things he seemed to neglect. One minute you cannot do without one, and then for weeks on end it has is no use at all.

Crane was thankful that the road twisted and turned; at least he could keep the much faster Mondeo in sight. The man in the Mondeo felt satisfied. He had got away with it. Despite the man's friendly banter, the child sat, without a seat belt, wide-eyed in the back seat; staring into the interior mirror at the stranger's face. After the initial shock of being taken, his tears had dried up, leaving stained trails across his cheeks.

Crane was now lagging some distance behind, but he managed to see the Mondeo turn off into a lonely wooded area near the country area of Danbury. Crane felt somewhat elated as he realised that there was now only one way in and out – the Mondeo was trapped. Crane pulled his Transit right up to the rear of the Mondeo and jumped out. The stranger and the boy were still in the car. Crane rattled on the passenger door window.

'Whadda yuh want?' The stranger called out.

'Open up and let the boy out.'

'Whad's the idea? He's my nephew and we're gonna have a picnic, now bugger off.'

Crane was getting impatient, 'I saw you snatch the kid at the supermarket, now open up and let him out.'

The stranger quickly got out of the car. He was a big man with slicked back hair that seemed to flop either side of his face. He looked about thirty years old, a couple of inches taller than Crane's six foot frame and a little broader. Considering his size, he was nimble on his feet.

As Crane walked round to the other side of the car to

confront him, the man's hand groped in his jacket pocket and came out holding a stiletto. A scowl spread across his face as he waved it wildly in the air and pressed a button; the blade sprang out of the handle with a metallic swish. 'Get out of here or you'll get some of this,' he said waving the knife around.

Crane paused, and stood facing him about four metres away. A relaxed, confident smile spread across his face. His right hand quickly dipped into his jacket pocket and came out holding the toy pistol that the boy had dropped at the supermarket car park. The fat man's eyes widened; the scowled expression disappeared and was replaced by fear. From that distance, it seemed like the real thing. Suddenly there was a deep menace in Crane's voice as he took careful aim at the stranger's head and said calmly, 'Well now, I believe this is something a little better, and I'll put one right between your eyes if you don't drop that knife right now. I'm very good with one of these, you'd better believe me!'

The man's face whitened and his jaw sagged. He loosened his grip on the knife and let it slip to the ground. Andrew, the young boy had been watching the drama unfold with interest. His face was pressed against the inside of the car window; eyes darting from one man to the other.

Keeping the toy gun trained on the stranger, Crane walked slowly towards him until they were about two metres apart. Andrew let himself out of the rear door of the car; his head continually turning from one man to the other. His young mind became confused as it experienced the animosity between the two men. Then, suddenly his gaze rested on Crane and he became animated; he immediately found his voice. 'Hey, that's my gun!'

The stranger stared at the weapon and his face broke into a smile as he began to reach down for his knife, but he was far too late. Like a sprinter at the starting line, Crane thrust himself forward, and lashed out with his right foot. It made contact with the stranger's stomach. The man went down like a felled tree and remained there; curled up and gasping for breath on the ground. Crane picked up the knife and closed the blade. He crouched down and handed the little boy his toy pistol. 'What's your name, son?' he enquired.

The boy looked happier as he reached out, took the toy gun and replied in a quiet voice, 'Andrew Barker.'

Crane gave Andrew a reassuring smile and said, 'Okay, Andrew, I think it's time to take you back home.'

Andrew began fiddling with his toy gun; grinned and simply replied, 'Alright.'

Crane picked the lad up and carried him over to the Transit van. After adjusting the seat belt around Andrew, he returned to the weighty man; he had not moved and was still lying prone on the ground curled up, suffering from Crane's heavy kick. Crane looked at him without sympathy and said, 'Who are you? What's your name?'

The man did not answer. Crane asked another question. 'What were you going to do with the boy?'

The man remained silent.

Crane's easy-going manner was sometimes mistaken for a sign of weakness; and this seemed to be one of those occasions.

'Don't feel like talking eh?' Crane said casually. 'Well, I've wasted enough time on you; I don't much care for perverts.' Crane pressed the button on the stiletto and the blade shot out from its handle with a menacing metallic swish. 'I think

I'll just leave you here then; with this knife sticking out between your shoulders; you'll find it very difficult to pull it out.'

'Ryan – name's Ryan,' he blurted out – in between taking huge lungfuls of air. 'And I'm not a bloody pervert I was taking the boy for someone… someone who wants him.'

'Keep talking,' Crane urged, toying with the blade a few inches from his face.

'That's all I know – honest.'

Crane's eyes hardened as he bent down and scraped the blade against Ryan's whiskery face. 'No, you're not an honest man Ryan; you're not the type. Tell me and make it quick.'

'Okay, okay. I'm supposed to be meeting a man right here and hand the boy over to him.'

Crane straightened up. 'Who is he? What's his name?'

'Bradley. Bradley Kemp.'

'What's his interest?' Crane demanded.

'I don't know.' Ryan gasped. 'He promised me two hundred quid to make the snatch and meet him here afterwards.'

The sound of a car pulling up at the entrance to the wooded area made Crane and Ryan turn their heads; it was a Jaguar. The car paused momentarily and its driver poked his head out of the car window. Upon seeing Crane and the prone Ryan, the driver put the Jaguar into gear and sped off.

'That's the guy I'm supposed to meet,' Ryan stated flatly.

Crane turned back towards Ryan, 'This Bradley, is he into car theft?'

Ryan hesitated, but mindful of the knife Crane held replied, 'I think he does a bit.'

'Where does this Bradley live?'

'I'm not sure. My dealings with him were done at Jim's Cafe in Chelmsford, but I think he's got a place, a farm, around this area, somewhere between Danbury and Maldon. And that's all I know.'

Crane was pensive for a moment before saying, 'I should be handing you over to the police, but I'm more interested in getting the boy back to where he belongs.'

Crane backed off towards his van. He stabbed the knife hard into a tree; twisting and breaking the blade as he did so. Ryan was tempted to tackle Crane, but satisfied himself with the thought that there may be another time.

*

Penny sat in her bright red Mini Cooper in the supermarket car park. She was feeling tense and anxious. The temptation to report the missing Andrew to the police was great, but she surmised that maybe Crane knew something about it and decided to wait until she had heard from him – if only he had his mobile phone switched on. After an hour, much to her relief, Crane's van pulled into the car park and young Andrew leapt out and ran across to Penny's red mini. She seemed puzzled when Crane explained what had happened, wondering what Bradley Kemp was up to.

'It's a fair bet that if you find where this Bradley's farm is located, you'll find your sister,' Crane commented.

Penny bit her lower lip and said, 'It doesn't make sense except maybe getting her son, Andrew, would be some kind of sop to keep her there, after all she hasn't seen him for three months.'

'There's a lot of farms, all shapes and sizes, in that area.

It'll take ages to check them all out and what we don't want to do is to let him know we are on to him,' Crane replied. Crane finished their meeting with, 'Keep in touch and let me know as soon as you hear of the next theft.'

*

Two hours later Crane headed back towards his home in Palmers Rise, Canford. He had bought the cottage from his parents years ago with a view to getting married but things did not work out. In between army life he had spent his spare time renovating the cottage. Since his retirement from the army, most of his time had been taken up looking after his garden as well as several others in the area. The extra cash earned from doing this supplemented his army pension.

Crane turned his white Transit van into the lane. On either side lay coils of bramble interspersed with blackthorn bushes. They gave the lane an untidy, but natural appearance. It was not quite scrubland; in between the bushes sprouted a number of tall, willowy ash and sturdy oak trees.

Deep in thought, Crane parked the van on the drive adjacent to his double garage, jumped out and headed towards the front door of the cottage. As he turned the key in the door, the latch snapped back and then all went black.

# CHAPTER FIVE

Crane slowly opened his eyes whilst lying face down in the entrance hall. His mind was a-whirl as consciousness began to return. Slowly rising to his feet he gingerly touched a sore lump on the back of his head. A sharp pain shot through his ribs as he moved; especially whilst taking a deep breath. He guessed that he had suffered a kicking whilst lying unconscious and checking his watch, realised an hour had passed. He assumed whoever did this would not hang around – they were long gone. Crane looked around inside; nothing seemed to be missing. The quiet was interrupted by a sharp warble drilling into his head. It was the phone. Crane moved painfully towards it, and with fumbling outstretched hand, managed to scoop it up.

'Mr Crane, it's me, Penny.'

Crane managed to grunt an incoherent reply.

'You okay?'

'Just about.'

Penny's words sounded urgent. 'It's your car, the Mustang; they've got it again.'

'That must have been the reception committee that I've just suffered,' Crane groaned. 'Is it there at your place?'

'It was, but only for five minutes or so; it's been whisked away in their big van. What happened?'

Crane explained that he had only just regained

consciousness and can only surmise that they found his address through the car's registration number.

'I thought you couldn't get that kind of information from the number plate.'

'There are ways and means. It can be done,' Crane sighed.

'Are you sure you are alright? I mean, I could come over and…'

'No,' Crane interjected, 'I'll be fine, besides you never know whether someone is going to keep tabs on you. Best stay where you are for now. Let me know if anything new turns up.'

Crane hung up the phone and wandered into the bathroom. Rummaging through the medical cabinet he found a roll of crepe bandage and proceeded to wind it tightly round his damaged ribs; this eased the pain, giving him a great deal of relief. He went to the freezer, took out an ice pack, in the form of a packet of frozen peas, placed it directly over the lump at the back of his head and eased himself down on his most comfortable armchair.

After some while, Crane went outside to find the garage door wide open and the tyres of his van slashed. The local tyre dealer could not send out replacements until later on the following day. The only wheels that he could make use of were on a rusty old bicycle which leant against the wall at the back of the garage. It had been a year since he last resurrected it, but now it seemed that it would be put to use once more. First he needed to fix one of the tyres; the last time he used the machine he punctured one of them and had not bothered to fix it.

Crane walked a mile or so down to the village shop in

the hope that they still sold puncture outfits. Mrs Trent, the shopkeeper cast her eyes around and saw what she was looking for. 'You're lucky, Mr Crane; it's the last one. Don't seem to have had much call on them lately. By the way did the man – who said he was a friend of yours – manage to find you? Said he couldn't find it on his satnav.' The shop was often a centre for local gossip, with Mrs Trent at its head, but Crane never felt inclined to add to this.

He just mumbled a quick, 'Yes thanks,' as he was about to leave, when suddenly, he noticed a CCTV monitor fixed on the wall displaying four mini screens. He nodded towards it and said, 'Is that something new?'

Mrs Trent couldn't hide her satisfaction that it had been noticed. 'Had it installed last week,' she stated proudly. 'Security and all that, it will help keep the insurance bill down, so I'm told.'

Crane thought this to be a real stroke of luck. 'I'm impressed. Can you show me how it works?'

Mrs Trent bubbled with delight. 'Of course, Mr Crane, I can show you your friend arriving if you like.'

Crane smiled and replied, 'That would be nice.'

The monitor gave a clear view of a Jaguar parked outside the shop, with fat Ryan sitting in the passenger seat. Also on the monitor was a good image of a man, whom Crane assumed to be Bradley; it showed him entering the shop. Crane made a mental note of the car number; he thanked Mrs Trent and, with a newspaper tucked under his arm, bid her good day. Elation rippled through him as he made his way back home. The spring in his stride caused a few extra aches, but he did not care – it now seemed all the more bearable – it was nearing payback time.

Within a few minutes of entering his cottage, Crane phoned an old army colleague at Whitehall. If the Jaguar had been stolen then it would have scuppered things; but a search found that it was legitimate, and he soon had the name and address of the Jaguar's owner; it was Bradley Kemp, living on a remote farm on the other side of the River Crouch – no more than forty-five minutes away.

Crane scanned the used-car pages of the *Southend Echo* and soon found the set of wheels that he wanted; a vehicle that was cheap and reliable. He had to act quickly to stand a chance of recovering his Mustang. His limbs ached as he cycled through the back streets of Southend where he had purchased the car and, with his cycle hanging from the car boot, he rode back in the old, tatty white Mercedes saloon; its five-litre heart was all there as it roared through Rochford back to Canford.

Dusk began to surround the area as Crane neared Bradley's farm, and after two passes in front of the property, he parked his newly-acquired, old, inexpensive white Mercedes near some bushes and approached the entrance gate on foot. Still aching from the kicking he had suffered earlier in the day, he did not want to encounter further confrontation at this stage. He eased himself past the five-barred wooden farm gate and crept silently, sidling like a ghost, along the grass edge of the gravel driveway until the house came into view. A pheasant suddenly fluttered noisily across the path ahead; it was soon followed by a fox, picking and sniffing its way across the gravel surface, until they both disappeared through a gap in the hedge.

The Jaguar was parked at the side of the thatched house. Crane stopped for a moment. From his position, by a hedge in the drive, it was difficult to see whether floodlights were installed. His caution proved right. Suddenly the area was flooded with bright light as the front door opened. Bradley and Ryan stepped outside and walked towards the Jaguar. Crane strained his ears and could only just make out part of their conversation which was carried by a slight breeze. A voice, which he presumed to be Bradley's, said, 'I'll run you back to your place on the way to Southend.' He recognised Ryan's voice answering and a harsh laugh ensued and what may have sounded like a reference to Crane, 'Should've broken a few limbs.'

Within seconds they were in the car and heading out of the drive. Like a rabbit, Crane quickly dropped down on hands and knees, painfully hopping and squeezing through the small gap in the hedge, through which the fox had disappeared a few moments earlier, just as the Jaguar's headlamps swung round, splashing the vegetation with its bright halogen beams. The car disappeared into the lane and Crane eased himself back through the gap. To avoid any of his movements being detected by the external floodlight sensors, he crept forward in a wide arc stealthily towards the rear of the house. It worked – the floodlights remained off. Although the curtains were drawn, a diffused glimmer could be seen filtering through them, together with the faint glow and the muffled sound of a television. It reminded him to remain cautious.

Through the grey light of dusk, Crane saw the outline of a huge barn, sited some twenty metres away from the rear of the house. The front of the building was covered by a wide dull-grey steel-ribbed shutter, with a small Judas door set in one corner. The Judas door lay partially open. He walked towards it, peered through the opening and saw that the inside was pitch black. Standing by the entrance, he groped in his jacket pocket and pulled out a small pencil beam torch; its shaft of light stabbed into the darkness. He turned his wrist and the narrow beam revealed several car-sized dust covers. He was about to move further into the barn when a bat flickered erratically into the ray of torchlight; its wings flapping audibly as it flew across the barn. But, another sound made him freeze. It was the unmistakable hollow metallic sound of a shotgun's barrels snapping shut against the stock and the menacing, barely audible click of the safety catch being released.

# CHAPTER SIX

A shrill continuous noise resounded throughout the house. It was the doorbell. The hand pressing it was impatient; irritable. There was some delay in getting to the door, because Penny had just put a very tired Andrew to bed. She scampered breathlessly down the stairs and caught sight of the perpetrator of the noise through the wide frosted-glass panel and a stab of fear shot through her body. It was Bradley; his tall lean frame was rocking up and down on his heels. As Penny opened the door, he shouldered roughly past her and went straight into the lounge, then stood by the fireplace until Penny had caught up with him. Pushing back a mop of brown hair with one hand, Bradley got straight to the point, 'Perhaps you can tell me what the fuck is going on.'

Although feeling tense and nervous, she tried to keep her feelings under control and replied calmly, 'What do you mean?'

Bradley glared threateningly, 'Don't bullshit me! Tell me about this guy Crane.'

Penny knew she had to give him something. 'He... he threatened me.' She stammered.

'Go on.'

'He was in a white van passing by when he saw his car being loaded into the transporter van. Apparently he followed it and took it back. Then he called here and started pushing me around.'

Bradley eyed her with scepticism. 'What is he?'

'He does gardening – so he says. Anyway, I received all sorts of threats from him unless I told him about the next job. Maybe he wants some of the action. I told him to meet me in the car park and then someone tried to kidnap Andrew; so he followed them and brought Andrew back; and that's the last I've heard of him.'

Bradley, fully aware of her acting skills, was still not quite convinced. 'Why didn't you tell me about this before now? He could have ruined everything and if he had, it would not have been too good for you.'

Penny was feeling more confident now as she replied, 'How would you feel? I'm getting threatened from both sides. He said if I mentioned it to anyone, I would get a damn good beating.'

Bradley decided to leave it at that and as he walked towards the front door said, 'You had better tell me if and when you hear from this Mr Crane in future.' As he stepped outside he paused then suddenly spun round on his heels, and taking a step towards her, pushed his face close up to hers and with a snarl emphasised, 'Got it?'

Penny nodded mechanically, and breathed a sigh of relief as he walked down the path got in his car and left.

*

Crane turned around slowly. A bright lamp made him screw up his eyes and squint. The silhouette of a man holding a powerful torch stood a few paces away and barked, 'What do you think you are doing here?'

Crane surmised that he had, at some stage, been

observed on CCTV monitors and, sounding as innocently as possible said, 'I've run out of petrol near the end of your drive. I was hoping to find some fuel lying around and I'd leave some money; I suppose I should have knocked on the door, but it didn't seem as though there was anybody at home.'

The voice behind the gun said, 'Well you won't find any in there.' He used the gun to point the way to another outbuilding and continued, 'There's some in a can in that shed over there – you got a tenner?'

Crane fumbled in his wallet and produced a ten pound note. A hand sprung out from the shadowy figure, took it and backed off.

'Thanks, I'll return the can,' Crane said.

'Don't bother,' the gruff sounding shadowy voice replied, 'it's only an old five litre oil can – keep it, it'll save you running out again.' And with some emphasis added, 'And it'll save you bothering me again!'

Under the watchful eye of the shadowy figure, Crane removed a can from the shed and walked back down the gravel drive to the road. Footsteps on the loose gravel had followed him and surreptitious glances told him he was being watched as he stood on the grassy lay-by and poured the fuel into the tank of the car.

When Crane had departed, the shadowy figure pulled out his mobile phone. 'Bradley, it's me, Stan. Just after you left a bloke came sniffing around, he was near the barn, said he'd run out of fuel.'

'Really? I'm intrigued; what did he look like?' Stan gave a good description of the man he had seen and Bradley responded in a hushed tone, 'Crane.'

When Crane arrived back home in Canford, he phoned Penny and told her all that he had found out. She in turn, related her encounter with Bradley.

'You've done well,' Crane remarked. 'Phone him up and tell him that I've phoned to say that I've a few broken ribs and I'm going to claim on my insurance. Hopefully, that may reinforce your trust with him.'

Crane rang off and thought about his next move. To begin with, he would need to know of any future visitors arriving in Palmers Rise, and so he decided to reinstate an alarm system, one that he had used in the past. It comprised of a pressure switch, set near the end of the lane, which would activate an alarm in his cottage. Upon leaving the lane, he would scatter a layer of cement dust from side to side so that any vehicles entering or leaving the lane would leave an impression of their tyre tracks. Crane had no intention of being caught out again.

*

The following morning, Bradley's curiosity was gnawing at his brain. Questions hung in the air. Who was this guy, Crane? Why didn't he go to the police? He contacted a private investigator to no avail but it was suggested that he contact another; Toby Finder, based in Southend-on-Sea who might be able to give him information about Crane.

Finder's office was dingy, which was not quite what Bradley had expected, however he had been told that Finder was the longest-established private investigator in the area and was well worth checking out.

'Mr Taylor,' Finder greeted, offering a limp sweaty hand. 'What can I do for you?'

Bradley stood, momentarily transfixed; staring at this gaunt willowy figure with a sallow complexion. Toby Finder was not the suave archetype private detective that the movies led you to believe existed.

'Do you know anything about a man by the name of Jack Crane?'

A slight shiver ran through Finder at the mention of that name. 'Jack Crane, you say?' he repeated.

Finder motioned Bradley to a chair by the side of a wide desk. Finder could have told Bradley everything that he wanted to know from personal experience and memory, but he wanted to appear to be earning his fee. He then sauntered across the room towards a large metal filing cabinet, delved through the files, pulled out a sheaf of papers and sat down behind his desk mumbling the name, 'Jack Crane; so what do you want to know?'

Bradley exhaled noisily, 'Anything you can tell me.'

'As a matter of interest,' Finder enquired cautiously, 'what's your connection with Jack Crane?'

Bradley was equally cautious and gave a vague reply, 'Oh, it's just some kind of business arrangement that I may get involved in; I just like to know what I'm up against; who I am dealing with that's all.'

A wide tight-lipped twisted smile spread across Finder's face as he flicked a photo across the desk. 'That's him; taken about a year ago – age forty-six. He's not a man to mess with you know. One of my best clients tried a year or so ago; he disappeared after Crane followed him to the USA. Jack Crane is an ex-SAS soldier from a very different mould. I was fortunate at the time to find this out from a fellow that was also ex-army, although he was of a different breed. He too, appears to be no longer around. He told me that Crane was permanently stationed at Whitehall and was an integral part of what is known as a ghost squad.'

'Ghost squad?' Bradley echoed.

'No one is supposed to know of their existence. A select group of men – hand-picked from the SAS – who do all sorts of covert jobs; jobs that cover a wide variety of dangerous missions for our government. If they get caught, they're on their own – so to speak.'

Bradley left Finder's office somewhat comforted with the knowledge of what he was up against; and smiled to himself with the thought, *"Dangerous eh? Forewarned is forearmed, but the man that can outsmart me hasn't been born yet."*

*

The air was chilled at four am the next the morning when Crane returned to the farm. It was still dark. The shadowy outline of a Ford Mondeo was parked directly outside the front door of the house. Dressed entirely in black, Crane skirted around the back of the building and made his way towards the barn.

He paused beside the ribbed steel shutter listening intently. All was quiet. He paused again and put an ear to the partially open Judas door; and satisfied that there was no one around, produced his torch and stepped inside. The pencil beam hit a blank timber wall and the door slammed shut behind him. Crane pushed against the sides to no avail. He was trapped in a cage – a small shed within the barn. He tried lifting it from underneath, but it was firmly anchored down. A hissing noise and pungent turpentine-like smell filled the air. He recognised it immediately and was already beginning to notice the effects. It was ether gas. In spite of feeling light-headed, he cupped a hand over his mouth; holding his breath as he did so. He knew it would not take long to succumb to its sleep-inducing qualities. Using the torch, Crane frantically looked around the walls until the beam fell on a large brown knot halfway down the planking. Holding his breath, he used the torch to push hard on the knot and slammed it with his other hand until it popped out. Leaning heavily against the wall, he put his mouth over the hole and felt a sharp splinter dig in his lip, but he didn't care about the pain, as he pinched his nose tight and drew in lungfuls of clean fresh air.

\*

Ryan stood back from the barn and gave a satisfied, smug glance at Stan – his accomplice – as he reached for the mobile phone in his pocket and dialled Bradley's number.

'It worked a treat, just like you said it would; he fell for it good and proper. It's all quiet in there; he must be well under by now. What do you want done with him?'

There was a pause at the other end before Bradley replied, 'Like I said before, give it a few minutes or so then drag him out and use that iron bar leaning against the side of the barn and break his fucking legs; you got that?'

'I've already got it. It'll be a pleasure.'

Bradley continued, 'And after that find the car he is using – he's probably parked down the road somewhere – stuff him in it. Then one of you guys drive it back to his area and leave him there and I'll see you both back at the farm, okay?'

Ryan was in jubilant mood as he paused in his conversation with Bradley. He looked at Stan and said, 'You can drag him out now.'

Stan nodded in eager expectation as he flipped on a gas mask and strode towards the Judas door.

Ryan continued his chat with Bradley, pacing up and down as he did so. His face lit up in wonder when Bradley told him that he would be returning within the hour with a Ferrari.

\*

Crane managed to stay alert. As soon as he heard approaching footsteps, he drew a deep breath through the knothole and held it as he moved swiftly to the opposite side of the shed, pressing his body against the wall adjacent to the door. Stan flung the door wide open with a clatter and stepped inside. Crane's balled fist struck him in the neck; leaving him silent and gasping for air. The second blow, a hard punch behind the ear, felled him instantly. Crane ripped off the gas mask and put it on himself. He closed the door and stepped outside into the dull moonless night. It would have been difficult to distinguish anyone's features – shadowy outlines were the order of the night. Ryan looked towards the approaching figure and ended his phone call.

'Where's Crane?' he began.

'I'm right here,' Crane replied. 'Your friend is having a rest.'

Ryan stared in disbelief but he recovered quickly enough and gripping the iron bar, moved menacingly towards Crane; who had not quite recovered from the kicking he had received from their last encounter. Crane's hand dipped into his pocket and holding the pencil-beam torch between forefinger and thumb said, 'You don't think I came here unarmed, do you?'

Ryan stopped dead; eyes straining at Crane's outstretched hand. All he could make out was an outline of something that could be a gun.

Crane pushed home the point with venom. 'Why have you stopped? Come on, give me an excuse to put a nine mil slug in your fat face. Now drop whatever you're holding and move over to that barn door, and be quick about it.'

Without taking his eyes off of Crane he walked towards the Judas door. He paused outside for a moment until Crane, by way of motioning him forward, waved the pencil-beam torch a bit too dramatically; and the light came on.

'A fucking torch,' was all that Ryan could utter as he picked up the iron bar and charged, like a raging bull, towards Crane. Without hesitation, Crane flung the lamp down, turned and ran, but when Ryan was within arm's reach, Crane dropped suddenly to the ground and curled up his body. Ryan tumbled helplessly over Crane's encumbered hulk and crashed heavily to the ground. Within a split-second, Crane sprang up and placed his foot heavily across Ryan's neck. 'Don't move an inch unless you want it broken,' he hissed. 'Now, where's Bradley?'

By way of reply, all that Ryan could manage was, 'Agh! I'm choking.'

Crane kept the pressure on and said, 'Consider yourself lucky, I usually wear boots. I'm only going to ask one more time and, you'd better tell me – and no bullshit.'

'He's on his way here,' Ryan managed to gasp.

'When?'

'In about an hour or so.'

'Where is my Mustang?'

'I dunno.'

Ryan sensed that Crane was about to increase the pressure and in a panic he blurted out, 'It's the truth. It's probably gone out of the country by now.'

'Keep talking.'

Ryan was sweating and gasping for air as he spoke, 'All I know is that Bradley takes some cars abroad, on the continent and Thailand and places like that. '

Crane took his foot off of Ryan's neck, picked up the iron bar and waving it around said, 'Who else is in the house?'

'No one.'

'Then I think we had better wait inside the house, and then you can tell me more about the continent, but don't try anything silly or you'll get some of this.'

Ryan gave a rueful glance at the cudgel as he scrambled to his feet and rubbed his neck. Crane used the iron bar like a cattle prod as he shuffled Ryan towards the house and through the back door. The house seemed to be unoccupied, but he was mindful that there may be somebody else inside. They passed through a narrow passage leading to a room at the front of the house. Crane directed Ryan to an easy chair and, after dimming the lights, sat down opposite him. From this position he had a good view of the driveway but at the same time, was able to keep an eye on Ryan. It had crossed his mind to ask the crook about Penny's sister, Jean, although, if things did not go as planned it would jeopardise both himself and

Penny. He decided to wait until he had cornered Bradley.

Ryan, still rubbing his neck, remained silent. After a few minutes, a ringing sound filled the room; it was Ryan's mobile phone. He picked it up and looked at the screen; it was Bradley. Before pressing any buttons, he glanced across at Crane, who leapt up.

'You'd better answer it, but turn the speaker on; I want to hear both sides of the conversation; and be very careful what you say.' And motioning with the iron bar added, 'Or else this could break a few bones.'

Ryan did as he was told. His hate-filled eyes flicked from Crane to the keypad.

'Yeah?' he rasped.

'Where are you?'

Ryan looked questionly at Crane who mouthed the words, 'Tell him.'

'We, erm, haven't left yet.'

'Is there a problem?'

Ryan hesitated and once again looked at Crane, who mouthed the word, 'No,' followed by, 'tell him it's all okay.'

'No. No Bradley, everything's fine.'

'Well, I'll be there shortly, so you can take him back later.'

Bradley hung up and Ryan was about to pocket his mobile when Crane pointed at the table and Ryan leaned forward in his chair, and with a scowl put it down. Glancing around the room, Crane saw a nylon sash dangling by the closed curtains. He picked it up and said, 'Hold out your hands, and no tricks.'

Ryan's mean eyes were fixed on Crane as he slowly stretched out his arms and, in doing so, he made a grab for the iron bar, but Crane was too quick to be taken in by this obvious move and Ryan slumped back into his chair with a feeble groan. Crane left him securely bound and then wandered into the kitchen, returning a few moments later with a fresh mug of coffee. Ryan was still out cold.

After checking the sideboard drawers, Crane decided to have a quick look around the house, but could find nothing incriminating. Whilst upstairs, he heard a sound coming from one of the rooms. Slowly he edged his way towards the door, paused and listened; it was the noise of sleep. Opening the door quietly he inched his way into the room. An old lady lay on her back with a duvet pulled up to her chin. She was snoring softly and occasionally grunting. Crane assessed her to be in her eighties. He stood for a moment when suddenly her eyes blinked wide open. Crane raised a finger to his lips and whispered, 'Shh, it's alright, go back to sleep.' She seemed to obey this command, lowering her lids slowly and with a snort and a grunt, drifted back into her slumber.

Crane went downstairs and stood by the curtains. He checked his watch; it was a little after five am. He surmised that Bradley would be here anytime soon. Inching back the drapes he witnessed the early morning light filtering across the nearby open fields; it coincided with the local bird-life beginning their dawn chorus. A noise from behind made him turn around. It was Ryan fidgeting and regaining consciousness. A draught swept lazily around the room; a draught that Crane had not previously been aware of. A harsh voice snapped from the shadows in a corner of the room, 'Drop the iron bar.'

Crane turned towards the voice to find a Glock semi-automatic handgun pointing at his chest. He let the iron bar drop to the floor. Bradley's face was still in the shadows as he motioned Crane to a chair by the table. 'Sit down.'

Crane sat on a chair and rested his arm on an old oak dining table. Gun in one hand and without taking his eyes off of Crane, Bradley put his other hand in his pocket, produced a switchblade and cut through Ryan's bonds before prodding him with his left foot and saying irritably, 'You awake?' Ryan responded with a weary groan.

Ryan scrambled out of the armchair, staggered out of the room and headed for the bathroom. He walked towards the sink, stuck his head under the tap and turned it on.

Bradley was quiet for a moment, looking hard at Crane. It was their first direct meeting. Crane stared back defiantly at the lithe sinewy man. They were of a similar height, but Crane was broader. He guessed Bradley was no weakling. His hollow cheeks emphasised a mean character; even when he smiled, and Crane guessed he was dealing with a very cruel man. Bradley continued smiling and broke the silence with, 'You could have claimed on the insurance.'

'That car has sentimental value,' Crane replied.

'That kind of sentiment can get you killed.'

Crane, adept at thinking on his feet, became motivated when his eye caught a slight movement by the door that led to the hall and looking at Bradley said, 'I'd put that gun down if I were you.'

As Bradley scoffed, Crane quickly added, 'I didn't come alone; my old friend, Tony, by the door, has you covered.'

The confident Bradley sneered, 'You think I'd fall for that one?'

The door creaked as it was pushed open wider and Crane, looking over Bradley's shoulder said, 'It's about time you got here.'

Bradley spun round and came face-to-face with the old lady. She mumbled irritably, 'What time is it?'

Crane was ready. In a flash, he sprung from the chair and lunged at the gun; knocking it from Bradley's hand; sending it slithering across the hard surface of the lino. In the brief time it took Bradley to recover, Crane had scrabbled across the floor and scooped up the Glock. In a panic, Bradley quickly pushed the old lady out of the way, causing her to lose her balance. He made for the open door and into the hall and exited the way he had entered; by vaulting through an open sash window in an adjacent room. The old woman had inadvertently barred Crane's pursuit. By the time he had gently set her to one side, Bradley had managed to sprint down the drive and speed off in the newly-acquired Ferrari; its high-pitched exhaust note resounded into the distance.

Ryan was totally oblivious to everything that was happening. He turned off the tap in the cloakroom and began groping around for a towel.

Crane walked back into the house and came face to face with the old lady. He quickly tucked the handgun out of sight into the waistband at the back of his trousers. She squinted and peered into his face. 'Where's Stanley?' she demanded.

Crane shrugged his shoulders.

'He's always bringing people here and they stay for months,' she moaned. 'And they fills the barn up wiv their motors. Then he buggers off abroad somewhere for a few days. He should be taking care of the farm, he should. Ever since his dad died he hasn't lifted a finger on the land. When you find him, tell him to keep the noise down, I needs me sleep.'

The old woman trudged up the stairs to her bedroom.

For a moment Crane was left standing in the hall, contemplating his next move. Ryan, his senses returning, had seen Bradley hot-footing it down the drive and decided to follow suit. Peeping through a crack in the door, he saw his chance when Crane re-entered the front room. Slowly at first, Ryan edged his way across the hall into the opposite room and in a sudden panic, hurled himself through the open window. Crane heard the sound of heavy boots on the stony driveway outside. He pulled back the curtains and caught sight of Ryan jumping into the parked Mondeo. Ryan brought the engine to life. In a panic, he crashed it into gear and with wheels churning and spraying gravel everywhere, sped out of the drive.

There would be little or no chance of catching up with the pair, so Crane decided to have a chat with Stan, so he walked over to the barn and unlocked the Judas door and swung it wide open. The early morning light flooded in and made Stan blink as he sat on the floor; the remaining ether gas had, by now, dispersed. He looked at Crane quizzically. He rose slowly to his feet and moved unsteadily towards the open door but he stopped dead when he saw the Glock pointing directly at his head.

'I don't want to use this; it may wake your mother,' Crane said, 'but I will if you try anything.'

Stan, still a bit groggy, looked beyond Crane. There was no sign of Ryan or Bradley. 'Where's the others?' he rasped.

'Oh, they've left in a bit of a hurry. Now tell me, where do you think they have gone?'

'I dunno. You were the one who's not supposed to be here.'

'Well, I am.' Crane replied firmly. 'Now where is this place on the continent that Bradley goes to?'

'I don't know anything about that.'

'Your mother seems to think you do. Now I'll ask you one more time and if you don't tell me... ' Crane paused and pulled back the slide on the Glock before adding, 'I'll put a nine mil slug in your foot and one in your knee. Do you want to be crippled protecting the pair that abandoned you?'

Put like that, it did not take long for Stan to make a decision and with resignation said, 'Okay, okay. All I've done for Ryan and Bradley is take a few motors through the Channel Tunnel for them and then spend the day in Calais before getting a ferry and train back home.'

'Where do you drop them off?'

'A public car park right in the centre of the town, it's easy enough to find. I don't even see who picks them up. I lock the car up and leave the keys on top of the front tyre.'

Crane lowered the gun, 'Take my advice. Unless you want to end up in jail or get hurt, you'd be better off here – looking after the farm.' With that, Crane quickly turned and hurried down the drive to the old Mercedes that he had left partly hidden in some bushes off the main road.

Stan felt light-headed with relief as he walked across the yard, opened the door of the house and nearly bumped into his mother. Her finger was raised in the wagging position, but Stan shrugged his huge shoulders, held up his arms and said, 'Need to see about getting some grain in the ground before winter sets in.'

She was about to reply, but instead she stood with jaw agape as he walked past, picked up the phone and spoke to his local seed merchant.

Crane tossed his jacket onto the back seat, started the powerful V8 motor and pointed the Mercedes Benz towards Canford. During the uneventful drive back to Canford, his brain was awash with what had taken place over the past few hours. He drove with all the windows down in the hope that the fresh morning air would remove some of the ether fumes, still wafting from his clothing. He pulled the car into Palmers Rise, and after a few metres, stopped dead. A set of tyre tracks were plainly visible in the cement dust; and whoever made them, had not left. They were still there.

# CHAPTER SEVEN

Bradley's mean face was set in anger as he drove the Ferrari around the country lanes like a maniac. He eased up only when he reached the main A130 route. He cursed himself for miscalculating Crane's resolve; bringing his shady enterprise to a premature halt. A shrill warble resounded around the inside of the car and Bradley's hand automatically dipped into a jacket pocket to pull out his mobile phone. His eyes quickly flicked at the caller's number; it was Ryan.

Bradley answered with an irritable, 'Yeah?'

'I left just after you – through the open window.'

'You alone?'

'Course I am – in the Mondeo.'

'It's a good job we cleared the cars from the barn before Crane's visit. Things are finished here. We'll meet up in Suffolk to shift the last of the cars to the docks before we make for Cap Nez, okay?'

\*

Crane leapt out of the Mercedes; leaving it in the middle of the lane. As he put on his jacket, a weight pulling down on one side reminded him of the Glock. He took out the handgun and stuffed it into the waistband at the back of his trousers. He kept close to the bushes, which lay on either side and slowly made his way along the lane, edging his way towards home. He gradually rounded the slight bend and the cottage came into view. He felt a surge of relief as he realised that the tyre marks, which had been left at the end of the lane, belonged to a police car which was now parked in front of the cottage gate.

Crane checked his watch. It was nine am. 'Good morning, Constable Travers, you're up early.'

'It seems I'm not the only one, Mr Crane,' Travers smiled. 'I was driving down Alders Hill, and being as I know you, so to speak, I thought I'd give you a look in – my Chief Inspector informed me about the theft of your Mustang; that's the second time in as many days isn't it? Unfortunately, so far, we haven't had any luck in tracing it. Have you?'

Crane pursed his lips and shook his head. 'No, not yet, I'm of the opinion that it may now be somewhere on the continent.'

'You may well be right. There's been a whole spate of car thefts right across the county and into parts of Suffolk. There's reason to believe a well-organised gang is involved.' Constable Travers shuffled his feet and continued, 'Oh well, I'll be on my way. Let us know if you are successful.'

Crane did not want to reveal the cement dust trick and said, 'My newly-acquired car has run out of fuel and is blocking the lane.' He walked towards his parked Transit van, opened the rear doors and continued, 'Luckily I've got a spare can of fuel in here.'

As Travers moved towards his police car, his nose caught a whiff of Crane's clothing. He paused, raised his head, flared his nostrils and sniffed the air.

'Strange smell,' he remarked.

Crane replied quickly with, 'Probably some of the weed killer and fertilisers I've been using lately; I think they have been messing around with the formulas.'

'Hmmm, smells more like ether, eh?'

Crane, now with his head in the back of the van said, 'Oh, I wondered what it reminded me of; you never know what they are mixing up these days do you?'

*

Crane was enjoying a good soaking in the bath after putting his clothes in the washing machine. As he idly wallowed in the hot, steamy water, the raucous sound of his alarm resonated throughout the cottage. He sat up and scrambled out of the tub. There was no time to run through the scrubland to see who was approaching, so he hastily wrapped a towel around his waist. Crane was in no mood for physical confrontation; his ribs were still sore from the kicking he had received a few days earlier. So he placed the newly-acquired handgun in a strategic place completely out of sight, at the end of the narrow hallway. He was well aware of the UK's gun laws and had meant to dispose of the weapon, but in view of the past few hours, he thought it prudent to keep hold of the gun for a while longer.

An urgent rattle on the front door ensued. Stooping low, Crane peered around the wall at the end of the hallway. He recognised the shadowy figure through the frosted glass straightaway. It was unmistakably Penny. At a lower level, Andrew's face rested on cupped hands. His eyes were screwed up tight; trying to stare through the opaque glass. She rattled on the door again, only this time, the noise was more prolonged. Crane pulled on a pair of jeans and ran bare-footed towards the door. An excited Penny began a breathless chatter until Crane motioned for her and Andrew to come inside. He directed them towards the cosy beamed sitting room and said patiently, 'Okay, now start from the beginning.'

Penny brushed the hair out of her eyes and began in a calmer voice, 'I had a phone call from Bradley. He said he was on his way to the house and if I was still there when he arrived, he would beat me to a pulp. I was terrified.'

Crane looked at her for a moment. Even in her distressed state, he realised that she was a very attractive young woman. Crane looked at his watch, 'When did he call?'

'No more than half an hour ago. I hurriedly packed a few things for Andrew and myself, jumped in the Mini, drove around for a while, tried your phone, but there was no reply, and thought I had better come here to warn you. He sounded absolutely furious.'

Crane told her the details of his confrontation at the farm and finished with, 'One thing's for certain, he won't be going there again. I've discovered from the owner of the farm that he has use of a barn in France; somewhere near Calais, I'm going to follow it through when I catch up with him. Hopefully I'll also find out what has happened to your sister. But meanwhile, I'll pay a quick visit to your house, just in case he is still hanging around.'

Penny gave Crane a nervous glance, 'Do be careful, I really believe he's capable of anything.'

Crane smiled in an easy-going manner as he ran a hand over Andrew's mop of curly brown hair. 'I'm sure he is, but I'll be okay. I think for the moment, it would be safer if the pair of you stayed here until I get back.'

Crane finished dressing and dashed outside into the Mercedes. Within fifteen minutes he was standing by the front door of Penny's house. There was nobody in sight. There were no vehicles parked nearby and the house appeared deserted. However, Crane was taking no chances. Using Penny's key, he turned the latch slowly and stepped cautiously inside. All was quiet. He slipped off his shoes and padded softly towards the lounge. It was dark; the heavy velvet curtains were still drawn. He felt something brush against his leg. It was Felix, the cat, head-butting against the lower part of his trousers, mewing and purring; it was obviously his breakfast time and he had missed out.

Crane thought he heard something and stepped back into the hall. As he did so, Felix, vying for attention, sprang into action; running around and dashing in and out between his legs. Crane ignored this unwanted attention as he put an ear to the wall. A faint whining noise – an electric drill – could be heard from below. There was somebody still around. He moved to the end of the hall, stepped into the kitchen and peered through the window. From there he could see the twin doors of the basement garage. They were flung wide open. Crane replaced his shoes and stepped outside onto the brick pathway that sloped down towards the end of the rear garden onto the service road. Beside the path, a series of flag-stone steps led to a steep concrete ramp which connected the underground garage to the rear service road. Crane walked cautiously down the steps following the sound of the drill and paused when he saw a Volkswagen camper half in and half out of the garage. The sound of the drill was coming from the rear of the camper – its noise was continuous. He edged his way along the side of the camper van, paused and bent down and caught sight of the drill lying on the floor – running continuously. As he straightened up, a man in a blue boiler suit was rushing towards him swinging a hammer. The assailant's weapon missed Crane's head by a millimetre – smashing heavily into the side panel of the camper; causing a neat round dent. The man's grunt of effort was quickly followed by a deep yelp of pain as Crane, dropped to the floor and grabbed hold of the attacker's scrotum. Twisting hard, Crane pulled on the unfortunate part until the man fell to the floor with a heavy thud. In a split second, the would-be attacker felt a knee pressing firmly into his neck. Fearful eyes looked up at the ferocious expression on Crane's face as he hissed, 'If you move, I'll kill you.'

The man remained still and Crane continued, 'We need to talk. Now, what's your name?'

'Harry,' the man replied quickly and, without taking his eyes off of Crane he grunted hoarsely, 'Look mate, I don't know nuffink.'

Crane gave a tight smile, stared coldly into Harry's eyes and said quietly and matter-of-factly, 'Well then, Harry, you are no use to me whatsoever. I was going to let you live. You would have killed me with that hammer,' Crane glanced at the dent in the side of the camper and added with malice, 'that's for sure – so you can die right now.'

Harry began to panic as he felt the pressure on his neck increase. 'Wait… wait,' he gagged. 'Ease off, what do you want to know?'

Crane raised his knee slightly and said, 'Where's Bradley?'

'He's gone.'

'I can see that; tell me where exactly?'

'He's meeting Ryan at the barn in Suffolk. He came here in a bit of a hurry, picked up some vehicle documents and left.'

'What's the address?'

There was panic in Harry's voice as he said quickly, 'I don't know, honest, I've never been there. All I know is it's near Felixstowe; he's going there to put a consignment in containers ready for shipping.'

'Consignment? Stolen cars you mean.'

'Yeah, whatever.'

'How about France?'

'He's going there sometime this week.'

'Where do you figure in this?'

'I do a few alterations to some of the vehicles.'

'Like changing number plates,' Crane added.

'Yeah now and again.' Harry stopped abruptly as though he did not want to add to this.

Crane was intrigued, and as a prompt, he momentarily increased the pressure on Harry's neck, 'Go on.'

'Alright, ease up! I source most of the donor vehicles too.' Harry fell silent again.

'I'm getting impatient,' Crane said, grabbing hold of the hammer lying on the floor and holding it aloft.

'Alright, alright. This camper for example; I buy an old wreck of a van; legitimate like, then nick a motorhome of the same make; Peugeot or VW. Swap the ID plates over then send its log book off to get it re-registered as a camper and then take the wreck – minus its identity – to a breaker's yard for scrap. The stolen vehicle becomes legitimate. Similar thing with the cars, only sometimes we get hold of a damaged car from insurance companies' auctions – Bradley has good connections. All we need is the log book, the damaged car is taken to the breaker's yard and crushed – and the nicked car is made legitimate.'

Crane lifted his knee from Harry's neck, stood up and said, 'Don't move.'

Harry, remained on the floor, and feeling somewhat relieved said, 'You're that Jack Crane fella that Bradley told me about.'

'What did he tell you?'

'He just said to watch out for you in case you turn up here.'

Crane took his eyes of off Harry and looked around the back of the camper van. Harry gradually propped himself up on his elbows and slowly inched his way backwards until he was level with the passenger door. As soon as Crane's head disappeared, Harry sprang up, leapt in the side door and quickly pushed the central locking into place. He jumped into the driver's seat and turned the ignition key and the engine burst to life. Looking into the rear-view mirror, he sighted Crane at the rear end and swiftly knocked the camper into reverse gear, hoping to pin him to the rear wall, but Crane quickly side-stepped. The camper shuddered violently and the bumper split with a cracking sound as it thudded into the wall. Realising the futility of his actions, Harry jammed his foot hard down on the accelerator and wheel-spun the camper up the gradient, laying a trail of black rubber on the grey concrete surface, until he reached the service road at the top. Carelessly pushing his heavy hand against the gear lever, so that the cogs grated and clattered noisily, he sped off towards the direction of Southend.

Crane ran up the steps and back through the house, slamming the front door behind him as he raced towards his parked car. By the time he reached the main road, there was no sign of the camper – it could have gone in either direction, but Crane decided to turn left. The Mercedes screamed down the road towards Southend and after a few tight bends, Crane had the camper in sight, so he eased back on the throttle to follow at a distance. Hopefully he wouldn't alert Harry to the fact that he was being followed. After a few miles, the Mercedes coughed and began to fall back. Crane snatched a glance at the fuel gauge. It was registering half full. Hoping it was only the fuel gauge at fault, he stamped on the brakes, leapt out, grabbed hold of the spare fuel can from the boot and poured its contents – a couple of litres – into the tank. Within a few turns, the starter brought the engine back to life, but by then, Crane knew he had insufficient fuel, and realised there would be no chance of catching up with Harry. After a visit to the nearest filling station Crane made his way back to Palmers Rise and stopped dead at the scattering of cement dust strewn across the lane; fresh tyre tracks had left their mark in and out of the lane – and they did not belong to Penny's Mini.

# CHAPTER EIGHT

Bradley and Ryan met up at an old barn on the outskirts of Felixstowe in Suffolk and the iniquitous pair began stocktaking. The barn had a good roof and, despite huge cracks in some of the black weatherboards, it remained reasonably dry. The building was well suited for their purpose; because it nestled, partially concealed, amongst overgrown scrub. Its original use had been lost in the mists of time. The owner, who was a retired farmer, had sold off parcels of land surrounding the barn and did not mind earning some hard cash for storing a few cars – on a no-questions basis.

A huge grin spread across Bradley's face as he said, 'Do you think Crane has met up with Harry the Hammer yet?'

Ryan grinned back, 'He may well have done after you warned Harry about Crane. You left him back at the house working on a VW camper didn't you? That guy, Harry; he's not normal he ought to be in a home for the criminally insane.'

Bradley gave a half smile and said, 'Not again I hope.'

'What do you mean?' Ryan queried.

'He's been working for me ever since he came out of Broadmoor.'

Ryan's jaw dropped, 'Broadmoor? The mental hospital? You're having a laugh.'

'I wish I was – he's really great at sourcing vehicles, you can't deny him that!'

Ryan looked troubled and replied, 'He's gonna kill somebody one of these days, if he hasn't done so already. You never see him without that bloody ball-peen hammer. I was at the bottom of the hill when I saw Crane dash out of Palmers Rise in that old Merc. Then I nipped down the lane. Penny's Mini was parked in his drive. The boy, Andrew, was playing in the front garden. It was a piece of cake; the boy must have thought it was Christmas when he got in my car and found toys and sweets and all that. Penny must have been inside the cottage. She never even realised I was there; piece of cake!'

As he spoke, Ryan used his thumb to indicate where his car was parked. Bradley peered through the vegetation. He was unused to kids. Andrew's chocolate-smeared face had just consumed half a giant slab of Cadbury's Fruit and Nut. He appeared totally absorbed, playing with an electronic video game, whilst sitting in the back seat of Ryan's Mondeo.

*

Crane pulled into his driveway and saw a distraught Penny chasing around the garden calling out Andrew's name. She was a little relieved when she caught sight of Crane. 'I can't find Andrew,' she gasped, 'I've looked everywhere. He seemed to have disappeared when I was watching the news on TV, I should have kept a closer eye on him.'

'I don't want to worry you, but I believe someone else has been here whilst I've been away,' Crane replied grimly.

Penny looked at him aghast, 'How… how do you know?'

Crane shrugged his broad shoulders and told her about his cement dust trick.

Penny seemed uncertain by this and she said, 'How about the postman? Milkman?... ' Her voice trailed away as Crane shook his head, 'I collect my mail from the village Post Office, and I don't have a milkman or anyone else calling here on a regular basis. Someone must have seen me leave and I wouldn't mind betting on that someone being Ryan – the guy that tried it before.'

'But... why?' was all Penny could mutter.

'I'm not sure, maybe to join his mother perhaps, to placate her, wherever she is being held. Do you think it's time to inform the police?'

'I don't know what to do. I keep thinking that he may harm my sister and now he'll hurt Andrew as well if I do something like that.'

Crane moved towards his computer and switched it on. 'I'll have a look at the Google map around the Felixstowe area. It's a long shot, but I have a few clues as to their immediate whereabouts. All things considered, they can't be more than an hour or so ahead.'

After a few minutes Crane said, 'There's one or two barns that might be worth checking out,' at the same time he entered the coordinates onto a portable satnav and headed towards the front door.

Penny grabbed hold of her fleece jacket and said, 'I'm coming with you.'

Crane hesitated, 'Are you sure that's... '

'I'm sure,' she interrupted, 'it's my nephew that's been taken. Come on, let's go.'

Penny's resolve left no room for argument as she

brushed past Crane when he stopped to lock the front door. She headed towards the parked cars on the drive and stood between her Mini and the Mercedes, waiting for Crane to catch up. 'Your car or mine?' she enquired wryly.

Thoughts of trying to get her to change her mind were swept aside as Crane replied, 'If you insist on coming, I insist on driving, we'll take my car. Get in.'

Penny jumped into the Mercedes and as he was pulling out of the drive, she noticed his mobile phone lying on the floor. She picked it up, 'Does this thing work?'

Crane grinned at her sheepishly and said, 'I'm the world's worst mobile phone keeper you wouldn't believe how many I've ruined or... '

His voice trailed off as Penny, examining the device, interrupted, 'Battery's flat; you got an in-car charger?'

'No I've never... '

'Stop the car,' Penny cut in, 'I'll get mine from the Mini; you never know when they come in handy.'

Penny was in and out of both cars rapidly and as the Merc was backed out from the cottage, she was busy connecting the mobile phone to the dashboard charging socket. With a degree of satisfaction she said, 'There, that'll do it.'

Crane sped out of Palmers Rise and aimed the car towards Ashingdon and Hullbridge. At a sharp bend he turned into the aptly named Watery Lane, and after splashing his way through to Battlesbridge, picked up the A12 dual carriageway heading towards Ipswich.

A little over an hour later, they were travelling on the A14 and were within five miles of Felixstowe Docks. For the second time in as many minutes a mechanical voice announced, 'In one hundred yards, you have reached your destination.'

'Let's hope we are lucky enough to find something this time,' Crane mused as he pulled the car onto the hard shoulder. Slowly inching the car forward, two pairs of eyes scanned both sides of the dual carriageway. Penny caught sight of a gap in the hedge, 'How about there?'

Crane's head turned, his eyes following her well-manicured finger, then nodded in agreement and brought the car to a halt. Immediately Penny's reaction went into overdrive; she thumbed the seat belt release button and at the same time her other hand snatched at the door lock. 'I think it would best if you...' Crane's words trailed off; his eyes were focused on the door mirror; concentrating on a flashing blue light. A police car seemed to have appeared from nowhere and was chasing along the hard shoulder towards him until finally it screeched to a halt behind. It was only when a policeman got out of his car that in a hushed voice Crane finished his sentence, '... stay in the car.' But it was too late; Penny had disappeared through the gap in the hedge.

Crane lowered the driver's window and the policeman enquired, 'Is there a problem with your car, sir?'

'No, no problem at all. It's the erm, the wife,' he replied with a smile, 'she's been taken short – bladder problem – so she's gone for a pee behind the hedge. I'm sorry about this, shan't be here more than a few minutes.'

The policeman smiled knowingly and said, 'Alright, sir, in that case we'll leave you alone.' With that, he sauntered back to his patrol car and, after chatting to his companion for a moment, drove off.

Penny was thankful for her choice of flat shoes when carefully stepping around numerous muddy puddles; as she picked her way along a worn cart track which lead to an old rustic barn that stood, hemmed in by boundary fences belonging to adjacent farmland. Parked nearby was Ryan's Mondeo. Penny became excited as she got nearer; Andrew's chocolate smeared face had caught sight of her through the rear window of the car. A huge smile spread across his face and he began to wave excitedly with both hands. Spurred on by this Penny waved back and quickened her pace towards the car. She yanked and pulled at the car's rear door, but it was locked and she tried each of the car's doors, in turn, without success.

'You need these.'

After ferrying the stolen vehicles to the docks, Ryan had been left behind by Bradley in order to tidy up and make sure there were no old number plates or any other equipment, lying about. Now his chilling tone made Penny spin round. He was approaching the car twirling a set of keys with an inane grin on his face and repeated, 'You need these, but you're not getting em!' There was real intimidation in his voice as he flicked the remote control, and with a snarl said, 'Get in.'

Penny did not move and was about to argue, but Ryan moved menacingly towards her and repeated his threat, 'Get in the back and make it quick!'

Without taking her eyes off him, she scampered into the back seat next to Andrew who sat unfazed and said matter-of-factly, 'Uncle Ryan is taking me to see Mummy. Are you coming too, Auntie Penny?'

Penny gave Andrew a tight-lipped smile and a hug.

Regaining some of her composure she replied, 'Oh, that does sound nice.' Ryan slumped heavily into the driver's seat, firing up the engine as he did so.

As the car was turned around, Penny gingerly tried the door lock but to no effect; the child-proof locks were in place. The vehicle now turned into a narrow strip of road where Ryan spotted Crane walking some metres ahead. He put his foot hard down on the accelerator and aimed the car at the man who had caused him so much hassle.

Crane leapt out of the way by flattening himself into the hedge and as he did so he felt the tyres brush against his legs. He recovered in time to see a distraught Penny looking out of the rear window. He ran along the track splashing through muddy puddles towards the Mondeo. Ryan checked his rear-view mirror and scowled as he slammed on the brakes; slewing the car to a halt. With a grinding of cogs he thumped the gear lever into reverse towards his approaching victim. The hedge was too high for Crane to leap over so once again he managed to flatten himself into the spiky greenery, out of reach, as the rear of the Mondeo rammed into the bushes. Ryan pulled the car away from the hedge, spinning its rear wheels in the ruts and splattering Crane, from head to foot with watery mud. Ryan checked the rear-view mirror again and looked at the erect figure of Crane. He glowered, snorted and decided to give up; he was wasting time, so began to make his way towards the main road.

Penny could not take her eyes off of the receding figure of Crane. She looked at Andrew; playing with a toy car on his knee; he was blissfully unaware of what was happening. 'Where are you taking me?' she spat at Ryan.

He glanced at her through the mirror and said, 'Dunno till I talk with Bradley.'

'Why do you want the boy?'

'Bradley said his mother wants to see him.'

'Isn't he going to let *her* go?'

'Dunno. I just follow instructions. Now do me a favour; don't ask any more questions, right!'

Ryan turned off in a country lane and Penny guessed that this may be a ruse to ensure that Crane did not follow. It suddenly occurred to her that although her bag was in Crane's Mercedes, her mobile was in her pocket. She looked at Andrew; he was still preoccupied with his new toys. Her eyes darted surreptitiously towards Ryan and she saw him lean over to one side, grope around his jacket pocket, until his fat sweaty hand came out clutching a mobile phone and he began dialling one-handed. Slipping the phone from her pocket and holding it low she began to text Crane both the road number and the town that they were heading for.

*

Crane hurriedly splashed his way through mud puddles along the cart track back to the dual carriageway of the A14 and stared into the distance; there was no sign of the Mondeo. Opening the boot, he found some old rags and wiped off the surplus mess from his hands and face. Inside the car he had just began to study a map of the area when the trilling of his mobile alerted him to Penny's text. Immediately he sprang into action, voicing the instructions to the satnav. Instantly the gear lever was put into drive, and with the wheels screaming like a banshee, he thrust the car from the hard shoulder and back onto the dual carriageway.

*

Ryan thumbed in Bradley's number and held the mobile to his ear. The response came through immediately, 'Where are you?'

'On the A130 to Yarmouth. I picked up that woman, Penny. I'm taking a roundabout route just in case that bastard Crane tries to follow.'

'What!'

'I don't know how, but they found the barn. I'd just finished tidying up when I saw her trying to open the car door, so I made her get in.'

'Is Crane following you?'

Ryan glanced in the mirror and replied cockily, 'No. I left him lying in the mud. He'll find no sign of me by the time he gets back on the road.'

'Well you'd better get rid of the woman. Drop her off somewhere, anywhere. I only want the boy so you can tell the kid that I'm taking him to his mother. Give me a call when you've dumped her, okay?'

Ryan grunted, 'Yeah,' and put the mobile back in his pocket. Some miles further down the road Ryan spotted a lay-by sign and decided to offload Penny. Heavy rain had started to fleck the side mirrors of the Mondeo and the rear window had begun to mist up. If he had been able to check his rear-view mirrors, Ryan may have noticed that, in the distance, some way behind, a dirty white Mercedes saloon was gradually moving closer.

The Mondeo slewed into the lay-by and with a snarl Ryan turned in his seat and said, 'You can get out here and stretch your legs.' Nodding towards the direction of a toilet he said, 'You may want to use that.' And as though to justify his actions added, 'We're in for a bit of a long run.'

Penny tried the door lock, but it wouldn't open. Ryan grinned and to emphasise his control, stared at her and slowly pressed the release button. Penny guessed what was happening, but an idea came into her head and voicing out loud, echoed, 'There's a toilet? I could use that. That's very thoughtful of you.'

Ryan grinned once more; his plan was working, until Andrew suddenly became fidgety and started to undo his seatbelt. 'Toilet, I need to go too, Auntie Penny.'

Penny laughed inwardly, it was what she expected.

'It's all right, I'll take you.' Ryan breezed. 'You don't want to go to the ladies' loo now, do you?'

But it was too late. 'Want to go to toilet with Auntie Penny,' he called back as he scampered out through the open rear door. She held his hand tight as they both raced across the wind- and rain-lashed tarmac. Ryan leapt out and tried to catch the pair up as they headed towards the ladies' toilets, but he was too late.

As he was pacing around outside the toilet block, he noticed a dirty white Mercedes pull into the parking area. It stopped briefly for a second and then moved slowly towards him. Ryan cupped a hand over his eyes; squinting through the splattering rain. The wipers on the Mercedes were racing furiously across its windscreen, but there was no mistaking its driver. It was the mud-stained face of Crane. The Mercedes followed Ryan's movements and inched menacingly towards him. Fear showed in Ryan's face. He began to back away, then suddenly, he swerved his body to one side and broke into a sprint across the car park, leapt into his Mondeo, slammed it into gear and sped off.

Penny was standing on the toilet seat looking through an open window; she had witnessed the whole episode. Andrew, now with the chocolate stains removed from his face, stood nonchalantly beside her in the cubicle, still fascinated with the latest electronic pad that he held, firmly between his hands. As soon as Ryan drove off, Penny hurried out of the toilet and with both arms held high, began waving and running towards Crane. Her chest felt heavy with tension, but at last she felt as though she could breathe again.

'*Am I glad…* to see you!' she gasped.

Crane got out of his car and smiled broadly, accentuating a row of white teeth against a semi-camouflaged muddied face. His clothes were caked with dry mud. Penny stared for a second, laughed and with a huge sigh said, 'Look at you, covered in mud,' and placing her arms around his waist, gave him a hug. It was a reflex action. Andrew barely glanced up as he trailed slowly behind – eyes still focused on the small screen, fingering his games machine. It was the first time, in the short while he had known her, that Crane had seen Penny laugh or even smile. It suited her and Crane, despite feeling ominous about the whole situation, hoped that the final outcome would be a happy one. He then headed for the gents' and removed some of the dirt from his mud-encrusted face, while Penny phoned her brother Trevor, to bring him up to date with what had happened since he had left for work early that morning. She gave him Crane's address and suggested that he call there after he had finished work to discuss their next step.

\*

Ryan sped along the A130, wanting to put distance between himself and his adversary. His eyes were constantly fleeting towards the rear-view mirror. He steered the Mondeo carelessly with one hand whilst dialling Bradley's number with the other – stabbing at the buttons with his fleshy thumb. The ringing tone resounded in his ear for some time until eventually Bradley answered and Ryan blurted out, 'Crane's got the boy and that Penny woman.'

Bradley was clearly irritated, 'What! Where are they now?' he growled.

'I left them at a lay-by a few miles back.' And as if to defend his actions added, 'He took me by surprise as I dropped off the woman. Came at me in his car and tried to run me over.' As he was speaking, Ryan's shifty eyes, darted around the rear-view mirrors, and he added with confidence, 'I took off like a bat out of hell. Drove like the devil was after me and took a few side roads. He's not in sight. There's no way he can catch up with me now.'

Bradley was quiet for a moment, until eventually he sighed, 'Okay. Let me think on this one and I'll get back to you. By the way, on a more pleasant note, all our stock has been placed in containers and will be leaving the docks tonight.'

Ryan mumbled a, 'Thank fuck for that,' and hung up.

Bradley dialled Harry the Hammer's number. A gruff voice answered.

'Harry,' Bradley said cheerfully, 'have you met our Mr Jack Crane yet?'

Harry did not want to go into details with his embarrassing encounter and responded with, 'Briefly, so what?'

'He is a bit of a thorn in our side, Harry. Would you care to see to it? Sort of dissuade him, you know.'

Harry was a man of few words. This bolt from the blue – the very idea – excited him. He would be delighted to have another go at Crane, only this time it would be on his terms; he wouldn't make any mistakes and grunted, 'Where's he live?'

Bradley gave him Crane's address and added, 'He should be home within the hour. You may want to take someone to help.'

A plan to waylay Crane was already forming in the monosyllabic Harry's devious head and he grunted confidently, 'Who me? No worries; leave it to me.'

Bradley informed Ryan and they both laughingly agreed that the 'criminally insane' Harry the Hammer, would take good care of things for them.

# CHAPTER NINE

Crane had no intention of chasing after Ryan, especially with Penny and young Andrew onboard, so he decided to head for home. After a while, the light filtering through the car was gradually blotted out by a dark overcast sky. It was early September and the days were getting shorter. The gloomy clouds remained static, hovering above until eventually they completely blackened the sky, swallowing up the horizon. Suddenly, the windscreen was swamped by heavy rain and Crane's foot gently touched the brake. The car slowed down and, with headlamps blazing, it battled against the torrential downpour.

'I'm hungry,' he announced, 'fancy stopping for a bite to eat? There's a drive-in not too far from here.'

'Sounds fine,' Penny replied, 'all this excitement has made me feel peckish.' She turned her head and threw a glance at the back seat. Andrew – safely strapped in – was fast asleep with the games machine clutched against his chest. She turned back and said in a hushed voice, 'I really don't know why they want the boy. That is the second time they've tried to snatch him. Ryan told me his mother wants to see him, but he would not give any further information. It's obvious that they are not going to use me any more. I just don't understand why that crook is still holding on to my sister.'

'Maybe Bradley wants to wait until he has disposed of all the vehicles before he lets her go,' Crane mused, 'perhaps letting her go too early would be risky. Once he has covered his tracks it wouldn't matter who she tells everything to.'

'Mmm... ' Penny sighed, and sat quiet for a moment pondering, until Crane interrupted her thoughts with a half-hearted, 'I'm afraid this will have to do,' as he turned the Mercedes off the main road and into a drive-through eatery. Penny shared Crane's lack of enthusiasm, but her peckish feeling had turned to hunger and; a "when needs must" attitude took over.

*

Trevor dodged and weaved his way through the crowded Liverpool Street Station in time to board the packed 6.15 pm Southend-bound train. It was dusk when fifty minutes later, he leapt off at Hockley Station and walking at a brisk pace, collected his car from the station car park. Penny's phone call recounting her traumatic day's events had been playing on his mind, and he had decided to leave work early. The drive to Canford would take no more than fifteen minutes.

The clouds had darkened and it was raining hard as he pulled into Palmers Rise. He cursed angrily as the car's bright halogen headlamps illuminated the shape of a large waste bin, seemingly abandoned in the middle of the narrow lane. It meant leaving the dry comfort of the car and getting wet. He yanked the handbrake on, leapt out of the car and walked quickly towards the obstruction. As he positioned his hands on the sides of the bin, the lid raised itself high in the air, and like a jack-in-the-box, Harry the Hammer rose up. His maniacal eye-bulging stare was enough to make anyone jump out of their skins and Trevor was no exception. Before he could recover his wits, a ball-peen hammer smashed cruelly against his temple and he slumped to the ground.

Harry leapt out of the huge bin and with a great deal of satisfaction quickly strutted around the still form of the rain-soaked body. He then, in a mad rage, ran to Trevor's car and struck the panels several times with his hammer. Despite the heavy rain, Harry felt compelled to take a closer look at the still form lying on the ground. He wanted him to move so that he could strike him again. Trevor's head lay to one side and using his foot, Harry nudged it face up. Fumbling in his pocket, he produced a small torch, and bending down slightly, he sent a beam of light directly onto his unfortunate victim's head. He focused it onto a solitary mark in the centre of Trevor's forehead where a trail of blood, slowly oozing from the wound, was being washed away down the turned neck to mingle with the muddy surface of the lane.

Harry straightened up, and the beam widened, moving across Trevor's turned face. Harry suddenly became transfixed. He knew he could never forget Crane's features after all, he had the experience of staring up into his face for some period of time. He remembered feeling Crane's hot angry breath and the full weight of his knee – Harry's poor neck still ached from their last encounter. Realisation came to him slowly. The face he was looking at was not the face he remembered. Wide-open eyes – dead-looking eyes – were staring back accusingly at Harry. They sent shivers down his spine. It was the wrong man – and he was dead.

Harry had never killed anyone before; he had maimed a number people – smashing their limbs with his hammer; but not killed. Panic began to set in and he ran; slipping and sliding through puddles, almost falling over, as he made his way to the place where he had partially hidden his old Escort van. After falling into the driver's seat, sweat began to mingle with the rain dripping from his sodden hair. It began to sting his eyes and rubbing them seemed only to make things worse. To try and gain some relief, he blinked hard several times whilst turning the ignition key. Screwing his eyes up tightly, he gradually squinted through the rain-lashed windscreen and then crashed through the gears jerking the van violently forward.

There was no room to spare as he tried to coax the van past Trevor's car. The car still had its engine purring steadily and its headlamps brightly illuminated the twisted prone figure on the rain-sodden ground. He made several attempts of metal scraping and grating against metal on one side, together with the chafing of woody brush on the other side, before he finally made it through to the main road and sped off in the direction of Rochford.

*

Crane drove out of the fast-food car park and eased the Merc along at a steady pace as he headed back home to Palmers Rise. Penny felt on edge and said, 'Do you think they'll try to take Andrew again?'

'They've tried twice now without success, I think they may leave things as they are for a while, but if they are that determined, they'll try again when you least expect it.'

Penny stared vacantly through the windscreen as she spoke, 'I have an apartment which I was forced to leave while living in that house. For some reason I always had to be on tap, so to speak. Now I'm worried about going back to my own place.'

'You can stay at my cottage if you like,' Crane offered.

'That's very kind of you,' Penny sighed, 'but it's even more remote. I know it's cowardly, but I'd be scared stiff of being left on my own, and you can't leave a boy like Andrew locked up inside all of the time.'

Crane thought for a moment and said, 'Maybe it's time to get the police involved. Tell them the whole story. I'm sure they will find a safe place for you both until it all blows over.'

'If it had not been for my sister, Jean, I would have done so from the start, but I suppose these attempts to take Andrew change things.' Penny turned to look at the boy – he was still asleep. 'If I told the police everything, I would probably get arrested for aiding and abetting. I'll talk to Trevor about it this evening. I phoned him whilst you were getting the mud off your face and brought him up to date. He's leaving work early and instead of going home to his apartment, he's coming straight over to your place this evening.'

\*

Bradley met up with Ryan to discuss their next move. They were seated in a Little Chef on the A12 near Ipswich. 'Things were better until that Crane came onto the scene,' Ryan mused. 'Maybe we should have let him keep his car.'

'What? And throw away the best part of forty-odd grand? His car is a '*Shelby*' Mustang in pristine condition – rare as rocking horse shit – and it's worth that kind of money anywhere.'

'Yeah I suppose you're right. Let's hope Harry sorts things out.'

Their conversation was interrupted by a noisy ringtone. Bradley plucked a mobile from his jacket pocket and eyed the tiny screen. 'Talk of the devil,' he said, 'it's Harry the Hammer. Don't tell me he's done the job already.' Bradley put the phone to his ear and said, 'Yes,' whilst Ryan looked on in anticipation.

'I've done the wrong bloke.'

'Who is it?'

'I dunno, I think maybe I've seen him at the house, it could be… '

Bradley cut him short; 'Trevor, the brother,' he stated flatly.

'Yeah, that's it.'

Bradley remained calm and said, 'How bad is he?'

It was quiet for a moment and Bradley thought he had been cut off until he heard Harry's low voice mumble, 'He's erm… dead.'

Bradley remained calm and said, 'Are you sure?'

'Oh yes. I'm sure. I need to get away.'

'Of course you do. You had better pack your things and find somewhere to go until things settle down; oh and erm, don't call me for a while, I'll get in touch sometime next week.'

Bradley looked at Ryan and simply said, 'The silly fucker has topped the wrong man; he's done in Trevor! Still there's nothing to connect us.'

Ryan shrugged and they both carried on eating their meal.

*

Crane swung the Mercedes into Palmers Rise and immediately stopped. The blue iridescent lights of an ambulance and a police car reflected through his windscreen; eerily illuminating the pair of wide-eyed faces staring at the scene. Crane leapt out of the car and hurried towards the carnage. After checking that Andrew was still asleep, Penny followed Crane.

The rain had eased off slightly and, upon seeing Crane approach, PC Travers motioned him towards the back of the ambulance and said sombrely, 'Evening, Mr Crane. I don't suppose you know anything about this.'

It was a statement rather than a question. Crane had known the local bobby for a few years. Crane shook his head. Travers continued in his serious, concerned tone, 'About fifteen minutes ago, I was just passing by and noticed a stationary car in the middle of the lane with its headlamps blazing and driver's door wide open. I drove up behind and saw the body lying in front of the car. It's murder all right. Single blow to the head – killed outright; I thought it might have been you at first. Do you know him?'

Crane climbed into the ambulance with PC Travers. He looked down at the lifeless form of Trevor and in a hushed voice said, 'Yes.'

Then as Penny got out of the Merc, he nodded towards her and said, 'That's his sister.'

Travers glanced towards Penny as she approached and said to Crane, 'Have you any idea what may have happened?'

'No. We arranged, rather his sister, Penny, arranged to

meet him at my cottage this evening.' As an afterthought he added, 'If only we had got here sooner… ' His voice trailed off as Penny climbed up the step at the rear of the ambulance.

A look of horror spread across Penny's face when she recognised the lifeless form of her brother lying on the ambulance stretcher in the back of the ambulance. Without saying anything, her head turned, looking from Crane to Travers the policeman, searching for some kind of explanation. Crane stepped up to put an arm around her shoulders and her eyes began to fill with tears until suddenly they began to flow uncontrollably.

Travers broke the silence with, 'I'm so sorry, miss. We don't know exactly what has happened here, but we'll find whoever's responsible.'

Vehicles were moved and the ambulance headed for the mortuary at Southend General Hospital. After parking Trevor's car further down the lane, it was decided that it would be best if Penny and Andrew spent the night at the cottage. The young lad seemed to like the idea and after supper he settled down in bed.

Penny kept her voice low, 'Have you any idea who… '

Crane interjected with, 'Oh yes. The guy that left his trademark on your brother's head is Harry, the guy I came across when I went back to your house. He nearly caught me with that hammer of his. Do you know anything about him?'

Penny thought hard for a moment until she came up with, 'Harry the Hammer – Hammerteen,' she stated flatly. 'He does work for Bradley. I overheard Bradley refer to him several times. Strange name, not easily forgotten. Always carries a hammer – either in his hand or in a pocket. I've seen him a few times. He's a strange kettle of fish – weird, creepy. A slim, lithe-looking bloke, but muscular. Shifty, weasel-like eyes – always stares at me if we are in the same vicinity. About five foot eight tall. I'm not sure, but I believe he lives on Canvey Island.'

Crane blew some air between his teeth, 'That's a perfect description. Look, Penny, now that it's murder, as well as kidnap, don't you think it's time to get the police involved, you know, tell them the full story?'

'I guess you're right, but I'm so worried about my sister – wherever she may be.'

Crane had been thumbing through the telephone directory as Penny was talking, and now questioned, 'How long has it been since you actually heard from your sister?'

'I've not heard a word from her since she disappeared three months ago.'

Crane kept the thought, *"She could be dead,"* to himself and he suddenly announced, 'Hammerteen; H Hammerteen, it's in here, and he does live on Canvey. Maybe I should pay him a visit, take him to the police and *then* we can tell all. What do you think?'

'Do you think that he'd go home?'

Crane checked his watch, 'Harry's initial attack would have happened barely an hour ago and as far as he's concerned no one would be looking for him – at least not yet. If he's going to do a runner, he will have time to go home and pack first.'

Crane tossed the directory onto the table, grabbed a padded jacket and headed for the door, then turned and said, 'Keep it locked till I get back. I'll call you on the mobile.'

Penny felt weak in the knees at the thought of being left

alone in a strange home, 'Don't let the battery run flat then,' she managed to say feebly.

'I've still got your charger – remember?'

Penny gave a nod and a weak smile as she followed him towards the door and turned the latch after he left.

*

Harry chased around his rented accommodation, a small terrace house off the main road near Small Gains Corner on Canvey Island. Thoughts and plans whirled around his head in a kaleidoscopic manner; *'Passport, passport, car insurance, drivers licence,'* as he rushed around gradually filling a large suitcase. It had not been much joy on the road travelling back home. The traffic had been particularly heavy, plus a front tyre had punctured – probably caused by something in that damn lane. He considered himself lucky to find a service station in the nick of time. So all-in-all, it had taken him much longer than expected to get home.

Harry felt dry-mouthed and kept looking at the large clock hanging high on the wall, each ominously loud tick jerking into his brain and reminding him to hurry up, *'But don't forget anything.'* He forced himself to remain calm. He had never killed anyone before, just smashed their bones. His plan had been to bring the hammer down hard on Crane's collarbone and then smash it into his knees. *'That would put him out of action,'* he thought at the time. How was he to know it was the wrong man? Now the police will get involved and it will be a murder hunt, but *'Nobody knows it was me.'* Harry's mind was in overdrive, *'After all, it's not as though anybody was chasing me, I could walk if I wanted to.'* But the nagging doubt would not go away, and it spurred him on. He was now packed and ready to leave.

The sound of a car door slamming made him drop his suitcase. His right hand sprang up, like a switchblade, and flicked off the light before dashing across the room, in the dark, to the window. His hand slowly eased a tiny gap in the curtain and he peered into the shadowy greyness outside, only to find it was a neighbour arriving home late from work. Like a sentinel, he remained in the same position for some time until he felt confident it was safe enough to leave and he grabbed hold of his suitcase and exited through the rear door.

Harry walked cautiously round to the front of the house and made his way towards his old Escort van that was parked amongst a row of assorted vehicles. He intended to drive to the lock-up garage where he had left the Volkswagen camper; he could then switch the vehicles over and head for the continent in the camper van.

Crane drove into Harry's road in time to see a shadowy figure leaving the side of a house, then toss a suitcase into the back of a van, before driving off. There was no doubt in Crane's mind that the shadowy, almost macabre, figure, was Harry.

Crane followed the van at a distance whilst figuring out his next move. He did not have to wait long. After approximately a mile, the van turned off the main road and entered a small courtyard. Crane parked his car nearby and leapt out. Approaching the yard with caution and keeping close to a wall, he peered around the edge of the building. In front of him he noted there were twelve double-sized detached garages. In the dim light, he saw that one garage door was fully open and that an Escort van stood in the yard to one side; its door was flung wide open and the engine was still ticking over.

The sound of another vehicle engine starting up, prompted Crane to make his move. The clatter of both engines camouflaged the noise made by the sudden rush of his feet against the gravel surface of the yard. He darted towards the stationary Escort and found a suitable gap, where he could press himself in between two garages. He made it in time to see the camper now emerge into the centre of the yard. Harry jumped out – leaving the camper engine running and the driver's door wide open. He then ran frantically to the Escort to garage it. As the Escort disappeared into the garage, Crane darted from his hiding place up to the camper, turned the engine off and swiftly removed the ignition keys, before retreating to his hiding place. Harry pulled hard on the up and over garage door; crashing it down noisily. Then, without bothering to lock it, he darted like a ferret back to the camper van, jumped in and slammed the door violently.

Crane left his hiding place and sauntered towards the driver's door of the camper. As he approached, he could see the frantic movements of Harry, who was scrambling about in the front of the camper searching high and low for the ignition keys. In the now suddenly quiet surroundings, Harry turned his head sharply as he heard the crunching sound of heavy feet upon gravel. His weasel-like eyes strained as they peered into the light of his headlamps, diffused and laced with rain. His eyes widened as he recognised the well-built figure of Crane approaching, holding aloft a set of keys. In a flash, Harry snatched at the central locking with his right hand; all the locks snapped shut. A wide grin of delight suddenly spread across his face. Then his left hand delved into his jacket pocket and produced a spare set of keys. Without delay he plunged them into the ignition, started the engine and, with the rear wheels displacing a generous mound of gravel, left the yard.

Crane cursed as he hurled himself towards his Mercedes. He leapt in, fired up the engine and slotted the auto transmission into drive, aiming his car at the receding haze of tiny red lights in the distance.

Harry knew he was lucky to escape another face-to-face confrontation with Crane. He was beginning to feel invincible; he had got away with it for a second time. The road ahead was empty, so he slammed his foot down hard on the accelerator as soon as he entered the long stretch of Canvey Road. The shock of seeing Crane was subsiding, but he could not stop his eyes from continually darting to the rear-view mirrors.

Far in the distance, two pin pricks of white light appeared; it worried him – *could it be Crane?* Further along the road, he nearly lost control when taking a roundabout too fast and the camper slithered on the wet surface into the kerb. This made Harry feel more edgy as he sped towards the bridge that spanned Benfleet Creek. As though mesmerised, he could not take his eyes off of the camper's door mirrors, because the pin-pricks of light that they reflected had steadily grown into much larger orbs; *"Is it Crane? If not why are the lights catching up?"* He watched, as the car behind also slithered at the roundabout and was now less than a hundred metres away.

Crane was in no doubt that he was following Harry's

camper van. He was surprised that the villain, given a head start, had not tried to hide in any of the side roads, but was instead making a straight run towards the bridge that joined the island to the mainland. Crane, foot hard down, was catching up by the second but then he suddenly braked, slithering to a halt.

Harry was fixated; he was concentrating on the rear-view mirror, more so than looking at the road ahead. If he had done so he would have noticed that one side of the bridge was sectioned off. It was closed for repairs to the barriers. His enthralment with the road behind was interrupted by flashing amber warning lights that filled the cab of the camper van. Harry's right foot tramped down hard on the brake pedal, as he tried to veer away, but it was far too late. A look of terror spread across his face as the camper smashed through the warning signs and slithered towards the area where the barrier had been removed. Shocked workmen threw themselves to one side as the camper slid towards the side of the bridge. Bright floodlights, set up by the workforce to facilitate the repairs, illuminated the camper as it teetered on the edge – balancing for a split second – before it plunged headlong into the murky depths of a high tide. The camper bounced up on the surface of the creek and floated on the swift current, but as gallons of water rapidly seeped through door seals, cracks and openings, the vehicle quickly began to submerge. Harry frantically tried to open the door; but the outside pressure of water made it impossible. His hand repeatedly stabbed at a button controlling the windows, but the electrics had short circuited. He was trapped.

Crane watched fascinated as the camper gradually sank

to the muddy bottom. It would not be seen again until some hours later when the tide ebbed once more. There were enough witnesses around. Having recovered from the shock of jumping out of harm's way, the work crew stood by watching helplessly. One of them contacted the emergency services. Crane, not wanting to get involved, managed to slip away unnoticed. He would send an anonymous note to the police informing them of the Escort van's location and of Harry's involvement of Trevor's demise.

Crane drove back to Canford through patchy squalls of heavy rain and was glad when he swung the car into Palmers Rise. Penny heard the car in the lane, long before Crane pulled into the drive. She stood anxiously in a front room by the window, watching as he got out. By the time he reached the front porch, door keys in hand, Penny was already standing by the front door and with a look of relief swung it open and said breathlessly, 'Any luck? Did you find him?'

'Sort of,' Crane replied briefly, as he stepped inside and continued, 'things didn't turn out quite as I'd planned.'

Penny, with a puzzled expression on her face, followed him into the kitchen, and as he filled the kettle and put it on, he brought her up to date on the past hours' events. She stood silent for a moment, watching Crane make a pot of tea, until eventually she said, 'Are you sure he's dead?'

'Oh yes, unless he has aqua diving gear on board.'

Penny continued with her questions, 'And you're sure it was him?'

'Yeah, the Escort van had a sample of paint all along one side, and the other side still had bits of bracken poking out. Plus the fact I had a good look at his face before he sped off.'

And pushing a mug towards her said, 'Tea?'

As Penny lifted the mug she gave him a steady gaze and remarked, 'You're a cool one, Mr Crane.'

*

The two thieves had finished their meal in silence. Bradley was now thumbing through a small diary as they were mulling over their next move.

'We have six left-hand drive classic Yanks containered at Southampton docks. They are due to be shipped to Jacksonville next week; very collectable in the States. And three left-hand drive motorhomes stored at Dover; they need to be taken over one at a time.'

Ryan was deep in thought; wondering whether now was the time to quit. Underneath it all Crane was beginning to bug him and he reasoned he would not stop until he got his Mustang back. Bradley interrupted his thoughts, 'It's a pity that Crane has hastened our departure, I owe him big-time, but in the meanwhile, I'll make sure that our stock is on its way out of the country before I make it up to him.'

At that moment a raucous sound reverberated between the two men. Bradley snatched at his jacket pocket, plucked out his mobile phone and looked at the tiny screen. A smile spread across his face as he answered. 'What have you got Davy?'

Ryan watched with interest as Bradley's eyes widened as he listened to the caller until eventually Bradley finished with, 'Yeah, I'm interested, I'll call you back later this evening.' The phone remained clenched in his fist for a while until he broke the silence with, 'That was Davy Porter.'

'What's he got?'

'Three good un's.'

'Really, what are they?'

Bradley smiled and continued, 'Late cars – about two years old. A Jag, a Merc, and a Beamer.'

'Are they hot?'

'All cold metal, so he says. Cleaned up and ready to ship. I was about ready to suspend things, but this is an offer I can't refuse.'

\*

It had been a long tiring day and Penny, feeling totally exhausted, settled down in the same room as Andrew and soon fell into a fitful sleep. The tragic loss of her brother and the dangerous situation of her sister, were scored deeply into her soul and she awoke tearfully several times. Crane, after setting the alarms and locks also turned in – his mind awash with the past few days events; *"Penny's sister could be dead. Why did they want young Andrew? As a lever to get Penny to do their bidding? Or to take him to his mother?"* At present there was no next move. Things mulled around in his mind until eventually he fell asleep.

He awoke early next morning to find Penny and Andrew up and already dressed. She looked at him, gave a half smile and said, 'I thought it best to go back to my apartment now I'm not forced to live in that house any more.'

'Do you think Bradley will go back to the house?'

'I don't see why, he only rented the place. I suppose I fitted in to his plans very well, but not any more.'

Crane suddenly had an idea, but decided to keep it to himself for the time being. It was a long shot, but then he was used to taking long shots; it was what he did.

# CHAPTER TEN

Crane watched as Penny turned her Mini out of the drive; Andrew gave a quick glance and a wave before looking down at his electronic game. Now they were gone, Crane prepared a few sandwiches, got in his car and headed for the house in Denisons Lane, in the hope of finding something that may lead him to the whereabouts of Bradley. As soon as he arrived there at the lane he parked the car some distance away from the house and walked along the pavement and then past the building before turning into the service road at the rear. After satisfying himself that he was alone and unobserved, he used the keys that Penny had given him, and slipped in the house through the back entrance. He had figured, if anyone was going to come to this place it would be sooner rather than later.

After he had checked over every room in the house, he looked in the garage – there were no clues as to what had been going on there. He was fairly certain that the place was exactly as he had left it on the previous morning. At lunchtime he settled down with a sandwich and a mug of coffee. By mid-afternoon, his patience was about to be rewarded. Peering out of the front window, he saw a small car transporter pull up and park adjacent to the driveway. Its single occupant, a man, about five foot ten in height and of stocky build, got out and sauntered towards the front door.

His bunch of keys rattled and as one of them entered the lock, the man hesitated when he heard the urgent ringtone of his mobile. Crane stood near to the front door and listened intently to one side of the conversation. The man had a gruff London accent; 'So you made your mind up then. Where do you want them delivered?' There was a pause and the conversation continued, 'Okay, but I want readies, large notes will do nicely okay? Oh, and don't forget you owe me for the rent.' There was a pause and then he finished the conversation with, 'I'm at my house now, I'll meet you at the docks around four this afternoon.'

He returned the mobile to his jacket pocket, turned the key and stepped into the hall and walked straight into the kitchen and switched a kettle on. It was then his heart skipped a beat as he noticed Crane casually leaning against the wall drinking a mug of coffee.

'What the fuck are you doing in my house?'

'I've come to ask you where I might find Bradley,' Crane replied pleasantly.

The man took a step towards Crane and said aggressively, 'What? Me tell you? Are you fucking mad? There's more chance of a one-legged man winning an arse kicking competition! Now get out!'

Crane didn't move, 'I'll go when you tell me where I can find Bradley.'

'You get out of here now or I'm throwing you out!'

Crane did not move.

At that moment the man's mobile rang; he ignored it and with a look as dark as thunder he rushed towards Crane. In a flash, Crane tossed the full mug of hot coffee straight into the man's face. An agonising scream followed and the unfortunate victim's hands shot up towards his eyes. Crane pulled him down to the floor sat on his chest and leant a knee across his neck, and with his free hand wiped the man's face with a tissue. 'There,' Crane remarked calmly, 'let's start this all over again shall we. First off, what's your name?'

'Davy, Davy Porter,' he gasped. 'Ease up on my neck, will yuh?'

Crane raised his knee slightly, 'Okay, Davy. It's a nice place you got here. Now once more, tell me, where's Bradley?'

'I don't know anyone called Bradley.'

Crane sighed loudly and increased the pressure on Davy's neck, 'You'd better.'

'Alright, alright. He's just a tenant, I rent this place to him.'

Crane kept up the pressure on Davy's neck and said, 'You're going to have to do better than that.'

'Bradley will kill me if he finds out I've told anyone.'

There was menace in Crane's voice as he said, 'I'll kill you right now if you don't,' And with that said, he increased the pressure once more. 'I haven't got all day, this is the last time: tell me or I'll crush your windpipe.'

'Alright, alright,' Davy gasped, 'I don't know where he is, he could be anywhere but,' he hastened to add, 'I'm meeting him later this afternoon.'

'What time and where? And don't lie to me; I picked up some of your conversation just now.'

'Four o'clock; Harwich Docks.'

'That's better. What have you got for him?'

'Some motors on a transporter.'

'Okay. Now this is what's going to happen. First of all, when you get up, you are going to give me your mobile so that you won't be able to contact Bradley. I'll be right behind you when you drive to Harwich. When I catch sight of Bradley, I'll leave you alone.'

'Yeah okay. Why do you want this so bad? I mean, what's he done to you?'

'He stole my car, an old Mustang and I want it back.'

'Oh.'

Crane straightened up, and as he did so he looked down at the prone figure of Davy and said, 'Just so you know who you are dealing with, don't try any tricks if you want to get out of this in one piece – is that clear?'

Davy propped himself up on his elbows and said, 'Alright, I know when things are stacked against me. Can I get up now?'

'Yeah, but remember what I've just said.'

Davy got to his feet and at that point, his mobile rang. He removed it from his jacket pocket and looking at Crane, hesitated. 'Answer it with the speaker on,' Crane warned, 'and if it's our friend Bradley, be very careful about what you say – it could cost you dearly.'

Crane's assumption was correct. Bradley's voice resounded around the room. 'Davy, I meant to warn you; there's a guy called Jack Crane that's poking around. He knows about the house, that's why we moved out. He's about six foot tall fairly well built, ex-SAS, so don't tangle with him; give him a wide berth – okay?'

Davy shot a quick forlorn glance at Crane and with some resignation replied, 'Yeah thanks, I need to know that,' and hung up.

*

Bradley and Ryan had spent the night at a boarding house in the back streets of Westcliff-on-Sea, during which time Bradley had made phone calls and arranged for his new assignment to be shipped from Harwich.

It was lunchtime and Ryan was busy re-fuelling the car that they were both using. Bradley leant back comfortably in the front passenger seat, flicking through the pages of his diary as Ryan replaced the petrol pump nozzle and went off to pay the bill. Waiting to be served inside the kiosk, the front page of the *Southend Echo* caught his attention: 'Camper Drives off Bridge'. Ryan grabbed hold of a copy before he left the kiosk and dashed across the forecourt to show Bradley. Together they stared wide-eyed at the bold print and colour photo of the camper, which was partially submerged near the bridge, 'That's Harry's latest camper alright.' Ryan said, 'It explains why we haven't heard from him.'

'Do you think Crane has had anything to do with this?'

Bradley shrugged and looked askance as he replied, 'There's no mention of a third party being involved. Witnesses say he couldn't have been concentrating. They say the vehicle braked too late and skidded straight through the temporary traffic lights, through the open rails and into the drink.'

'It's a bloody coincidence though, all the same.'

'Yeah, I guess we'll never know.'

Bradley turned the page and another report stared back at him; 'Murder in Canford'. He grinned at Ryan and said, 'That should have been Crane; he's one lucky sod.'

Ryan shrugged a reply, 'Yeah, but it won't be long before his luck runs out; his turn will come soon enough – I promise you.' There was a pause and he continued, 'By the way, how did you meet up with Harry in the first place?'

Still scanning the newspaper and without looking up, Bradley replied, 'In Broadmoor.'

Ryan stared at the nonchalant Bradley expectantly, as if awaiting some kind of punch line of a joke. There was none. Bradley rustled the paper as he turned a page and added, 'I was there for a short time, being assessed, as they call it. I met Harry, realised his potential and helped him escape.'

Ryan felt a little uneasy at these revelations, but did not dare show it. He began to regret asking and said simply, 'Oh well, we'll miss him,' but the unease remained. However, he managed to brush things aside and concentrated on only one thought; *"Bradley's helping me earn a lot of money."*

\*

Crane trailed the car transporter, lagging behind at a hundred metres or so distance. Porter grinned to himself, eyeing the rear-view mirrors and picking up his spare mobile phone he dialled Bradley. 'I've got that Crane bloke on my tail.'

'What! How… '

Porter bought Bradley up to date with his encounter with Crane. Bradley was furious, but he managed to hold it back as he almost whispered a reply, 'And you told him about our meeting place?'

'I had no choice. When you called first, I was outside the house. I didn't know he was inside; he'd heard part of our conversation. I tried lying but he was choking me – I had to tell him – didn't I?'

Bradley was quiet for a moment. An idea was gradually forming, and he replied slowly, 'Okay… be sure to contact me before you turn off at Ipswich on the A14 Felixstowe road.'

'Sure thing, Brad.'

Bradley hated having his name shortened, but he let it go; he had more important things to think about. He looked at Ryan and said, 'Crane's on Davy's tail. He's driving an old white Merc 500. Give Terry a shout – find out where he is.'

Ryan dialled Terry's number and almost immediately the call was answered. After the usual salutations, Ryan said, 'Are you in the Ipswich area?'

'It's where I live innit?' came the jovial reply. 'What are you after?'

Ryan smiled, nodded at Bradley and said, 'There's a guy giving us a bit of aggro; he's following Davy in a white Merc 500. Can you tap him off the track for us?'

There was amusement in Terry's voice as he said, 'No problem; what, when and where?'

Ryan gave Terry the details, hung up and gave Bradley a satisfied look, 'That's Crane sorted out.'

Within the hour Bradley's mobile rang. It was Davy. 'I'm approaching the A14 junction now. He's still behind me.'

A brief smile and an, 'okay,' escaped from Bradley's lips and he dialled Terry's number. 'He's on his way.'

'Right. I'll be waiting.'

# CHAPTER ELEVEN

Penny's head seemed to be in a whirl. She felt like bursting into tears as she rummaged around her apartment, cleaning and tidying things up. Her mind was torn between the grief she felt for her dead brother and the constant worry about the fate of her missing sister, but she knew that she had to hold herself together for young Andrew's sake. She cast a glance in his direction; he had found a quiet corner and was amusing himself drawing on a pad with coloured felt-tip pens. She stood for a moment watching him, and it seemed to give her a sense of purpose and a calm strength of resolve.

*

One thing that can be relied upon in England is the unreliable weather. The sun was bright and cheerful when Crane took to the road. He had followed Davy's transporter through Rochford and Ashingdon, but by the time they reached the roundabout on the outskirts of Ipswich, ominous groups of heavy cloud had taken its place. As they turned onto the A14 road to Felixstowe, a heavy downpour ensued causing automatic headlamps from the passing traffic to switch on, their beams reflecting a silvery path as they trundled along at a steady pace.

Crane was surprised when a heavy truck sped past, its

rear wheels splattering water and dirt onto his windscreen. Then suddenly, its driver swung the vehicle in front of his Mercedes, blocking his view of the transporter. Instinctively Crane eased on the brakes. Without warning, the truck in front began to slow down. Crane, keeping an eye on his rear-view mirror, waited until the outside lane was clear, and then pulled out in an attempt to pass the slow moving truck. Terry, the driver of the truck, had other ideas and swung his lorry out directly into Crane's path. Crane's reactions were swift. He slammed hard on the brakes, the tyres aquaplaning on the drenched surface sending the Merc towards the hard shoulder. By now, Crane surmised that the truck driver was involved with Bradley. Every time Crane tried to pass, the truck blocked his path. It was a dangerous game. Crane saw a chance of escape when a daisy chain of cars raced past in the outside lane. He tried to tag on the end, but the truck swerved out, braked and once again confined his movements.

Meanwhile Davy, keeping a watchful eye on his rear-view mirrors, saw what was happening. He grinned to himself as he rammed his foot hard down on the accelerator and outpaced the jousting pair. A mile or so on, he breathed a sigh of relief and seized upon the opportunity to leave the A14 unseen. He stopped to contact Bradley in order to meet up at a different location near the docks.

Crane pulled up on the hard shoulder whilst the truck drifted ahead. He stabbed his finger on the satnav for an alternate route to Felixstowe docks. He was in luck, it was only half a mile away. The sound of high-pitch whining of gears and a screaming engine made Crane look up from the small screen. He saw the truck hurtling backwards along the hard shoulder towards him. Instinctively he slammed the Merc into reverse. He half turned in his seat and with one hand on the steering wheel quickly guided the car up an adjacent narrow ramp, normally used by police to observe traffic speed. The bulky truck roared past with barely inches to spare. The truck driver, Terry, rammed his foot hard down on the brakes. The rear end of his truck slewed wildly out of control on the rain-drenched surface; it slithered into the main highway and straight into the path of an approaching police car. The quick acting driver of the police car slid to a halt and switched on his hazard lights. Terry frantically tried to restart the stalled engine as the policemen cautiously approached.

The police did not seem to notice Crane as he gunned his vehicle down the ramp and sped off. Unfortunately, his speed meant that he did not have the pleasure of witnessing the truck driver being tasered as he tried to run away from the law.

Crane trawled around the docks area for half an hour before spotting the stationary car transporter. It was down a side road but its cargo of three vehicles were missing. Crane parked the Merc directly in front of it and leapt out. Davy remained motionless in the driver's seat. Half-open eyes stared vacantly through the windscreen. There was no reaction as Crane marched up to the driver's door, swung it open and bellowed, 'Where's Bradley?'

There was no reply. Davy remained inanimate; with glazed eyes staring through the windscreen. There was a tortured expression on Davy's face and he was panting heavily and gasping for breath. Crane noticed a dark red, wet stain on the seat and on Davy's jacket. It was blood. Slowly, he lifted the edge of the jacket; the hilt of a long kitchen knife was visible. The knife had pinned Davy to his seat. He became aware of Crane's presence and whispered hoarsely, 'Help me. Take it out.'

Crane examined the area around the knife and replied, 'The blade seems to have missed bones, but if I take it out it may cause more damage; you need a doctor. Who did this? Bradley?'

Davy waited a few seconds and gasped, 'Yeah. I'm no saint, but that man's evil. He didn't have to do this to me. He meant to do me in. He would have done so, if I hadn't seen it coming. I turned to one side as he drove the knife in me. It hurts like hell.'

Crane saw Davy's mobile in the door pocket and picked it up. 'I'll call an ambulance.' As he dialled, Crane continued, 'Meanwhile tell me, how can I find Bradley? Do you know where he lives?'

'No one knows. It's one of life's mysteries.'

Davy winced with pain with each intake of breath, 'He rents places here and there. He has a barn full of motors in France.'

'It's a big country, do you know whereabouts in France?'

'Ryan told me, he was boasting about it. Near Calais; a farm at Cap Nez, that's it. He may go there next. Bradley is an evil bastard. I wasn't gonna deal with him any more. I mean, nicking cars is one thing, but he's got no conscience; he'll steal anything or anybody.'

'So he's not just into cars then?' Crane echoed. 'What else does he take?'

'You don't know the half of it. Bradley thinks I overheard something I shouldn't have when he was on the phone, but I didn't hear it all. I think that's why he's done me.' Davy winced with pain once more and was quiet for a moment.

'Do you know which car he is using?'

'He was using a white Transit van – 'bout three years old; probably just nicked it. He's cunning, that's for sure. He gets others to do all his dirty work.' At that point Davy passed out.

The wailing noise of an ambulance siren sounded in the distance and Crane, deciding it was time to leave, straightened up. The sudden movement caused Davy to stir and wincing with pain gasped, 'If you find Ryan, Bradley won't be far away; they're always together.'

Crane drove out of the cul-de-sac as the ambulance turned in. He parked the Mercedes on the edge of town in a lay-by adjacent to the A14, reflecting on Davy's last words; the registration number of Ryan's dark blue Mondeo came to mind.

*

Bradley was in ebullient mood as he sat chatting with Ryan. They were gulping cups of tea in a cafe near the town centre of Felixstowe. Ryan pulled a face as he sipped the brew, 'The bloke that made this should be put in prison for spoiling good water.'

Bradley shrugged and said, 'Give Terry a call, see how he got on with Crane.'

As he palmed his mobile and dialled Terry's number, Ryan grinned at the thought of Crane being knocked off the road.

A muffled raucous noise of a mobile phone resounded

around the police cell in which Terry was housed. He reached deep into his trouser pocket and responded with a desultory, 'Yeah?'

'It's Ryan. How's it going?'

'I'll tell you how it's fucking going. I managed to delay the guy in the Merc, but that's all. I got nabbed by the law and tasered as I tried to hop it.'

Ryan looked at Bradley and shrugged, 'Crane's still on the loose and Terry's in the nick.'

Bradley laughed out loud, 'Silly bugger, he wants to be more careful.'

Ryan joined in the mirth and said, 'Still, at least he put Crane off the trail. When you paid Davy did he say there was anything else to be had?'

This caused Bradley to laugh again, the money he had promised Davy was still in his pocket. 'No, I don't think he'll be getting anything else for us.'

Ryan did not know why, but for the second time in the last few days, he felt uncomfortable during the silence that followed this terse reply and he wanted him to elaborate. 'Is erm… Davy, is he retiring or something then?'

Bradley grinned as he gave another brief answer, 'Dunno, I just got the feeling that erm… somehow he'd had enough.'

Realising that was all the response he was going to get, Ryan left it at that.

\*

Crane sat in his vehicle parked in the lay-by pondering his next move. Traffic streamed past and his eyes were glued to the door mirror in the hope that the villainous pair he was seeking were still in the neighbourhood and that they would suddenly materialise in the mirror. He was having no luck and was beginning to think that the whole country drove white vans, when suddenly, he saw a dark blue Mondeo in front of a line of vehicles. It was them, it was definitely the vehicle that Ryan had been using. At the same time, Crane's sharp eyes quickly noted the registration number of a Transit van with dirt-streaked finger-marked sides, following behind. He immediately gunned his Merc off the lay-by into the mainstream of traffic but, in order not to be seen, he trailed a few cars behind. At last he felt confident he would catch up with them.

Now driving on the A12 Colchester Road, Crane was certain that he had not been spotted. Unfortunately the Mercedes engine missed a beat and began to pull back. Crane groaned, *"Fuel... I should have fixed the fuel gauge,"* and at the same time, the car slithered to a halt on the hard shoulder. Crane leapt out, opened the boot and cursed when he saw the spare fuel can was empty. Luck had not entirely abandoned him; a service station was visible just about half a mile away but he realised that there was no hurry because his quarry would now have plenty of time to get beyond his grasp.

\*

Bradley and Ryan headed for a boarding house in Folkestone, Kent. During the evening meal they made plans to cross over to Calais via the Channel Tunnel. Bradley said, 'Later this evening, take one of the left-hand drive motorhomes and I'll meet you sometime tomorrow at the Cap.'

Ryan, with a full stomach and a glass of ale down him, looked at his watch and replied, 'No problem, I'll make the ten o'clock crossing. By the way, at one stage after we left Felixstowe, I could have sworn Crane's white Merc was following us, but after twenty minutes or so it disappeared. Still, I guess there's more than one white Merc flying around.'

*

Crane fuelled up his car and headed for home. He knew he had dented Bradley's nefarious operation, but he had not done enough to get his Mustang back. So he decided that it was time to go to France. He would have a look around the Cap Nez area that Davy had mentioned, but thought it pertinent to change his car. After the incident with the truck he was beginning to think the white Merc was becoming too well known.

When Crane drove into Palmers Rise, he noticed that the heavy rain had washed away his cement dust warning indicator from the surface of the lane, so he approached the cottage with caution. Once inside he checked the telephone answering machine; there were three calls, two of them had left no message, but the third was from Penny asking for an update. Crane grabbed a bite to eat and called her when he had finished. He decided against telling her that he was travelling to France in case things turned out to be a disappointment. Crane checked his watch; it was not too late to call on Eddie Edwards, a local motor dealer he knew well.

With a hand stretched across his brow, Crane scanned

the neat rows of cars for sale. Edwards spotted Crane from his office and hurried over to greet him.

'What are you looking for Jack?'

'Something not too ostentatious – you know – a bit run-of-the-mill, but with some poke in it, and not too expensive.'

Eddie stood for a moment as though deep in thought. He had put a bit more weight on since Crane saw him last, but this did not affect his genial manner, in fact it seemed to add to it. Suddenly he enthused, 'You know, I might just have what you're looking for; a real wolf in sheep's clothing. In fact I don't really know if it's legal.'

He led the way across a large sales forecourt to a remote corner at the rear of the yard, and like a showman, swept both hands towards a saloon car. Crane glanced at the dull grey body of a Rover 620, grinned hugely and said, 'You've gotta be joking!'

Not put off by Crane's remark, the dealer defended the few small scratches and shallow dents as a trivial matter. 'It's a few years old. Trust me, Jack, you can see it's had a few arguments, but only little ones – minor cuts and abrasions like, and, erm, it's reflected in the price. It's only just come in. The engines been changed for something a bit livelier. It's got a big lump under the bonnet; three litre with high lifts and, wait for it… twin-turbos. Goes like a bastard.' Then, looking over to a man hard at work leathering off a row of used cars, he called out, 'Herbert, tell Jack how it drives.'

Herbert grinned and replied with enthusiasm, 'Like shit off a shiny shovel mate.'

Crane grinned at the colourful description Herbert had given the car and Eddie continued, 'Take it out and let Jack drive it.'

Herbert grunted a reply and went off to get the keys. Eddie turned his attention back to Crane and knowing that his Mustang had been stolen said, 'No luck in finding the 'Stang' then?'

Crane pursed his lips and replied, 'I'm working on it.' They both watched as Herbert returned with the keys and began to manoeuvre the car out of the yard.

Crane got behind the wheel and Eddie said, 'Tell you what, if it don't drive like I said it does, I'll give it to you for nothing – how's that!'

Crane smiled and eased the car down the London Road. He could feel the engine's responsive growl as he gained speed. Herbert said nothing throughout the test drive, but after he had left the vehicle, if anyone had cared to look, they would have seen deep impressions in the thick pile carpet, that were made by a pair of nervous feet, as well as finger pressure marks on the sides of the front passenger seat.

A deal was struck and Eddie and Crane shook hands. They had known each other for twenty years or more and Eddie finished with, 'I'll give it a full service and new MOT test for good measure – be ready tomorrow.'

Crane could only foresee trouble ahead and needed all the help he could get, including the old 'wolf in sheep's clothing' car.

# PART TWO

PART TWO

# CHAPTER TWELVE

Despite the long queue of traffic, Crane did not have to wait long at the Folkestone terminal before being directed, by efficient marshals, towards the waiting Channel Tunnel train. Within minutes he was driving aboard and being herded into a carriage full of vehicles, where he was tucked neatly behind a dirty white Transit van. His sharp eyes instinctively scanned the registration number but, as expected, it turned out to be different number plate from the one belonging to the vehicle he had previously followed.

With the handbrake on and the engine switched off, he sat back and relaxed for a short while until the train moved imperceptibly smoothly out of the station and into the tunnel. It was a signal for his hand to dive into a holdall on the front passenger seat and come out clutching a thermos flask and a pack of sandwiches.

The hot black coffee and food had a refreshing effect as he leant back with his seat in the recline position and scanned the daily newspaper. The news, as usual, was all doom and gloom so he put the paper to one side and tuned in to the Channel Tunnel radio station.

The train was near the end of its short journey when he stepped outside of the car, into the carriage, to stretch his legs and make use of the toilet facilities which were in the next compartment. He strode past the dirty white van and two cars on the way there. On his return something scratched at his brain – swirling and nagging – but he could not really pin it down then and there. He checked his watch as he slumped back into the driver's seat of the car, just a few minutes before the train was due to arrive at Calais.

A pair of anxious blue eyes below a thatch of flaxen hair suddenly caught Crane's attention as they peered through the grimy rear window of the white van in front. He surmised they belonged to a child, probably a girl, and he gave a friendly wave of the hand. At that point, he half expected her to rise and show her face, but kids are sometimes shy and unpredictable. Her eyes seemed transfixed on Crane and her eyelids fluttered lazily, as if she were half asleep.

The van suddenly lurched forward; it was time to leave the train. The movement caused the girl's nose to flatten against the glass and she disappeared from view. The vehicles were herded off the train and Crane trailed behind the van, together with a daisy chain of vehicles that were also being directed towards the passport control area where on production of their passports, an officer nonchalantly waved them through the checkpoint.

Crane was still quite close up behind the white van as they cleared the port area. The eyes appeared again at the back of the van and Crane thought they still seemed worried. Then suddenly he was certain. Just before the van sped off ahead, the rest of the young girl's face appeared together with her hands propped against the rear window for support; they were bound at the wrists with black adhesive tape and a wide strip was spread across her mouth.

Crane was concerned by this turn of events and decided

to lag behind the white van as it sped along the 940 coast road towards the direction of Boulogne; he had intended to head in that direction anyway. It was then, that his brain entered the recall zone; the dirty finger-marked swirls on the side of the van. This was too much of a coincidence. There was now no doubt in Crane's mind, that this was the van that Bradley had been driving, albeit with different number plates, but whoever was behind the wheel, was obviously up to no good.

*

Penny was in the local supermarket when her phone shrilled loud and tuneful in her jacket pocket. She let go of Andrew's hand, snatched at the mobile and without looking at the tiny screen to see who was calling, pressed the answer button, 'Yes?'

'Penny, my dear,' the voice began. It was Bradley.

'What do you want and where's my sister?'

'That's exactly what I'm calling about. She would like to see you and the boy.'

'Why don't you bring her back here then?'

Bradley cleared his throat and said, 'It's kind of awkward you see. I'm finishing my erm… operation here and I erm… believe the police are taking an interest in things. Well to cut a long story short – she's in France.'

'France?' Penny echoed.

'Yes, and she told me that she would like you to fetch her, to take her home.'

Penny was lost for words momentarily and Bradley continued, 'Take your own car and fetch her. Follow me up, so to speak, across the channel, and I'll take you straight to her. It's not far from Calais.'

Penny was speechless for a moment and Bradley prompted her with, 'Well?'

'When?

'Oh, let's say we leave tomorrow around noon. We'll do the Channel Tunnel crossing and you'll be with her around early evening.'

'Alright, where do we meet?'

'I'll be waiting in the parking area of Rochford Station. Oh and by the way, don't forget to bring the boy will you? And most important of all, don't even think about telling that interfering busybody, Crane, or the whole thing is off – is that clear?'

'Alright, as you wish. See you tomorrow morning then.'

Feeling somewhat elated, by the possibility of being reunited with her sister, Penny abandoned the idea of shopping and took Andrew out of the supermarket. Once outside she sighed and took in a lungful of fresh air, walked straight to her Mini, strapped Andrew inside and dialled Crane's mobile number.

'The number you are calling is unavailable.'

*

Crane eased his foot off the accelerator when he saw the white van turn off of the main highway. He quickly pulled into a convenient lay-by and watched from a distance. All he could see was the white roof of the van as it bounced along the narrow farm track set between huge fields of ripe corn, until eventually it disappeared over the brow of a hill.

He was tempted to follow, but caution held him back and he decided to find another parking place which would be less conspicuous. One kilometre further down the road, beyond the farm track, seemed the ideal place. He groped around the glove-box and produced a small pair of binoculars. Bringing them up into focus, he was just in time to see Ryan, behind the wheel of a motorhome, as it swung off the main road and into a dusty farm track. Satisfaction welled up inside Crane. If he was a wolf, he would have salivated; knowing that there was absolutely no doubt whatsoever that he had found Bradley's lair, his French hiding place, and hopefully, the Mustang. Without taking his eyes off the farm track, he sat back and drained the last of the coffee from the flask and ate the last sandwich and thought about his next move.

Apart from a farm tractor, there was no further vehicular activity, either entering or leaving the area and it was dusk before Crane decided that the time was right to make his move. He chose a moment when the main road was quiet and turning the ignition key, raced the car up to the opening and slowly turned his car into the farm track.

With the Rover's headlamps switched off, he drove at a snail's pace along the dusty trail. It was like driving through a darkened tunnel, towering shafts of corn maize shivering and rattling in a light breeze, hemming him in on both sides. He brought the car to a standstill just short of the brow of the hill and leapt out, as he decided to walk the last few metres to see what lay ahead on the other side. A crimson horizon outlined dark shapes. Using his night glasses he peered into the distance. About a kilometre away, he could see the outline of a house, its diffused lights surrounding the immediate area. Nearby several barns lay in complete blackness, silhouetted against a darkening sky.

Crane got back into the car and powered it to the top of hill, where he switched the engine off. He threw the gearbox into neutral and coasted the Rover silently down the hill. He came to a halt, neatly alongside a sleek Audi Coupe and well out of range of the lights coming from the house. He got out and stood by the car for a moment, listening intently, scanning the open spaces around the house with the night glasses. When he was satisfied that all was quiet, he took a few steps towards the house but halted when a mangy dog made an appearance. Without stopping, the animal glanced disinterestedly in Crane's direction and then it ambled past the house towards a small shed. The dog's presence assured Crane that there were no bright security floodlights and his sure-footed steps scarcely made a sound as he edged his way towards the side of the house.

Shafts of light that faded and melted into the dark, filtered through one or two of the knot holes on the old worn shuttered windows and Crane boldly stepped forward to look inside. The child, that he had seen in the van, sat at a table. In front of her lay an untouched meal; she was quietly sobbing. She looked up red-eyed when a door suddenly opened and a man entered the room and said in a kindly tone, 'Haven't you eaten your supper yet dear?' All the child could say – in between sobs – was, 'I want to go home.'

The man, forced himself to be patient and sound friendly, 'We'll see about that later, now eat up there's a good girl.'

The child was old enough not to buy that one and said, 'I want to go home to my mummy, now!'

The man's patience was short-lived, 'If you don't do as you're told I'll tape your mouth up again. Now shut up!'

Crane circled the house. Peering through the kitchen shutter, he counted four men; three of whom he did not recognise. Ryan was unmistakeable as he sat at a table gorging a mound of food off a huge plate and swigging red wine from a large goblet.

Shrinking back in the shadows, Crane reached for his mobile phone and switched it on. His command of the French language was not good enough to hold a conversation with the local gendarme, so he would contact his old office at Whitehall in London and hopefully get their assistance. As he tapped in the UK number, the phone bleeped once and the tiny screen went blank: the battery was flat. It was at that point that he realised he had left the in-car charger in the glove box of the Merc which he had part exchanged for the Rover. It was obvious that he would be unable to inform the authorities. He reckoned he would continue looking around alone.

Three barns were situated in the open space which stood about one hundred metres away from the house. They were in total darkness. Peering around, he walked cautiously to the nearest outbuilding. Finding it unlocked, he stood back and flashed his pencil-beam torch through the open space. Inside there were at least twenty vehicles, but his Mustang was not amongst them. He left the barn and proceeded with vigilance to the next one; it was full of cars, but again, not the one he was looking for.

Success came with the third building. The Mustang was nestled amongst the first row of, mostly American, cars. It had been fitted with false number plates, no doubt together

123

with all the cars that were being stored there. The ignition key was missing, but despite this, a feeling of elation swept through Crane – he had found his cherished car.

A bright wide-angled flashlight illuminated the whole of the car and a voice from behind startled him. '*Bon n'est pas?*'

Crane turned around and the man lowered his torch. Recovering quickly from his surprise Crane managed to respond with, '*Oui magnifique. Parlez-vous Anglais?*'

'My English is pretty good,' came the heavy-accented and confident response. 'I am Henri Girard, 'ave you just arrived?'

'Yeah,' Crane replied, 'I'm erm, just getting my bearings.'

'Bearings?'

Crane smiled. He guessed the well-built man to be in his late twenties. 'The word '*bearings*' means looking around. There are many cars here, are you one of the forty thieves?'

Girard's puzzled expression meant that Crane's flippant remark was wasted and he followed it up with, 'What do you do here?'

'I walk around the whole area and try to make sure that nobody steals anything.'

Crane stifled his inner thoughts and bit his tongue before replying, 'That's good isn't it.'

The Frenchman nodded in agreement and said, 'I am very hungry and going for supper are you coming?'

'Me? No I've already eaten; I'll catch you up at the house.'

Crane guessed he was now on borrowed time; the Frenchman was bound to mention their meeting – it was time to leave. Keeping in the shadows he made his way back to where he had left the Rover. He sat for a while, deep in thought, keeping a watch on the front door, half expecting a flurry of men to burst out looking for the stranger in their midst. But it didn't happen. Maybe the newly-arrived Frenchman with a full stomach and a bottle of wine simply forgot to mention it.

Suddenly Crane's attention was distracted in the opposite direction by headlamps flickering in the dark sky, like searchlights, as they danced above the brow of the hill signalling the approach of more than one car. Crane slid down low in the seat of his car as a Jaguar swept past followed by a Mini – Penny's Mini – with Andrew asleep in the rear child's seat. Crane was intrigued by this turn of events and he rightly surmised that she had somehow been lured away from home; perhaps on the pretext of seeing her sister. If that were so, Crane suspected there must be a more sinister reason behind it. From his experience so far, Bradley and the people around him were nothing short of plain evil.

Thoughts of the Frenchman were cast aside as Crane watched the cars pull up directly outside the house. Like a sentinel, Crane kept his eyes on the front door and about half an hour passed by without any further movement, so Crane got out of the car and stealthily approached the house. As he neared, he thought he could hear the sound of raised voices, but they were indistinct and carried away by gusts of wind that seemed to have built up. He made straight for the side of the house, where the girl from the van was being held, and again made use of the holes in the window shutters by covertly peering through them.

Crane was in time to see Bradley leave the room. Penny, looking distraught, immediately began to pace up and down.

A sleepy-eyed Andrew sat motionless, yawning and clutching a soft toy. The young girl, who was in the white van, sat with her elbows propped on the table, her head cradled in her hands. An idea ran through Crane as he looked at the shutters; they were bolted top and bottom on the outside. Carefully he began to ease one of the bolts back. It offered no resistance; it was well oiled and slid back noiselessly. The lower bolt behaved in the same way. Inch by inch he eased one of the shutters open and, as he did so, he managed to catch Penny's attention whilst pressing a finger against his lips. Her face lit up with surprise as she bounded towards the window and threw the locking lever across. Crane stepped to one side as the windows swung outwards. The children were tired and they took little notice of her movements. Crane and Penny spoke in low hushed voices and her whispers confirmed his suspicions.

'Bradley told me that my sister, Jean, would be here and I am to take her back home. Now he says that she will be here in the morning. I can't believe a word he says. I just don't trust him.'

Crane told Penny everything he knew about the young girl he saw in the van. Penny looked horrified, 'Kidnapped?' she echoed. 'Now I'm worried. Where do you think Jean is? What do you think has happened to her?'

In the present circumstances Crane did not want to add to this lovely woman's worries and tell her what he really thought. 'I'm not sure,' was all that he could offer.

Within seconds Penny was handing the dormant Andrew through the open window into Crane's arms. Penny put her finger across her lips and signalled to the young girl that it was now her turn to get out. After the little girl had leapt out onto the soft earth, she looked up at Crane and said quietly, 'I hoped you would come.'

Crane smiled warmly and said, 'What's your name?'

'Samantha. My friends call me Sammy – you can call me Sammy. What's your name?'

'Jack.'

'What's you second name?'

'Just call me Jack, that'll be fine.'

'I will, but my mummy said it's impolite to call adults by their first name.'

Crane briefly threw his eyes heavenwards and said, 'She's absolutely right, Sammy, but sometimes we can make an exception and this is one of those times. You like your friends to call you Sammy and I like my friends to call me Jack.'

Sammy warmed to this idea and said, 'I guess that's okay then, Jack.'

'How old are you Sammy?'

'I am eight.' Sammy thought for a few seconds and continued, 'well, really I'm seven years and eight months.' And in order to justify her earlier statement said, 'but I am really in my eighth year.'

'I think you are a very brave young lady, Sammy, but we all need to get away from this place as soon as possible.'

Finally Penny stepped out of the window and she took in a deep breath of night air, made sweet by an old straggly jasmine bush that leant against the wall, before she took Andrew, from their rescuer, back in her arms. The quartet made their way quietly towards Penny's car, creeping around to the front of the house, where it was still parked.

Before approaching the car, Crane poked his head

around the corner; the curtains were drawn. The noise from a television set would hopefully camouflage any inadvertent noise they might make. Penny carefully opened the door of her Mini and laid the sleeping Andrew across the rear seat, where he nestled down sighing in his sleep. In a hushed voice, Crane suggested they push Penny's Mini as far as possible away from the front of the house before attempting to start the engine. Penny released the handbrake and together they managed to push the Mini down to the base of the hill until they came to a halt in front of Crane's Rover. Penny got into the Mini and Crane motioned Sammy to get into the front seat beside her, but the child said, 'You were the man in the car who waved to me. Please let me stay with you.'

Crane was not about to argue the toss so he grunted an assent and Sammy quickly followed him to his parked car and got in. He flicked his headlamps as a signal and both cars started up simultaneously, with Penny in the lead. They drove up and over the hill, bouncing and swaying along the farm track. Penny turned the Mini onto the main Calais Road, but just a second later, a motorhome pulled off the main road and into the farm track, blocking Crane's exit. There was no alternative for him but to back up his vehicle because, if Crane had pulled his Rover off the narrow track it would soon have been up to its axles in soft damp earth. His reversing light was just bright enough for him to see a way back up the hill where he could pull the car out of the way and over to one side enabling the motorhome to pass.

Crane breathed a sigh of relief as the motorhome slowly lumbered by him heading towards the house but now there was another problem. A farm tractor – lights blazing – had suddenly appeared from an adjacent field and had come to a halt, straddling the track, blocking his escape. Hasty feet clumping along the gravel made him look in the opposite direction. Three men silhouetted against the lights of the house, were running towards him. They were clearly armed. Sammy's wide-eyed face registered a look of dismay. Her lower lip remained in a firm pout as her eyes darted between her rescuer and the approaching men. Crane threw a glance at Sammy and shrugged; there was no way out.

# CHAPTER THIRTEEN

Penny, anxious to get home, kept her foot down all the way to the Channel Tunnel. Her eyes kept flitting to the interior mirror, looking for signs to show that Crane was following. As she pulled into the Channel Tunnel parking area at Calais, she was worried that he had not caught up with her but she decided it best to press on; she would catch the next available train to England.

\*

Crane remained in the driver's seat, switched the engine off and pocketed the keys. The approaching group of men stopped within a few metres of him. Then one of them motioned with a shotgun for the seated Crane to get out of the car. A fourth man, following up at the rear, strolled casually amongst them; it was Bradley. He gave Crane a cursory glance before he turned to one of the men and said, 'Take the girl back to the house.' The front passenger door to Crane's car was snatched open and a gruff voice ordered Sammy out. Surprisingly she did not whimper. Crane reasoned that, helpless as the situation maybe, there was some comfort in seeing someone else in the same sinking boat as herself – albeit her rescuer.

Ryan and another armed man had guns pointed at Crane,

whilst Bradley stood and watched Sammy being led back to the house. When the door of the house slammed shut, all eyes were on Crane. With a hand resting on his chin, Bradley looked down, as though deep in thought. 'Jack Crane.' It was an announcement, not a greeting, and it was not directed at Crane. Bradley was thinking aloud. 'Now what am I going to do with you... ' His voice faded and all was quiet for a moment, until suddenly he spoke to his men, 'Take him to the secure room.'

Crane stood by the car quietly weighing up his chances as Ryan and the other man signalled for him to move towards the house. A pair of twelve-bore shotguns were prodding at his back so there was nothing he could do, as they marched him purposely towards the farmhouse. Once inside Ryan growled, 'That's far enough.'

They stood in the entrance hall whilst Ryan's cohort threw back a door and nudged Crane towards the opening. Crane stood at the top of a steep flight of stairs and looked down into the bowels of a darkened cellar. Without warning, Ryan thrust his heavy boot hard into Crane's lower back, sending him plummeting headlong against the narrow walls and concrete steps until he lay unconscious on the dank quarry-stone floor.

Ryan secured the cellar door as Bradley walked into the hall. Bradley paused at the entrance to the cellar and gave a grunt of satisfaction as he examined the heavy bolt and five-lever padlock. He felt satisfied and strolled, with Ryan in tow, towards a large room at the end of the hall. As they entered, Ryan said, 'How the hell did he find this place?'

Bradley shrugged and said with some emphasis, 'Well he *did*. At least we know where he is now.'

'What are you planning to do with him?'

'I haven't decided his fate yet, but rest assured it will be a permanent solution.'

'What about that Penny woman? Do you think she'll go to the police?'

'Nah, not while she believes her sister, Jean, is in trouble. She's probably on her way back home. If I can't persuade her to come back here, I'll have to arrange for them to be picked up later. Now, the thing is, are we ready to move out the stock?'

Ryan nodded and said, 'Some transporters will be arriving here any time now to deliver them to the ports of departure; we should be clear of most of them within a few hours.'

Bradley nodded his approval.

*

Crane lay prone on the hard cellar floor and, as consciousness returned, his memory gradually flooded back. Opening his eyes slowly, he became aware of complete darkness. Limbs were stiff as he sat up and checked himself over; a few bruises and grazes, but fortunately no broken bones. Remaining on the floor, his hand fumbled around his jacket pocket, until he produced the small pencil-beam torch. He flicked the switch and its narrow blade of light penetrated the darkness. His hand guided the light around the room to reveal four bare brick walls with a ceiling height of about two metres. A wire was dangling from the rafters with its bulb missing. The room was empty apart from some wooden boxes stacked in one corner.

He stood up and heard muffled voices filtering through the wooden floorboards above and then the walls started to resonate dully, along with the sound of vehicles being manoeuvred outside. He checked his watch; it was six-thirty am; he had been comatose for half of the night. He climbed the stairs and gingerly checked the door handle; as expected, it was shut tight. Descending the stairs, he aimed the torch at the ceiling once more, methodically examining the areas between the rafters. Just as the torch battery began showing signs of wear, he found just what he was looking for in one corner. It was a trapdoor that had once acted as an outside chute for winter fuel. It straddled the outer wall connecting the cellar with the outside world. Raising his arms he gently pushed against the closure and found it offered little resistance; he had found a way out.

*

Bradley and Ryan directed the vehicles onto the transporters, which were being used to move the illicit cargo to various shipping areas. Bradley checked his watch; he had an early-morning appointment at an old country chateau outside Boulogne with a man interested in a very different kind of merchandise: human beings. After Crane's aborted rescue attempt, Sammy had been kept in a locked room upstairs. She had slept soundly for a few hours but the continual noise of cars being moved around, had disturbed her sleep. Upon awakening, her stomach had got the better of her earlier stubborn resistance to food offered by her captors, so, discovering milk and cereals on an adjacent table, she hungrily helped herself to a large bowlful.

Crane stood on a wooden crate that he had found to one side of the dingy cellar. He listened intently, for some time; his ear close to the trapdoor, until the resonance of the vehicles had abated. When all was quiet, he gently eased up the trapdoor, sending a flurry of dust and dirt down onto the front of his clothing. Mindful of the dust, he screwed up his eyes and peered through a slit into the darkness. Nothing could be seen. With a little extra effort he lifted the trapdoor and slid it over to one side and then eased himself up and out into the early morning air.

*

After a non-stop drive, Penny arrived home at her apartment in the early hours. She felt exhausted but found it impossible to sleep and spent the time pacing around her apartment, occasionally gulping from cups of strong black coffee. She tried Crane's mobile number several times only to receive the familiar, 'Sorry I am unable to connect you,' response. She was about to try again when her phone rang and she reached out and snatched it off the table; it was Bradley.

'You're not going to get your sister back by running away, *and* I did say tell no one, especially that meddling Crane.'

'You lied to me. Jean wasn't there; and you kidnapped a child.'

Bradley laughed out loud. 'Penny, my dear, you've been well and truly misinformed. Your sister, Jean, is staying in a hotel – a particularly nice one I might add – just a few kilometres outside Boulogne. I was going to take you there this morning, she will be so disappointed. As for the child, she's Ryan's niece. He was taking her to her parent's new home. She had been staying with some friends and was a bit upset about leaving them.'

Bradley sounded very plausible, but Penny did not believe a word that he was saying. 'Where's Jack Crane?'

Bradley laughed again. 'Oh, I wondered when you'd come round to him. He's cooling off. I'll send him back home when he's no longer a nuisance. Now look, you've got nothing to worry about, so why don't the pair of you come back to the farm and take Jean back? She'd really love that.'

Penny thought for a moment. 'Why can't you just send her home, on a train or something?'

'Because, my dear girl, I want certain undertakings from you, and also your sister, not to harass me. I don't want you to notify the police or anyone else in authority. Surely you must understand that. It won't take long for you to get back here and after that you'll both be on your way.'

Penny did not trust him but she really could not think for what other reason he would want her in France, other than to collect her sister, Jean. She looked at her watch and said, 'Okay, I'll be there after lunch.'

\*

Crane heard voices and flattened himself against the side of the house; it was Bradley talking on the phone as he got into his car. Thoughts of rushing him were quashed; he was too far away, besides an armed man could be standing by the front door, so he watched frustrated, like a cat losing sight of a mouse, as Bradley got into the car, started the engine and drove off. Crane remained where he was until the car's rear lights became diffused, fading into the early grey light of dawn until they disappeared completely out of sight, sinking over the other side of the hill.

A few moments after losing sight of Bradley, Crane inched his way around the side of the house towards the front door; it was closed and all seemed quiet. He decided to check out the room in which Sammy was held prisoner and peering through a gap in the faded green shutters, he could see that the room was now unoccupied. He unbolted and pulled back the shutters, it seemed the best way to get inside, and after a few careful strides across the room, he eased back the door and cautiously stepped into the dimly-lit entrance hall. Noises could be heard. They sounded as though they were coming from a kitchen or dining room. Crane edged stealthily along the hall towards the sounds. Through a gap in the door he saw three men sitting and eating but unfortunately Ryan was not amongst them. It was showtime.

Crouching low, Crane inched towards them, like a cat about to spring. Suddenly, at the last split second, he rushed forward roaring like a lion, scooped up the table, tipping it upside down and sending the three shocked diners to the floor. He grabbed hold of an up-ended wooden dining chair and felled the first man who tried to get up. As the other two recovered and tried to stand, Crane used the chair like a scythe, mowing them down flat, like cut wheat, on their faces. The room was filled with stifled groans until they were silenced with hefty blows from Crane's boot. He searched their pockets and waistbands and was surprised to find that none of them carried a handgun. Foraging in the next room, he found the ideal weapon to move the men around; propped against the wall in one corner was a loaded double barrelled shotgun.

Crane questioned the battered men as they began to recover. None of them knew, or they wouldn't say, where Ryan was. So he bundled the light-headed trio, under the threat of death into the cellar before he slid the bar across the door and turned the key in the padlock. Remembering his own method of escape, he dashed outside and found some heavy stones to place over the trapdoor.

Crane entered the house again and made his way to the kitchen. There was hot coffee on the stove and food on the sideboard. He grabbed a coffee and a hunk of French bread, together with a wedge of cheese, and then made his way to the barn where he had last seen his car. It was still there, amongst a handful of other American cars. This was a fair indication that Bradley and his cohort Ryan were coming back. A noise made him turn around and he was confronted by Henri Girard. As Crane approached him, Girard's hand dived into a small haversack hanging from his shoulder. He seemed to be having difficulty in finding what he was looking for and quickly began foraging around with both hands, as though trying to dislodge something caught inside. All of a sudden, both hands appeared and one of them held aloft an M67 grenade. Crane halted in his tracks. Girard smiled and began bouncing it up and down in his hand, like a tennis ball and said cockily, 'You are not one of Ryan's men but maybe you know what this is, eh?'

Crane looked at him and remaining calm said hastily, 'Of course I do.' And with some urgency said, 'The pin's missing, and I believe it's cooking.'

The Frenchman's frivolous expression changed as Crane continued, 'We're only five metres apart; that thing is deadly within at least fifteen metres!' And with a greater command of urgency shouted, 'Unless you want to die throw it as far as you can and fall to the ground!'

Girard's reactions were fast. As the grenade left his hand Crane flattened himself to the grassy surface – followed by Girard a split second later. It was a good throw; the weapon exploded in the air – just above the roof of a parked car. Crane was the first to get up and he immediately snatched at Girard's haversack lying nearby.

Girard stayed on the ground. His eyes were fixed and his jaw drooped open as he looked at the damaged car. '*Merde! Mon auto!* My bloody car!' he shouted in frustration. The vehicle was a brand new Audi convertible. Crane could not suppress the wide grin that was beginning to stretch across his face as he listened to a string of expletives – in French and English – whilst he was rummaging through the Frenchman's bag. He discovered a small, but effective Jennings semi-automatic handgun, chrome plated, twenty-two calibre. It would fit neatly into the palm of his hand. Eventually the Frenchman got up and dusted himself down. He had a wrestler's build, gladiator's shoulders and a deep penetrating gaze, but he seemed unfazed when he turned and faced the pistol in Crane's hand.

Crane nodded towards the wrecked car. 'Claim on your insurance; that's what I was told when mine was stolen,' he said curtly.

Girard seemed to ignore the gun pointing in his direction. He looked back at the car and reflected vacantly, 'I can't. I only stole it yesterday and I erm, haven't had time to… make it legal.'

It gradually dawned upon Girard that Crane had the upper hand as he said, 'Ryan gave me the grenade and told me to toss it in the cellar; I couldn't really do that; I'm not here to hurt anyone. Why does Ryan not like you and want you out of the way?'

Crane made a backwards motion with his head towards the barn, 'That Mustang over there, it's mine. It was stolen from me in England; that's why I'm here. I want it back.'

Girard looked past Crane's shoulder and said with admiration, 'It's a very beautiful car and quite rare in this part of the world.'

The sound of an approaching vehicle made them turn. Girard bridged a hand across his brow and looking through a gap in some bushes said, 'It's Ryan. I don't like him, I'm going.' With that he ignored the gun trained on him and walked off in the direction of one of the other barns. Crane wasn't going to argue and he lowered the gun and walked back to the house, with the certainty that neither of them had been seen by the occupant of the approaching car.

Back in the kitchen Crane found the coffee pot still hot to the touch and he poured out another helping of the hot drink. The sound of heavy boots clumped into the house and stomped their way towards the kitchen. A look of shock spread across Ryan's face when he saw Crane standing with a mug of coffee in one hand and a gun in the other. The shocked look soon disappeared and a smile spread across his face as he said, 'I see you're still playing with toy guns Crane.'

Crane returned the smile and said, 'Not this time. Where's Bradley?'

Ryan took a step forward. At the same time his left hand

eased back his jacket and exposed the butt of a Glock semi-automatic. His right hand inched towards it and Crane fired the twenty-two calibre pistol at Ryan's foot. In the confines of a small room, the noise was much louder than it would have sounded out in the open. Ryan yelped and hopped and Crane rasped, 'Take that gun out slowly and put it on the table or the next one goes in between your eyes.' Ryan did as he was told.

'Where's Bradley?'

'I'm not sure, he's gone to meet someone.'

Crane took aim at Ryan's other foot.

'It's the truth!' he screamed.

Crane lowered the gun and said, 'Where's the little girl?'

'Upstairs,' he said in a panic, 'she's in one of the rooms upstairs.'

'What were you going to do with her?'

There was a silence for a moment and Crane raised the gun, 'Well? You'd better tell me.'

'Okay, okay. Bradley has a sort of arrangement with someone he knows, childless couples like, they pay him for kids.'

Crane's face hardened, 'And what about Penny's sister, Jean; where is she?'

'I don't know, I've never ever seen her.'

With his free hand, Crane picked up Ryan's Glock semi-automatic from the table, hefted it, felt its balance and remarked casually, 'A nine mil,' and pocketing the small handgun, drew back the slide, remarking, 'this'll do a bit more damage, although not as much as a forty-five. Maybe two or three bullets in your leg would make up for that. The IRA called it knee-capping; I understand it's very painful and the damage is permanent.'

Ryan was sweating profusely. His eyes were awash with fear as words stumbled out from between dry lips, 'I think... she's... been... sold.'

'To whom, when and where?'

Tears began to mingle with sweat and stream down Ryan's face as he bleated, 'I swear I don't know. Bradley takes care of that end of things.'

Crane lowered the gun and said, 'Henri Girard didn't want to use the grenade you gave him. If you and Bradley think you can get rid of me like your friend Davy, you'd better think again.'

This revelation about Davy was another shock for Ryan, 'Davy, Davy Porter? What about Davy?'

'Didn't Bradley tell you? He stuck him with a long kitchen knife; pinned him to the driver's seat in that transporter of his.'

'What!' Ryan gasped. 'I knew nothing about that. He was supposed to be a friend of Bradley.'

Crane grimaced, 'If he's lucky, maybe he'll live, but then I don't really know, but I know one thing; I wouldn't put too much trust in Bradley if I were you, he could be the death of you. Right, get moving, it's off to the cellar.'

'My foot,' Ryan moaned.

'You've still got it,' Crane quipped as he grabbed hold of a roll of kitchen towel and tossing it towards and said, 'here take this with you.'

At the top of the steps to the cellar, Ryan flicked a nervous glance behind, expecting the same treatment that he gave to Crane – a hefty foot in the back – but this didn't happen. The three men already incarcerated in the cellar had hopes of release when the door suddenly opened. They shielded their eyes from the shaft of light that emanated from the door as it opened, but their hopes were quickly shattered when they saw Ryan limp towards them down the narrow staircase and heard the door slam shut firmly behind him.

After a quick rummage around in one of the front rooms, Crane found a box of car keys. He delved into it and soon found the set he was looking for. It was clearly labelled, '*Mustang.*' He swiftly pocketed them. The feelings of elation returned as he bounded upstairs and came across a room with the key dangling outside. As he opened it he called out, 'Are you in there, Sammy? It's me, Jack.'

Upon seeing Crane the little girl's face lit up and she ran forward to greet him, hugging him tightly around the waist. Crane gave her a huge grin, picked her up and said, 'Come on let's get you out of here.'

Crane and Sammy stepped outside savouring the relief of freedom. As he expected, there was no sign of Henri Girard. Together, the pair headed for the outbuildings and, while Sammy waited patiently by a barn door, Crane started up his Mustang. He drove it out of the barn and stopped for the excited Sammy to get into the front passenger seat. They drove up to the redundant Rover, where Crane paused briefly to transfer his possessions. Then they took the bumpy farm track and headed towards the main road.

When Crane turned the Mustang onto the 940 coast road, Sammy's face presented an expression of relief and she became more vocal. 'Before you came to my room I heard lots of noise like furniture being knocked over; what was that?'

'Oh... I had to make sure the erm... the bad guys were sort of, taken care of.'

'Did you kill them?'

Crane was unused to being interrogated by an inquisitive child and he grinned hugely at her directness, 'No, no nothing like that, I sort of got the better of them and managed to lock them up out of the way.'

'Oh.' She sounded disappointed and added, 'I think they were horrid.'

Sammy was quiet for a moment and suddenly she became animated once more, 'Why did they want to take me away from my mummy and daddy?'

'They are very bad people, Sammy. Do you remember how they took you?'

'Yes, I was walking back from the sweet shop on the corner – that's what I call it – and a van pulled up and a man opened the door asked me the way to St Andrew's.'

'St Andrew's?' Crane interrupted.

'It's our church; there was a fete there or something. When I got near the van he grabbed me and stuck a long pin in my arm. I don't remember anything after that. I woke up with my hands tied and horrid black sticky stuff over my mouth. I tried to get up; I kept falling down and then I saw you in your car. Where are we?'

'France, Sammy, we're in France; I'm taking you back home.'

Sammy looked around the interior of the Mustang and said, 'Jack, does the top come down on this car?'

'Yes it does.'

'Can we have the top down then?'

'If I do that it'll mean stopping and I think it best we get to England first and then I'll lower it.'

Sammy was satisfied with Crane's reply. After a few

kilometres, as they neared Calais, a bright red Mini Cooper flashed past going in the opposite direction. Crane's attention was mainly on the road, but Sammy turning her head and looking back, confirmed what he had only just glimpsed, 'Hey, I just saw the nice lady, erm Penny with her little boy in that red car going the other way.'

# CHAPTER FOURTEEN

Penny was driving her Mini to the limit. She had no idea that she had passed Crane on the opposite side of the road. Crane gripped the steering wheel and swung the car round, on a handbrake turn, in an effort to catch up with the Mini. It was then he remembered the mobile phone and said, 'Sammy, can you look in that compartment and take out the mobile phone. You'll find a battery charger in there too.'

Sammy found the phone and charger in the glovebox and following Crane's instructions, she plugged it into the dashboard. It took a few minutes for the phone's flat battery to come back to life and Crane thumbed in Penny's number but there was no response. Crane reasoned that there was no option but to try and catch her up and find out the reason why she had returned.

*

Henri Girard strode around the barn where the remainder of the American cars were stored. His imagination began to run riot. He wanted a vehicle to replace the Audi convertible that had been inadvertently blown up, but he soon discovered that there were no ignition keys belonging to any of these parked cars, so he decided to look in the house.

As Girard entered the house muffled shouts drew him

to the cellar door. He paused for a moment before sliding back the heavy bolt. Ryan was the first to limp out and red faced he screamed at the Frenchman, 'About bloody time you turned up. Where's that guy, Crane?'

Girard shrugged nonchalantly as Ryan shouldered roughly past and limped towards the bathroom for the first aid kit. The other three men lumbered slowly up the cellar staircase and, glancing sheepishly at Girard as he drifted into the hall, headed for the kitchen. Girard stood to one side while they filed past and he suddenly found himself full of admiration for Crane. It would, he knew, have been no mean feat to overpower those four men.

*

In the distance, Crane was just in time to see Penny's Mini disappear off the main road and then turn back into the farm track from where they all had just escaped. He checked his watch; it was two pm. He had been away from the farmhouse for no more than thirty minutes, but he knew a lot can happen in that time. He decided against charging down the track with Sammy in the car. Instead he stopped across the entrance.

'Aren't you going to drive back to the house Jack?'

'I don't think that would be a very wise thing to do just yet, Sammy. I need to find out if the bad guys are still there.'

Crane looked around and pointing to a clump of dense evergreen said, 'Sammy, see those bushes over there? Could you be a very brave girl and hide in them while I go and see if I can find out what Penny is doing?'

'Yes of course I can, but you won't be very long, will you?'

'I hope not. Don't come out until you see me or Penny, okay?'

Sammy nodded enthusiastically and said, 'I'm getting a bit hungry now?'

'I'll try and bring back something to eat, Sammy.'

As soon as Crane was sure that the child was safely tucked out of sight he gunned the Mustang down the track towards the farmhouse. Penny's red Mini Cooper was parked close to the front door. Crane brought the car to a halt at a safe distance and checked the newly-acquired weapons; the Glock semi-automatic had a full clip of eighteen rounds and the small twenty-two calibre pistol had five cartridges remaining. That would be more than enough firepower.

He left the car and, with the Glock firmly gripped in his right hand, slowly approached the house. All was quiet. A constant flurry of wind sent swirls of dust and dirt peppering excitedly around the entrance. The front door was ajar, idly swinging and moving freely on its well-oiled hinges. Crane flattened himself against the wall, before he crouched down, and looked inside. He gradually straightened up but then froze when he heard a voice from behind saying, 'Put the gun down carefully on the ground and step back.'

He did as he was told and turned to face one of the three men whose breakfast he had so abruptly disturbed. The tall wiry man was holding a shotgun and he was aiming it at Crane's head. The sound of heavy limping feet made Crane half turn and he saw Ryan, his foot bandaged, holding a mobile phone and stooping down to retrieve the Glock. As he picked it up an evil grin spread across his face, 'Didn't expect to see you so soon, Crane.'

'I'm surprised to find you lot still here,' Crane replied.

'The game's up. I thought the gendarmes would have been here before now. I must have beaten them to it. Probably loading their machine guns; they use them a lot in this country you know.'

A worried look spread across Ryan's face, 'You're lying.'

'Why would I lie? Do you think I'm stupid enough to have come back here for nothing? Car theft and kidnapping doesn't go down too well in France. It used to be the guillotine or Devil's Island a few years ago for that kind of caper.'

'Where's the girl?' Ryan spat.

'Where do you think? In the safe custody of the police.'

The man with the shotgun lowered it and looked at Ryan for guidance. Ryan tried to put on a brave face, but he was finding it hard. He had been caught out by Crane's deceptions before and the third time, he reminded himself, when he called his bluff, it had cost him a bullet in the foot. The unmistakable sound of a vehicle, approaching from the other side of the hill, was timely and gave Crane some impetus as he said, 'At last, better late than never eh?'

Crane looked at both of the men in front of him in turn and said, 'If they see anyone with a gun there's no talking, it's open season, they start shooting; their rifles have telescopic sights, they can pick you off from half a mile away.'

The man with the shotgun had heard enough; he stood his weapon, with the safety catch on, against the wall by the front door and stepped away from it. Ryan glared at him, he was still uncertain about things; his jaw was set hard; elation at having Crane at his mercy was rapidly turning to disappointment and frustration.

Crane was acutely aware that any second now, whoever appeared over the hill would be calling his bluff and he would likely receive a bullet for his trouble. In a final attempt, Crane raised his hands high in the air commenting, 'At least they can see I'm unarmed.'

Ryan finally snapped, with some effort, he stooped down and laid the glock beside his feet. As he straightened up and stretched his neck, he cursed Crane when he caught sight of Bradley's car bouncing over the hill. Unfortunately for Ryan, he was not quick enough in trying to recover the weapon he had so carefully laid on the ground. He paused half way down when he heard the chilling sound of Crane's casual sounding voice remark, 'Do you want the other foot done now?'

His eyes shot up and stared uneasily at the barrel of the Jennings semi-automatic pistol held unwavering in Crane's hand.

Ryan gradually straightened and Crane was certain that whoever was in the car, bumping along the dusty track, would have seen them by now and he quickly scooped up the Glock, grabbed hold of the shotgun and said, 'In the house the pair of you and make it quick.'

Ryan's other two companions were standing in the hall, uncertain what to do, until they saw Crane slide the safety catch off the shotgun and then they were all too willing to be herded back into the cellar.

Their incarceration was timely. Crane turned around at the sound of a car scraping to a halt on the gravel. He watched as Bradley stepped out of the driver's seat. There was a sound of hurried footsteps from behind as Penny dashed down from a room upstairs. 'Jack, what on earth are you doing here, I thought... '

'I was going to ask you the same question,' Crane

interrupted without taking his eyes off Bradley.

At that point Bradley was leaning on his car and he called out, 'This is like a reunion eh?'

Gun in hand, Crane stood by the door just inside the entrance hall. 'I don't think so,' he called back, 'I could drop you at any time, so don't try anything. Just hold your arms out where I can see them.'

Bradley smiled confidently and with closed hands, extended his arms, 'Of course, but this little gizmo, I'm holding in my right hand, will detonate the necklace that my passenger is wearing, so if I were you I'd put the gun down.'

It was then that Crane noticed Sammy, slumped low down in the front passenger seat. Bradley appeared to be unarmed, Crane let his right arm drop down to his side, but his hand still held on to the Glock.

Bradley, his arms extended like a showman, was enjoying himself. 'With your permission, perhaps a little demonstration would convince you of my sincerity.' He tossed a matchbox some metres away and his other hand held what appeared to be a remote control. Like a salesman with a great deal of panache, he held it aloft and pressed a button. There was a violent explosion. 'That's button one,' he announced. 'The other button is for… well, that's obvious isn't it?' The smile vanished. 'Now the demonstration is over; put down the Mustang keys and drop the fucking gun.'

Crane loosened his grip, allowing the gun to drop to the ground by his side and after delving into his pocket, tossed the keys towards Bradley. The smile was back on Bradley's face. 'Okay. Now what did you do with my bunch of bloody morons?'

'They're in the cellar.'

'Well they can stew there for a while.' Looking past Crane, Bradley called out, 'Come on Penny, get in the car and we'll go and see your sister Jean… oh, and don't forget the boy.'

Penny hesitated for a moment, but this was interrupted by Andrew shuffling down the stairs, 'I'm hungry Auntie.'

Penny gave Crane a nervous glance as she drifted past him and called out to Bradley, 'The boy's not eaten, it's well past his lunch time.'

'Should have thought of that before; bring him out, I've some chocolate in the car.'

Penny stepped outside with Andrew trailing behind and Bradley said, 'You can follow me in your Mini.' He stood and watched whilst Penny strapped Andrew into the rear seat and when she climbed into the driver's seat, Bradley focused his attention back towards Crane; who stood framed in the doorway. Waving the remote control towards him, as a reminder of his callous intent, said, 'Now you can open the cellar door.'

At that point the sound of heavy feet clumping on gravel seemed to put things on hold. Bradley turned his head towards the sound; it was Henri Girard lolloping towards them.

'*Bonjour*' he said as he slowly lumbered past the gathering and headed towards the front door of the house with his haversack dangling from his broad shoulders.

Bradley looked askance – it was his first encounter with Girard. '*Parlez-vous Anglais?*'

Girard threw a glance over his shoulder and simply replied, '*Oui.*'

The semi-arrogant reply irritated Bradley and he said, 'Well who the fuck *are you* then?'

'*Je m'appelle*, erm, my name is Henri Girard.'

'Where the fuck do you think you're going?'

Henri Girard looked at his watch and said, 'In the chateau. It is past time for my lunch and I am hungry.'

His *laissez-faire* attitude did nothing to enhance Bradley's mood as he leant on the roof of his car and he said snappily, 'Well, what the devil are you doing here?'

'Mr Ryan is paying me to keep away intruders. I walk all around the borders of the estate, many kilometres – it takes a long time.'

At the mention of Ryan's name Bradley calmed down and said, 'Right, okay, well pick up that gun and take that man, an intruder – the one you missed – inside, then release my men from the cellar and put him in it – is that clear?'

'*Oui* – no problem.'

Bradley watched the two men enter the house before striding over to the spot where Crane had tossed the keys. He picked them up, returned to the BMW, and carried the comatose Sammy over to where the Mustang was parked and placed her inside. Signalling to Penny to follow, he climbed into the driver's seat and drove off with Penny following behind in her Mini.

To Crane's surprise, Girard ushered him past the cellar door and into the kitchen, motioning him to sit down. Girard set his bag on the table, dropped the Glock inside and took out a bottle of red wine. He turned and looked around. There were plenty of glasses in the sideboard and he plucked two from a dusty shelf, examined them before setting them on the table. The Frenchman then removed a couple of stick loafs from the cupboard, tossed them on the table and took a large platter of cheeses from the fridge. ''Elp yourself,' he proffered.

Between mouthfuls, Girard said, 'You are erm, *sang froid* eh?'

'You seem pretty cool yourself.' Crane replied cautiously.

'I had to work on it. I am supposed to get a little excited once in a while because I am French, but no. So my friend, I am in no great hurry to get that Ryan out of the cellar. Why does the man who took your car want me to put you in the cellar?'

Crane explained the reason he was there, to retrieve his Mustang, and now hopefully to secure the release of the young girl, Sammy.

The Frenchman was very attentive and said, 'I would steal a car; I would steal money if I had to, but I would never steal children.'

'Your English is pretty good.'

'I went to university in Paris; I studied English and Spanish. I wanted to be a linguist, but life always seems to play a different hand.'

'How did you get mixed up with this lot?'

'By accident I suppose. For nearly a year now, I am wanted throughout France for theft and murder, but it was self-defence – one of those 'either him or me' things ya know, and I prefer it to be me, that is, the one that remains alive. Pierre Marcel, the man I killed was evil. He stole my girlfriend and turned her into a prostitute. When she realised what was happening, she ran back to me, but it was too late. I tried to help her, but the evil bastard tracked her down and killed her. He got off; the witnesses changed their minds, no doubt scared or bought off, so I confronted him, he pulled a gun, a semi-automatic, before he could pull back the slide, well we fought and I killed him with his own weapon; and now *I* am wanted for murder. Pierre Marcel's men may also be looking for me. They want to kill me for killing their boss.'

They both remained silent for a moment and Girard, looking forlorn, could see the empathy in Crane's face. Suddenly Girard stood up, drained his glass and stabbing his chest with his thumb announced with renewed vigour, 'I, Henri Girard, will give you all the help I can.'

*

Penny followed behind Bradley in the Mustang. They had been on the road for an hour and Penny had plenty of time to think. With the passing of each kilometre an ominous feeling began to engulf her, causing her to feel more and more uneasy. Her mind drifted back to the conversation she had with Crane. The feeling worsened when Bradley turned into a remote single track lane with a hand-painted sign pointing to a chateau, "Chateau du Lac". Its name plaque seemed to slap her in the face.

Immediately steering with one hand on the wheel, her free hand groped inside the handbag which lay on the front passenger seat until, eventually her fingers clasped around her mobile phone. Balancing the mobile on her lap, she began texting Crane her whereabouts in the hope that somehow he will eventually receive it. A sombre grey stone structure loomed up, which only added to Penny's fears and she shivered.

She stared at the large three-storey house, remote and

surrounded by wild and unkempt scrubland. To one side, there was a small dried up lake. The place seemed to reek of past despair. A dark green Bentley Mulsanne with darkened windows was parked outside on the wide gravel driveway. Bradley drew the Mustang alongside the Bentley and leapt out. Penny brought the Mini up behind the Mustang, turned the engine off and sat clutching the steering wheel. She was wondering whether to drive off or stay put until her sister came out of the house, but she could not convince herself that this was going to happen.

A movement at the front of the house caught her attention. A portly, rotund woman came out to greet Bradley. As they spoke, Penny noticed the woman glancing in her direction. Bradley turned and motioned her to join them. A bolt of fear shot through Penny's veins and she suddenly felt nauseous. Before reaching for the door handle, she checked her phone in the remote chance that she had missed a call from Crane, but then she remembered that he was in trouble before she left the farm and she tried to comfort herself with the thought; *'If he manages to get away my text would be his only guide to where I have been taken.'*

Penny managed to summon up enough courage to walk slowly towards the huge front porch. Bradley introduced the rotund woman as Louise. She had a stern face and seemed to be trying hard to smile, although her English accent sounded pleasant enough. 'Do come in, my dear, you must be tired. I have some freshly-made sandwiches inside for you and the boy.'

Although feeling weary, Penny could have sworn that she spotted a knowing wink aimed at Bradley and it only added to her feeling of angst. She looked back over her shoulder towards her Mini; Andrew was craning his neck wondering what was happening. She knew him to be hungry, but the only words she could utter were, 'Where's my sister, Jean?'

The portly Louise flicked a glance at Bradley, who answered with a smile, 'In the house; she's inside getting ready.' And as if to reinforce things he added, 'You can wait out here if you like, but it was her idea for you to have something to eat; it's up to you.'

Bradley sounded so plausible that it was hard to believe that he was not telling the truth. It was what Penny wanted to hear and believe, so she went to fetch Andrew from the Mini and they followed Louise inside. As they stepped across the wide entrance hall Penny's heart sank as she heard a loud audible snap of a key being turned in the lock. She was trapped.

# CHAPTER FIFTEEN

Crane regarded Girard for a moment. He seemed sincere enough in wanting to help and he still retained that youthful exuberance that was hard to dislike, so Crane said, 'I don't suppose you have any idea where Bradley is going?'

The Frenchman shrugged his huge shoulders, 'No, I am sorry; it's the first time I've met him; and I don't much care for him. How about the guys in the cellar? Maybe one of them knows.'

Crane straightened up and said, 'Let's give it a try.'

Girard became enthused and he bounded towards the cellar door, slid the bolt back and throwing the door open called out, 'You guys want something to eat?'

'We wanna get outta here you great French idiot!' Ryan shouted back as he moved towards the bottom of the stairs.

'First I want to know where Bradley has taken the child.'

'None of your bloody business, Frenchie. We're coming up.'

The sound of Ryan's heavy feet clumping on the first two treads prompted Girard to call back, 'Okay, if you say so. I have a grenade in my hand, you know? – The one you gave to me. The pin has just fallen out and I don't really want it any more, so I'm going to throw it down right now.'

There was a scurrying of feet scrambling away from the stairs and a frantic cries of, 'Wait, wait for fuck's sake. None of us knows where he takes the kids, he's never told us; he just drives off for a few hours and then comes back without them – it's the truth.'

Cries of, 'Yeah. Yeah, that's right,' were audible amongst the others.

Crane, standing behind Girard, said in a hushed tone, 'They could be telling the truth.'

Girard was enjoying himself as he answered quietly, 'Let's make sure, eh?'

Crane looked askance as Girard shouted through the open door, 'I don't believe you; I think you are all lying. You are all boring me. You had better brace yourselves, here it comes.'

Panicky screeches of, 'We don't know! We don't know,' reverberated around the confines of the cellar; echoing noisily up the staircase.

With his last remark, Girard, grinning like a Cheshire cat, glanced at Crane and removed a chromed orb from his haversack; it was a heavy-chromed steel boule, about the size of a tennis ball. With some deliberation, he carefully lobbed it through the open cellar door so that it bounced and thumped, with a menacing sound, slowly down the stairs. Slamming the cellar door shut and still grinning, he shrugged and said to Crane, 'You are right; I guess they don't know.'

There were no clues about the house as to where Bradley might have taken Penny and the children and after a short while Crane said, 'It's a long-shot, but I'm going to drive to the next town, just in case they are nearby. I suggest you let those villains go one at a time and make sure that they leave the farm, but not Ryan. He may be of some use later.'

They exchanged mobile numbers and Girard offered the Glock handgun to Crane, 'You may need this, it may be of help.'

Crane palmed the weapon and handed back the small Jennings semi-automatic, 'This is yours. Oh, and by the way, one bullet's missing; I left it in Ryan's foot.'

The Frenchman grinned, showing a row of healthy-looking teeth, 'If he gives me any trouble… ' His voice faded away as Crane dashed out into the yard.

Crane climbed into the old Rover 620 and, as he drove along the farm track, pulled the mobile out of his pocket. The battery was flat. He cursed to himself when he realised, that he left the charger in the Mustang's glove box. He turned into the 940 coast road and headed towards Boulogne in the vain hope that he might catch sight of the Mustang or Penny's Mini but, at the very least, he would be able to buy an in-car charger for his mobile in the town.

*

Penny looked at the mouth-watering table that was laid out with food. Both she and Andrew were hungry and, seeing Bradley help himself, they too could not resist the fresh crusty French bread, or the mouth-watering cheeses and cold meats. Beverages were on hand and Louise offered a choice of soft drinks, wine or beer. 'I prefer tea, if possible,' Penny remarked.

Louise bustled off and within minutes returned with a jug of hot water and some tea bags, leaving Penny to help herself.

Bradley finished swigging from a beer bottle and said jovially, 'No doubt you'll be wanting to leave soon, I'll go and see if Jean is ready.'

Penny was beginning to believe she had overreacted and been mistaken about things. She threw a contented glance in Andrew's direction. He was no longer hungry, after having stuffed himself with an assortment of cakes, followed by a generous helping of cola and he was now lost in the folds of a large armchair. He looked tired and began to yawn. It was contagious. Penny sat down in an armchair beside him, her eyes felt sore and heavy; after all, she told herself, it had been a long day with so much tension and worry. The temptation to close jaded eyelids – just for a moment – was too great to resist. As she did so she whispered softly to Andrew, 'Mummy will be here soon.'

*

Crane plugged his newly acquired charger into the dashboard and waited patiently for the mobile to show signs of life. As soon as it powered up, a bleep warned him that there was a message waiting to be opened: it was Penny's desperate text – two hours old. Crane fed the information into his satnav. The location was twenty-five kilometres south-west of Boulogne.

He paced the Rover through narrow country lanes; at times, narrowly missing vehicles approaching in the opposite direction, until he entered the lane with an arrow pointing towards *'Chateau du Lac.'* Crane eased his foot off the accelerator and, after two kilometres, he braked and managed to tuck the car off of the road as soon as the grey, looming stone building came into view. Before climbing out of the Rover, he forwarded Penny's text to Girard's mobile.

Keeping to the hedgerows, Crane kept up a steady pace as he

hurried towards the ominous-looking house, sometimes pausing to use his binoculars. He felt apprehensive when he spotted Penny's Mini parked outside. It was the only vehicle to be seen so he quickly backtracked and jumped into the Rover. He drove up to the front door, leapt out and rang the bell. The door swung back almost immediately. Louise stood, one hand firmly clamped to the door and the other placed on her hip. She looked Crane up and down, '*Que voulez-vous?*' she rasped. 'What do you want?'

Crane smiled pleasantly and nodded in the direction of Penny's car, 'Penny, the woman who owns that car.'

Louise looked flummoxed, 'She's not here. Why do you want her?'

'She's a friend of mine and I know she would be glad to see me,' Crane answered with a smile.

'Well, she's out,' came the curt reply.

'When will she be back?'

'I don't know.'

'I'll wait if you don't mind.'

Louise was getting irritated, 'This is private property.'

Crane still smiling pleasantly said, 'That's okay, I'm a private person.'

Louise's jaw hardened as she said, 'The master won't like it.'

'Oh, and who is he?' Crane enquired.

'None of your business,' she snapped assertively.

Crane had had enough. He half turned, as though he was about to leave, at the same time his right hand snatched at the waistband of his trousers, pulled out the Glock semi-automatic and spun back round, pointing the gun towards her chest.

'You are beginning to annoy me,' he snarled.

Despite her portly size, Louise stepped back quite nimbly and tried to slam the heavy oak-panelled door, but Crane, anticipating this, was also quick and he barged against the door, knocking her off balance, so that she went sprawling and screeching across the polished marble floor of the spacious entrance hall. She lay there for a moment panting. Furious wide eyes stared at the business end of the Glock pointing downwards. As Crane stepped inside he kicked the door shut with the back of his foot.

'Let's start all over again, where is Penny, the owner of that car?'

Louise remained tight-lipped until Crane pulled back the slide on the gun and said with nonchalant chilling menace, 'Well then, you are not much use to me – you can die right where you lay.'

It was too much for Louise, her expression changed. '*Monsieur*, wait, wait,' she wailed.

Crane eased the gun to one side, 'Well?' he growled.

'The lady went away with Bradley and the master.'

'Where to?'

'I don't know.'

Crane raised the weapon again.

'Monsieur, I am never told such things.'

Crane held the gun steady, his jaw set hard, there was real menace in his face. 'Tell me what you do know, so that you may live.'

The eyes, of the portly-looking woman, widened with fear as she spouted slowly, 'The English lady, she came with a little boy. They ate, they drank… ' her voice tailed off as she looked down.

'What did they drink, sleeping draught?'

'*Oui*, yes. When they were sound asleep, we carried them out into the master's car.'

'What kind of car?'

'English car, called Bentley'

'And you don't know where they were going?'

'*No, monsieur. S'il vous plait*… please, they do not tell me. I keep house and do as I am told.'

Crane lowered the gun again, 'Was there anybody else here – a little English girl?'

'*Oui*, yes, very pretty, they all went an hour ago.'

'What is the master's name?'

'Claude Mullah.'

Crane pondered for a moment, 'That does not sound entirely French.'

'No, he was born in Algiers, has family there.'

The picture was now coming into focus; it would seem that the kidnap victims were being shipped off to North Africa.

'Is that where he takes the children?'

Louise was quiet; her eyes set on the floor. She looked up as Crane prompted, 'Well?'

'Yes,' she answered quietly.

'How many?'

Louise shrugged, 'I am not sure.'

'What do you know about Penny's sister, Jean?'

Still looking down she replied, 'They go to the same place as the children.'

'And that's into slavery for the rest of their lives!' Crane said scathingly, 'And you helped them get there.'

A noise from behind interrupted the proceedings. Crane quickly glance around and saw a man standing motionless at the foot of an oak-panelled staircase; he was holding a baseball bat. This was an opportunity that Louise was not going to let pass and from her position on the floor, she pounced towards Crane like a wild animal, clamping her arms around his legs, bringing him crashing down onto the floor beside her. The gun fell from Crane's hand and slithered across the polished surface. She scrambled over him – like a wrestler – using her weight to try and keep him pinned down. The baseball bat wielder wasted no time and rushed towards the writhing couple. With the bat held high the assailant aimed for Crane's head. Crane saw this move coming, but at the last second, using all his strength, he managed to manoeuvre Louise around and she took the full force of the blow. It knocked her out cold. The man repositioned himself to attack again, however Crane swiftly rolled away from Louise's comatose form. The man came in fast and as he stood between Crane's legs, raised the club again. Lying prone on the floor, Crane quickly turned his left foot inwards and brought it up behind the man's right calf. In the same instant he pushed hard with his right foot against the front of his attacker's leg, sending him crashing down. In a split second Crane was on his feet retrieving the Glock handgun.

The man had fallen heavily with the breath knocked out of him. He lay on the floor for a moment then recovering slightly, he propped himself up on his elbows to face Crane who was waving the gun and warning, 'You'd better stay there.'

The man's nervous eyes looked up from his position on the floor, following Crane's every move as he paced around the large hall. Gesticulating with the gun Crane said, 'Do you speak English?'

The man shrugged, 'Of course. I am English,' he grunted.

Crane said, 'What's your name?'

'Does it matter?'

'You'll need some kind of marker on your grave. Tell me, when is this Claude Mullah due back.'

'I dunno.'

Without saying anything else, Crane walked behind the prone figure and pulled the slide back on the Glock. The metallic sound of the gun and Crane's silence made the man flinch and turn his head.

'Who are you? Whadda gonna do?' he said uneasily.

'You're no use to me,' Crane said matter-of-factly pointing the gun at his head. 'If I'm going to hang around for a few days waiting for this Claude Mullah to return, I'd sooner have you out of the way.'

'Alright, alright. My name's Mackie. Claude is due back this evening, about nine.'

'Will there be anyone with him?'

'Maybe, Haj – a friend of his that helps out.'

'Where do you figure in this filthy business?'

'I used to do a bit of snatching for Bradley, until things got a bit too hot for me. So I ended up working here.'

'And,' pointing to the comatose figure of Louise said, 'where does she fit in?'

'Put's 'em to sleep and does whatever she's told.'

'Is there anyone else around?'

'No, not today; just me and her.'

'If I find out you're lying. I'll kill you.' Crane said coldly. 'Now there must be a wine cellar somewhere in the house – where is it?'

Mackie pointed, 'The door at the far end.'

'Does it have a key?'

'Hanging up by the door.'

'Okay, that's where you are both going. Get her up; drag her there if you have to, and no tricks.'

Louise groaned as Mackie pulled her along the slick marble surface and she managed to rise to her feet as he opened the wine cellar door. Crane stood by, watching them descend the wooden stairs and before closing the door he called out, 'Do help yourself to drinks.'

After locking the door, Crane made a quick reconnoitre outside, to make sure that there were no escape hatches from the cellar. When satisfied there were none he got in the Rover and again tucked it out of sight in some nearby scrub. Crane checked his watch; it was four pm.

Crane walked back to the chateau to look through the rooms but found nothing of interest or anything remotely incriminating. Two hours passed before the sound of a car, turning into the gravel driveway, made Crane rush to the window. It was Bradley and he was alone in Crane's Mustang. Crane stood for a moment and watched Bradley casually amble towards the house. Then, like a butler taking his place, he concealed himself by the front door with the Glock semi-automatic hand-gun hanging loosely by his side.

The bell clanged raucously and Crane, believing surprise to be on his side, during this elusive encounter with his arch-enemy, immediately swung back the front door to find himself facing an Uzi submachine gun pointing at his head. Bradley's face wore a twisted smile as he said. 'Gotcha! Now put my Glock down on the table, slowly.'

# CHAPTER SIXTEEN

Penny awoke to the sound of air being gently drawn in and out. It was Sammy and Andrew fast asleep. Nothing else could be heard. They were in total darkness. She felt movement, a gentle rocking feeling, like being in some sort of cradle. "A boat!" she correctly surmised. As her head cleared, she was certain that they were moored in a harbour. Thoughts of using her mobile were quashed, when she realised her handbag was missing and she began to lose hope fast.

*

Henri Girard, still at the farm, was spoilt for choice. With a box of car keys in his hand, he surveyed the remaining cars in the barn. Ignoring the classic cars, he settled on a year old dark-blue Porsche Boxster. Engrossed in the vehicle, he did not hear Ryan approach from behind until he saw a reflection in the glass windscreen. Girard turned and faced the overweight, sweating and seething man, who limped closer and barked, 'What the fuck are you doing with those keys?'

Girard shook the box he was holding and answered, 'I'm looking for the keys to this Porsche.'

Ryan snarled and held up a pepper spray, 'Well the Porsche

is not for you. Didn't expect to see me, did you. Luckily one of the others returned and let me out after you left me down in that cellar. Now, where's your friend Crane, eh?'

Girard shrugged his huge shoulders and lowered his lip, 'He had a gun, I had to do what he said. What could I do?'

'Come off it, a big bloke like you? Get back to the house now!'

Girard laughed and replied casually, 'No, I don't want to.'

This infuriated Ryan. Stepping forward, within two metres of Girard and waving the pepper spray canister he growled, 'You want some of this?'

Girard laughed again, only louder and said, trying to suppress his mirth, 'I wouldn't use that if I were you,' and he carried on looking in the box for the Porsche keys.

Ryan was apoplectic as he pressed down on the canister's button. A gust of wind sent a cloud of spray back into his face, sending him buckling to the ground, coughing violently with his hands held over his eyes.

Girard was grinning like a Cheshire cat and, between bouts of laughter, he began to chastise Ryan, as though he were speaking to a child. 'I did try, to erm… advise you. Is that the correct word? Advise? You should always check to see which way the wind is blowing before using any kind of spray.'

Ryan, with his eyes streaming and his lungs gasping for air, was not in a fit state to answer and Girard, finding the set of keys that he had been looking for, jumped into the Porsche and drove off.

Louise sat back in an armchair, nursing an egg-sized lump on her head whilst glaring accusingly at Crane who, under threat of being shot, had been forced to sit on the marble floor. Mackie had busied himself fetching ice packs from the freezer and he handed them to her. Bradley, having retrieved the Glock, gesticulated with the weapon, 'This ends here Mr Jack Crane. I don't know how you found this place, or the other places come to that, but I must assume that given your background, you are a very resourceful man. However, so am I.'

Crane looked up and said, 'You won't last, your kind never do.'

Bradley sneered, screwed up his face then turned towards Mackie, 'It's just as well there was a phone in the cellar and very fortunate I was nearby at the time. I must go soon, got things to do.' He turned and snarled at Crane, 'I'm sure Claude Mullah will know exactly what to do with him. Where can we put him until Mullah gets back?'

Mackie grinned, 'There's a concrete bunker on the edge of the drive, built by the Germans during World War Two. It's bomb proof; he won't get out of there in a hurry.'

Bradley was satisfied with this arrangement and watched as Mackie, using a twelve-bore shotgun, herded Crane towards the bunker and sealed him in with a heavy iron bar braced across a steel door.

Mackie stood confidently for a moment, with the shotgun tucked under his arm, as he waved Bradley off before returning to the house. Crane, peering through the narrow gun slit, also watched the departing pair.

*

Penny tried hard not to feel panicky as she lay in total darkness. The children were still asleep. Considering the circumstances, Penny thought it was a blessing. She could hear sounds outside, but they were muffled. Maybe it was her imagination trying to get through the tinnitus sounds in her head. However, she decided that, just maybe, there could be somebody in the vicinity; so she shouted for help at the top of her voice. The only response seemed to be the faint hum of an engine and a sensation of motion as the craft pulled slowly out of the harbour which just added to her feeling of despair.

*

Henri Girard was in ebullient mood as he put his newly-acquired Porsche Boxster through the paces. He loved the way the car handled, pulling it hard around the tight bends, he passed through Boulogne and headed towards 'Chateau du Lac'. His face beamed with satisfaction as he whispered to himself, 'It goes around corners like it's on rails,' he breathed out a sigh and began to sing out loud an old Disney classic that he had seen on video when he was a child, 'Zip-a-dee-do-daa, zip-a-dee-day... '

*

Crane positioned himself by the narrow gun slit – it was a source of warm, dry fresh air and a welcome change from the dank atmosphere inside. The bunker had been well sited;

it gave generous views of the long-winding driveway that led to the chateau. After an hour's confinement, he heard a vehicle approaching. He turned and stared into the distance. As it neared, he recognised the man behind the wheel; it was Henri Girard. Crane stuck both hands through the slit and began waving frantically and the car gradually slowed down to a halt. Girard jumped out of the Porsche and strolled up to the bunker; his eyes flicked between the padlocked steel door and Crane. ''Ello; I got your text. What are you doing in there?'

'Not much,' Crane replied and he went on to explain how he became imprisoned.

'Leave it to me,' Girard said before leaping into the Porsche and driving round to the front entrance of the house.

Girard walked boldly up to the door, rattling the huge knocker, pressing the bell at the same time. It was answered by Louise. Through the open door, Girard could see Mackie holding a shotgun.

With a wide grin Girard said, '*Bonsoir, Madame*, I'm Henri Girard. *Monsieur* Bradley sent me to collect *Monsieur* Crane.'

At the mention of Bradley's name, Mackie seemed to relax and leant the gun up against the wall. But, Louise was more cautious and she eyed him up and down with suspicion. Wanting to exercise her authority she said cockily, 'Do you have anything to authenticate?'

Girard's grin widened as he put a hand in his pocket and replied, 'But of course, it is wise of you to ask.'

Louise's shoulders relaxed until Girard slickly produced the small Jennings handgun, 'I have this.'

171

Louise stepped back a few paces at this unexpected move. Mackie immediately reached towards the wall for his shotgun but Girard was ready for this. The range of four metres was not too great for him to send a bullet smashing into the wooden stock of Mackie's weapon, sending it crashing to the floor. By now, Louise's eyes were wide with fear as she stared at Girard and heard him say, 'I don't really want to kill you, so you had better do as I tell you. I'm already wanted by the police for murder; well… I have nothing to lose. Put the key to the lock of the bunker on this little table and then both of you get outside… *s'il vous plait.*'

Girard turned the key in the padlock and withdrew the heavy bar. Crane stepped outside, with a feeling of relief, to get away from the confines of the humid, musty, damp atmosphere of the bunker, complete with German graffiti, with its echoes of the past also etched into its walls. Then Girard ushered Mackie and Louise inside. Their sullen looks caused Girard to say to them cheerfully, 'Don't look so worried, think of it as an exchange visit eh?'

On their way to the house, Girard said, 'I think we should cover up that porthole or else they may be waving their arms about to get the attention of their boss when he turns up.'

'Good thinking, but maybe it would be better to hand them a bottle of water with some of their sleeping draughts in. They'll soon get thirsty and that will keep them quiet.'

Within a short time, Girard was handing the water through the gun slit and after doing so, he paused for a second to hear the pair slurping it down their throats.

Back in the chateau, Girard busied himself down in the wine cellar. After some time, he had selected a bottle of red wine and came into the dining room. 'There is nothing special down there,' he declared and, plucking a pair of glasses from a cabinet, proffered, 'A little Bordeaux perhaps?'

Crane looked at his watch; it was seven-thirty. 'No thanks, I need to keep a clear head for when they arrive.'

Girard shrugged and poured himself a large glassful of the red liquid, '*Oui*, so do I. I'll just have one.'

Crane walked towards the door, 'I'll check up on our sleeping beauties; we do not need any more surprises.'

Girard grunted an assent between mouthfuls of crusty bread.

\*

At the farm, Bradley was somewhat fazed to discover his right-hand man Ryan was the only person around and that he appeared to be in a state of frustration because of his heavily bandaged foot. Bradley gave a cursory glance at Ryan's foot and unsympathetically dismissed it with, 'Shit happens.'

Ryan reluctantly recounted the details of what had happened since their last meeting and was somewhat consoled by the fact that Bradley had placed Crane under lock and key in an old German bunker.

Bradley looked at his watch before getting back into his car and said, 'A transporter should be arriving any time now to take care of the remaining stock. Pity you couldn't have stopped the French guy from taking the Porsche.' And looking Ryan straight in the eye added, 'It'll have to come off your share you know.'

Ryan was not too pleased, but at the back of his mind, he had by now, no reason to doubt Crane's story about Davy being pinned, with a long knife, to the seat in his vehicle. He was beginning to feel that if he was not more careful, he could share a similar fate and so he felt it pertinent to reply lamely, 'Yeah Bradley, that's only fair.'

Bradley left with a, 'Be back soon.'

\*

Crane walked from the front door of the chateau towards the concrete bunker. It was mid-afternoon and unseasonably warm for the time of year and he knew it would be hot and sticky inside the old wartime building, and maybe that fact would also help the drugged water on to induce sleep. He approached the building silently by walking on the grass verge and he stood outside for a while and listening intently. He heard the heavy sound of slumber coming from inside. He turned away and looked instinctively along the driveway. A large car was silently gliding along its surface; it was the Bentley returning home. There was no time for him to dash back to the house, without being seen by the driver, but he just had time to dart around to the back of the concrete structure, before the Bentley whispered past. The idea of surprising Claude Mullah and his companion Haj were rapidly evaporating and his thoughts now turned towards Girard, whom he had left in the sitting room reclining comfortably in a deep-piled armchair whilst swilling red wine.

# CHAPTER SEVENTEEN

The hatch above Penny suddenly scraped open and their confined space became awash with sunlight, its rays stabbing harshly into the children's eyes, causing them to wince. She gradually got used to the intensity of the light and looked up at a blue cloudless sky. Within a few minutes, a basket containing food and drink was being lowered from the edge of the hatch and a gruff voice in broken English called out, 'Somethink to eet and drink.'

Penny found it difficult to react at first, but after a moment she called back, 'Where are we? Are we at sea? Where are you taking us?'

There was no reply. The children were now wide awake and anxiety was beginning to show on their faces. Putting on a bold front Penny said, 'Who would like something to eat?'

Andrew was the first to reply and Penny dipped into the basket and handed him a bottle of fruit juice, a sandwich pack and some cakes. Sammy looked morose and said, 'Do you think Jack will be able to come for us?'

Penny looked down, 'I would like to think so, Sammy. I really would. Perhaps some food will help you keep your strength up, just in case he does.'

*

As soon as the Bentley had passed by, Crane moved from his position behind the bunker. He dodged behind the rows of bushes lining the drive, which twisted and turned, towards the chateau. The Bentley came into view once more, it was parked adjacent to the front door outside the house. Crane paused for a moment, to check for movement inside the car and, judging it was now empty, he kept low, as he ran deftly up to the front door. It was wide open and all was quiet. Feeling apprehensive, he remained there for a while, listening. There was not a sound to be heard.

Very slowly, he gingerly stepped into the large entrance hall, paused for a moment and listened again: nothing. It was as though the place was empty. Crossing the hall, he approached the door to the sitting room and gently nudged it open with his foot and looked inside. He saw Girard sitting in an armchair, looking decidedly relaxed. He had a half-filled glass of red wine in his hand and his foot was firmly straddled across the chest of one of the men from the car. The other man, lying prone on the floor, appeared to be out cold. Upon seeing Crane, Girard looked up. He smiled and said nonchalantly, 'Ah, there you are, I was beginning to worry about you. Are these the two men we have been waiting for?'

Crane, recovering from his surprise, grinned and said, 'I reckon they must be. Were they armed?'

Girard nodded towards the table, 'Large calibre Smith and Wesson magnum revolver and a brand new nine mil Glock.'

There was movement and a groan from the floor and they saw that the prone figure was recovering and coming round. Crane grabbed the revolver from the table and said,

'The man under your foot… is he still alive?'

Girard shrugged and wriggled his foot on the man's chest, 'I'm not sure.' There was a groan and he said, 'Yes, I think so. He is alive.'

'Okay, let's find out what they have been up to.'

The men began to sit up and Crane said, 'Okay, on your feet the pair of you and take a seat.'

The groaning men sat down in chairs opposite each other and looked scathingly at Crane. One of them complained, 'What do you want with us, money?'

Crane looked at the man who spoke, 'Are you Claude Mullah?'

There was an arrogant tone in Mullah's voice as he replied, 'What if I am? Who are you and what do you want?'

'I want the women and children who were here.'

Mullah smirked, 'I don't know what you are talking about. There were no women or children here. What have you done with my staff, Mackie and Louise?'

'They are locked up in the bunker. Now, tell me, where did you take the woman and two children this morning? And please don't lie to me.'

'What are you, police or something?'

'No, now tell me.'

'What are you going to do if I don't?'

'You'll be no use to me or to my friend Girard; he's already wanted for murder – we'll kill you, simple as that.'

There was no fear in Mullah's eyes; just hatred. 'They are at sea.'

'Get them back.'

'I cannot.'

Crane looked long and hard at Mullah. His face reflected

pure ferocity as he drew back the hammer on the .45 calibre revolver. He pointed the gun at Mullah's leg and said, 'You've got just one chance of coming out of this alive, don't ruin it! One bullet from this gun would blow your kneecap right off and that would be just for starters.'

Mullah's self-assured confidence drained rapidly. Rivulets of sweat began to run from his hairline and down the sides of his face. His eyes darted between Crane's savage expression and the handgun that was pointing directly at his knee.

'Mobile phone,' Mullah stammered, 'mobile phone.'

'Where is it,' Crane hissed.

'In the car. It's in the car.'

Girard leapt up, 'I'll get it.' Within a few minutes he was handing Mullah the phone. As Mullah began to dial Crane said, 'Turn the speaker on.'

Mullah reacted nervously by nodding several times. The quietened room was filled with the sound of a ringing tone, but before long the automatic voice responded in French with an, 'Unable to connect you; please try again later.'

Mullah shifted uneasily in his seat. His eyes darted from Crane, who stood leaning against the table, to Haj, who had remained silent throughout. They were both well-built men, but not as broad or as muscular as Girard. Crane guessed the ruthless pair to be in their late thirties.

'Try again,' Crane barked.

Mullah carefully dialled once more, but receiving the same response, looked up fearfully at Crane.

'When and where did the boat leave?'

Mullah looked at his watch, 'About an hour ago from a private mooring near Boulogne.'

'What kind of boat are they on and where is it heading?'

'A motor launch about ten metres long; it's heading for Morocco, but it will stop, refuel and take on supplies and more, erm... passengers at a private mooring near Le Havre.'

'And the arrival time?'

'I'm not sure. Three, four, five hours maybe.'

Crane checked the time and said, 'You can take us there.' Mullah looked at Crane askance but Crane continued, 'We can hire a helicopter from the airport at Le Touquet; it's about twenty kilometres from Boulogne. I take it you've got plenty of cash knocking around?'

Mullah nodded vacantly but was beginning to succumb to Crane's resolve. Haj's eyes alternated between Crane and Girard as he leant back in his armchair trying to hide the hatred he felt towards this intrusion. His mind was awash with schemes to get himself and Mullah out of this situation. 'There's a private airfield; it's nearer and has a helicopter service,' Haj offered.

Mullah nodded vacantly and Girard confirmed, 'I passed it on the way here.'

'Okay,' Crane said, 'we'll try that one first.'

Girard accompanied Mullah to the Algerian's Bentley and, using his remote control, Mullah opened the rear compartment. Under Girard's watchful eye, Mullah reached inside and grabbed hold of a large expensive-looking black-leather holdall and together, with Girard trailing close behind, they went back inside the chateau where Mullah tossed the bag onto a grandiose polished table.

Crane looked at the bag and said, 'How much is in there?'

'A little over two hundred thousand euros.'

'That'll do. Open it and tip the contents onto the table, slowly.'

Mullah did as he was told and feeling some of the fear evaporating remarked, 'You're a very cautious man, Mr Crane.'

Crane scoffed as he watched the neatly bundled notes cascade onto the table together with a small pearl handled revolver, Crane smiled and said, 'Yeah,' as he picked up the weapon and, turning around, he handed it to Girard and said, 'Give the airport a call to see if they have a chopper available, your French is better than mine!'

Mullah's eyes shifted from Haj to Crane, 'Look, Mr Crane, why don't you take the money and forget about everything else – eh?'.

Crane said, 'You're forgetting something – I've already got the money.'

Girard, rummaging around for a phone book, grinned at Crane's answer. Within a few minutes, the Frenchman was talking to a private charter company and, when he put the phone down, he said, 'When I mentioned cash, they seem to have a helicopter at our disposal.'

'Okay!' Glancing at Mullah, Crane said, 'We can only take one of you with us so your friend will have to stay here; in the bunker.' Haj looked up scathingly as Crane continued, 'We'll make sure there is enough food and drink to last until our return. If anything should happen to us, well the bunker is very remote and whoever is in there will rot there. Do I make myself clear?'

Mullah, unused to being ordered around, nodded sullenly. Haj remained silent, but Crane was not seeking approval as he watched, gun in hand, while Haj and Mullah took supplies from the kitchen, and ferried them over to the bunker. Haj was then locked up inside the bunker with Mackie and Louise, who were still lying there sound asleep.

Crane was beginning to feel he was getting somewhere, when the three of them, in Mullah's Bentley, headed off in the direction of the airport. With Girard at the wheel, they made good time and upon turning into the main entrance, followed the signposts to *Heli-hire*. As the car approached the building, the occupants saw a man, drawing heavily on a cigar, standing framed in the open doorway, his free hand resting casually on the door post. As the car pulled up he propelled himself off the door frame and greeted Girard and Crane with a huge grin as they leapt out. Mullah took his time getting out of the car and trailed behind. The laid-back man introduced himself as Pierre Durand and directed them into his office. It was soon apparent that he spoke good English, 'Where exactly do you want to go to?'

Crane and Girard turned towards Mullah, who, considering his circumstances seemed to be somewhat ebullient. As Mullah strode forward, he gave a quick glance at Durand and stabbed his finger on the map. 'There!'

Durand thought for a moment and said, 'No problem, but I need to file a flight plan.'

Crane nodded and said, 'How long will that take?'

'Not long. Once I've got that cleared, we'll be there within thirty minutes or less.'

Whilst the pilot was busy Crane looked at Mullah, 'Are you sure your man will refuel the boat at the place you pointed out?'

'There is no doubt; it's my own private mooring complete with fuelling facilities.' Mullah checked his watch, 'We should be there before the boat.'

Crane detected an almost cheerful note in the tone of voice, which seemed inappropriate considering the situation that Mullah had found himself in. However, like it or not, Crane dismissed this observation as being over cautious.

Within minutes, a thin-faced willowy young man in his early twenties came into the office. He was introduced as Simon and Durand announced, 'All is well. Let's fly.' They followed him as he walked towards an adjacent shiny red, Polish-made, Mi-2 helicopter which was parked close to the office. There was plenty of room inside the eight-seat aircraft, but Girard made a point of sitting close behind Mullah. The twin-turbo engines whined into action and with rapidly spinning rotors, they were airborne in seconds.

*

Since rousing from their induced sleep, the warmth and the cramped surroundings had taken their toll with Penny and the children. They had quickly got through the bottled water, which had been left down below with them. Their throats were now parched and they felt keen to move around and stretch their legs. Penny thumped on the hatch and shouted, 'Is there a loo on board this boat, a toilet?'

The sound of feet shuffling across the deck and a heavily-accented voice resounded, 'You can come out for a little while, eh, then you go back, eh!'

The hatch was thrown back and Penny clambered up a short flight of steps. As she stepped on to the deck, her hand shot up shielding her eyes from the bright intense sunlight. Sammy and Andrew were quick to follow; eagerly scrambling up the narrow ladder. When the sun's rays spread across their faces, they closed their eyelids tight shut with discomfort. A gruff-looking man stood by, with a helping hand, making sure the trio found their sea-legs as the launch bucked and swayed over a heaving grey blanket of sea. Penny could see the land quite clearly as the boat hugged near to the coastline towards Le Havre.

Penny let the children visit the toilet first and she asked her jailor, 'Where are you taking us?'

The man remained silent. After using the toilet Penny repeated the question – again there was no answer. Instead the man handed over a plastic shopping bag containing bottled water and snacks before directing them back to their confines below deck.

\*

Bradley returned to the farm in time to see that the remaining vehicles were being taken out of the barn and that they were now being driven onto the car transporter. He stood leaning against his BMW – watching every move until they had finished loading. His eyes did not leave the huge, now fully-loaded, vehicle until it reached the hill and disappeared from view. His trance was interrupted when Ryan limped out of the farmhouse, 'Okay, it's tidied up inside and the owner's been paid. Where to now?'

Bradley thought for a moment before replying, 'Our work is all done here, but before we head for home, I think a quick visit to Mullah's chateau would be in order. It won't take long. I'm curious to see what he has done with Crane.'

Ryan grinned at the prospect of Crane's demise as he hobbled towards the BMW.

*

The helicopter drifted around the desolate grounds of an tall old house, a typical French maison. Crane scanned the remote area for signs of life, but there were no other houses in sight nor any towns or villages to be seen. After a moment, the aircraft hovered over the area while the pilot considered a suitable spot for landing. Then the craft floated gently down and settled onto a dry, grassless patch of earth.

Crane stepped out of the machine, followed by Mullah and Girard. They turned to face a modern newly-built boathouse complete with a jetty. It was sited some hundred metres away from the isolated house and it was an ideal location for the kind of business that Mullah was involved in.

Crane looked at Mullah. 'Anyone in the house?'

Mullah shrugged, 'There is a housekeeper, but she is not always here.'

Crane stood for a moment, looking towards the house, but he could see no signs of life. He turned his head in time to see Durand with his arm outstretched, holding a revolver. It was pointing at his chest. Mullah sneered at Crane and Girard as he shouldered past the pair and rushed towards Durand, beginning with, 'You took your time… ' However in his haste, Mullah crossed Durand's line of fire and Crane, seizing the opportunity, snatched the purloined Glock from his waistband, flipped off the safety catch, then aimed and fired in a split second. A look of pain and surprise spread across Durand's face as he clutched at his arm. His gun, held in a vice-like grip, pointed uselessly towards the ground.

184

Mullah turned to face Crane, his eyes registering disbelief. Crane held the Glock steady and said, 'Drop it now, Durand, or the next bullet goes between your eyes.'

Durand, through gritted teeth, allowed the pistol to slip from his grasp. Girard casually strode forward, shaking his head and wagging a finger at Durand, chiding him like a naughty schoolboy, before stooping and retrieving the handgun. Crane called out to Durand's co-pilot, Simon, who appeared frozen, his face registering a look of terror.

'I'm sure there's a first aid kit in the chopper,' Crane snapped, 'get it and no tricks!'

Simon became reanimated. Wide-eyed, he nodded fearfully and scampered towards the helicopter.

Girard offered the revolver to Crane, 'I have to admire the way you handle difficult situations.'

Crane pursed his lips with a feeble smile; he always felt awkward being praised for something that seemed to come naturally and said, 'My pockets are full, can you shove it in your carrier?'

Girard held out his hand, pursed his lips, shrugged – as the French tend to do – and took the weapon. He shuffled the haversack from his shoulder and looking inside said, 'I already have the magnum and two others in there; it's like I am walking around with an arsenal.'

There was a distinct clinking of glass as the handgun dropped into his bag and noting Crane's expression he added quickly, 'And of course two very good bottles of wine from Mullah's cellar.'

Simon returned with the first aid kit and discovered Durand had suffered a flesh wound in the upper arm and so under the watchful eyes of Crane and Girard, he set about applying a bandage. Girard suddenly took his eyes off them and said, 'Where's Mullah?'

Their eyes searched around the area and came to the conclusion that Mullah had probably made a run for the boathouse. 'Keep your eyes on those two,' Crane yelled as he ran off towards the large boathouse by the jetty.

*

The chateau stood cold and empty but in the confines of the bunker the sun was shining through the wide slit. All three occupants were wide awake and sweating profusely as they paced around like caged animals in their prison. Louise was bemoaning her plight and insisted she would have to pee in the corner rather than wet herself, while stifled groans of protest enthused from Mackie and Haj. Their rhetoric was interrupted by the noise of an approaching car. Mackie sprung up and looked through the gun port; 'It's Bradley,' he enthused, and extending his arm through the gap, began to wave frantically.

Bradley put on the brakes, leapt out of the BMW and noticing the padlock holding the bar in place, called out, 'It's locked.'

Mackie replied, 'I have a spare key here in my pocket,' and tossed it outside through the gap.

When eventually they were inside the chateau, Bradley listened intently as Haj recounted the details of what had happened.

Bradley's mean face turned into a grin as he said, 'And Mullah used our friend the helicopter pilot, Pierre Durand eh? Well Durand may have nailed Crane and his big lout mate, the Frenchman, but I wouldn't bank on it. So we need to be prepared. Meanwhile, Ryan and I, we have a few things to clear up in England. Get in touch if you hear anything.'

Mackie grunted an assent and Haj added, 'If he comes back here, he will die here and I will bury him here.'

# CHAPTER EIGHTEEN

It was the third time Penny and the children had been allowed to go up on deck and she observed that they were heading towards the coast. On this occasion they were allowed to remain up on deck in the fresh air, but while there, Penny was careful to accept only drinks from unopened bottles and only factory-wrapped snacks when offered anything for them to consume.

Sammy, watching the coastline draw nearer, appeared to be a little more relaxed than before, although Penny could see the underlying concern that was showing on her young face. Andrew, however, was content and seemed to be treating everything as an adventure; there were plenty of biscuits and chocolate on hand and he still held onto his favourite electronic game.

*

Girard's observation that Mullah was missing had stirred Crane into action. It was an easy run for him, as he stormed down the gentle grassy slope leading to the boathouse. Within a few metres, the raucous whine of an electric starter motor spurred him on. With a final effort, he increased his pace and burst through the rear door – gun in hand. He was in time to see Mullah adrift on board a speedboat in the calm waters of the boathouse, desperately trying to start the engine. Crane bent down and thrust his hand into the water and grabbed hold of the mooring rope trailing on the surface. Mullah turned to face Crane, who continued to wind the rope around a capstan. 'Get out!' Crane shouted angrily, levelling the Glock handgun.

Mullah's face whitened. The boat was a few metres from the landing stage and he called back, 'Pull the boat in then.'

'Get in the water! If you don't I'll start shooting.'

'Alright, alright,' Mullah replied feebly, 'I'm coming,' and he jumped over the side of the boat. The water in the boathouse came up to his chest. Crane stood back and watched as, with some effort, Mullah clambered up spluttering onto the decking.

'Try that again and you'll end up dead,' Crane barked. 'Now we get back to the helicopter and you'd better just hope that your friend turns up.'

They returned to the helicopter landing site close to the house, where Durand was sitting on the grass nursing his wound with Simon close by. Like a sentry, Girard was keeping a close watch over the pair of them and turned when he heard Mullah approach with Crane trailing close behind.

Girard looked on approvingly and said, 'I've got the keys to the helicopter in my pocket. I think one of us should take a look inside the house.'

Crane glanced across at the tall narrow building, with its steps leading up to a central front door, and said, 'That's a good idea, I'm not in the mood for any more surprises.'

'My turn,' Girard said, 'so far there's been no sign of life, so I'll see if there is anyone at home,' and delving into his

189

bag, produced the magnum revolver, adding with a grin, 'at least I can speak French.'

Crane smiled at that light-hearted remark and said, 'Okay, but take care.'

As usual, the devil-may-care, big man shrugged his great shoulders. Crane stood for a moment and watched as Girard casually ambled off towards the chateau. Then he turned his attention back towards Mullah, 'Sit down, you can join your friends on the grass.'

Holding the handgun behind his back, Girard approached the oak-panelled door and as he leant on the bell push he saw a weathered sign attached to the wall displaying the name of the house: 'Maison Rouge'. A shuffle of feet could be heard trampling softly across the floor towards the entrance. All was quiet for a few seconds and suddenly the door snapped open, restrained by a security chain. The curious face of an elderly woman looked Girard up and down.

Girard put on his best disarming smile and said, 'Good afternoon. I'm Henri Girard, Monsieur Mullah sent me over.'

At the mention of Mullah's name the woman's face relaxed and she undid the chain and pulled back the door. She looked petite in a long dress which accentuated a straight upright back. Her long grey hair was tied back in a ponytail which did not seem to match her age and frail appearance.

'My name is Giselle.'

'Such a beautiful name, madame.'

'Why thank you, Henri.' A sweet coy smile spread across her face as she instantly warmed to Girard, 'You are so kind. Does Monsieur Mullah need anything?'

Keeping the smile intact Girard said, 'He's in conference

at the moment, Giselle, he's expecting a boat to arrive anytime from now.'

'Hmm, I guessed it might have been today,' she offered, 'Monsieur Mullah's always such a busy man.'

Not wishing to frighten the old lady, Girard surreptitiously tucked the handgun down his rear trouser waistband and said, 'In fact he has invited me to look the place over because he is thinking of selling it.'

'Is he now? Very well,' she replied and stepped back to allow Girard in.

It did not take long to satisfy Girard that the old lady seemed to be the only person in the building, but when finally he came to the last room, he peered round the door and found two little girls staring at him, their blue eyes wide with curiosity. Girard reckoned them to be three or four years of age.

'Who are they?'

Giselle smiled warmly and said, 'They are such little dears, Monsieur Mullah's nieces, you know. He has many nieces that stay here of different nationalities. Those two are due to leave today by boat.'

The children were surrounded by toys and were absorbed playing together with a doll's house. When Girard spoke to them they answered in French. Girard was shocked when they told him they were waiting for their mummy to collect them.

'Do you realise these children have been kidnapped?' Girard chided the housekeeper.

Her hand shot up to her face, which registered a genuine look of shock at the accusation. She was quiet for some minutes before answering, 'If what you are saying is true then I have been a fool. This place is a long way from the village. Monsieur Mullah always arrives by helicopter. I see no one. Everything is delivered here and I am allowed to live here for nothing as a reward for looking after the children.'

'How long have you been here?' Girard questioned.

'Three months.'

Girard tended to believe her and left her in a state of bewilderment as he led the children outside.

Crane stood by the helicopter, with Mullah and his two cohorts seated on the ground. He watched, with arms folded and became somewhat bemused, when Girard made an appearance through the front door of the house holding the hands of two little girls, clutching several soft toys between them. Girard led them towards the helicopter and seated them inside, before reporting what he had discovered to Crane.

'We'll need to notify the police,' Crane said.

'You can, not me. I cannot go anywhere near a police station.'

'Well one thing's for certain; we shall take the girls with us. We'll have to find somewhere to secure Mullah and his two villains.'

Crane and Girard locked up the three men in one of the most favourite places in all French houses, large or small; the wine cellar, although to Girard's chagrin, this one was devoid of wine bottles and was completely empty. As an added security, Crane suggested that the old lady be locked in a separate room.

'I feel sure she was telling the truth,' Girard said.

'You may be right, but let's not be too complacent about anything.'

They then went back to the helicopter. Crane checked his wristwatch, it was early evening and it had been four hours since they had landed. From then on, they took turns in going back to the boathouse, to keep watch and look for signs of the incoming launch. Their key element was surprise.

When Crane's turn to keep watch on the boathouse came round again, he caught sight of what appeared to be a speck on the horizon. He grabbed hold of a pair of binoculars that were conveniently dangling from a hook on the wall and saw a large motor launch ploughing through the surf. From its current position it appeared to be heading in the direction of the jetty. As a precaution against being seen, he moved deep into the boathouse and tucked himself out of sight. He kept a watchful eye on the launch, until he felt confident that the approaching craft was the one that belonged to Mullah.

Girard stood by the helicopter and kept an eye on the house. He was surprised to see Giselle suddenly come out of the front door and walk towards him; she was carrying a tray covered with a white cloth. Girard had locked her in himself and he still had the key in his pocket. She obviously must have had a spare, it would never occur to Girard to frisk such a sweet old lady.

Girard kept a curious eye on Giselle as she tripped casually along the grass, like a maid bringing her master lunch al fresco. Her wide smile was infectious and Girard beamed back. Within three metres she paused and, like a cordon bleu chef, she held the tray in one hand and skilfully whipped off the white-cloth cover with her other hand, to reveal a .38

Smith and Wesson revolver on a platter. Snatching at the weapon, she dropped the tray and pointed the gun at Girard, 'Nobody locks me in, you bastard,' and she pulled the trigger. Girard had recovered from the shock rapidly and dodged to one side. The bullet thudded harmlessly into the side of the helicopter and a second bullet followed soon after. Girard ducked under the machine and pulled out the .45 magnum from his waistband, just as a third shot ricocheted with a whine off the helicopter.

With shouts of, 'Keep still you bastard,' Giselle began swearing profusely at her own inability to bring her quarry down. Girard did not like the idea of returning fire, but equally, he did not like the idea of being killed. He paused briefly and holding the gun with both hands, took careful aim and fired. The weapon flew out of Giselle's hand and Girard blew a sigh of relief, but the relief was short lived. As he ducked and ran around the helicopter to face her, the three men who had been locked up in the cellar, were running towards him like mad animals – and they were armed.

They stopped abruptly when Giselle lost her gun. Mullah swung up a Mossberg pump-action shotgun, levelled it and fired. Girard threw himself to the ground as the pellets whistled past, grazing Giselle on their way before peppering the aircraft. From his position on the grass, Girard took aim and fired. Mullah screamed in pain as a bullet passed through his right calf and he crumpled to the ground.

The pilot, Durand, standing next to Mullah, was instantly reminded of his wound and earlier involvement. He was not anxious for any more gun play, especially when he had witnessed Girard's skill with a handgun. He froze and his co-pilot, Simon, followed suit, dropping their weapons and throwing up their hands. Girard looked towards Giselle disappointedly. His sympathy towards her had waned. He considered her fortunate enough to have only suffered a sprained hand.

Without a saying a word, Girard used the gun in his hand as a pointer. He motioned for her to sit down, and to join the groaning Mullah who lay prone on the ground. This invite was extended to Durand and Simon, shepherding them together in a close-knit group. Girard kept a mistrusting eye on the motley bunch whilst gathering up their weapons. When he had finished, he paused, slowly pulled a bottle from his shoulder bag and took a generous swig of *vin rouge*.

\*

From his concealed position in the boathouse, Crane saw the approaching launch slow down. The craft's engine altered pitch and it went from an incessant drone to a gentle throb as it drifted lazily towards the jetty. As far as Crane could tell, there were two swarthy-looking men on board, but no sign of Penny or the children. One of the men leapt off onto the jetty and his companion tossed him a line from the boat, which he swiftly tied around a capstan and immediately began refuelling.

The other man that Crane had seen, left the boat and joined his shipmate on the landing stage, Crane decided it was time to play his hand and pulling out the Glock semi-automatic, he slid a nine mil bullet into the breach. As he casually approached the two men, they looked up at him in surprise and then turned towards each other with puzzled expressions on their faces, as though searching for an explanation, before turning back to face Crane.

'Change of plan,' Crane announced, motioning them off the jetty with the Glock semi-automatic handgun. In an instant and without hesitation, the man nearest the edge of the jetty leapt into the sea and sank out of sight, swimming underwater and resurfacing around the other side of the boat. His mate took one step forward and Crane sent a bullet in between his legs. The man looked down at the splintered hole between his feet and froze. Meanwhile his companion the swimmer, had hauled himself aboard the launch and had dashed to the main cabin, where he grabbed hold of an Uzi sub-machine pistol. Crane was half expecting this kind of move and he quickly positioned himself so that the man on the jetty would be in the line of fire. Within seconds the swimmer reappeared on deck holding the weapon, trying to aim past his shipmate, but Crane sent a bullet into his shoulder causing the Uzi to fall from his hands and clutter across the deck and into the water. The wounded man's eyes were transfixed on Crane's gun as he winced with pain. He clasped a hand across his shoulder and feeling somewhat shaky, got off the boat. Crane motioned the pair towards a bench, 'Sit down,' he barked. 'Now tell me, where are the woman and children?'

The two men scowled and said nothing. 'Okay,' Crane said quietly, 'maybe after I've emptied the magazine into the pair of you, you'll tell me… or die,' and with that he pulled back the slide and took aim.

'They're under a hatch, below decks,' Jacques the wounded man stammered.

Crane pointed to the other man, Emile, 'You – the one without the bullet – get back on board and open up the hatch and no tricks, I'll be right behind you.'

Emile, a big brute of a fellow, got up and led the way, leaving the groaning Jacques sitting on the bench nursing his wound. Crane kept his distance as they clambered aboard the boat. He followed Emile across the deck but stopped suddenly to look down at a square hatch about a metre across.

'Open it!' Crane growled.

The heavy-set Emile crouched and pulled back four clips, one on each corner and as he lifted it off, threw it at Crane. The gun was knocked forcefully from Crane's hand. A slight grin of satisfaction spread across Emile's face as he charged like an enraged bull but Crane had recovered quickly. With split-second timing he sidestepped the onslaught and spun round, thrusting his foot hard into the centre of Emile's back. Crane stood and watched as the big man toppled over the side and into the water and, to the sound of Emile splashing and gasping, Crane picked up his gun and peered down the hatchway.

'Penny, are you down there?'

An uncertain voice called back, 'Jack?'

'It's me. Everything's alright, you can all come up now.'

Penny's face suddenly appeared through the open hatch, her eyes squinting against the bright late-afternoon sun. Sammy, followed by Andrew, slowly made their way up and onto the deck whilst Crane kept an eye on Emile, who was still floundering in the water around the boat.

Sammy was the first to find her voice, 'I just knew you would come, I just knew it,' she said reaching up with a hug.

Penny's expression was one of intense relief and she said, 'I've never been so glad to see anyone in my whole life. I was absolutely terrified, it's only the children that have kept me intact, they've been marvellous.'

Crane looked at all three and smiled, 'Tidy yourselves up a bit if you want, I should imagine all the facilities are on board. Meanwhile I'll figure out what to do with your two captors.'

Crane looked in a nearby locker. There was a first aid kit and a roll of elephant tape on one of the shelves. He grabbed hold of both items and moved towards the edge of the boat, pointing the gun at Emile, who was standing shoulder deep in the water. 'Get on to the jetty now or I'll start-shooting,' he commanded.

Emile looked up at Crane with a face like thunder as he grunted an assent and began moving towards the jetty. He hauled himself out of the water to face Crane as he stood, gun in hand, ready to bind Emile's hands behind his back.

Jacques was sitting despondently on the jetty, still nursing his wounded shoulder. Crane tossed him a lint pad out of the first aid box, 'If there's any more trouble from you, you may not be so lucky next time.'

Without a word, the weary-looking Jacques took the pad and set it against his wound. Crane felt sure that of the two of them, Jacques at least, had had enough.

After they had washed and freshened up, Penny and the children stepped off the boat and joined Crane on the landing stage. Together they all made their way towards the house. On the way, Penny explained what had happened to them and Crane briefly recounted how he came to be there, finishing with, 'The helicopter that brought us here will hopefully take us all back to England.'

As they neared the parked helicopter and chateau, they saw the motley villains bunched together on the grass. Crane directed Jacques and Emile to join them. Girard explained to Crane what had happened during the past hour.

'You've been practising with a hand gun?' Crane remarked.

'I was in the army; a marksman,' Girard stated proudly.

'I'm impressed, how long were you in for?'

Girard stifled a grin and looked down, 'Well, technically, I am still in the Legionnaires, The French Foreign Legion, you know.'

Crane looked skywards and said, 'Yes, I've heard of them. Don't tell me, desertion from the Legion is also amongst your catalogue of crimes?'

Looking slightly sheepish about his confession, he said, 'What could I do? The police want me for murder and theft. And also maybe, some friends of Pierre Marcel, that evil bastard I killed – maybe they also want me. It was self-defence. There was a struggle and Marcel was shot with his own handgun. The police, with the help of that bastard's men, did not believe me.'

The sound of a police siren drawing near made them look up and, without hesitation, Girard darted off like a frightened hare. Within a minute, tyres scrunched on gravel as two police vehicles pulled up in front of the chateau. There were two uniformed men in the car and two in the van behind. Guns were drawn as they approached the party sitting on the ground. A look of relief spread across Penny's face as she whispered to Crane, 'At last, now perhaps this lot can be locked away.'

One of the officers approached Crane and Penny, 'We

have come to investigate. Someone reported hearing gunfire.'

Between them, Crane and Penny explained what had happened. 'We will take care of everything now, Mr Crane, please hand me your weapon.'

Crane gave him the Glock and within minutes, they were herded, together with the four children, into the back of the van. Penny looked at the children and smiled at Crane, 'I'm beginning to feel like Mary Poppins.'

Crane smiled back, looking at the children, who seemed none the worse for their ordeal, 'Hopefully they'll soon be back where they belong.'

*

From the cover of a thicket, Girard pulled a pair of binoculars from his haversack and watched the proceedings. When the van disappeared from sight, the remaining two policemen helped Mullah to his feet and they all headed towards the house. There was laughter in the air. This was not police procedure. Girard stared after them, frustration running through his veins. The police, or whoever they were, were obviously in league with Mullah. He was now certain that Crane and the people they had rescued were in extreme danger.

# CHAPTER NINETEEN

Ryan was happy to be back in England. He could now eat the food that he liked regularly and relax; things were more ordered and predictable. He was staying at a boarding house in Southend and was enjoying bracing walks along the promenade each day. He was anxious to get his hands on the money which Bradley had said was due to him. There was one difficulty for him, in that he could not put aside the nagging feeling about trusting Bradley. He had been told that, when all the money was collected, he would get his share. He knew Bradley well enough to know it was always cash only that changed hands when the vehicles were passed on. He kept running all these things over and over in his mind. He wondered if the story, that Crane had told him, about Davy Porter being impaled with a knife to the seat of his transporter, was true. He hoped it wasn't, but then why would Crane lie about it? He did not dare broach the subject with Bradley; if it were true it may rile him and in a fit of temper he could get the same. However, to reassure himself, he decided that it would be an easy task to check up on Crane's story. He phoned the hospitals in the area where the incident had happened. Within the hour Ryan had got his answer: Davy Porter was dead.

\*

The bench seats either side of the police van were spartan. Lap belts provided little stability as the vehicle bumped and swayed along the uneven track, leading to the main road. The driver and front seat passenger were cut off from the occupants seated in the rear, by a metal divider, so Crane shouted out as loudly as he could, 'Take it easy!' It made no difference. He looked out of the tiny rear windows for signs of the other police vehicle; there were none.

*

From his hiding place in the thicket, Girard checked the Mossberg pump-action shotgun that he had taken from Mullah; there were four cartridges in the magazine. With his eyes fixed on Mullah and company, who were entering the house, he ran keeping low, commando style, past the stationary helicopter, up to the police car and looked inside; no keys. Without a moment's hesitation he ran towards the front door of the house and, just as it was being closed, kicked it back forcefully with his foot. 'Everybody on the floor now!' He shouted, and, to reinforce his command, pointed the shotgun at the ceiling and pulled the trigger, sending a shower of plaster falling like snow everywhere.

'Keys to the car and guns, slide them over to me,' he commanded, 'and be quick, or some of you are going to feel the weight of some buckshot.'

The pseudo police did as they were told and, as Girard scooped up the guns, Mullah said, 'You don't know what you are getting into.'

As he exited through the front door, Girard twirled the

shotgun, John Wayne style, and in a relaxed, slow tone replied, 'Neither do you!'

Without a care for the potholes and ridges, Girard pushed his foot hard down on the accelerator pedal and aimed the Peugeot 508, bucking and jumping, in a straight line along the worn dirt track. The suspension clonked and groaned its way towards a narrow road that led to a village some five kilometres away. The road was straight and Girard spotted the van in the distance. Within a few minutes he was up behind it, flashing his lights. Suddenly he overtook the van, slewed to a halt in front of it and leapt out. The van driver and his accomplice were taken by surprise, when confronted by the maniacal appearance of Girard swinging the shotgun. 'Get out', he screeched.

They clambered out throwing their hands in the air. 'Weapons on the ground, carefully,' Girard ordered.

Gingerly they put their hands in their jacket pockets and laid the guns down on the road. Girard scooped them up and stuffed them in an already overloaded and heavy rucksack and said, 'You are working for Mullah, eh?'

The pair looked at each other to see who was going to admit it first.

Girard wanted an answer and said impatiently, 'Look, I want an answer now or perhaps you would prefer me to shoot the pair of you here and now.'

'Alright, we work for Mullah, but not all the time,' one of them volunteered hurriedly.

'Where were you going to take these people?'

'Nowhere, we were told to keep them locked up in the van and wait for further instructions.'

'Where did you get the vehicles and uniforms?'

'We borrowed them.'

Girard eyed them suspiciously and pointed to the grass verge, 'Get down there and don't move.'

The pair sat down on the edge of the road.

Girard unlocked the rear doors of the van. To everyone's relief, he announced with a flourish, 'They are not police,' then added, 'if they are, they're bent.'

'I was beginning to have my suspicions,' Crane replied, trying to repress the smile that was forming on his lips in response to Girard's *savoir faire*.

Girard looked skywards, 'It'll be dark soon. We are about three kilometres from that *maison*.'

'Are you thinking what I'm thinking?' Crane offered. 'We have unfinished business with Mullah. I think we should return to the house and give them all a surprise.'

Girard nodded in agreement, 'But I think, maybe it would be better if we went on our own.'

Penny overheard this and pleaded, 'Don't leave us on our own – please!'

Girard regarded Penny momentarily and smiled. It was the first time he had seen her and she returned the smile as their eyes locked together briefly. As if to offer some reassurance Girard said, 'Don't worry, *mademoiselle*, you'll be safe, stay in the van until we return.'

Penny seemed comforted by Girard and said, 'What are you going to do with those two men sitting on the verge?'

'No problem,' Girard said, 'I'll secure them with the handcuffs hanging on their belts.'

Mullah's two henchmen were made secure; handcuffed uncomfortably together, straddling a telegraph pole, still wearing their stolen police uniforms. Crane and Girard drove their two vehicles away and parked them in a secluded spot, behind some bushes, about one kilometre from the house. When they had got out of the vehicles, Girard sat on the moist grass, opened his haversack and gently tipped the contents onto the ground. 'You're a walking arsenal,' Crane remarked as Girard offered him a choice of handgun but, as he picked up the Glock and Colt magnum, he noticed a medal; a cross on a long ribbon lying amongst other odds and ends. Picking it up and regarding it for a moment, Crane blew through his teeth, '*Croix De La Valeur*, yours?'

Girard shrugged and remarked, 'That's what the inscription says.'

Crane regarded the cross for a moment, 'How did you get it?'

'I was saving my commanding officer's life and took a bullet in my shoulder when I pushed him aside – one of those reflex actions I guess.'

Crane handed it back without comment as Girard nonchantly set about repacking his haversack.

Girard kept the shotgun and chose a semi-automatic Walther handgun for himself and left the remainder in his haversack, which he stowed in the boot of the hidden car. Wasting no time, they stealthily made their way back towards the house.

*

Ryan was caught in a stream of traffic as he drove through Rochford so he decided to turn towards Canford, although it was the longer route to Hullbridge. He was surprised to see the car in front, with a woman at the wheel, turn into Palmers Rise. Curiosity got the better of him and compelled him to turn his car around and enter the lane. He knew Crane would not be there so he drove boldly up to 'Bramble View', Crane's home. He stopped his car and looked out of the window. The car that he had seen was now parked in Crane's drive; a Peugeot 207 and the rear window's sticker showed it was a hire car from Southend Airport.

Within a minute, a hurried patter of feet caused him to shift in his seat and turn his head; an attractive woman was approaching. She picked her way daintily through a bevy of rose bushes in full blossom, which filled the air with their sweet fragrance. Her corn-coloured hair was tied at the back into a short pony tail. He guessed her age to be somewhere in the late thirties, early forties. Misty blue eyes looked at him inquisitively before an eager smile spread across her face and she enquired, 'Is Jack around?'

Uncharacteristically, Ryan stumbled with his words as he took in the trouser-suited woman standing on the path. He was momentarily taken aback by her charm and good looks, 'That's… erm, what I was wondering. Perhaps he is still away on business,' he mumbled.

The smile was replaced briefly by a small pout as she replied, 'Oh, I should really have let him know I was coming. Oh, well, I do have a key, I'll wait until he returns. I don't suppose you know how long he will be?'

Ryan noticed her accent was not English, but he couldn't place it, however he was feeling more confident as he replied, 'Not really, you know what Jack is like; he's sometimes difficult to get in touch with, but I know someone who may know his whereabouts. If you give me your mobile number, I'll get him to call you.'

'That's very kind of you,' she produced a business card and handed it to Ryan. He stared briefly at the card, noting that it was foreign, before he drove off, feeling somewhat elated. He now had an excuse to contact Bradley and maybe get paid what he was owed.

\*

Crane and Girard could have been taken for elusive shadows as they approached the tall narrow French house, which was now ablaze with lights. They approached from the rear and gradually circumnavigated the property. In the main downstairs room, the curtains were not drawn tight and they could clearly see Mullah between the gaps, resting his wounded leg on a footstool. One of the other occupants seemed to be having trouble using a mobile phone, pacing up and down the room with the instrument clamped to his ear. He twisted and turned, held it at arm's length, when suddenly he gave up the idea of trying to use it and threw it down on a couch.

'Bad reception here,' Girard whispered quietly, more to himself than to Crane. They remained crouched surreptitiously peering in through the curtains now and again.

Pierre Durand, the helicopter pilot, was seated next to Mullah. He had a bandage neatly wound around his arm and could be heard to say, 'I can probably start the engine without a key, but to do that, I need to hot wire it properly in the daylight tomorrow.'

There was no sign of the two men, Emile and the wounded Jacques who had driven the motor launch. Giselle tripped into the room carrying a tray piled with bread and wedges of cheese. She wore an elastic support around her wrist. 'She looked so innocent when she approached me,' Girard whispered to Crane, 'the bitch. If I hadn't moved so quick she would have killed me for sure.'

As they stood unobserved near the window, the sound of footsteps made them slink deeper into the shadows. It was Emile approaching the front door. Oblivious to their presence, he rapped it loudly several times. It was opened by Simon, the pilot's companion. At that moment, Girard with outstretched arms, rushed at Emile, propelling him forward, sending him crashing into Simon. The pair of them ended up sprawled in a heap on the floor of the hall.

Crane stepped in behind Girard, and announced, 'We're back. Now all of you group together.'

The ceaseless chatter was abruptly followed by a hushed silence as all eyes focused on Crane and Girard. The two phoney policemen bunched up with the others as Jacques, the wounded boatman came down the stairs.

'Who do you think you're dealing with?' Crane said menacingly as he held a gun in each hand. 'Unless you tell me what I want to know, none of you will leave here alive.'

Mullah's face was ashen, 'What do you want?'

'Where is Jean, Penny's sister? And don't tell me you don't know.'

Mullah looked uncomfortable and shifted uneasily in his chair, which prompted Crane to bellow angrily, 'Well?'

Mullah looked down and clearing his throat said awkwardly, 'At my home in Boulogne.'

Crane stared hard at Mullah, who ran a tongue around dry lips, before continuing, 'She's buried somewhere in the grounds of my chateau,'

'You killed her?' Crane snarled.

Mullah shook his head nervously, 'No... no, it was Bradley, he killed her.'

'When? How?'

Mullah's voice was hoarse as he spoke, 'About three months ago; Bradley wrote a letter addressed to Jean's sister in England – the one you call Penny. The letter purported to be written by Jean. Bradley asked her to sign it; she refused.'

Mullah paused and Crane said, 'What was in the letter?'

'I'm not sure, probably to help him steal cars.'

'And people,' Crane added.

Mullah looked down and continued, 'She refused to sign the letter he had typed. They began to argue, when suddenly, in a fit of rage, he grabbed her by the throat and squeezed the life out of her. I swear I had nothing to do with it. I was upstairs when it all happened. When I heard all the shouting I came down to see what it was about. She was lying on the floor, dead.'

'How long have you been involved in kidnapping?'

Mullah hesitated before replying, 'Two, maybe three years.'

'Where do you take them?'

'Algiers,' and he hastened to add without much conviction, 'I am reassured that they are all well looked after.'

'Who do you sell them to?'

Mullah's eyes flicked nervously, 'I cannot tell you that.'

Crane said calmly, 'You know, my friend Girard put a

bullet in the fleshy part of your leg… ' and pulling back the slide of the Glock continued, 'right now I'll put a bullet in both of your knees if you say that again. Who do you sell them to; name, address and contact number!'

'They will kill me if I tell you.'

'I will kill you right now if you don't!'

Mullah was sweating profusely as he looked around the room; all eyes were focused on him.

'Pen… paper,' he said in a whisper.

Girard looked around the room until his eyes fell on Giselle, the housekeeper, who sat on the edge of her seat and with a wave of the gun said, 'Get something to write on, *s'il vous plait.*'

Giselle scurried over to a large sideboard set against the wall, opened a drawer and returned with a notepad and pencil. Girard took it from her and handed it to Mullah.

'You had better write all you know,' Crane said, 'and don't make any mistakes, your life depends on it, because I'll not let you go until it is checked out.'

Mullah wrote with trembling hand. It seemed to take him some time and he paused briefly when his hands became clammy, running them down the sides of his trousers. When he had finished writing, he handed the pad to Crane and said in a hoarse whisper, 'They'll kill me for sure if they find out I've done this.'

Crane gave him a disdainful look, as he took the notepad and, after a cursory glance, handed it to Girard with the remark, 'It's in your language.'

Girard quickly translated what Mullah had put down and said, 'I know where this place is. There's enough information here to hand over to the authorities but Jack, you'll have to do the handing over. Let's hope some of the poor souls can be found.'

Crane checked his watch and said, 'One of us should check up on Penny and the kids in the van. Bring them here first and then we'll drive to the nearest city gendarme police station.'

Girard was keen to see Penny again, 'I'll go,' he offered enthusiastically.

'Okay, meanwhile I'll figure out what to do with this lot.'

The evening light had vanished when Girard slipped through the front door. Once outside, he paused for a moment – allowing his eyes to adjust to the dark – before trundling off along the gravel driveway towards where they had left the van. The scrunching of loose stones beneath his feet bothered him. Each footfall kicked up gravel, making it sound as though there was somebody trailing along behind. He wanted to move quietly, without distraction, animal-like, and tune his ears into the night sounds, so he stepped deftly onto the moist soft grassy edge along the side.

Before long, the dark outline of the two vehicles came into view and Girard began to feel less apprehensive as he approached the rear door of the van. All was quiet, except for the snap of a twig. Too late! As Girard spun round, a series of blows were hammering onto the side of his head causing him to slump heavily to the ground.

*

Crane decided that the best place to put his prisoners was back down in the cellar. Only this time he would make sure that nobody had a spare key. He ensured that they had all emptied their pockets onto a large table whilst paying special attention to the scowling housekeeper, Giselle. He checked his watch and realised that Girard had been gone for almost half an hour which was far too long for the task in hand. This sent his alarm bells ringing. He managed to find a small torch before stepping outside but as he passed the door, he stood for a moment and stared into the darkness. The moonless night was blanketed by clouds. He decided to take a roundabout route and arc round to where they had left the vehicles. Minimal use of the lamp meant his progress was slow going in the dark, but within fifteen minutes he was staring at the empty space where the vehicles had been parked.

Crane tried to get quickly back towards the house but the torch batteries were about to expire and he lost his footing once or twice, tumbling to the ground. As he neared the *Maison Rouge* again, he realised that the Glock handgun had slipped out of his waistband and he arrived back just in time to see the helicopter, lights blazing, suddenly lift into the night sky.

Crane moved towards the front door of the house and paused; it had been left wide open and inside was in total darkness; everyone had gone. He turned and walked towards the barely visible path that led to the jetty. Suddenly he stopped halfway and listened. The reverberation from the launch's engines told him that it was too late. Crane had underestimated Mullah's resourcefulness. Everyone had left and he was stranded in the middle of nowhere, miles from the nearest town, in the pitch black dark.

# CHAPTER TWENTY

That evening Ryan arranged to meet up with Bradley in the cafe at the Cliffs Pavilion, situated in Westcliff-on-Sea. He was the first to arrive and sat staring out across the Thames Estuary. The tide was out and pools of water, left in the estuary mud, gleamed metallic in the sun. Ryan was finding it difficult to contain his excitement. Bradley arrived within a few minutes, grabbed a coffee and drew a seat up next to Ryan beside the huge panoramic windows of the Pavilion Cafe. Bradley listened with interest as Ryan, not wishing to leave anything out, told him of the day's events. 'She even had a key to his front door,' he added, as he passed her business card to him.

'Did she now,' Bradley said thoughtfully as he took the card, held it at arm's length, scrutinised it and read out loud, 'Hmm... Doctor Daniella Mersch, with a Romanian address.' A twisted smile began to spread across his face as he ran his thumb along the edge. 'A little trump card in case it's needed. One way or another, I'll nail him into the ground. You've done well Ryan.'

Ryan beamed and took the opportunity to mention as casually as possible, 'By the way, do you happen to have my share of our earnings?'

The smile vanished from Bradley's face as he pursed his lips and with a sombre expression said, 'I wish I had.'

Reaching for his wallet he snatched out a pair of fifty pound notes and stuffed them into Ryan's hand. 'A little bonus – you deserve it. It won't be long now before you get what's coming to you.'

It was not the answer he was hoping for. Ryan managed a weak smile as he pocketed the money and in a hushed voice said, 'Okay, thanks,' before they parted company.

\*

The two men that Girard had left hand-cuffed and straddled to a telegraph pole, grinned with satisfaction as they manhandled Girard's limp body towards the rear of the van. One of them unlocked the door and Penny looked horrified as the pair bundled the Frenchman onto the floor between the rows of seats either side.

'You've got company,' the driver said jauntily before locking them in again. The children, who had been keeping themselves amused throughout, stared down at Girard's prone form. Andrew said, 'Is he dead, Auntie Penny?'

Penny gave him a stern look, before unbuckling her seat belt and then she knelt on the floor beside Girard. Checking his pulse, she looked at Andrew and said, 'Not yet thankfully.'

Andrew nodded and fished his computer from a pocket whilst the three little girls looked on with concern.

The sound of the vehicle starting up made them look towards the front, but there was nothing to see, just a miniscule window – a peephole – through to the cab. The van rocked and swayed on the uneven ground for a few kilometres, before reaching the tarmac surface of a public road. Penny remained on the floor, cradling Girard's head on her lap. She found herself attracted to his handsome features and despite suffering discomfort, she preferred to protect him from further damage as he lay on the bare metal floor of the van.

*

Crane reasoned that there was no point in stumbling around in the dark and so he made his way back to *Maison Rouge* and went inside. The electricity had been turned off. It was too dark to hunt around for the main power switch. He had no choice but to wait until dawn. He made himself comfortable in one of the armchairs near the front door and, whilst contemplating his next move, drifted off into an uneasy sleep.

Throughout the night, sleep came and went as Crane twisted and turned in the folds of the armchair. A crack of light pierced between one of the heavy drapes at the window and as he stirred from sleep, a sound scratched at his brain. He shot up, like a hare alerted to danger and paused for a moment, stretching like a cat, before following the shaft of light and peering through the curtain.

A steamy haze preceded the early morning sun. Two men were standing on the gravel outside. They puffed misty breath into their cupped hands until one of them produced a pack of cigarettes. An Uzi submachine gun dangled from each of their sides. They looked around and seemed uncertain which direction to take.

*"Amateurs,"* Crane smiled to himself as he crossed the floor of the large sitting room and padded up the stairs into one of the bedrooms. There was a side window in the

bedroom and the curtains were not drawn. He moved slowly towards it and looked outside. About a hundred metres from *Maison Rouge* stood a dark coloured Mercedes SL sports car; it would be an escape route for him, if the keys were still in the ignition.

The scraping of heavy feet on the gravel drive and the thud of the front door being thrown open, interrupted his thoughts. Without delay, Crane eased back the double windows. He then pushed the single bed from the middle of the bedroom and set it underneath the window ledge. He snatched up one of the covers and laid it over the window ledge. Within minutes, the stairs began to creak and groan under the weight of large-booted feet as someone clumped their way up.

Crane squatted behind the door as it opened and watched a man enter the room, pause and then walk straight towards the open window. As he poked his head through the gap, Crane sprang like a panther and upended the thug through the opening, who screamed loudly as he hurtled down onto the ground below. Then all was quiet. Crane did not bother to look, but snatched up the abandoned Uzi as again the heavy thud of another set of boots raced up the stairs. The next man followed the same route, out of the window, as his predecessor and Crane left the room mumbling to himself, 'Amateurs, bloody amateurs.'

Outside, Crane walked towards the two semi-conscious men prone on the dewy grass. On hearing his approach, one of them moved his head. Crane looked down at him and said nothing. Fearful vulnerable eyes stared back at Crane. They were a well-built pair, but now they were helpless. Taking no chances, Crane pointed one of their Uzis at them whilst he rifled through their pockets. The other man began to stir, flickering puzzled eyes, as Crane searched him, found the keys to the sports car and extracted them from his pocket. Crane looked at him contemptuously and said quietly, 'You're very lucky to be still alive. If I see you again, I'll kill you.' He was uncertain whether they understood what he had said as he relieved them of their mobile phones and headed towards their parked car.

He checked the inside of the car. The fuel gauge registered that the tank was almost full. Upon opening the glove box he found a handgun, a semi-automatic nine mil Glock with a full magazine, so he tossed the two Uzis he had taken from the men into the boot. Crane reasoned that his first port of call should be on Pierre Durand, the helicopter pilot. The built-in satnav told him that it would take two and a half hours of drive time, to reach the Boulogne area. He glanced in the rear-view mirror and saw the pair of would-be assassins sitting up dishevelled, on the grass by the side of the house; no doubt bitterly regretting their involvement.

\*

Within two hours of Crane's departure, a dark sombre looking vehicle, scrunching its tyres on the gravel drive, pulled up outside the *Maison Rouge*. The driver leapt out of the hearse and stared agape at the pair of would-be assassins sitting up on the grass outside. 'What happened?'

Through clenched teeth one of them said, 'He got away, that's all I'm saying. Now help us up and get us to a hospital and be careful, we've got broken bones.'

After helping the pair into the hearse, the driver said, 'I'd better phone Mullah, I was supposed to be taking a corpse to Chateau du Lac for burial.'

When he heard the news, Mac, Mullah's manservant, put the phone down and immediately dialled Bradley. 'I haven't disturbed Mullah. He went to bed early. He copped a bullet from the Frenchman yesterday, caught him in the leg. Anyway we've now managed to get him under wraps, but this Crane guy is still on the loose and causing us grief.'

Bradley was quiet for a moment; Mac thought he had hung up, 'You still there?'

'Yes I'm still here. I believe I have the answer to our problem. I'm assuming he is going to arrive at Chateau Du Lac, simply because you have the woman and kids there. If and when he does, let me talk to him.'

Mac's face registered a puzzled expression as Bradley continued, 'As it happens, I have found someone he knows, someone he must care about because she has a key to his cottage.'

*

Two hours had passed and Girard lay on the floor in the back of the van, his head still cradled on Penny's lap. In the dim interior light, she had found some used paper tissues and gently dabbed at a gash on the side of his head until it stopped bleeding. By now, the four children were thoroughly bored and looked on wistfully. They sat in a row opposite, strapped in their seats, leaning forwards curiously with their chins supported by cupped hands and elbows resting on knees.

The van suddenly stopped. The driver jumped out, gun in hand and walked to the rear doors, rattling them open.

Without a word he looked inside and Penny shouted out in French and English, 'This man needs a doctor and... ' her voice trailed off as the man gave a cursory glance, stepped back, slammed the doors shut and locked them again. By then, his companion, who was following up in the car, had leapt out and joined him at the rear of the van. They both lit cigarettes. 'What are we supposed to do we do with these people?'

The van driver said, 'I'm assuming we are taking them to Chateau du Lac, but I must phone Mullah to confirm this.'

'But we have no mobiles.'

'I know, we must use a pay-phone. There's one in a quiet part of the next town.'

It was Mac who picked up the phone and, after listening for a short while, put it on hold while he spoke to Mullah. Returning to the phone he said, 'What's happened to your memory? Mr Mullah's instructions were for you to bring them here and not to worry about the health of Girard. He's a wanted criminal, murder, robbery and so on. There's plenty of land here at Chateau Du Lac where he, or anyone else, can be laid to rest.'

*

Crane drove along the perimeter of the airfield. To avoid instant recognition, he made use of a pair of sunglasses and a well-worn baseball cap before driving into the parking area of 'Heli-Hire'. He got out of the SL and glancing around, was satisfied by the sight of Durand's red Mi-2 helicopter, laying squat in its parking zone. *"At least Durand may be around,"* he reasoned.

Looking towards the ground, Crane ambled casually towards the office. A young man, whom Crane did not recognise, was sitting down with his feet propped up on the desk. The man looked up as Crane entered and immediately swung his feet to the floor.

'*Bonjour,*' Crane began, '*parlez-vous Anglais?*'

'Yes, I speak some English.'

'*Ah bien.* Is Pierre around?'

'Monsieur Durand should be here any moment. I am standing in at short notice, but I must leave soon. His other assistant, Simon, I believe his name was, apparently he quit the job in a hurry.'

'Can't get reliable staff these days eh,' Crane muttered.

The smell of coffee attracted Crane to a machine and he helped himself to a cupful of espresso whilst studying some charts on a wall. His thoughts were interrupted by the man slipping out of the office, saying as he left, 'Ah, here he comes now, cheerio.'

As the temporary assistant leapt through the opening, a shadow filled the door frame to take his place. Crane had his back towards him – coffee in hand – and remained staring at the charts on the wall.

'*Je suis désolé…* ' Durand began, apologising for his late appearance. It was only when Crane turned slowly around to face him, he paused in mid-sentence, staring as though trying to look through a bank of mist. He thought there was something strangely familiar with the man standing in front of him. Crane removed the baseball cap and sunglasses. Durand's face turned ashen; it was as though he had seen a ghost. His eyes shifted nervously when Crane peeled back one side of his jacket, exposing the handgun that was tucked neatly into the waistband of his trousers.

'So nice to see you again,' Crane said between gritted teeth, 'but I'm sure the feeling is not entirely mutual. I trust the arm is healing. Now tell me – where are they?'

Durand; getting over his initial shock gasped, 'Mullah's Chateau Du Lac.'

'What do you know of their plans?'

'Nothing; I swear it. I just dropped them off at the chateau and returned a few hours later to fetch Mac, his manservant. I brought him back here to collect Mullah's Bentley.'

'Has the woman, Girard and children turned up?'

Durand hesitated before saying, 'No, they were not there.'

Crane stared hard at him for a few seconds, 'Are you sure? I'd hate to come back here, which I would do, if I find out you are lying.'

Durand felt hot under the collar at the thought of what Crane could do, 'Come to think of it, after picking up Mac, I caught sight of a van moving along the drive that leads to the chateau.'

Still glaring at Durand, Crane said with suspicion, 'It would have been dark. How do you know it was a van?'

'I'm a pilot. It was easy to distinguish. There was a car following up behind it with its headlights on low beam.'

Durand looked down at the floor for a second, as though conjuring up signs of remorse. Straightening up he said, 'Look, I've really had enough trouble with this whole thing. I know I bend the law on some things, but gunplay and kidnap is another thing; taking Mullah's money is not worth the risk.'

'Then you might *just* have saved your bacon.'

Durand looked puzzled by this expression and uttered, 'Eh?'

'Forget it,' Crane said, 'My problem is this, I don't trust you. What can I do to stop you warning Mullah?'

Durand shrugged and said weakly, 'I won't contact him. My word on it.'

Crane shook his head, 'I don't think so – past experience and all that – I think it best you accompany me on a drive to Mullah's chateau and, when we arrive, you can drop me off outside and then you can drive yourself back in the Merc, I already have another car parked there.'

Durand pressed his lips together and nodded fervently in agreement, 'Okay,' and they both left the office and headed for the car parking lot.

*

Earlier in the morning the van, holding Girard, Penny and the children, had come to a halt just inside the estate of Chateau du Lac. The driver of the van leapt out, walked up to the car behind and settled in the front passenger seat beside his accomplice and said, 'It's best we wait until daybreak before rattling on Mullah's front door.'

The car driver grunted an affirmative through a yawn, reclined his seat, then closed his eyes and said wearily, 'Do you think they are comfortable in that van?'

'Who gives a shit? I haven't heard a peep out of them, they are probably fast asleep right now.' With that he yawned hugely, reclined his seat and shut his eyes.

A full moon appeared from behind heavy clouds, sending a stream of the silvery light through a small glass panel in the roof of the van. The diffused light caused Girard to open his eyes. He looked up into Penny's face. Her chin lay wearily on her chest. She had her back propped awkwardly against a long bench seat. The moon's light gave her face a monochrome appearance. 'Are you asleep?' he whispered.

Penny jerked her head up and said wearily, 'I wish, more like a semi-coma, how are you feeling now?'

'Apart from a sore head and stiff limbs, I feel okay.'

She shifted her legs uncomfortably, 'Do you feel like sitting up now?'

A smile spread across Girard's face as he said, 'With your permission, *mademoiselle*, I would much sooner stay where I am. Your lap, it is so comfortable, I thought I was in heaven just now. It gives me a sensation as though I could rest on it forever. Despite my aching head, it senses the softness of your lovely skin but,' he hastened to add, 'I do not want to wear out my welcome, and thank you for caring for me.'

Penny returned Girard's smile and said, 'Only a Frenchman could think up so much bullshit in such a short space of time.'

Girard's smile turned into a grin, 'The ladies – they like to hear these nice things about themselves.'

'We haven't been properly introduced; my name's Penny.'

'My name is Henri Girard – and I am at your service.'

'That's an old-fashioned term, I like it.' Penny said warmly.

They both moved onto a seat next to each other. Girard checked his watch; it was five-thirty.

'Why have we stopped?' he said quietly.

'I don't know. The van stopped a few times since we left that place and one of them opened the rear doors and looked in, you were still unconscious. I must have drifted in and out of sleep several times. Just now, I heard the cab door open and close, together with some footsteps.

In the vague light, they looked at the children; they were fast asleep, sagging forwards against their seatbelts.

Girard moved quietly to the rear of the van and peered though a tiny gap in the darkened glass. 'We are in a narrow lane; it looks familiar, it could even be the one that leads to Mullah's Chateau du Lac. Their car is a few metres behind us,' he whispered, 'maybe they are resting.'

Gingerly he raised his hand and tried the door handle; it was locked tight. 'Once they get me into the chateau, I'm dead. They won't harm you and the children.'

Penny looked at Girard and knew he was right. Girard continued, 'When they unlock the door again, I'm going to make a break for it. They won't be expecting it – it's the only chance I'll have and if successful, I'll see what I can do to get you and the kids away.'

A worried look spread across Penny's face, 'You must be very careful. When the driver opens the door, he holds a gun, at the ready, in his left hand.'

Girard grinned at her concern, 'I am used to taking risks; I was a Legionnaire. It's a matter of do or die.'

Penny sighed, 'It sounds all very romantic but... '

Girard cut in warmly, smiled and said softly, 'You are so attractive when you look at me like that. I see romance as something different; love, kisses and passion. I cannot stay here until they execute me. I'm damned if I do and I'm damned if I don't – I must try to escape.'

224

# CHAPTER TWENTY ONE

Bradley contacted Ryan and said, 'I had a call from Mac; it seems they still have aggravation with Jack Crane. I want you to pay a visit to his place in Canford and find out if that woman is still staying there, but do it *without* being seen and report back. Got it?'

'Yeah sure thing, Bradley, I'll leave in five minutes. I'll park at the end of the lane and walk down to his place from there.'

The roads were clear and it took no more than fifteen minutes for Ryan to park at the end of Palmers Rise. Keeping to the edge of the lane, he tramped at a steady pace but slowed down as he neared the cottage. The Peugeot 207 hire car, was still parked in the drive. Ryan snatched the phone out of his pocket and called Bradley. 'I'm outside the cottage now; the woman's car is still here,' he said quietly.

'Okay, Ryan, that's all I need to know.'

'Any news of my money?' Ryan enquired anxiously.

'I'll sort that out sometime this week.'

At that moment, Daniella was tidying the front bedroom, when by chance she glimpsed through the net curtains and caught sight of Ryan. His flabby frame was tucked into a hedge, but she recognised him straight away, only this time he appeared to be without his car and he had a mobile phone pressed against his ear. Intrigued, she noted he was talking in a low voice and his eyes were continually flashing across towards the cottage. Alarm bells began to ring and she dashed into the kitchen, picked up the phone and dialled Crane's mobile number but there was no reply and so she left a message together with a description of the man outside.

Daniella quietly opened the back door and walked across the rear patio and into the adjacent woods. From there she followed a path that Crane had shown her some time ago, which led almost to the end of Palmers Rise. She ran light-footed along the trail and stopped just before the end, then waited. Totally unobserved she stood and watched as Ryan sauntered towards his parked car, climbed in and drove off. Daniella was now confident that something was not right and she ran back to the cottage and packed her bag. She had decided it would be best to leave and wait until she heard from Crane.

After locking up and returning the key to Crane's hiding place, she threw the bag into the boot of her car and jumped into the driver's seat. The engine sprang to life, she slammed the gear lever into reverse and looked into the rear-view mirror just in time to see a dark coloured BMW straddle across the drive, blocking her exit.

\*

Dawn was breaking over the Chateau Du Lac, giving it an even more sinister appearance. A short distance away, Girard, still crammed in the back of the van, heard a noise from the car behind; it was a door snapping shut. He held a cautionary hand up to silence Penny and listened. They heard the sound of footsteps, casually moving towards the rear of the van. A key scraped clumsily against the rear door until it found its way into the lock. Girard's eyes were riveted on to the movement of the door handle. As it completed its turn, he braced himself and thrust both feet hard against the rear doors, flinging them wide open and sending the van driver toppling with arms flailing backwards onto the ground, unfortunately the fall did not dislodge the handgun that stayed gripped firmly in his left hand.

The man sitting behind the wheel of the car saw everything and was swift to react. He grabbed hold of a silenced Glock off the back seat with one hand and snatched at the door handle with the other. Girard did not hang around; he crashed through an adjacent hedge like a rampaging bull and ran across the open field in front of him and towards a thicket some hundred metres away. It was a wide stretch of land, sparsely vegetated. Patches of ground mist eddied over the field and spiralled skywards. His pursuers were quick to follow, but they found it difficult to take aim at their quarry, because he ran low, zig-zagging continuously as he headed towards the copse. The gunman with the silenced Glock stopped and steadied his weapon with both hand then squeezed the trigger several times at the receding figure. A nine-mil bullet struck Girard just as he leapt into the safety of the woods.

A triumphant shout of, 'Got him,' resonated between the attackers as they saw Girard recoil sideways and fall to the ground. He lowered the Glock and said to his companion, 'I'll make sure he's finished, you had better take the van to the chateau. I'll catch up with you shortly.'

The van driver hurried back and, after a cursory glance inside, turned the key on the rear doors and continued the short journey to Mullah's chateau.

\*

Crane was sitting in the passenger seat, next to the pilot Durand, who was driving the Merc SL towards Chateau du Lac. It was not long before they entered the long tree-lined lane that led to the front entrance. After they had driven a kilometre along the drive Crane said, 'Right, you can drop me off here.'

Durand stopped the car and, before getting out, Crane retrieved the pair of Uzis that were lying on the back seat. As a parting shot, Crane said harshly, 'It's up to you what you do with the car; the previous owner no longer has a use for it. Oh, and if I find out that you have contacted Mullah... well, I'll leave that to your imagination.'

Fear spread across Durand's face as he replied, 'I meant what I said earlier; I'm finished with Mullah.'

Crane stood and watched as Durand turned the car and drove off in the opposite direction. He guessed it was now about a one-kilometre hike to the chateau and, keeping close to the edge of the lane, he jogged along at a steady pace.

After a while, giant poplars on either side of the lane gave way to an unruly hawthorn hedgerow. Crane paused as he rounded a bend and sighted a parked car. His left hand shot up, tugging expertly on the lanyard of one of the Uzis and it slid off his shoulder. When he neared the vehicle, it became apparent that it was the phoney police car. He approached it with caution and looked inside; it was empty, with the keys still positioned in the ignition. Looking around he noticed a freshly-made gap in the hedge and keeping low he peered through the opening. Three sets of newly-made footprints trailed across the dewy meadow towards a wooded area.

Crane made a split second decision – he was curious. With eyes focused on the ground, and keeping low, he followed the tracks across the field and paused halfway. There were now only two sets of footprints; one set had veered off returning to the lane. With gun at the ready, safety catch off, Crane moved stealthily towards the copse. Reaching a sturdy elm at the edge, he stopped, as a sudden breeze rattled through the trees sending clusters of leaves spiralling towards the ground.

During the brief lull that followed, he heard a noise. It was a deep groan. Inching forward towards the sound, he almost tripped over the body of a man lying face down on the ground who was wearing nothing but his underwear. His trousers had been utilised; ripped apart and used to bind his arms and legs. Crane bent down and carefully turned the man over and recognised him as one of the phoney policemen; a trickle of blood was beginning to clot on the side of his head. The snapping of loose bracken made Crane drop down into a crouch. His fingers began to tighten around the trigger of the Uzi, when a shape appeared through the shadowy light. As the figure lumbered nearer, he relaxed when he saw the familiar bulk, 'Girard; what kept you?'

*

While still parked on the cottage drive, Daniella kept her eyes on the rear-view mirror. With some trepidation, she watched as the dark-suited man got out of his car. Her hand groped at the central locking button as Bradley nudged the door shut of the BMW and casually sauntered up to confront her.

'Would you mind moving your car, I'm just about to leave; I have an appointment.'

Bradley smiled casually and said, 'So have I. Get out of the car.'

'I can't be late,' Daniella said weakly.

Bradley produced a nine-mil Walther semi-automatic, pulled back the slide, pointed it at the side window and said coldly, 'You don't have to get hurt but I'll pull the trigger right now if I have to. Now get out!'

Bradley stepped back as Daniella got out. She looked at him defiantly and said, 'What do you want with me?'

Bradley sneered, 'Not you, my dear, you're just an innocent pawn. It's Jack Crane I want. Now let's go inside the cottage, shall we?'

\*

A huge grin spread across Girard's face and he said, 'I managed to escape,' and, nodding towards the prone figure on the ground, he added, 'two of them chased me. A bullet caught my arm and I went down. One of them, the van driver I believe, returned to his vehicle but this one came to see his handiwork, and that is when I had him. He was going to kill me. I do not know why I have let him live. I needed a piece of his shirt for my wound and well… as you can see, I had to secure him, so the trousers came in handy. I made use of his jacket too; I don't like holes in clothes. We must now rescue the lady, Penny,' he paused and added, 'I believe she likes me and the feeling is mutual.'

Crane couldn't suppress a grin and Girard continued, 'I promised her I would come back, any way I could, to get her and the children.'

'How long ago did all this happen?'

'No more than twenty minutes perhaps.'

'Okay, there's a car with the keys in the ignition where this guy left it. It will make it easy to approach.'

They left their assailant groaning miserably and made their way back across the field and got into the car. Girard ducked low in the seat as the vehicle pulled up outside the front entrance of the chateau. The van Girard had escaped from, was parked over to one side, adjacent to Mullah's Bentley. Crane stooped down over his steering wheel and Girard kept out of sight, laying down low in the rear seat in the hope that the front door would swing open. They did not have to wait long. Mac, the manservant, bounced out leaving the door ajar and he walked towards the car. 'You alright mate,' he called out as he approached.

Crane straightened up and pointed the Uzi at Mac's chest and said, 'Yes, we're fine thanks. Don't move, I've just found out that this thing has a hair trigger.'

The colour drained from Mac's face as he stammered, 'Alright, alright, take it easy.'

Girard wound down the rear window and kept Mac covered as Crane got out of the car and the three men walked towards the house.

As the three of them entered the large hall, Louise came scurrying out of the kitchen. When she saw them, she spun round immediately but Girard barked, 'Take one more step and it will be your last.'

As she froze, Crane walked up to her and said, 'Where's Penny and the children?'

She looked at Crane nervously and replied, 'Upstairs, they are all upstairs.'

'And Mullah, where is he?'

'He is in his room upstairs. I was just about to take breakfast up to him.'

Crane ushered both captives to a seat and while Girard covered them, he walked into the kitchen and came out with Mullah's breakfast tray, setting it down between himself and Girard. In between mouthfuls, Crane asked the captives, 'Who else is here?'

Mac and Louise looked at each other. 'Well?' Crane said impatiently.

Mac said, 'Just Albert, the van driver; he told us he was tired and he's in one of the spare rooms upstairs.'

At that moment Girard detected a slight movement out of the corner of his eye. A shot rang out – sending a bullet smashing into the panelled wall behind. It was followed by excited shouting in French and English. Without taking his eyes off the man on the staircase, Girard knew he had no choice and carefully laid his weapon down. Crane followed suit.

The colour returned to Mac's face, 'So good of you to join us, Albert, we were just talking about you,' he said smugly as he looked at the dejected pair. Mac crouched down and scooped up their weapons and placed them on a chair.

The gunshot brought Mullah limping out of his room and he stood watching on the landing. Albert moved slowly, cat-like, down the stairs holding a Glock nine mil, 'Where's Andre?' he spat.

'Who's Andre?' Girard answered innocently.

'Don't fuck with me; the car driver who thought he had put a bullet in you.'

'Oh, him. I left him in the woods.'

'You killed him?' Albert snarled.

'No,' Girard answered casually, 'he's okay. He's just resting.'

Albert's attention had been focused on Girard and it was now Crane's turn to act. He whipped the Glock from behind his waistband and, in rapid succession, sent several bullets into the stair where Albert was standing. A shocked Albert tossed his gun to one side – like it was red hot – and threw up his hands. Mac eyed the Uzis laid out on the chair, but realised it would be suicide to attempt to reach out to try to get one of them. Girard took the initiative and strode purposefully over to recover them.

The raucous sound of gunfire was momentarily replaced by a deafening silence which was only broken when the sound of the phone resounded noisily throughout the hall. Mac looked at Crane for approval to answer it. Crane nodded and said, 'Put the speaker on.' Mac picked it up and flicked the amplifier switch. A menacing metallic voice reverberated around the room, 'Hello, Mac, is Jack Crane with you yet?'

Mac uttered a limp, 'Yeah.' He looked at Crane and put the phone down and backed away from it, saying hoarsely, 'It's for you.'

A puzzled expression spread across Crane's face as he walked towards the instrument, picked it up, turned off the speaker and held the phone to his ear, 'Who is it?'

A loud chuckle resonated through the earpiece, before the voice said, 'It's me, Bradley. I heard your French friend has been put out of action for good – serves him right!' Crane smiled inwardly at this suggestion. 'Now down to business; I'm with someone who knows you.'

As Crane began, 'Who the… ' Bradley, at the other end, shoved the phone in front of Daniella; who was staring anxiously at the barrel of a gun.

'Jack, I'm sorry… '

'Daniella,' Crane gasped, 'where are you?'

'At your place. It was supposed to be a surprise visit. Look, I don't know what's going on but… '

Bradley snatched the phone away and said, 'Now, Crane, you listen to me and do as you are told if you want your attractive playmate to stay in one piece.'

'She's got nothing to do with… ' Crane began.

'That's where you are wrong. She is now involved and has everything to do with this.'

'If you want to talk hostages, I've got Mullah and his lot right here at his chateau.'

Bradley was unfazed by this and said, 'That's your decision; I'm telling you what I will do if you do not cooperate. Your cottage; it's so quiet and peaceful, miles from anywhere, so to speak. I expect you could get away with anything here without ever being disturbed, am I right? So, what's it to be?'

Crane knew he was right. His mind raced for a few seconds until he received a prompt from Bradley, 'Well?'

'What do you want me to do?'

Bradley was enjoying himself as he said, 'Leave Mullah's Chateau du Lac right now and simply, come home. Mac will contact me when you leave. Meanwhile, your friend will be tucked away in a place where nobody can find her, so if anything happens to me – she'll die, so don't try any tricks or get in touch with the police or anybody.'

# CHAPTER TWENTY TWO

Daniella's eyes flashed defiantly at Bradley, 'Perhaps you can find the time to tell me what this is all about.'

Bradley sat on the edge of the kitchen table sipping cola from a can and looked disdainfully down at Daniella, who sat on a chair nearby. Her hands were securely tied behind her back. A dog collar, with a two metre length of chain attached, had been placed around her neck. Her movements were restricted. He was in control and could move her around and secure the fetter wherever he wanted. She was helpless; he could lead her around like an animal.

Daniella was furious inside, but tried not to show it and maintained a steady calm; she repeated her question. Eventually Bradley answered curtly, 'I took his car and he got in my way; nobody gets in my way! End of story.'

'What are you going to do when Jack gets here?'

'I haven't quite made up my mind about that. Anyway, why should I tell you?'

Daniella shrugged, 'It will not be pleasant, no doubt.'

Bradley sneered and said, 'I must make preparations for your stay,' and he walked out of the room.

*

In the hall of the Chateau du Lac, Girard had been collecting the motley bunch of villains that they had overpowered. Through the open door, he saw Crane standing motionless by the phone in the main room. Crane had remained transfixed, Bradley's message and threats whirling around his head. When he saw the Frenchman, looking at him through the door, he flicked his head, motioning Girard over towards him. Crane told him what Bradley had said. Girard thought for a moment, 'There is only one thing to do; I will phone the gendarme and get them here. They can see for themselves the missing children. I will of course stay and make sure it is done and then, well… the police, they can do what they like with me.'

Crane looked at him and nodded his approval, understanding the sacrifice the Frenchman could be making. He went upstairs and unlocked the room where Penny and the children were being held. Upon seeing Crane, Sammy came rushing up. He bent down and the small girl threw her arms around his neck, 'I'm so happy to see you, Jack. I told Penny you'd come. Is it nearly time to go home?'

Crane stroked her hair gently and said, 'Very soon Sammy,' and with a hug she went back to join the other children. Penny looked at Crane, 'I've been worried sick about Girard. When he escaped from the van… those two men, is he… '

'He's okay,' Crane interjected, 'he's downstairs on the phone to the police.'

Penny let out a sigh, 'Thank goodness for that.' She seemed to melt with relief.

But Crane suddenly looked solemn, 'Your sister, Jean...' he began.

Penny's eyes widened and her mouth dropped slightly in expectation, as Crane continued. 'She died three months ago, I'm so sorry.'

Penny's eyes filled with tears as she whispered, 'Bradley?'

Crane nodded, 'Mullah told us that she is buried somewhere in the grounds of this chateau estate. Apparently she wouldn't sign a letter that Bradley typed, so he killed her and forged her signature. She was trying to protect you.'

'So, that letter wasn't her doing after all.'

She clung on to Crane for a moment and in an attempt to offer some comfort, he put his arms around her. She sobbed bitterly whilst resting her head on his shoulder. Between tears she said, 'First my sister and then my brother.'

Crane stood there for some minutes before saying gently, 'I've got to go soon. In an effort to get at me, Bradley has got hold of someone that I know who is very dear to me.'

Penny straightened up and reached for a tissue, 'You must go then. I hope he pays dearly for what he has done.'

'He will if I have anything to do with it.'

Crane went downstairs. Girard, gun in hand, was still on the phone to the gendarme headquarters in Boulogne. The Frenchman cupped a hand over the phone and said, 'You had better go, if the gendarmes find you here your departure could be delayed.'

Crane felt a sticky patch as they shook hands and noticed a dark area on the sleeve of Girard's jacket: it was blood. 'Are you sure you are alright?'

The Frenchman managed a weak smile and said, 'Yes, I'm fine, go on and take care, *mon ami.*'

Crane left the chateau and walked to the Rover; it was still parked in the place where he had left it. He got into the car, turned the key and the oversized engine roared to life. Listening to the beat of the engine ticking over, he reached inside the glovebox for the mobile phone; the battery was flat, so he plugged it into the dashboard before he drove off. He guessed it should take no more than four hours to get home, providing he could get a channel crossing through the tunnel. This would make it early afternoon when he would reach home and hopefully have time to somehow do something to stop Bradley.

*

Daniella heard the front door of the cottage close and then the muffled sound of a car starting up. This was her first, and maybe only, chance to try and escape. She sat, tied to a wooden dining chair, and with the uncomfortable collar and chain still around her neck. The other end of the chain was coiled around the leg of a heavy solid oak table. Her hands were bound at the back of the chair and her legs and waist securely tied to the seat, keeping her static.

Daniella gradually shuffled the chair closer to the table. She tucked her bound legs and feet under the cross member of the table and managed to raise it slightly. She then began to jostle it. The continuous movement caused the chain, which was looped around the table leg to gradually fall to the floor. However the chain still remained attached to the bottom of the leg and the work was tiring.

The next part was more difficult; she had to lift the corner of the table and at the same time, shuffle backwards on the chair to get the chain from under the leg. She was aware that too much movement could cause the chair to slip back and she might be strangled by the pull of the dog collar. Daniella made several attempts, but at last she was successful. Now she could stand, albeit leaning forwards as well as being tied to the chair. She hopped and hobbled on both legs towards the knife stand, then bent forward and knocked the stand over with her chin so that it lay flat on the work surface on one side. She turned around and grabbed hold of one of the blades. It took some time to manoeuvre the knife on the work surface into position and, with restricted movement, slowly, very slowly she hacked away at the bonds on her wrists until, at last her hands were free and she could use them to finally cut the rope that was binding her to the chair.

Daniella removed the dog collar and rubbed her sore red wrists and neck. Looking at the kitchen clock she noted that Bradley had been gone for an hour. *"He could be back at any time,"* she thought fearfully, as she grabbed hold of her handbag and ran towards the front door. She turned back the latch and was about to swing the door open when the sound of Bradley's car pulling up outside nearly made her heart stop. Easing the door shut, she hurried through the passage towards the rear door and stepped out into the garden.

Once more, with legs shaking, she ran along the path adjacent to the lane, ignoring the small branches that swished into her, and stopped breathlessly when it came to an end. She would now have to get into the lane and run like hell for the last fifty metres to reach the main road and maybe safety. She hoped that Bradley did not beat her to it.

Still breathing heavily, Daniella stepped into the lane and made a bold dash for the main road. As she neared the end of the lane, the throaty roar of an engine coming up from behind spurred her on. She knew he was catching up.

At last she turned into the main road. Suddenly a feeling of hope surged through her as a single decker bus flashed past and slowly pulled up at a stop a few metres ahead. The bus driver caught sight of Daniella in his mirror as she was running and panting towards his vehicle so, with a deft flick of his thumb, he had opened the automatic doors in expectation. Daniella was exhausted as she reached the door, but she somehow found the energy to clamber aboard. The driver, smiling gently at the expression of relief on her face, pressed the button to close the doors. If the driver had stayed looking in his rear-view mirror a split second longer, he would have seen Bradley, face contorted with rage, chasing along the pavement after her. However, the driver knew he had checked the road and nonchantly put his vehicle into gear and the bus pulled away. Daniella flopped into a seat shaking, exhausted and gasping for air but with the deep satisfaction inside her: she had made it!

*

The police from Boulogne wasted no time in reaching Chateau du Lac. Three police cars and a van arrived in quick succession. Girard had called Penny and the children from upstairs and bade them to sit and wait on chairs outside whilst he kept a watchful eye on Mullah and his cohorts.

Two of the armed policemen entered the building and one of them relieved Girard of his weapon. The detective in charge stood outside and was taken aback when he saw Penny with the missing children. Using her best French accent Penny explained how they came to be there.

'This is fantastic,' the policeman exclaimed, 'they have been missing for over a week and we were beginning to fear the worst.'

'It's all down to Girard, it would never have happened without him and an English gentleman.'

'English gentleman, where is he?'

'He had to go back home to England. One of the perpetrators is holding someone he knew as a hostage.'

'I hope he is successful. I would like to meet him if that is possible.'

'What about Girard, I mean, he's a wanted man isn't he?'

'Not any more, at least not by us. We discovered the truth about the criminal activities of the men who framed him, but alas, the Foreign Legion may see things differently.'

As they were speaking, one of the police cars pulled into the drive with a half-naked man sitting in the back seat. They had found him lying bound up, exactly where Girard described, deep in the woods a little further down the lane.

Mullah and company were handcuffed but, as they were shepherded into the van, Girard exclaimed, 'One of them is missing,' and looking around he said, 'the woman, Louise – she's not here.'

A look of concern spread across Girard's face when he noticed that the housekeeper, Louise, was not amongst Mullah's little group. Thinking back, he realised that she had not returned from using the toilet and reasoned that she must have escaped through the toilet window. He mentioned this to the Detective Inspector in charge and together they walked around the side of the chateau and discovered the toilet window to have been left wide open. A set of footprints in the grass led to the old World War Two concrete bunker. The door was shut and locked from the inside. Girard called out her name in a taunting voice, 'Louise, are you there? It's time to leave.' But there was no response. He turned to the detective, put a finger across his lips and said quietly, 'One moment.'

The detective registered a puzzled expression and watched with curiosity as Girard walked over to a nearby cluster of fruit trees – which grew within an unkempt small orchard. Branches hung low and were sagging, heavy with over-ripe fruit. Girard cast his eyes around the trees and soon found what he was looking for, a dead branch about two metres long, drooping so low that it was almost touching the ground. Snapping it off, he slowly moved towards another tree that had a large oval shaped bees nest suspended from one of its lower branches. Very carefully he expertly reached out with the stick and gently removed the swarming drone hive from its resting place.

Within a few minutes he was outside the bunker with his buzzing bundle gently singing an old Maurice Chevalier tune, but slightly altering the words, "Every little bee seems to whisper Louise," much to the amusement of the detective. He called out once more, 'Are you there, Louise?' Once again there was no response, so standing on tiptoe, he pushed the nest through the opening. Within seconds, a yell and a terrified scream resounded throughout the concrete bunker and frantic hands scrabbled at the door until suddenly it burst open. The shocked woman stood before the two men with her hands frantically whirling and thrashing about her.

'*Ahh! Voila* – Louise,' Girard said in a mocking tone, and extending an introductive hand towards the detective added politely in his best French, 'may I introduce you to Detective Inspector Laronde?'

They walked back to the chateau and Louise was bundled into the van with the others.

Penny was about to accompany the police back to headquarters to give a full statement but, upon seeing Girard, she ran over and planted a kiss on his cheek.

Beaming widely he sighed heavily and said slowly with some deliberation, 'I shall never wash that part of my face again.' And with that, he collapsed onto the ground.

*

Daniella slumped deep into the padded bus seat. There was enough breath left in her to produce a sigh of relief. The bus had made a few stops in Hockley and was on its way towards Rayleigh. She felt recovered enough to turn around and glance out of the rear window. There was a thin line of traffic, but five vehicles behind, she clearly saw Bradley's dark-coloured BMW. Panic almost set in as she thought, *"He's following me."* She delved into her handbag and pulled out her mobile, switched it on and waited until there was a signal. After an agonising spell, she frantically dialled Crane's number. At last, for the first time, she heard the ringing tone. Whilst waiting for an answer, she turned around again. Her heart skipped a beat when she saw Bradley's car was now immediately behind the bus. As the phone continued to ring she almost said out loud, *"Please be there, please answer."* The thoughts raced through her mind until a mechanical voice said, 'Sorry unable to connect you; please leave a message after the tone.'

# PART THREE

PART THREE

# CHAPTER TWENTY THREE

Crane was casually watching sea gulls swooping around the queue of traffic as he sat in his car awaiting customs clearance at Dover. His mobile rang and he picked it up reluctantly, expecting it to be Bradley, 'Yeah?' He had missed the call, so he pressed the recall button; it was answered immediately and the voice at the other end raised his spirits.

'Oh, Jack, you're there, thank goodness. I've managed to get away from that maniac. I'm on a bus, but he's following it. I've got to get off it sometime.'

'Whereabouts are you?'

'It's just gone past a church in a town called Rayleigh.'

'Another two or three stops will bring you more or less outside the Police Station; get off there, go straight inside and wait for me. I'll be there within an hour and a half.'

Bradley watched scathingly as Daniella jumped off the bus and ran into the front entrance of Rayleigh Police Station. He circumnavigated around the block of shops and parked his car out of sight in a lay-by. On the opposite side of the road to the police station, he noticed J D Weatherspoons, a pub with tables and chairs set outside on a large forecourt. Within a short space of time, Bradley had found an ideal position from which to observe. His eyes remained fixed on the doorway that Daniella had rushed through and, whilst waiting to be served a drink, he picked up a discarded newspaper and pretended to read.

After some minutes he fished the mobile from his jacket pocket and dialled Ryan. 'I'm at the pub opposite the cop shop in Rayleigh. Are you anywhere nearby and if so would you care to join me?'

Believing that the money due to him from Bradley was at last going to be handed over, a surge of elation swept through Ryan and his response was, 'I can be there in ten minutes or so.'

*

Crane's right foot was pressed hard down on the accelerator pedal of the old Rover as it tore down the dual carriageway towards the Dartford crossing, a tunnel and bridge system that spans the River Thames connecting Kent to Essex. An inbuilt warning system flashed and sounded on the dashboard which was to give the driver plenty of notice when approaching speed cameras and the car dealer's warning flashed through Crane's mind, *"It goes like a bastard, I'm not sure this car is legal."*

The crossing was unusually quiet and he zipped through the tunnel in record time and, before long, he was racing down the Southend Arterial Road towards Rayleigh.

Daniella sat patiently in the waiting room, situated at the front of the police station. The reception desk was unmanned although it had a hatch and a bell to summon staff. At one stage she was asked if she needed any help, but she declined, saying she was waiting for somebody.

Ryan crossed the road, weaving his way through constantly streaming traffic. He ordered a drink and sat down at the outside table next to Bradley.

'She's over there,' Bradley spouted, nodding with his head.

Ryan thought he detected an almost maniacal look on Bradley's face as he replied with some hesitation, 'Who, Crane's woman?'

'Yeah.'

'But how?'

Bradley did not want to go into details, 'Does it matter? That's where she is,' and looking at his watch said, 'been there about thirty minutes.'

'What you gonna do?'

Bradley looked at Ryan coldly and said, 'Not me – you!'

'Me? What can I do?'

'Go inside and, if she is in the waiting room, get her out.'

Ryan looked askance, 'You mean just wander into the nick and drag her out?'

Bradley ignored Ryan's remark and delved into his jacket pocket, pulled out a narrow box and taking out a hypodermic needle offered it to Ryan, 'Use this; it's fast acting.'

Ryan gaped at the needle wide-eyed, 'You've got to be kidding. I'll never get anywhere near her. She'll recognise me straight away, start screaming and I'll get nabbed.'

'No you won't.' Bradley said irritably, 'Shield your face as you walk in; pretend you're reading a newspaper, here take mine. It's the last thing she will expect to happen. Just go inside, sit down next to her and give her the jab. When she's sleepy, help her out, like you're an old friend,' and with a degree of finality he added, 'simple as that!'

Ryan reluctantly took the needle and newspaper, but a plan of his own was forming in his mind as he crossed the road. He knew Bradley would be watching his every move and so he crossed the road and sauntered casually towards the police station. The bullet hole that Crane had put in his foot, was still aching and for Bradley's sake he was going to make the most of it and exaggerate the limp. He walked past the door, feigning to look in, and after a few yards, using his mobile, called up Bradley. 'Can't be done; she's talking to a copper in there,' and with that he slowly limped back.

Bradley's face looked angry when Ryan rejoined him. He glared at Ryan accusingly, but Ryan had been ready for that and he put on his best disappointed expression, 'Pity, but there's nothing you can do. Just have to wait until she comes out.'

Bradley looked at his watch and said slowly, 'Have you considered that Crane could be here before much longer; she may have been in touch with him.'

Ryan looked thoughtful for a moment, 'We could still lay in wait at his place; you know, get there before him; hide the car at the far end of the lane.'

It was Bradley's turn to look thoughtful, 'You know... that may be the best answer.'

Ryan felt relieved and was bold enough to ask, 'Have you got my money?'

Bradley was irritated by this, but he managed not to show it, 'Erm, tomorrow. I'll sort it out tomorrow after Crane has been taken care of.'

They were about to get up and leave when an old Rover zipped past, swung across the road and parked in the lay-by near to Bradley's BMW.

'That's him,' they said simultaneously in hushed tones.

*

Crane dashed into the police station and Daniella leapt up from her chair and ran into his arms. A policeman appeared at the desk, 'Can I be of assistance to anyone?'

Crane smiled, 'No thanks, we're just leaving.'

The policeman tried not to return the smile, looked down and said firmly, 'This is not a meeting place you know,' but when he looked up, they had slipped out through the door.

Throughout their journey to Palmers Rise in Canford, Daniella calmly related everything that had happened from the time she had arrived at Crane's cottage.

*

Ryan and Bradley stared after Crane's departing car. Ryan leant across the table and said tentatively, 'Do you think it's worth pursuing him any more? I mean, the damage has been done; you know, cut and run, so to speak. After all, you've still got his car and we are both leaving the area anyway.'

Bradley's dark eyes bored deep into Ryan's skull, making him shiver inside until eventually he turned his head away. 'It's become personal,' Bradley hissed. 'I'll figure something out. There is no way he is going to be let off the hook, and that's final!'

The pair sat in front of empty glasses for a while saying nothing to each other until a waitress appeared and scooped up the empties. Looking at Ryan she broke the silence with, 'Would there be anything else?'

Ryan flicked his eyes at Bradley for guidance on answering such a mundane question, 'No we're leaving. Give us the bill,' was Bradley's gruff response as he shuffled back his chair and stood up whereupon she turned on her heels and left.

They walked towards their parked cars in silence until suddenly Bradley became animated and said, 'I have an idea. I'll pick you up this evening about six-thirty.'

Ryan felt impotent; he did not want any more hassle, but neither did he want to antagonise Bradley and so he replied lamely, 'What's the plan?'

A smile spread across his face as he said, 'That woman escaped via a path from the back of Crane's place; there's no other way she could have got past me.'

He paused briefly leaving Ryan's brain to speculate a *'Not me, don't even suggest it.'*

Bradley continued, 'We'll park my car on the main road and I'll walk into Palmers Rise and find the pathway that leads right up to Crane's back door; and then wait to see if she comes out, and if she does, I'll nab her.'

Ryan looked at Bradley and was relieved he was talking in terms of the first person.

'What if… '

'There's no, *"what ifs"*, I'll try again the next day and then the next day, until I'm successful.'

*

On the way home Crane leaped out of the car and did a quick shop in the local supermarket, snatching up a copy of a newspaper in the process. Before continuing their journey home Crane lingered in the car park and spread a copy of the *Southend Echo* across his lap headlined, "Kidnap Girl Sammy Found Alive In France".

The little girl told the story of how she was rescued, together with an English woman named Penny, with her nephew and some French children. They were rescued by a mysterious Englishman known only as 'Jack'. He was helped later by a Frenchman who was now recovering from wounds in hospital, but neither of them knew Jack's surname. Many arrests were made and the information received by the French police had culminated in the breakup of a major kidnapping ring extending to Algiers.

Daniella blew some air between her teeth and remarked, 'The last time I laid eyes on you was barely four months ago. You rescued me from that dreaded sea fort, it was terrible and now you get up to your neck in trouble again.'

Crane grimaced and said, 'Not of my choosing.' And Crane told her how it all started with the theft of his Mustang.

'Well,' she sighed, 'hopefully – things will settle down now.'

Crane looked at her wistfully and said casually, 'I haven't got my car back yet.'

Daniella raised her eyes skywards at the thought of Crane in trouble yet again, but from past experience, she was confident in his resourcefulness. When they arrived at the cottage Crane set about reinstating the alarm system that had been set up in the lane and, as he tested it out remarked, 'They may try again so it's not worth taking any chances.'

\*

Bradley pulled up on the road just past Palmers Rise. It was quiet and the first shades of dusk, with its long grey shadows, were preceding a cloudy sky. He had left Ryan sitting pensively in the driver's seat, ready for a quick getaway, whilst he stepped into the lane. He walked slowly at first, scrutinising the thick hedgerows on the right hand side. Within a few minutes, he found what he was looking for; a neatly semi-concealed gap. Amid a tinge of joyful anticipation, Bradley entered and followed the trim path that lead to the rear of Crane's cottage. It was getting darker by the minute and it occurred to him that, without a torch, it would be foolhardy to attempt a snatch. He also considered bursting in on Crane and shooting him, but wary and forewarned by Crane's past, he knew the man might also be armed and return fire.

Bradley's final decision was to play a waiting game, but he wouldn't have to wait too long. Daniella suddenly came out of the back door carrying a basket of laundry; she stepped off the patio and walked up to a rotary clothes line. Bradley was waiting concealed in the shadows. Like a cat stalking his prey, he could not believe his luck. She turned, and her back was towards him as she began pegging out the washing on the line, softly humming to herself. A few metres separated them as he inched his way towards her. Then he struck. A hand was pressed firmly over her mouth and a hypodermic needle was plunged into the fleshy part of her upper arm. Bradley held on tight until she gradually stopped struggling and her body became heavy as it began to relax. Using a fireman's lift, he whisked her up and strode back the way he came, down the path.

Ryan stared in disbelief when he saw Bradley carrying Daniella across his shoulders. He leapt out of the car and quickly opened the rear door of the vehicle for Bradley to lay the unconscious Daniella unceremoniously onto the back seat. They sped off in the direction of Southend.

*

Crane had finished shaving two days' growth. He entered the kitchen and found the door of the washing machine wide open and the back door ajar. The evening was closing in and the light outside was fading fast. His hand slid towards the rear garden light switch and as he stood by the rear door, called out Daniella's name, but there was no response.

He stepped outside with a look of concern spread across his face. A hollow pit occupied his stomach; the laundry basket lay on its side and Daniella's clothes were scattered over the ground. Crane guessed straight away what must have happened, but he knew it could only have been a matter of minutes ago.

Rushing back inside, he grabbed hold of a jacket, ran through the cottage and straight out of the front door towards the parked Rover. Jumping in and slamming the car into gear, he raced bumpily down the lane, getting to the end in record time. He reaching the main road and slewed heavily into a right turn. Crane trusted his instinct to make the right decision and sped towards the direction of Southend.

The raucous sound of his mobile suddenly resounded throughout the interior of the Rover. Crane's hand flew towards the phone and switched on the loud speaker to hear Bradley's self-satisfied voice, 'Ah, *so you are* there. It's so difficult to get hold of you on the mobile.'

'What do you want?' Crane replied bluntly.

'Surely you must realise by now that I have your lady friend, Daniella – or perhaps you are half asleep inside your delightful little cottage?'

'I'm in the cottage,' Crane lied, as he peered through the dusky evening sky at a distant set of very distinctive BMW rear lights.

'Well you'd better stay there and I'll be in touch very shortly and then we can resume my original arrangement. Bye for now,' and the phone cut off.

Crane put his foot down hard and the Rover's twin-turbos cut in and thrust the car into a sprint that would have been appreciated at the Brands Hatch racing circuit. Crane eased his foot off when he clearly saw the BMW turn into an industrial estate. The estate was quiet at that time of the evening. It was deserted and sparsely lit. Crane flicked off the lights and turned into the estate. Keeping his distance, he followed the bright beams of Bradley's car. When it came to a halt, some hundred metres ahead, Crane swung the Rover into an unlit warehouse parking space and turned off the engine. He surmised that the kidnappers were armed. He had left his acquired weapons in France and without them he knew it would be foolhardy to confront them at this stage.

Bradley parked the BMW in front of a small, detached brick building. He quickly got out of the car and hurriedly unlocked the front door. Once inside, he threw back a heavily padded door to reveal a four metre square, windowless room. The two men carried Daniella inside and laid her down on a thick-piled carpet floor. Catching his breath, Ryan looked around the dimly lit room and remarked, 'No windows.'

Bradley displayed one of his rare mean smiles and said, 'This place was once used as a recording studio. It was advertised in the local paper, so I've rented it for a month. It's purpose built – completely soundproof. When she wakes up, she can make as much noise as she likes, no one's going to hear her through the walls or the two sets of doors.'

'How long are you going to leave her here?'

'Does it matter? I want Crane, that's all that matters.'

'We'd better leave some water and... '

Bradley cut him short, 'Oh just shut the fuck up!'

Ryan looked down and was silent. He was getting increasingly concerned over Bradley's oppressive attitude towards him. He felt this especially so when there was any mention of the money which he considered was due to him.

Bradley locked the building then the two of them got back into the BMW and drove off.

Ryan remained quiet for a while, but he was curious and tried to make pleasant conversation, 'When are you going to contact Crane?'

'After I've eaten; he can sweat for a while,' he snapped.

'What will you do to him?'

He growled a response, 'I'm not sure. I'll either maim him or kill him. Now don't ask me any more stupid questions!'

*

From his place in the shadows, Crane watched them drive off and, as soon as they were out of sight, he started up the Rover, drove up to the brick building and leapt out. It was now completely dark. He removed his pen-light and examined the door locks. They were substantial and he considered that his bunch of lock-picks may not be up to the job of opening them.

He walked around the building and dismissed the idea of a window entry; they were small and far too high, sited up near the roof line. He tried the lock-picks and, to his surprise, they did work and well-oiled mechanisms sprang back with ease and he stepped inside.

The door to the soundproof room was fastened with a pair of heavy bolts on the outside, which Bradley had fitted in an attempt to make the room more secure. Crane slid these back and pushed the door wide open. Stale air filled his nostrils and the sound of Daniella's heavy breathing could be heard within the empty room. Using his pencil beam, he located the light switch and flicked it on. In the dim light he saw Daniella lying prone on the floor. He crouched down beside her and whispered softly in her ear; she was in a deep sleep and did not rouse.

A raucous, 'Gotcha!' startled Crane and the door slammed shut. Bradley could not hide his gleeful expression as he slid the bolts across and locked the outer door then strode back, cock-a-hoop, towards his car. Slumping into the driver's seat he said, 'It was a good job I spotted that pile of junk he drives around in. He won't get out of there in a hurry; it was worth paying the two month's rent in advance.'

Ryan felt no sympathy towards Crane, but could not help remarking, 'Pity about the woman though.'

Bradley seemed to ignore this and continued, 'They won't last very long without water and when their bodies are found. I'll be long gone.'

Ryan wished Bradley had included him and had used the word 'we', so he tagged on weakly, 'Me too.'

*

Crane heaved his broad shoulders against the padded door; there was no movement at all. There was nothing in the room he could use; it was bare. The ceiling had two small vents, but they were closed. He looked down at Daniella and was thankful that she was still asleep. Eventually he sat down on the floor with his back leaning against the wall. The day for him had been a long one and he was beginning to wilt and succumb to the warm stuffy atmosphere of the room. Apart from the sound of Daniella and his own breathing, the silence was absolute. He squinted at his watch; he had been there for nearly two hours. Heavy eyelids flickered and began to droop, until finally, they closed.

A sudden rush of cool air brushed against Crane's face and he opened his eyes. A man with a torch stood at the door waving it around the room, 'What's going on?' he groused.

Crane straightened up, 'We were accidently locked in,' he began.

'Good job I came along then, I keep an eye on the place for Mr Adams, the owner. I didn't know he had rented it out.'

'Well I'm certainly glad you didn't know,' Crane replied. 'Do you have Mr Adams's phone number?'

'Certainly, sir,' and the watchman produced a notepad and writing the number down handed it to Crane.

Crane looked at the number and noting it was a local one, thanked him and gently lifted Daniella up to carry her outside. The fresh air caused her to stir from her repose. Her eyes flickered responsively, as Crane set her down in the front passenger seat.

Crane thought for a moment and had to admit to himself that he had underestimated Bradley's resolve. Putting himself in Bradley's shoes, Crane guessed that his adversary would check up some time later by driving past the building and so he thought it best to leave his old car parked there as a decoy. Making use of his fully-charged mobile, he called a cab. Crane's surmise proved to be right, when later Bradley cruised past the building he felt smug and reassured when he saw Crane's old Rover still parked there.

By the time the taxi arrived Daniella was awake and reliving the moment when she tried to hang out the washing.

Although tired, Crane had more than enough adrenalin flowing through his veins and, with plenty of fresh evening air, Daniella seemed to have fully recovered from her induced sleep. It was approaching midnight when Crane and Daniella flopped into bed. After a shower, they lay naked for a while, content to remain quiet, nestling against each other's arms under the cool covers which moulded around them. Their bodies gradually warmed from under the quilt, it was then, Daniella propped herself up on one elbow and ran her soft lips down the side of Crane's face. 'You haven't shaved properly,' she chided gently, 'but I don't care.'

Crane sat up and rubbed his whiskers. 'I did earlier on', he offered. Then, as their eyes met briefly, he left it at that and gave her a gentle peck on the cheek. She reacted by throwing her arms about his waist, nearly tilting him off balance, before they embraced and kissed, gently at first and more passionately as they explored each other's nakedness. He was aroused by the feel of her warm breasts heaving sensually against his chest. Daniella responded passionately, moving slowly but purposefully into the act of love as they rolled over from edge to edge of the bed, until exhausted the pair drifted off into an uneasy sleep.

The morning came too soon; they were both awake at first light. After coffee, Daniella insisted on accompanying Crane wherever he went and, in the light of her recent experiences since arriving in Canford, Crane readily agreed. He was anxious to nab Bradley, however he was unsure where to start. For openers, he would try to find out his address and he dialled the telephone number, of the building's owner, that had been given to him by the nightwatchman. Unfortunately the response was on answerphone and Crane was reluctant to leave a message in case the owner contacted Bradley to sanction it.

The notion of keeping watch on the building, where he and Daniella had been incarcerated, was perhaps the only other alternative; in the hope that the villainous pair would check up to see if their prisoners were still in situ. Crane decided to use his Transit van and found an ideal parking place, partially concealed in a nearby cul-de-sac, as an observation post.

After several hours Crane was reluctant to quit, but having consumed two flasks of coffee, Daniella began fidgeting and was keen to visit the toilet. 'There's a bucket in the back of the van,' Crane remarked casually. Daniella gave him a look that only women can accomplish in such a situation and crossing her legs, remained firmly in her seat.

A few minutes went by and they saw Ryan drive past and pause outside the building; one glance at the Rover satisfied him enough to drive off. Crane's hand darted towards the starter and he pulled the Transit into the road; keeping a steady distance behind Ryan's Ford Mondeo. They followed him through Southend until he pulled up outside a boarding house in Westcliff with a "Vacancies" bedsit sign outside. Crane drove past and, checking his rear-view mirror, watched Ryan enter the building. Daniella seemed to have forgotten her needs momentarily and looked anxiously at Crane as he left the parked van and strode up to the bedsit.

Crane walked up to the front door and, trying the handle, found the door to be unlocked, so stepped inside. He was surprised at the neat and tidy hallway. A name plate was typed and fixed to each of the four doors. Not knowing which name Ryan was using, Crane paused at each one, listening for sounds of movement. He did not have to wait long, Ryan's voice could be heard and Crane, listening intently, guessed he was reporting back to Bradley on the phone.

When the phone conversation finished, Crane tapped lightly on the door. A few seconds passed before the heavy thud of Ryan's bulk resounded across the wooden floorboards. The sound of the latch snapping back echoed through the hall and, as the door inched open, Crane propelled all his weight against it, sending Ryan hurtling backwards across the room. At the same time, Crane leapt into the room, pushing the staggering Ryan forward until he ended up flat on his back on top of a bed. A strong forearm leant against Ryan's throat as he stared up into Crane's face.

'How's the foot, Ryan?' Crane hissed.

Ryan's eyes bulged fearfully as he stared at Crane in disbelief. 'It wasn't my idea to... ' he quietened as Crane increased the pressure.

'Tell me, where does Bradley live?'

'I don't know, nobody does,' Ryan rasped hoarsely, 'he always contacts me by mobile phone.'

Crane eased up the pressure on Ryan's neck and said, 'What's his number?'

The fear remained in Ryan's eyes as he said throatily, 'It's in my mobile; the number's in my mobile.' He raised his hand and pointed towards a hook behind the door, 'Jacket pocket.'

Crane straightened up and said, 'Don't move.'

Ryan remained stock still, hardly daring to breathe as he watched Crane walk towards the door to collect the jacket. He returned and upending the coat to shake the contents out over the bed. He picked up the phone and thrust it towards Ryan, 'Call him and arrange a meeting,' Crane said.

At that point Ryan did not know who he was more afraid of, Bradley or Crane, but then all things considered – Crane was there.

'What... shall... I say?' he stammered.

'Just tell him you want to see him.'

Ryan went quiet and looked down. He was pensive for a moment, until suddenly he blurted out, 'You were right about Bradley knifing Davy Porter; I found that out the other day. He died in hospital. If I call Bradley he'll want to know why; if he suspects you're involved he'll kill me. He's mad you know – round the bend. He was in Broadmoor.'

Crane's face hardened as he said, 'That's your problem, I'm not going to wait all day.'

Ryan was quiet again. He closed his eyes for a moment and he opened them to face Crane's steady gaze. Without a word, Ryan dialled Bradley's number and Crane said, 'Turn the speaker on.'

The ringtone seemed to fill the room until a voice said, 'Yeah?'

'It's me, Ryan.'

Bradley sounded irritable 'I know that, what do you want?'

'You said that you would have my share of the money today.'

'Did I?'

Ryan's voice was a little shaky as he said, 'Yeah, where can we meet up?'

'You sound a bit edgy, what's troubling you?'

Ryan cleared his throat and replied, 'Got a bit of a cold. I need the wedge, I've got bills to pay.'

It was silent for a few seconds before Bradley said, 'Thought you were going to do a runner, you know – get out of the country.'

It was Ryan's turn to be quiet for an instant. Bradley waited patiently, listening to Ryan's heavy breathing, before he came up with, 'Erm… not just yet, I was relying on getting some dough in.'

'Are you alone?' Bradley enquired suspiciously.

'Alone?' Ryan echoed with a forced laugh, 'Yeah, course I am, I'm in my bedsit.'

There was a slight pause before Bradley came back with, 'Okay, I'll call you back shortly and tell you when and where we can meet.'

Ryan glanced at Crane and shrugged nervously. Crane looked at his watch; he suddenly realised that he had left Daniella in the van and hoped she had not wandered off in search of a toilet. However, it would be foolhardy to leave Ryan on his own in case he contacted Bradley or vice versa and so he said, 'You're coming with me and please, don't do anything foolish. You won't get off so light next time and bring your mobile.'

Without taking his eyes off Crane, Ryan eased himself up off the bed, put on his jacket and they both left. As they approached Crane's van, Daniella appeared from the opposite direction with an expression of relief and satisfaction.

Crane smiled tightly and said, 'I'm afraid we're stuck with this guy for a while.'

Daniella looked at Ryan disdainfully, shrugged and got back into the van. At that moment Ryan's mobile rang and he looked at Crane who mouthed silently, 'Speaker.'

'Ten o'clock this evening,' Bradley announced. 'In the car park opposite the Kursaal, by the Aquarium, pull up alongside and I'll settle with you.' Ryan barely had time to acknowledge before Bradley hung up.

Crane checked his watch; it was seven-thirty in the evening and, in spite of a clear sky, dusk was approaching fast. He turned to Ryan, 'I'll tail you and trap him in the car park.'

'What are you going to do with me?'

'Nothing, for the moment, it's that scum Bradley I'm after.'

A slight feeling of relief swept through Ryan, but the *for the moment* part of Crane's sentence stayed in his mind.

There were two hours to wait; Crane and Daniella were hungry so they coerced Ryan to accompany them to the local fish and chip shop for a takeaway and they all ended up eating on the hoof and hanging around in the Transit van. Near the appointed hour, Crane relieved Ryan of his mobile phone. Ryan climbed into the Mondeo and headed towards his meeting place with Bradley. Crane followed at a distance. Throughout the drive to the car park, Ryan felt slightly elated at the prospect of being paid off; he considered he would be in with a chance to get away from both Bradley and Crane. As soon as the money was handed over, he intended to make his excuses and tear away, leaving Bradley to his fate. Ryan checked the rear-view mirror noting that Crane trailed some distance behind in his van.

As they drove along Eastern Esplanade, Crane glanced at Daniella and said, 'I'm not keen on you being here, things could end up with some bullets flying around. I'd much sooner drop you off somewhere.'

Daniella looked at Crane and smiled, 'Are you trying to scare me? I'm the one that pulls the bullets out – remember?'

Crane tried to remain solemn and said, 'Just thought I'd better warn you... '

Daniella cut in, 'Look, since arriving in this country, I've been kidnapped, drugged, incarcerated in a erm... soundproof room, dined out with the fish and the chips whilst we walk in the company of a man that tried to murder the pair of us and *now* you foresee the possibility of some erm... gunplay – erm, gunplay is correct word, eh?'

She looked at Crane for confirmation and, he nodded at the same time stifling a grin. Daniella continued, 'Okay then, and as they say in the American movies, bring it on! I'm not going to miss out on anything – I stay with you!'

By now Crane was laughing as she finished with, 'From past experience – you always know how to give a girl a good time.'

'Okay, okay, I give in, we stick together.'

They remained quiet for a short while, until they saw Ryan's Mondeo turn into a car park. A moment later Crane pulled into the parking area. He quickly doused the lights on the van, turned off the engine and remained parked near the exit. In the patchy light ahead, he could just make out the shape of Bradley's black BMW as its rear lights were suddenly extinguished. Ryan's Mondeo pulled up close alongside and the shadow of a man briefly covered the gap then disappeared into Bradley's car.

Like a cat waiting for a mouse to emerge, Crane scrutinised the pair of silhouettes – they were contours that were indistinct blurs in a dark corner. Within a few moments, there was the sound of a door slamming which echoed around the area. At the same time, the Mondeo suddenly burst into life and, with headlights gleaming bright, shot like an arrow across the car park, the rear end swaying violently from side to side. Slithering tyres scraped and squealed on the surface until the car reached the exit, turned into the main road, and was absorbed by the mainstream of traffic.

Bearing in mind the fact that Crane had mentioned bullets, Daniella automatically slumped low in her seat as Crane brought the Transit to life. With all lights blazing, the Transit raced across the path of the stationary BMW, blocking it in. Like a wraith, Crane slithered out of the van and swept into the shadows. Keeping low to the ground, he ran towards Bradley's car. Crouching down, he reached up and snatched at the driver's door handle, throwing it wide open. Bradley was not there. In the diffused light Crane saw Ryan sitting bolt upright and immobile in the passenger seat. His eyes were screwed tight as rivulets of sweat ran down his face and a patch of blood, staining his shirt, oozed out of his side where a long bladed knife remained, pinioning him to the seat. Crane immediately removed the mobile phone, which he had previously taken from Ryan, and called the emergency services.

As Crane finished the call, Ryan gasped, 'Thanks for that… He did me like Davy Porter… Bradley had no reason to do this to me… he doesn't know that you escaped… I hope you get the bastard.'

'I'll try, but I need to know where to start. Have you any idea where he may be heading for?'

Ryan was quiet for a moment and Crane thought he had passed out when suddenly, with some effort, he managed to say between clenched teeth, 'No… My mobile, you've got my mobile… look in that, I've never taken anything off… he's used it once or twice… it may help.'

The ambulance arrived as Crane pulled out of the car park. He couldn't stop the scene running through his mind, *It's like déjà vu – I've seen this before.*' On the journey back to Canford, Crane told Daniella what had happened to Ryan and its similarity to the fate of Davy Porter.

Daniella looked appalled. 'Is he mad?' she remarked.

'Maybe, I don't know, but what I do know is that he is just plain evil.'

Back at the cottage, while Daniella put the kettle on, Crane plugged Ryan's mobile phone into his computer and switched it on. The phone was crammed with old text messages, telephone numbers and notes. Bradley was listed as having three separate mobile phone numbers, but no landline. Sifting through the mail, Crane found several text messages from him emanating from a hotel in Athlone in Ireland. The last one, sent a month previously, mentioned a date for his return. Crane looked at the calendar and it was to be within two days.

Daniella entered the room with two mugs of tea and set one down beside Crane. 'Ever been to Ireland?' he said.

'No, I haven't.'

'Well you're in for a treat; I'll book a couple seats right now for a flight to Dublin and, from there, we can hire a car and drive to a town called Athlone.'

'What do we do there?'

'Book into the Hotel Lana and hopefully we shall be ready to greet Bradley when he arrives the following day.'

# CHAPTER TWENTY FOUR

Bradley left the mainstream of traffic lining Marine Parade, the road adjacent to the seafront, and headed for the outskirts of town towards the direction of the industrial estate, where he had incarcerated Crane and the woman. He was curious to know if Crane's car was still there and that they were still locked up. It was dark, apart from the street lights dotted about the estate, but as Bradley drove slowly past the disused recording studio, there was no mistaking Crane's old Rover, parked on the forecourt and he felt a sense of triumph. Crane was to blame for Bradley's criminal operation finishing earlier than planned, but he was satisfied in the knowledge that his adversary was no longer a problem. He had dealt with Ryan and would keep his share of the money. That was, he considered, adequate compensation. It was time for a break and flicking the switch on his mobile he confirmed his visit to Hotel Lana.

*

Crane and Daniella arrived at Southend Airport at 8.30 am and within a short time boarded an Aer Lingus aircraft bound for Dublin. Within an hour and a half of landing, having by-passed the city of Dublin, they were on the M6 motorway heading towards Athlone.

It was lunchtime when Crane and Daniella reached Hotel Lana, and booked a room for two days. It was essentially a small guesthouse with only seven bedrooms, but the building was situated on the banks of the beautiful Lough Ree. Their room, on the first floor took in panoramic views across the lake.

Crane stood looking out of the bay window at a grey rain-spattered sky, whilst Daniella made use of the en-suite to freshen up. He noticed a jetty, with a boat moored at the end, a short distance away and assumed it belonged to the hotel. He spotted a small yacht, its sails flapping loosely in the breeze as it turned and headed towards the opposite shore. It suited his purpose to note that, from the bedroom window, it was possible to see anyone coming or going to the hotel; the road was a dead end. Another useful feature transpired when the sash window was slightly open, he could also hear any vehicle that entered the cul-de-sac. However, being off-season, visitors appeared to be in short supply. There was only one other couple staying at the hotel and they were checking out in an hour's time.

Breakfast was the only meal served in the hotel and they had to drive for fifteen minutes to the town of Athlone for main meals. Crane went downstairs to look around; the proprietor, Kathleen, a widow in her mid-forties, was busy dusting around the entrance hall. She seemed friendly enough and this prompted Crane to enquire, 'Not good weather is it?'

She paused briefly in her chores and replied in a cheerful Irish brogue, 'Ah but it should brighten up a bit later on I should think.'

'Let's hope so,' and Crane asked casually, 'do you expect any other guests this week?'

'There's just one person arriving tomorrow,' and carried on dusting adding, 'one of my regulars.'

'That's nice,' Crane commented as he walked into the sitting room.

*

Bradley felt agitated even though he was certain that he had rid himself of Crane. On leaving Dublin Airport, he collected a hire car then flipped open his mobile to telephone his cousin, the proprietor of Hotel Lana. He gave her an arrival time and also casually enquired if anyone else was staying there. His cousin's description of Crane and Daniella was unmistakeable and he said, 'Do me a favour, Kathy, can you put them on ice for me?'

'No problem,' was the short reply. She laid the phone down and thought for a moment, before picking it up again and dialling out. After a few seconds, a gruff throaty voice responded, 'Yeah?'

'Is that yourself, Mickey Finn?'

'Who wants to know?'

''Tis I, Kathy, yur great lump; ya know? Kathy from the Lana Hotel. I just love the sound of your name.'

There was a laugh at the other end and he replied, 'Well do you now? I earned that moniker when I was a cocktail waiter. Now what can I do for you, Kathy, me darling?'

'Me cousin's arriving soon, but there's a couple staying here, that to use his own words needs "putting on ice". Could you do me a favour and see to it for me?'

'When?'

She looked at the clock; it was eight thirty. 'Well now, there's no time like the present is there?'

'Consider it done, my dear. Are they around now?'

'No, they've gone to Athlone to eat, but they know I lock up every evening at ten o'clock.'

'That's fine, we'll keep the trouble out in the open then. I'll be over with a few of the boys within twenty minutes or so and perhaps afterwards,' he chuckled, 'it's been a long time, so perhaps we can get together for a wee while.'

Kathleen felt herself blushing as she put the phone down and straightened up. She looked in the tall mirror in her bedroom, patted her mousey hair into place, sighed and drew in a slightly overweight stomach.

*

Crane and Daniella had enjoyed a fine meal at one of the Athlone restaurants and it was nine forty-five when their hire car pulled into the floodlit hotel's cul-de-sac. They clambered out and walked towards the hotel entrance. Three men were seated, drinking at one of the outside tables, and seemingly chattering amongst themselves. As they walked past the row of tables, a distinct unmistakeable metallic sound echoed in Crane's ear and he froze. It was that of a slide, snapping back and forth, of a semi-automatic Colt, followed by a gruff, 'Alright you two; that's far enough.'

Crane and Daniella turned around slowly to face the three men who had been drinking at the table, who were now standing.

'What do you want with us?'

'Me? Nothing, it's nothing personal. It's somebody else that's doing the wanting.'

'Who?'

'You'll find out soon enough, meanwhile, I'd be obliged if you do as you're told like,' and to reinforce the issue, waved the gun around adding, 'so I don't have to use this thing and believe me – I will if I have to. So I hope you're going to be sensible, that way nobody will get hurt.' And using the weapon as a pointer finished with, 'So, sit yourselves down for a while and keep quiet.'

Crane glanced at Mickey Finn and his pair of heavily-built companions; they appeared to be in their late forties or early fifties. Their eyes were focused menacingly on him whilst they spoke in hushed tones to each other.

'What are you guys, IRA?'

They gave each other knowing looks and one of them said, 'Wouldn't you be after knowing, that those days are long gone.'

'Ex-IRA, then?' Crane said with a degree of finality.

An audible snap resounded from the direction of the hotel as Kathleen locked the front door and dimmed the entrance hall light.

Crane and Daniella cast a compliant glance at each other and sat down at a table opposite the aggressors.

No more than fifteen minutes had passed before the headlights of an approaching car turned into the cul-de-sac, its bright halogen beams spreading rapidly across the lush green lawns, like white fire, until they came to a halt and were extinguished. All eyes, except Mickey Finn's, were on the figure that slowly emerged from the driver's door and as the figure neared, Crane whispered under his breath, 'Bradley.'

Bradley's fierce eyes remained upon Crane as he stomped towards the seated men. He passed Finn and said, without faltering in his stride, 'Won't be a moment,' and headed towards the hotel entrance door. Bradley drew heavily on a cigarette whilst pressing the doorbell and Kathleen came scuttling across the hall to let him in. A quick peck on the cheek served as a greeting as he stepped inside.

'You want these folks out of the way don't you?'

Bradley nodded and said, 'What have you got in mind?'

'I had an idea,' Kathleen ventured.

Bradley looked at her with a "go on" expression.

'I've been after thinking now, if you want to be permanently rid of that pair, there's an old row boat on the beach by the end of my jetty. I've been meaning to get rid of it; it leaks like a sieve. If someone was to be set adrift in the middle of Lough Ree, I know for a fact it won't go far. The waters of Lough Ree are very cold this time of year; a few people were drowned in them this very summer.'

'They are hardly going to row themselves out are they?'

'No, no, my dear,' she smiled, 'Mickey Finn can tow them out in my wee motor boat.'

Bradley rubbed his chin thoughtfully and said matter-of-factly, 'I was going to put a bullet in them and get Mickey to dump the bodies.'

Kathleen shrugged and said, 'Well it's up to you. It was just a thought but you know for a fact, that bullets always attract more police investigations than an accident would.'

'How bad is that boat? I mean you are sure it will sink?'

'Like a stone. It's very old and its timbers are rotten. Anyway it could always be helped along by using a hammer.'

Bradley looked sceptical but he understood the merit of

Kathleen's reasoning and so he agreed, as she smiled sweetly, and commented, 'The things I do for you.'

The gun in Mickey Finn's right hand never wavered or strayed. It was constantly pointed in the direction of Crane. There was no chance of him being able to overpower Finn without getting in the way of a bullet. He surmised that all three men were probably armed, but they seemed content to leave things to Finn. About twenty minutes had passed, before Bradley came out of the front door of the hotel. He spoke quietly to Finn and, without so much as a glance to Crane, sauntered back towards the hotel reception again.

Without taking his eyes off Crane, Finn motioned to one of his men with his hand. The man sprung up and moved smartly forward. After a few hushed words, Finn's eyes narrowed and he stared at Crane. 'Right, up you get,' he commanded, 'the pair of you – follow me.'

Without a word, Crane and Daniella fell in line between the three men. By now, the other two men had produced their handguns. Crane rightly guessed that these men were used to this kind of work; possibly they were ex-IRA or some other illicit organisation. 'Where are we off to?' he questioned. There was no answer.

The short walk to the jetty took just a few minutes. Under the watchful eye of Finn, his two companions attached a tow line from the motor launch to an old rowing boat on the beach. They started the motor launch engine and gradually dragged the old wooden boat into the water.

'Get in,' Finn barked gruffly.

Crane and Daniella waded and splashed through the water, until it came up to their knees, then clambered aboard and sat facing each other. No sooner had they sat down, when Finn, with his gun still trained on them, jumped into the motor launch. He positioned himself with his back to the driver so that he could face the unfortunate pair. One of his men slammed the boat into forward gear and the powerful Johnson engine responded, with a roar, as the boat pulled away from the jetty. The old rowing boat jerked violently forwards and the shoreline began to recede. Crane felt the water sloshing around his shoes as it seeped through the planking. He bent forward close to Daniella and said, 'Can you swim?'

She had also noticed the leak and nodded grimly. She tucked her long-sleeved cardigan in her waist and wrapped her cold arms around her shoulders.

'I reckon their idea is to tow this tub to the middle of the lake and, then when it sinks, leave us to drown.'

'It figures,' Daniella said, through chattering teeth adding, 'or to die of hyperthermia.'

Crane looked towards the dim lights of the hotel in the distance and said, 'It's pitch-dark all around but I remember seeing an island over to the right-hand side. When this thing sinks, we'd never make it to the shore; our only chance is to try and head for that island. Hopefully, we can use the lights from the hotel as a guide.'

Crane called out to Finn, 'This thing's leaking; we can't swim.'

There was no reply. Suddenly Finn threw the rope off his motor boat then circled around the row boat several times; it churned the water up in its wake, until the lake's surface was only a few centimetres from swamping the old boat. Finn grabbed hold of a lamp and aimed its beam, sending a blinding flash piercing into the darkness. He could see clearly that the boat he was towing was finished. Satisfied his part was done, he ordered the driver to head back to the jetty.

Bradley was there to greet them on their return and handed Finn a wad of Euros for his trouble.

*

As soon as Finn's motor launch began to head for shore, Crane and Daniella felt the boat begin to drop away below them and they rolled over the side into the bitter-cold waters.

Before leaving the boat Crane had warned, 'Stay on my left-hand side, so I don't lose sight of you.'

Keeping an eye on the dimly-lit shoreline, Crane headed for what he hoped would be the island that he had seen from the hotel window. Swimming fully dressed, with clothes billowing in the water, was no easy task; it was hard going. However, they knew that their lives depended on keeping it up but, after ten minutes or so, with the cold and exertion gnawing into her bones, Daniella felt her energy was being sapped away fast and her tired body was beginning to flag. Crane was also feeling tired. He had fully expected to have reached the island by now and was beginning to hope against hope, that in the pitch darkness, he had not misjudged their position and had bypassed that life-saving piece of land. It was then, he realised that Daniella was no longer swimming by his side.

# CHAPTER TWENTY FIVE

Bradley sat with his cousin Kathleen each downing a large globe, full of iced Sheridan's. The silky liquid soothed his throat together with his bad mood. 'I have to leave in the morning,' he said.

'Oh, so soon?' she cooed with disappointment. 'Aren't you going to wait until the bodies have been found?'

'Business, I'm afraid.'

'What are you up to this time?'

Bradley looked pained as he said, 'Organising my final consignment of cars, just two of 'em, a pair of old American antiques – worth a fortune over there. I now have the correct paperwork; proving they are mine, so I'm shipping them to New York first thing in the morning. That bastard Crane ruined my operation at home and in France. I must thank you, my favourite cousin, for helping me to get rid of him.'

Kathleen reddened slightly, smiled warmly and chided gently, 'Your *only* cousin, who will help you with *anything* you want. You'll be staying for breakfast of course?'

Bradley nodded and said, 'I look forward to it, but for now, I must rest. It's been a long day.'

Kathleen pressed a room key into his hand, 'I always save the best room for you.'

\*

Crane splashed and turned round. Treading water he stared into the inky blackness, but could see nothing. He threw his head back and shouted desperately, 'Daniella! Where are you?'

He listened intently above the splattering waters and thought he heard a strained gurgle in reply. Adrenalin rushed through his veins and with a burst of energy, immediately flailed his way towards the sound before he nearly bumped into a floundering Daniella. Reaching out, he wrapped his arm around her neck and brought her head up above the water. Treading water again, he held his position for a moment and, whilst looking around, he tried to regain his bearings, but the shore lights had disappeared and there was nothing to be seen, only darkness. He was beginning to feel disorientated when the realisation struck him. It must be the island that is blocking the light from the shore. His ears were muffled by the gentle ripple of the surrounding waters but he became enthused by another noise. It was the sound of water lapping against land. With a final effort Crane supported the semi-conscious Daniella and with all his strength he swam towards the sound. Within minutes, his feet scraped against the bottom of the lake and within seconds, when his shoulders were clear, he picked up Daniella, carried her ashore and laid her down on a grassy bank, then began a resuscitation procedure. He was beginning to feel desperate, but he could not give up then suddenly some water trickled from her mouth and it was not long before she appeared to be breathing normally.

Now fully conscious but also very cold, Daniella began shivering. She propped herself up on her elbows.

Crane sat beside her and said, 'How are you feeling?'

Through chattering teeth she said, 'Alive, thanks to you. Where are we?'

'We're on the island.' Crane stated flatly.

In between bouts of severe trembling she managed a half-hearted quip, 'Oh, how romantic.'

'Hmm,' he mumbled awkwardly, 'we need to find somewhere a bit warmer than here. Do you feel as though you can you stand up?'

Daniella held out her arms and Crane pulled her up and, with his support, they made their way slowly – feeling with their hands – through some trees and into a clearing. A darker outline stood out and, as they approached, they found it to be a shelter of some kind. There was no door, just an opening and slotted windows all around. 'It's a hide.' Crane said, and by the musty smell of it I believe the local wildlife have taken up residence.'

'What is hide?'

But before Crane could answer, they felt a draft from a beat of wings as a large barn owl, indignant upon being disturbed, gave a loud hoot and flapped his way out through the door.

'A hide,' he continued, 'is a place where people can watch birds without disturbing them, but it appears that the roles have been reversed here, but it'll suit our purpose. We'll need to get some of these wet clothes off and hang them up. Hopefully they will dry overnight.'

Feeling their way around the small hut, they found an old tarpaulin lying on the floor as well as cushions for the long wooden benches, 'That's all there is but I suppose it's better than nothing,' Crane commented. The pair made use of the items and huddled together trying to keep warm. In between shivers Daniella said, 'Like the babes in the wood, yes?'

Crane gave her a squeeze and said, 'You're a very brave woman, Daniella.'

They closed their eyes, but it was much too cold for them to get any sleep. They were still in each other's arms when the first cracks of dawn appeared through the narrow gap of the windows used for bird watching. Crane checked his watch; six thirty on a late September morning. Their underwear had dried on their bodies, but the clothes that had been hung up to dry, were still very damp.

Crane dressed and went outside. Nearby, coils of bramble were heavily laden with ripe fruit and he picked a couple of handfuls. He took some to Daniella, before he set about reconnoitring the small island. From its west shore, he could clearly see the hotel and the two other islands that lay to the east. Their best, and only hope of getting back to the mainland, would be to try and attract the attention of a passing boat.

It was around mid-morning when Crane sighted a pair of white billowing sails furling through the lake on a stiff breeze. As the yacht neared, to pass between the islands, he took off his jacket and waved it frantically in the air, high above his head until his arm ached. The boat tacked sharply, altered course and headed towards the island. Feeling elated, Crane called out to Daniella and they both stood together on the beach while the craft gently moved towards them.

The yacht's sails loosened – flapping noisily – as its prow front eased onto the beach and two men leapt off. Crane recognised them straight away. It was Mickey Finn's pair of cohorts. They were big men and the larger of the two bounded towards Crane whilst the other ran towards Daniella.

Crane remained still until the last second, then deftly side stepped, spun around as the brute went past and barged with all his weight against his assailant's back. This sent the thug sprawling awkwardly down flat on his face, breaking his jaw. Witnessing this, his companion looked shocked and abandoned Daniella. Swearing profusely he charged furiously towards Crane, who had started to run away but, within a few metres, when the thug was within arm's reach, Crane dropped low to the ground, curling his body up into a ball. His attacker was unable to stop the momentum. He fell over the top of Crane and ended up lying on the ground in front of him. Crane grabbed hold of the man's arm then sprang to his feet wrenching the arm up high, twisting it and tearing sinew as he dislocated it. A screech of pain was silenced when Crane delivered a heavy blow behind the ear.

Regaining his breath, Crane looked at Daniella and said, 'Let's go.'

They pushed the boat off the beach and clambered aboard. Crane set the sails and steered the craft between the islands. They headed northwards until the small boat was about three miles upriver from the hotel. Sailing close to the shore they found a convenient spot to beach the yacht but before leaving, they searched the yacht's tiny cabin and found two mobile phones, a nine mil Walther semi-automatic handgun together with a little over one thousand euros in cash, bound tight with an elastic band. As he pocketed them Crane remarked, 'This little lot may come in very handy.'

They were relieved to be on dry land and trudging no

more than half a mile, found themselves on the main road to Athlone. Within a short time they managed to hitch a lift to the town and its main shopping centre complex, where, using the money they found, they replaced their clothing.

Suitably attired, they took the escalators to reach ground level and left the shopping mall. They walked across the bridge towards a grey and ominous medieval building, Athlone Castle and had a meal in a cosy restaurant nearby. Over the meal Crane checked his watch; it was 4.30 pm. 'We'll wait until dark before getting a cab to drop us off just short of the hotel and then, I have a few ideas in mind to take them by surprise.'

Daniella shuddered at the thought of returning and, noticing this, Crane added, 'It may be best if you wait in the hire car; assuming it's still there.'

She smiled weakly and nodded.

*

Mickey Finn was dressed in his best suit when he called upon Kathleen at the hotel. She had invited him to dinner and, with Crane and Daniella out of the way and Bradley now gone, they had the place to themselves. She had laid a table for the pair of them, complete with an opened bottle of red wine. Upon greeting him at the front door, she took him by the arm and led him to the dining room, where a welcoming log fire crackled brightly, showering sparks against a mesh guard.

They sat down opposite each other and Finn cast his eyes approvingly over the table, poured himself a glass of wine, which he then gulped down quickly, before commencing the first course of the meal. He gave Kathleen a lecherous look as she replenished his glass. 'Which room are we going to have dessert in?' he leered.

'Depends what you have in mind for your dessert,' she replied, trying to sound modest.

At that moment, the sound of the front door opening and closing made her pause and cock an ear to one side. 'What was that?' she said out loud.

'Didn't hear anything,' Finn said as he slurped noisily away at the wine.

Kathleen got up and walked into the hall and looked around; there was nobody there. Believing that Finn hadn't closed the door properly when he had stepped inside, she returned to the dining room and sat down again. After a few minutes, she heard another noise; it was the sound of footsteps descending the staircase. She leapt up and walked back into the hall, leaving Finn to help himself to more wine. When she saw Crane standing by the desk holding his small wheelie case her face went as white as a sheet. 'I've come to check out,' he said.

For the first time in her life, Kathleen remained speechless, until she finally stuttered, 'Oh... I... thought...'

Crane interrupted her, 'By the way, where's Bradley?'

To her it was like a bad dream and she heard herself saying trance-like, 'He left first thing this morning... business; to erm, send cars to America.'

'I get the feeling that you didn't expect to see me again; who's in the other room?'

Her composure was slowly returning as she said, 'A friend.'

'It wouldn't be Mickey Finn by any chance?'

She looked down briefly and glanced over her shoulder and Crane said, 'Let's go in and find out shall we? After you,' and he edged the door open with his foot.

Finn had overstuffed his mouth with a wholemeal bread roll, softening it in between gulps of red wine when he saw Kathleen enter with Crane. He spat it out hastily and jumped up from his chair as though his pants were on fire. Taking one step forward he halted when Crane produced the Walther. 'It's your turn for a boat trip now,' Crane hissed, moving towards the fireplace. 'And if you're lucky, you can join your two mates on the island.'

Finn began, 'Look, perhaps we can... '

Crane cut him short with a venomous, 'Shut up!'

Perhaps for the first time in Finn's life he knew he was facing fury in its purest form and it worried him. Kathleen, looking at Finn for guidance, could see the fear in his eyes as she began to shrink back towards the door, but she stopped dead when Crane barked, 'Take another step and it will be your last!'

Her brain raced, she wished Bradley were here – he'd know what to do. But then, she considered it was because of him that she found herself in this position. Crane had his head turned towards her for a split second but it was enough time for Finn to try his hand and, picking up a chair, Finn hurled it clumsily towards the armed intruder. Crane saw it coming and moved to one side. The chair smashed and splintered on the stone hearth, knocking the fireguard aside and sending a shower of red hot sparks cascading onto the rug. Crane squeezed the trigger of the Walther and a bullet smashed into Finn's elbow. Ignoring his cries of pain, Crane said calmly, 'The next one goes in between your eyes!'

Cordite, from the spent bullet of the Walther, mingled with the smoke from a singeing rug and made a strange cocktail that spread across the room. Crane hooked his free hand around the small wheelie case that he had recovered from his room and waved the handgun to usher the pair outside. Together they made their way towards Finn's car. 'Keys,' Crane demanded, 'put 'em on the boot lid.'

Crane took the keys that Finn had placed on the car and without taking his eyes off the pair, felt inside the glovebox of Mickey Finn's Audi coupe. His left hand came out with a Colt semi-automatic. The weapon was somewhat weighty and he recognised it as a forty-five calibre with a full magazine. From there he marched the pair to the jetty – lit up by a large moon in a cloudless sky. 'Get in that boat!' Crane said harshly.

'My arm… ' Finn began, but before he could finish Crane said, 'Get in right now or you'll have both arms to complain about.'

Finn and Kathleen sat in the front of the craft, behind the steering wheel and Crane said, 'It won't steer. I've fixed your course for the middle of the lake and there should be just enough fuel in the tank for the ride. If you're lucky, maybe you can make the island and join your friends.'

Crane untied the boat, but before sending them off he added, 'Oh, there's just one more thing, you need the holes.'

With that he pulled back the slide on Finn's Colt and emptied the magazine into the bottom of the fibreglass hull. As the noise of gunfire abated another sound took its place; that of water pouring into the craft.

Tossing the rope to one side he called out, 'Off you go then, before I empty the other gun.'

Finn looked at the gun. He had no choice. He started the boat and it roared off. The throttle was jammed wide open and the wires controlling the rudder were bound up.

Crane stood momentarily until an orange glow made him turn. It was the hotel and it was on fire. With some haste, he strode to the hire car, placed the wheelie case in the boot and with a reassuring smile at Daniella drove off towards Dublin Airport.

Within an hour and a quarter, Crane was returning the hire car. One of the hire companies staff drove them to the nearby Airport Hotel, where Crane booked their return flight. The following morning, feeling refreshed, they boarded the nine am flight to Southend. A complimentary *Irish Times* was thrust in their hands and, as they flipped through the pages, they came across a colour photo of Hotel Lana completely engulfed in flames. It was reported that the hotel was believed to be unoccupied at the time and the Garda were trying to trace the owner.

Crane and Daniella arrived back at Canford just after 10.30 am. Crane felt, once again, that he had underestimated Bradley. He had fouled up big time, in such a way that it could have cost them their lives and so he once more delved into Ryan's mobile phone searching for further clues as to where he may find Bradley.

\*

Believing that Crane was now out of the way, after witnessing him being dispatched in an old, leaking rowing boat in the pitch-black dark of night, Bradley felt on cloud nine. So much so, that he had no worries about returning to his favourite hotel in Southend. However, two days after his return, one of his mobiles chirped. He stared momentarily at the tiny screen; he did not recognise the number, but he was familiar with the code; the call was from Ireland. He pressed the receive button and cautiously mumbled, 'Hello.'

'Is that you, Bradley?'

'Kathleen, so nice to hear from you my dear.'

There was a slight pause, 'You won't think so in a fecking minute.'

Bradley thought she sounded distressed, 'Why what's up that can't be fixed?'

For the first time in her life, she became irritated by her English cousin's laid-back attitude, 'Where shall I fecking start?'

Bradley tried to sound calming and replied, 'Tell your favourite cousin, Bradley, all about it.'

'That fucker Crane.'

Bradley suddenly felt edgy, 'He's dead, isn't he?'

'In your fecking dreams. Him and that woman, they got away to an island. Finn's two mates found them there but Finn's mates were busted up and left on the island while that Crane got away on their boat. Then he comes to my hotel, he puts me and poor Mickey in a boat and shoots fecking holes in it and my hotel has been razed to the ground – burnt to a frazzle – finished.' She stopped to catch her breath.

Bradley was silent for a moment trying to take in what he had just heard.

'Are you still there?' Kathleen screeched.

'Yeah, I can't believe it. I did say a bullet would have been better to get rid of him, didn't I?'

She ignored his remark saying, 'Well you'd better fecking

believe it; I had to swim for me life, it's a good job that I'm a fine swimmer, but poor Mickey, he didn't make it.'

'Mickey Finn is dead?'

'That's what I said, didn't I?'

Bradley had heard enough. He disconnected the call and turned the mobile off. His ebullient mood sank to a new low and he immediately turned his thoughts towards leaving the area. He knew that Crane would not give up, but then his ego allowed him to believe that nobody can outsmart or get the better of Bradley Kemp. The thought of, *'How did Crane know about his Irish retreat,'* whirled around his brain. No one knew about it, not even Ryan. He laid the puzzle to one side and resolved that the next time he encountered Crane, it would be Crane's demise for sure.

*

Jack Crane was tempted to find out whether Ryan had survived Bradley's vicious knife attack and if so, and if it was possible, he would question him in hospital for any information as to where Bradley might be heading. A quick phone call to Southend Hospital confirmed that Ryan was lucky; he had survived.

The nurse in charge of intensive care allowed Crane to visit Ryan. It was on the understanding that he was related, a deception that Crane used reluctantly. The nurse advised him not to stay too long. Crane poked his head around the door; Ryan was propped up in a semi-upright position, tubed and wired up. Doleful expressionless eyes stared up at Crane when he entered the small room.

'Can't get over Bradley knifing me,' he said unhappily.

'I've been through your mobile; I just missed Bradley in Ireland,' Crane said, but he did not elaborate on what had happened. 'Have you any other ideas where he may go?'

'Your car,' he said with some effort; 'your Mustang, it's tucked away in France somewhere not too far from Boulogne; Avenue de Parvenu in a place called Bellebrune, don't know where exactly, but it's just off the N42. I think he's going to keep your car for himself for a while. I also overheard him talking to a movie company about using the Mustang on one of their sets. They were offering to pay good money.'

Crane looked puzzled, 'Any idea which one?'

'No, but I do know it's in Spain, somewhere in Almeria. That's all I can tell you. I'm sorry I ever got mixed up with him you know. You're alright, Crane; I never thought I'd ever be thanking you, but if it weren't for you I'd be dead for sure. I hope you get your car back and when you do, sort him out good and proper.'

Crane left the hospital and, arriving back at the cottage, looked up the area of Spain on the computer. With a little more researching, he found that there were two movie studios near Tabernas in Almeria; both used for making western movies, although nowadays one was strictly a 'mock up' for tourists and the other combined tourism with movie-making. He considered that a trip to Spain would perhaps be something of a 'last resort' and returned to scanning Ryan's mobile once more. He realised that he had no idea how much information the phone held, although there were phone numbers and text messages that had never been deleted.

Daniella sidled up with mugs of steaming coffee as

Crane stared at the screen, 'Any luck?' she enquired.

'Not yet,' he replied. 'I reckon Bradley knows by now that we are still in one piece. If he came back to Southend, then maybe he would move on fairly soon. In any event, for now, I assume my car is still in France.'

Daniella nodded, 'I shudder at the thought of that man still on the loose.'

Crane picked up his coffee and talking through the mug he said, 'Fancy a trip to France?'

She looked at him and remarked, 'Never a dull moment, eh! I have said it before – where you go, I go!'

Crane stood up, put his mug down and curled his arm around her waist, 'It could be… '

She pressed a finger against his lips and finished his sentence, 'Dangerous? When is it *not* dangerous around you? I shall never forget how we first met, in that damn sea fort and I shan't forget Ireland in a hurry. So, when do we leave?'

Crane put his other arm around her waist and gave her a prolonged kiss, and when they came up for air he said, 'I think we should leave right now before I get other ideas!'

# CHAPTER TWENTY SIX

On the spur of the moment, Bradley decided to leave for France a few days earlier than he had planned; he was feeling paranoid. The same things had been continuously playing on his mind. He was confused as to how Crane seemed to be able to predict his whereabouts. This had happened on more than one occasion, but it was Ireland especially that puzzled his brain because not even Ryan knew about his cousin's hotel in Ireland. His body jerked involuntarily and his thoughts were suddenly interrupted, by the abrupt, raucous sound of his mobile. He picked up the phone, thinking it may be his cousin, but then stared briefly at the unknown number, before answering the call.

Within minutes of receiving the phone call, Bradley felt more positive, he perked up a little, packed his suitcase and on leaving his room, he paused at the top of the stairs, briefly scanning the wide entrance hall. He settled his account at the reception desk and headed for the front door. He stood outside for a moment, in the dark. His eyes soon became accustomed to the change of light and he looked in both directions, seeking shadows lurking in the streetlights that might belong to his adversary. Then he took a deep breath and sidled hurriedly out of the hotel. As he walked quickly towards the rear car park, his head darted from side to side; he stared cautiously around, like a nervous wild animal.

When he reached the sanctuary of his newly-acquired BMW, he quickly leapt inside and his hand shot towards the central door-locking mechanism. Powering up the engine, he slammed the car into gear and left the hotel parking area, like a bat out of hell, aiming for the Southend Arterial Road and the Dartford Crossing.

*

Crane fuelled up his Rover, then he and Daniella headed for the Channel Tunnel. It was a late night crossing and, by the time they arrived, they were among the last to drive on board the end carriage of the train. As fate would have it, Bradley had boarded earlier and he was situated near the front carriage. It was one o'clock in the morning, when the train completed its journey to Calais and, after disembarking, Crane and Daniella drove to Boulogne. They found an automated hotel to bed down in for the remainder of the night.

Meanwhile Bradley had driven to a left-luggage depot in Calais and retrieved a large holdall that he had deposited there, the last time he returned to the UK. It contained an Uzi machine gun and a Glock semi-automatic handgun with some spare clips of ammunition. He now felt comfortable about the situation and he would retrieve the Mustang around mid-morning.

*

Crane woke up early and nudged Daniella, 'Time to get up,' he said quietly. She looked at him sleepily, turned to her side and slid reluctantly out of the bed. Within ten minutes they were dressed and on their way out, stopping briefly in the lobby, where they grabbed coffee and croissants from the hotel's vending machines, before heading for the parking area.

It was eight am and the chill morning air struck the pair full in the face, causing them to exhale small clouds of misty breath as they approached the Rover. As soon as they were inside, Crane warmed up the engine and in between mouthfuls of hot coffee he set the satnav for the area of Bellebrune.

Within thirty minutes he had found the place where his Mustang was being kept. It was quite visible and plain for all to see from the main road, tucked in an open-ended hay barn on the outskirts of town. Crane approached the barn, looking about him as he went. He paced up to the car, and quickly appraised its condition and was satisfied that it was intact both inside and out. Producing his spare keys, he unlocked the door and started its engine which fired up straight away. He also noted that it had a full tank of fuel.

Crane approached the nearby farmhouse, with some caution, and rattled on the front door. There was no reply. In the distance, he spotted a farm tractor with clouds of birds hovering above and around it. The farm worker on the machine seemed intent on ploughing the field and paid him no heed, so he walked back to the barn got in the Mustang and drove it to the road where he pulled up in front of the Rover. Daniella looked at him through the windscreen and, with a smile on her face, gave him the thumbs up. She slid into the driving seat of the Rover and together they headed back towards Boulogne.

Crane led Daniella to the hospital where Girard was staying and after parking both cars, they entered the building and were taken to a private ward on the second floor. The nurse swung the door open and held it back to let them pass through, gesticulating with an open hand and commenting knowingly in French, 'He's quite a celebrity.'

Girard was fully dressed sitting at a table laid with coffee and a large plate of croissants. Penny was seated opposite. As Crane and Daniella entered the room, Girard and Penny looked up and they both sprang to their feet, '*Mon ami!* Jack, it is good to see you,' and looking at Daniella said, 'and especially you *Mademoiselle*.'

Crane laughed and introduced Daniella. They shook hands and, with his infectious grin, Girard said, 'Jack has told me about you but he did not dare to say how beautiful you are; he is very fortunate.'

Daniella could not hide her amused embarrassment; she guessed Girard's archetypical comments would take a little getting used to as she blushingly glanced at Crane.

Girard continued, 'I too am fortunate; Penny and I are to be married when I leave here. I cannot believe it's been ten days; I came in a wanted man and now they are calling me a hero – *me* – *a hero*, can you imagine? And you, my friend, are the *"Mystery Englishman"*, that's what the newspapers are calling you. Penny and I, we kept your name away from the prying pens of the press, just like you asked.'

'I appreciate that,' Crane replied.

'Tell me, did you manage to catch up with that Bradley man?'

'Not yet, although we've had some near misses.'

Girard's eyes widened, 'We?'

Crane told him what had happened since his return to England. Girard listened intently and remarked when Crane finished, 'And I was beginning to think everything was settled but this Bradley is a very dangerous man...' Girard suddenly stopped talking as he stared out of the window into the car park. 'Look!' he said anxiously, 'there's a man out there and he's getting into your Mustang!'

Crane spun round and looked out of the window, his eyes narrowed and he snarled, 'Bradley!'

*

Bradley had been caught in a line of traffic on the outskirts of Boulogne and was about to turn into the N42 road to Bellebrune when he had spotted the Mustang by chance. To the chagrin of other road users, he managed a slick u-turn and, keeping a safe distance, he had followed the Mustang unobserved to the hospital. The notion of a, *"A slight change of plan,"* ran through his brain. Noting where the Mustang was parked, he drove a short distance to the central car park where he left the BMW and then took a cab back to the hospital.

His paranoia began to fade when he figured out that the only possible explanation for Crane's arrival on the scene must have been down to Ryan, *"It's just as well I did for him,"* he thought.

Bradley unlocked the Mustang, using the spare keys he kept in his jacket pocket, and drove the car to where he had parked the BMW and pulled up alongside it and then transferred his luggage into its boot. He placed the holdall, containing the weapons, on the floor in front of the passenger seat of the Mustang. Within seconds, he had started up the car and was chasing across the other side of the city.

*

Crane and Girard stared out of the second floor hospital window as the Mustang veered out of the parking area, through the gates and out of sight. 'I'm afraid your visit has cost you your car once more,' Girard remarked.

Crane shrugged and grinned laconically, 'I'll catch up with him. I have the new French licence plate number and hopefully it can be traced by that.'

Girard flexed his appendage and said, 'My left arm, it is still a little weak, I was lucky; the bullet lodged in an artery and it slowed down the bleeding, strong muscle I guess, eh?' And with a huge grin he added graciously 'but look at me; now I am fine and I am at your service.'

Crane raised a hand and said, 'Thank you, but no, you've done enough to help me,' and glancing at Penny continued, 'besides there's no way I would want to hold up your wedding plans. I'll take it from here.'

As Crane was about to leave, Girard rested a hand on Crane's arm and with a solemn look said, 'Did you know that Mullah is out on bail?'

Crane looked shocked, 'What?'

'At the bail hearing he pleaded health reasons and so with special conditions attached, which nobody thought he would be able to comply with, he got bail; two million euros worth of bail money. He had to surrender his passport, his Bentley has been confiscated and a twenty-four hour police guard stationed at his home; which incidentally, he must pay for until the trial.'

'We both know that kind of money is small change to him; he's got to be up to something.'

Girard nodded as he said, 'That is a fact, *mon ami*.'

'It's a bit of a coincidence that Bradley happens to be in this area; perhaps if I paid a visit to Mullah's helicopter friend Durand, he may have wind of something.'

They spent an hour or so mulling over the possibilities, before they parted company. Crane was deep in thought as he and Daniella left the hospital. Girard stood by the window and rubbed his chin reflectively; staring after them as they walked towards the car park.

'Which direction are we heading for?' Daniella enquired.

'My curiosity has got the better of me; I want to take a peek at Mullah's chateau.'

'Won't the police stop you?'

'I'll say I'm a tourist, looking at old country homes.'

'What do you hope to see there?'

'I don't know – that's the reason I want to go there.'

Daniella shrugged, leant back in her seat and whilst listening to the satnav, browsed through a map of the area. 'There's an old chateau not too far from here,' she read out. Crane gave her a quizzical look and smiling she continued, 'Well, it'll back up your story to the police.'

Within twenty minutes, they passed the weathered sign of *"Chateau du Lac"*. Crane was familiar with the long winding tree-lined drive, which was commonplace throughout France. He slowed down as they approached the old wartime concrete bunker and inched the car towards the building at a snail's pace. Just before the chateau came into view he stopped the car.

Daniella sensed that there was something wrong, 'What's the matter?'

Through the windscreen, Crane's eyes flitted in all directions. 'It doesn't seem right; it's too quiet. I would have expected to see a policeman by now.'

'Maybe they are in the house.'

'Maybe; just keep out of sight and stay here while I take a look.'

Daniella gave him a sideways glance and slipped low in her seat, her eyes peering just over the top of the dashboard. Crane eased himself out of the Rover and crept up until he could see around the bend. There was just one car parked near the front entrance; an empty police car with the driver's door wide open. He began to walk slowly towards the Chateau, his ears and eyes alerted to danger. Suddenly he stopped dead in his tracks. What appeared to be a body lay propped against the wall near to the entrance of the building. A series of bullet holes scarred the wall either side of the victim. *"Machine gun,"* Crane thought as he moved cautiously nearer, until another body came into view sprawled out beside a large bushy shrub. Crane ran a hasty check on the two men; they were dead. Finally, when he rounded the police car, a third policeman lay gasping in front of his car; he was badly wounded. Crane looked around; there was no sign of anyone else. It seemed Mullah had flown and Crane guessed it was the work of Bradley. This was confirmed when the injured man whispered three words: '*American Mustang, Rouge.*'

Crane ran back to his Rover. Daniella, on hearing the rush of feet, straightened up as he jumped in and brought their car alongside the police vehicle, 'There's an injured man

300

lying in front of the police car; you'll find a first aid kit in the boot, see what you can do, meanwhile I'll see if I can get help.'

Daniella leapt out, grabbed the first aid kit and hurried to the casualty.

Wishing to remain anonymous, Crane plucked Ryan's mobile from the glovebox and relieved to find it had remained fully charged, dialled the hospital. '*Parlez-vous Anglais?* I need to speak with Henri Girard.'

'*Je suis désolé,* I am sorry, but he has just discharged himself.'

Crane was grateful that the voice spoke English and said, 'Okay, but an ambulance is urgently needed for a badly-wounded policeman at Chateau du Lac. Do you know of it?'

'*Oui,* satnav takes care of the whole area including buildings, I will see to it right away.'

'Oh,' and Crane added urgently, 'inform the police!'

Crane dashed back to the injured man. Daniella had just finished placing a heavy pad over his wound. 'It's bad, he would have been... how you say... a goner if we hadn't come, I believe he'll survive.'

'I couldn't get hold of Girard. I wanted him to contact the police but would you believe it, he's just left the hospital.'

Daniella looked puzzled, 'Can't you speak to the police?'

'We'd be held up for hours; it's best that the ambulance service sees to it.'

With assurances given to the injured man that help was on its way, Crane and Daniella jumped into the Rover and left.

Crane raced the car down the chateau's long road, its engine sounding like a high bred sports car. Daniella, gripping the sides of her seat asked, 'Where to now?'

'We have two places to call at; a small marina and an airfield.'

Just as they were about to enter the main road, Crane spotted Girard behind the wheel of Penny's Mini Cooper waiting to turn in; Penny was sat next to him. Slamming his foot hard on the brakes, Crane pulled the Rover to one side, allowing Girard to drive up alongside. They were surprised to see Crane. Powering down the window Girard said, 'We have come here to mark out the grave of Penny's sister so that she can be returned home.'

Unwillingly Crane brushed this aside with, 'Mullah has escaped. It's the work of Bradley. He's left two policemen dead and another badly injured. I phoned the hospital, they are sending an ambulance.'

Girard and Penny looked stunned, 'I knew it was wrong to grant him bail,' Girard said, 'where are you going now?'

'The marina and airfield. I'll call you later,' and Crane swung the Rover into the main road heading towards the direction of the marina.

The small, private marina was empty and there were no cars parked nearby. Crane delved into the glovebox and pulled out a small pair of binoculars, whilst Daniella looked idly around. Crane scanned the wide stretch of sea and declared, 'Nothing to be seen; they wouldn't have got away that fast, we'll try the airport.'

Ignoring the car park sign, Crane pulled the Rover up directly outside the office of Hele-Hire. Pierre Durand gave a cursory glance out of the window and froze when he saw who was getting out of the car. Crane pushed the office door and a breeze caused it to slam against the wall inside. Durand leapt up as Crane said, 'Where's your friend, Mullah?'

'I haven't seen him since you were here last,' and with emphasis added, 'and he's *not* my friend. I took his money on a no-questions basis and that's all. Anyway, according to the newspapers, he got bail; didn't he?'

'He jumped it; leaving two policemen dead and one badly wounded.'

Durand looked genuinely surprised and his jaw dropped with a 'What?'

'He got away with the help of Bradley – the guy that stole my Mustang.'

'We've had our differences, but there is one place they may head towards for a hiding place.' As he spoke Durand flipped open a map of the area and placed a finger on a spot, 'There!'

Crane looked at it and said, 'About twenty kilometres from here?'

'That's right, an old building, nice and remote and even nearer to his Chateau du Lac. I dropped him off there just once.' And looking earnest he added, 'Anyway, it's a long shot, but better than nothing eh?'

Crane nodded, 'Thanks for that,' and rejoined Daniella in the Rover.

*

Bradley was increasingly aware that the old Mustang was attracting too much attention. The iconic car turned heads when passing through small villages and country lanes. After dropping Mullah off and getting paid handsomely, he was anxious to take the car out of the area and head for one of the main autoroutes, where it would not be so conspicuous.

*

For the first time in days, Mullah felt at ease with himself. He had bought the old villa as an investment some time ago, before he had acquired the chateau, but he had done nothing with the old place and had no real interest in it, until now. He was always aware that things had to come to a halt sometime but strangely enough, he was totally unprepared when they did. He was a realist and surmised if it was not through Jack Crane, then it would be somebody else. The bloodbath to release him from the police guard, the bail money and confiscation of his chateau – well that was "par for the course" – it still left him a multi-millionaire. Most of his funds were banked in Algiers and he could live like a king anywhere in the world.

Mullah sat relaxed, watching a portable television and sipping wine. One of his henchmen had arranged to whisk him away and he would be calling later in the evening, under cover of darkness to transport him to Algiers.

*

Crane drove back into Boulogne and pulled up outside a hotel. He glanced at Daniella and said, 'I'd feel a lot better if you stayed here while I check things out.'

Daniella looked askance, but before she could reply, Crane put on his best pleading smile and said emphatically, '*Please*, I know what this guy is like, you know when rats are cornered… '

With a wry smile, Daniella raised both hands, 'Okay – just this once.'

Crane felt relieved and stayed in the car as she got out. He waited for a moment, with his elbows leaning on the steering wheel, his eyes taking in her neat figure as she elegantly ascended three shallow steps. She paused, turned and gave a small wave before entering the building.

Within thirty minutes, he entered the outskirts of Mornay and, going by Durand's description, it soon became apparent when the small villa came into view. He drove slowly along the deserted narrow country lane past the dull-grey building. There were no vehicles parked outside and there were no signs of life. All of its dark green shutters were closed. Durand's words – *"a long shot"* – echoed in his head.

However, Crane would not be satisfied until he had made sure the place was empty. Some metres along the lane, he found a convenient place where he could tuck the Rover out of sight of the villa. He clambered out and looked up; the sky was heavy with cloud, bringing the onset of dusk closer. He made his way along the narrow footpath, which edged the lane, towards the building; carefully approaching a windowless flank wall. He pressed an ear against the wall before slowly making his way around to the front. A faint noise wafted through one of the shutters; it was a TV or radio. At that moment, Crane wished that he was armed. Carefully he inched towards the front door, which was recessed in a porch. Gingerly, he placed a hand on the door knob and tried turning it, but without success. He was about to reach in his pocket for a small bunch of skeleton keys, when a well oiled metallic click made him freeze; 'Just turn yourself around slowly, Mr Crane.'

Crane did as he was told and came face to face with Mullah, whose right arm was extended, with a Glock firmly grasped in his hand.

'What now?'

Mullah's face was contorted with hate as he spat, 'Follow the path to the rear of the villa.'

# CHAPTER TWENTY SEVEN

Bradley had decided to have the stolen Mustang transported to Almeria in Southern Spain. If he drove the car himself there was a risk of being recorded on the numerous CCTV cameras en route. This, he thought, would also enable him to recover his BMW which he had left in the Boulogne car park. He was feeling smug because some days earlier, one of his nefarious contacts had given him a phone number suggesting that he could rent the iconic Mustang to a movie company, which was soon to film a short contemporary western commercial for a television station. He had phoned the company and the producer told him that the movie involved the use of classic American cars and he considered the Ford Mustang would be well suited for a part. He added that the company was prepared to pay twenty thousand euros, plus expenses, for a three-day shoot. Bradley loved that kind of money. It was not long before he was pulling up outside the removal company that would take the Mustang on one of its vehicle transporters – under wraps – to Southern Spain.

After all this had been completed, Bradley intended to drive the Mustang to the port at Malaga with a view to shipping it to the USA, where it would fetch a good price.

\*

Crane stared at the gun that Mullah was pointing at him. In the distance he heard the low-geared whine of a heavy vehicle and, as he saw it lumber along the road towards them, he looked over Mullah's shoulder and casually said, 'Refuse men calling, eh?'

Mullah flicked his head to one side for a fraction of a second. That was all it took for Crane to perform a high kick. He knocked the Glock skywards and sent a bullet soaring harmlessly into the clouds, while the weapon clattered, as it fell close to Crane's feet. Like a spring, he coiled down, snatched at the handgun and bounced upright again, now with the gun pointed at Mullah's head. Mullah's expression of hate turned to one of shocked surprise and fear. Crane's eyes darted from the Glock to Mullah, 'Latest model, eh?' Crane said calmly, 'Now what I want to know is, where can I find your friend, Bradley?'

There was no reply until Crane pointed the gun at Mullah's left leg. This kicked the Algerian into action as well as verbal panic. 'He has left,' he wailed, 'he's gone!'

Still aiming the gun Crane said, 'Where to?'

'South… Spain, Southern Spain!'

In the intensity of the situation, both men had ignored the sound of a heavy vehicle that had come to a halt a few metres beyond the front gate of the villa. It was some forty metres from where they stood. A sharp incentive for Crane to take heed of the vehicle came when he saw a swarthy scowling man on the path, gun in hand, walking slowly towards them. A bullet zinged past Crane's head and splintered into the wooden door frame behind. Crane grabbed Mullah, to use as a shield. He was shaking with fear, as Crane hissed scathingly, 'If you move, it will be last thing you'll ever do!'

The approaching, brutish-looking stranger, halted in his tracks. It was a standoff. They stood there, quiet for a few moments, then another voice with an accent that was music to Crane's ears came from behind the stranger, 'Put the gun down or I'll drop you where you stand.'

Now it was the swarthy stranger who hesitated, estimating his chances. He considered the voice, with a French accent, was convincing and urgent. He threw a glance at Crane, who was partially concealed behind Mullah. Then very slowly he bent down, to place his weapon on the ground but as he moved forward, he suddenly fell flat, rolled on his back, sat up and fired low at the voice behind him – Girard. In an instant, Crane jumped out from behind Mullah, ran forward and with both hands gripping the handgun, sent three bullets towards the stranger; two of which struck him in the shoulder. The man gradually crumpled and slumped to the ground.

Crane ran towards Girard, kicking the stranger's gun out of the way as he passed. Girard lay prone, eyes slowly blinking as Crane approached. As he bent down, Crane could see that his brave friend, Girard was unarmed.

'Good to see you again so soon, *mon ami*,' Girard murmured breathlessly.

Looking concerned Crane said, 'Where are you hit?'

Girard tried to smile and said, 'I'm not. I'm winded not wounded. When that guy turned and fired I tell you, I've never hit the deck so quick before in my life!'

Crane breathed a sigh of relief, just as they both heard the truck engine spring to life with Mullah behind the wheel. Crane was about to chase after him when Girard pulled out his mobile phone and said, 'Let the gendarmes take care of him. I've noted the truck's number; he won't get very far.'

Still feeling winded, Girard eased himself up, dusted himself down and remarked, 'Will you look at that, I've just soiled a clean shirt.'

'How did you know I was here?'

Girard shrugged and said, 'I spoke to the helicopter pilot, Durand, on the phone and he told me what he had told you, so... here I am.'

Crane smiled and said, 'Next time you threaten to shoot someone make sure you have a gun.'

Again Girard shrugged, in a way that only Frenchmen do, 'Our trade, it sometimes calls for bluff, wouldn't you agree?'

'Where would we be without them.'

*

Bradley was feeling pleased with himself as he leant back in the car seat in a relaxed state listening to a local station on the car radio. He had retrieved his BMW and was driving along the A16 autoroute from Boulogne. He was still congratulating himself when the music, that he had been listening to, was interrupted by a newsflash. His command of the French language was sufficient enough for him to understand that Mullah had been recaptured. Anxiety took hold of him; he hoped that Mullah would not implicate him. He felt certain that, sooner or later, the man would squeal, but then he began to feel confident again; at least he would be crossing the border into Spain long before that would arise.

*

Crane joined Daniella in the hotel where they intended to stay the night. Over the evening meal Daniella said, 'Well? I'm bursting at the seams. You haven't told me what happened?'

Crane made light of it and said, 'Not much really, Girard turned up and… '

'Girard! How did he get there?'

'It's a long story, but well… erm, the guy, Mullah, he got away, but Girard called the police and they eventually caught up with him.'

Daniella gave Crane a suspicious look and said, 'I feel there's something missing, but you're back and I guess I'm relieved at that.'

*

Bradley's conjecture about Mullah was correct. Within twenty-four hours, in order to save his own skin, Mullah had told the police everything he knew about Bradley. As a consequence, Bradley was a wanted man for the murder of two policemen and a woman found buried in the grounds of Mullah's chateau. Bradley had just crossed the mountains and was well over the border and into Spain when he heard the news on one of the French radio stations.

Bradley congratulated himself. He had the foresight to change the number plates on the BMW he was driving and on the Mustang that was being transported south. In case he was stopped at the border, he was wearing a false moustache and carrying a different corresponding passport.

*

Crane checked the flights to Almeria, but vacant seats were three days away and so there was no option; they would have to drive. According to the satnav, it would take about sixteen hours. He thought it would be a challenge to do it quicker, but then he would not want to give Daniella a white knuckle ride, besides, they would share the driving. Daniella looked fondly at her companion and said anxiously, 'This Bradley man, he has killed two French policemen and seriously injured a third. Do you think it may be better to help the police find him?'

Crane looked pensive for a moment before he replied, 'I tried the police right from the beginning at home in England; it comes down to time and evidence.'

There was a pause and Daniella began to worry again, 'The wounded policeman... '

Crane cut in, 'Probably didn't know what or who hit him, besides it's become far too personal; I'll do it my way... and if he's lucky, I'll hand him over to the police.'

\*

The movie studios were set amongst the arid hills of Almeria, a few kilometres from the small town of Tabernas. Crane and Daniella could not fail to be impressed by the grey, dry, dusty-looking terrain. In years gone by, the studios had been famed for producing hundreds of so-called "spaghetti westerns". Crane pulled the Rover into the parking lot and approached the main entrance of the studios. They stepped from an air-conditioned car into the dry stifling-hot day, that was totally lacking any kind of humidity. Eager attendants, with cameras at the ready, rushed to greet them. For a few euros, they would be ready to dress the pair up, complete with western-style guns, in less than a minute, in order to snap an authentic looking picture. Crane threw up both hands and said, '*Habla Inglais?*'

'*Un poco* – a leetle,' came the smiling response with shrugging shoulders.

Crane enquired about movie making. With shrugged shoulders and smiles, the attendants, who resembled Mexican bandits, said they were sorry and told them that movies were no longer made there; the studio location was for tourists only. As they were about to leave, one of the bandits called out grinning, 'Maybe the other one – leave here – go right – maybe three kilometres further on.'

Back on the road, Crane spotted a small insignificant signpost pointing in the direction of a grey, dust-laden desert trail. Leaving the main road they found themselves on a track, which was more fit for a wagon and horses. The twists and turns of the track where it skirted around dry riverbeds, made the area look as though water was a far distant memory. Crane glanced in the rear-view mirror at the dense cloud of shimmering dust spiralling skywards in the Rover's wake and began to wonder if there had been some mistake: a wrong turn, a wild goose chase, a sign misplaced perhaps. There was no sign of civilisation.

After several kilometres of anxious uncertainty, they suddenly came across a mock stockade with high wooden surrounds, the kind Indians attack in Hollywood movies, but this was not Hollywood, it was sited in the only desert in Europe. It was unbelievably desolate. Just beyond the stockade, like an oasis, lay a complete western town. Daniella giggled and childhood memories flooded back, as excitement mingled with anticipation.

Crane parked the Rover amid a number of classic American cars, some of which were covered and loaded on transporters. He paid the entrance fee at the car park kiosk and walked up to an area that was covered by cine-graphic equipment. Cameras and lighting were suspended on overhead gantries and there was a, far more realistic, Wild West town that lay in front of them. The film crew consisted of mixed nationalities, but were mainly Italian and English. They were told by one of the crew, 'Some of the places will be off limits while filming takes place.'

They also found out, from the crew man, that it was just as Ryan had told Crane from the hospital bed; a three-day shoot of an advertisement for some Italian television company. Crane thanked the friendly crew member for the information and together with Daniella skirted around the area. Men and women were busy setting up lighting on one of the boardwalks, and Crane felt satisfied that he had found the right place. This was at last confirmed when he saw his Mustang being offloaded from one of the transporters and set down at the edge of the mock town.

*

Bradley felt at ease whilst driving across Spain and, upon arriving at the port in Malaga, he sold the left-hand drive BMW that he had been using to a local Spanish worker at a 'knock down price'. This was on the proviso that the new owner would drive him to the movie set in Almeria.

Bradley was pleased with himself. In spite of recent setbacks, everything was going to plan. It took a little over two and a half hours for the BMW's new owner to drive him from the port to Almeria and then to the movie set near Tabernas. When the movie company had finished using the Mustang, he planned to drive it back to Malaga, where it would be containered for shipping to the USA.

Bradley arrived at the mock-up Western town in time to see the Mustang being offloaded from the transporter, under the watchful eye of the film company's props man. A small gathering surrounded the vehicle, extolling their approval of the vehicles appearance and condition. After brief introductions, one of the film unit's crew led Bradley to a refreshment trailer which was set up near one of the saloons.

In common with many people, Bradley had never been to a movie studio or a film set before, so he was invited to take himself and look around whilst preparations were being made for the company to start filming. The buildings were substantial and some of the interiors were used for inside takes. One of the rooms contained a wardrobe which was filled with prop clothes for current use.

Another room, much larger than the previous, was set aside with a selection of nineteenth century weapons. Winchester rifles were slotted in a long line on a wall rack. Single action Colt and Remington pistols were neatly laid out on a table. These were taken out and fired whenever a Wild West show was put on for the public. The weapons were working copies of the real thing; exact replicas made in Italy by Umberto.

Bradley could not resist picking up one of the old handguns. It was a short-barrelled weapon, the kind they use for a fast draw. It was known as a Colt Peacemaker and, as he spun the chamber, he noted that it was fully loaded with six cartridges. The handguns however, were very weighty, when compared to a much lighter modern piece like the Glock. Helping himself to a leather belt, he strapped it on, slotted a short barrelled Colt into its holster and walked over to a full length mirror. He stood for a moment, turning and admiring himself from different angles and began practising quick draw, although his attempts at this skill were somewhat clumsy. Whilst he was doing this the door opened. Bradley, feeling a little peeved at this interruption, stared hard into the mirror at the intruders who had just entered the far end of the room. They were no more than six metres away from him. Crane and Daniella stood, framed in the entrance, casting their eyes around the room until Crane noticed someone at the far end. He began with, 'I'm sorry I didn't realise… ' his voice trailed off.

Through the mirror, their eyes met and locked together for a split second. Both men, remained motionless, staring at each other in disbelief, astonished to be at such close quarters. Bradley quickly recovered, spun round, drew the Colt and levelled it towards Crane. Anticipating this obvious move, Crane pushed Daniella away through the open door. Bradley snarled as he thumbed back the hammer of the single action forty-five calibre pistol and pulled the trigger. A loud ear-splitting blast sent a flash of fiery flame spewing from its barrel.

Crane had already seen the neat display of guns spread out on a table in the centre of the room and he dropped down, rolled over on the floor towards them and quickly snatched at a long barrelled Remington New Army model. Bradley loosed off two more shots. Crane darted behind a cupboard but as he returned the fire, the realisation dawned upon him; the handguns were loaded with blanks.

Crane stood up and Bradley threw his head back sneering as he cocked the hammer once more and aiming at Crane's chest, pulled the trigger, quickly repeating the action. As the smoke cleared, Crane began to move towards him. Bradley felt cheated and muttered, 'Fucking blanks,' and in classic Western movie style, threw the gun at Crane's head and made for the open door. Crane dodged out of the way and ran across the room after him. Stumbling towards the exit, he bumped into a shocked Daniella. Relief spread across her face as she began, 'I thought you were… '

'Not yet; the guns were loaded with blanks.'

Daniella began to laugh nervously with relief as Crane said, 'Where did he go?'

She raised an arm pointing, 'Down the side alley,' and she remained by the door of the now empty room, as Crane chased along the narrow opening. Crane poked his head around the end and cast his eyes along the rear of the buildings. A cowboy gun-belt lay in the dust but Bradley was nowhere to be seen, so he guessed that, like himself, Bradley must have left his gun somewhere else. Crane remained still for a moment; listening intently for sounds that might betray Bradley's whereabouts, but all was quiet. Then, at the far end of town, a shout resonated, 'Action!' And the whole area was brought to life with instant shuffling, bustling and a general cacophony of noise.

Unseen, Crane and Daniella skirted the players acting out their scene and wandered back to where they had left the Rover. It was parked in a strategic position and when they got in it, they were able to eye everyone who was coming or going. They stayed there for some time, gazing at the actors, entering the saloons and lazily strolling along the boarded sidewalks on cue. There were many shouts of, 'Action,' and

'Cut,' until eventually there came a call for a lunch break. As they got out of the car, Crane pocketed the handgun which he had removed from the glove box. They walked over to a group of filmmakers. Crane sidled up to the director of the unit, whose face was buried in a huge sandwich, 'Excuse me, do you know the whereabouts of the guy that brought the Mustang here?'

In between gulps of coffee the director replied, 'Sorry – never even met him. You might try the props guy, he's around somewhere.'

However, unlike the director, who had his name on the chair, 'the props guy' was difficult to locate amongst the sea of faces.

*

Substantial white-washed replica buildings of a Mexican-style church and village were conveniently located immediately adjacent to the Western town but this area was not being used for filming. Bradley's view from the white church bell tower was restricted. He kept an eye on Crane and Daniella as they drifted across the parking area and out of view. He had sighted the refuge whilst scampering out of Crane's way, during which time he had managed to collect the Glock handgun from the holdall which he had left in one of the changing room lockers. He regretted, that given the distance, it would be pointless trying to use the weapon, he knew a rifle would have been ideal.

*

Crane eventually found the props man at the edge of the film set but trying to explain the ownership of the Mustang was difficult, because the man was Italian. He could not speak much English and his interpreter was unavailable. However, at this point in time, the director was now calling everyone back to their positions to recommence filming and Crane and Daniella were politely required to leave the set. Crane had no wish to incur the wrath of the security personnel and so, with a view to contacting the props man later, they withdrew from the area and wandered off the set into the replica Mexican town.

From his hiding place in the tower, Bradley watched the pair, like a hawk, as they sauntered around. He was in a quandary; he could either conceal himself or take them both by surprise. He decided to remain where he was but, as a precaution, he took out the Glock and screwed on a suppressor, ready for action.

Crane paused for a moment and regarded his surroundings. He spoke quietly to Daniella, moving to one side as he did so, 'Follow me.'

They were out of sight of the bell tower and tugging the handgun from his trouser waistband, Crane said in hushed tones, 'That church tower; it's an ideal place to snipe from.'

'Do you think he's still here?'

'I'm certain of it and there's only one way to find out.' Crane pulled back the slide on his semi-automatic, stepped into the middle of the road took aim and sent two nine mil bullets into the opening of the bell tower.

Bradley was well hidden at the top of the church tower and knew that he couldn't be seen, but the ricocheting slugs around the small space unnerved him. He concluded that

Crane was only guessing and he was not going to be drawn into a gunfight until he had the clear advantage. He slid down the ladder and exited through the back door, stealthily making his way behind the buildings until he came to the edge of the dusty road that turned into a Wild West section. Hoping to come up behind Crane and the woman, he gradually inched his way out onto the side of the road, but was disappointed to find they had disappeared.

Bradley dodged back into the shadows. He paused, standing framed in the doorway of a building. He listened intently but he found it difficult, because of the cacophony of sound that emanated from the movie makers in the adjacent street. Daniella, not daring to move, was propped against the shadowy wall inside. Her trembling hands were clasped firmly over her mouth. Her eyes were wide with fear as she watched every move of his silhouette a few metres away. A silenced gun dangled menacingly from his right hand. Bradley suddenly lifted his head and sniffed the air; his nostrils were filled with the unmistakeable scent of a woman's perfume.

*"They must be near,"* he thought, as he thrust his head out of the doorway and looked up and down the street. Empty. Bradley did not like a cat and mouse game, unless of course, he held a distinct advantage. To Daniella's intense relief, he slipped out of the doorway and keeping in the shadows, made his way back to the props room; he guessed Crane would not visit there a second time.

Crane decided that Bradley was no longer there – if he had been there at all – and walked back to where he had left Daniella. He was about to whisper her name when she rushed towards him, throwing extended arms around his body and said shakily, 'I felt certain he would see me. Don't leave me again, and I don't even care if bullets are flying!'

He comforted her until she calmed a little.

Crane and Daniella made their way back to the extreme edge of the western town and looked over the parking area. It was a haphazard arrangement; about fifty vehicles in all. They seemed to be scattered all over the place and Crane could not pin anything down that might have belonged to Bradley.

The pair eventually walked back to their Rover. Crane settled back in the driver's seat and said, 'I reckon we'll have to wait until they finish filming for the day. Most of the company guys will probably drift off except for security. Those that do stay here will use the large caravans.'

Daniella was relieved to escape the tension of the last few hours and, reaching for the thermos, poured out the remains of the coffee in two plastic cups and as she handed one to Crane said, 'Not very warm, but I need something to settle my nerves.'

Crane took the cup and with a smile commented, 'I thought you had nerves of steel.'

'Usually, but they are beginning to erm, wear thin. Wear thin, is that correct expression?'

Crane nodded and looked at her for a moment, he thought she was showing signs of strain, 'I'd feel a lot happier if you were to stay in a hotel until I finish this once and for all. Perhaps it won't take any more than a day to sort things out.'

She gave a half smile, inwardly pleased at his concern and began, 'I should only worry... '

'There's no need to,' Crane cut in, 'but it would be reassuring to know you are safe.'

*

'Cut!' The director's voice screeched bad-temperedly through a loudhailer. The raucous sound boomed across the set, bringing an abrupt halt to the filming. Everyone froze – like a photograph – and all went quiet, their eyes transfixed on the man standing next to a high camera boom.

The director used his loud hailer once more and pointing with his free hand shouted, 'You! Who are you and what are you doing?'

A sea of eyes followed the pointing finger and became focused on Bradley who was strolling nonchantly in the middle of the street. Bradley looked up and said calmly, 'I'm taking my car back now.'

The props man threw a glance at the director, signalled to his interpreter and together they rushed up to the strolling Bradley, 'You can't, we haven't finished with it, besides we have a contract and I paid you cash for three days.'

Bradley produced his Glock handgun and waved it at him, 'This is an amendment to the contract; it's now null and fucking void.'

The props man and his interpreter said no more; they shrunk back, their faces registering shock. The director couldn't make out what was going on, but he understood enough to call on security through the hailer. Two men moved forward, but stopped dead in their tracks, when Bradley loosed off a shot, sending a bullet in their direction, which thudded into a sign board above their heads. Bradley climbed into the Mustang and, spinning the rear wheels, exited the film set, shrouding it in a cloud of dust.

Bradley's unexpected move took Crane by surprise. A red streak, its rear wheels churning up clouds of grey, choking particles of dirt, which infuriated everyone in its wake as it flashed past their parked Rover. Daniella was the first to break the silence with, 'Isn't that… '

'My Mustang,' Crane finished.

# CHAPTER TWENTY EIGHT

Bradley kept his foot hard down on the Mustang's accelerator. He handled the car well, negotiating the twists and turns on the dusty track, by allowing the rear wheels to slither violently from side to side, at high speed, until he reached the main road. Without stopping or taking heed of any other approaching vehicle, the tyres screeched as its V8 engine powered the car in the direction of the E15, the route to the port at Malaga and then, for the Mustang, onwards to the USA.

Crane reacted like a lounging cat who had idly spotted a mouse, he came instantly out of his repose. In a split second, his hand rocketed towards the ignition and, slamming the car into gear, he brought the Rover around to follow in Bradley's dusty wake. Without comment, Daniella tightened her safety belt, bracing herself against this erratic performance by clinging to the sides of her seat and pressing her feet hard into the floor. Crane surmised that this may be his last chance to snatch Bradley. He paused briefly at the main tarmac road, waiting for the dust to settle, revealing fresh tyre marks clearly pointing towards the direction Bradley had taken – the E15 dual autovia motorway that leads to Malaga.

*

Bradley kept an eye on the rear-view mirror; he expected to be followed. The E15 was clear in both directions except for a tiny dark spec, like a dirty mark on the mirror, in the distance. He felt confident that the V8 Mustang, with its special Shelby conversion, now registering one hundred and fifteen mph on the speedo, would outrun Crane's old Rover. For a while, Bradley's mind focused upon Crane being able to predict his whereabouts all the time and concluded that it all pointed to Ryan. If Ryan had not told Crane in person, then somehow Crane must have got hold of his mobile phone; that idiot Ryan was too idle to erase anything. Bradley concluded his thinking with the question of the port at Malaga; he was absolutely certain that he had never mentioned the port to anyone.

As he drove, he could see in the distance to one side, the snow capped mountains of the great Sierra Nevada looming ominously against a deep-blue sky. His eyes flicked towards the rear-view mirror; the tiny speck had grown much larger but it was not yet identifiable, even so, it niggled Bradley. As a precaution, he decided that he would leave the motorway. Almost immediately, a series of bends came into view, and between two curves, he took an exit heading towards the Sierras. He kept an eye on the rear-view mirrors as the car glided down a gradient off of the main highway, and knowing he could not be seen by anyone behind, felt euphoric as the car disappeared from view.

*

Crane's Rover shot past the Sierra turn off, and after another curve, the motorway straightened out, stretching into the distance. 'Lost him,' Crane muttered more to himself than his passenger, 'he's turned off!'

Breaking all the rules, Crane jammed his foot on the brakes and slewed to a halt and, putting the car into reverse, he backed along the hard shoulder for three kilometres.

'Glovebox,' he said to Daniella. 'Inside you'll find a black plastic device that looks like a mobile phone; it's a tracker.'

Daniella leaned forward as her hand darted inside and came out holding the tracker.

'There's a switch on the side,' Crane added.

Daniella flipped it on and almost immediately a distinct beep filled the car with its repetitive noise. She held the tracker in her hand, steadily pulsing away. She looked at the tiny LCD screen, indicating direction and distance, while Crane swung the car into the Sierra exit.

'Do you know I almost forgot the tracker was in there. Never thought I'd need it. It's old army surplus but it only has a range of about fifteen miles. Tell me, what's on the screen?'

Daniella read out, 'He is three point two miles distant, direction North West. Would he know he is being followed?'

'Not unless he catches sight of me. There's a transmitter that I built into the chassis some time ago, it would be very difficult to find, so providing he is not out of range, we'll know exactly where he is heading and we'll eventually catch up with him. I hate to admit it, but this old souped up Rover is much faster than the Mustang.'

Bradley chided himself for being over cautious. There was no hurry to get to the port at Malaga. The ship, on which he had reserved space for the Mustang, was not due to sail for a week. The thought lightened his mood and also as he took account of the winding road, he eased up on the accelerator and resolved to stop at the next convenient roadside cafe.

Within two kilometres a small village came into view. Bradley pulled off the road and parked near to a small bar. There were only a few people inside the surprisingly cool and ornately tiled interior and the friendly waiter responded quickly to Bradley's, '*Cerveza, por favor*,' immediately setting down a San Miguel beer onto the table together with a plate of tapas. From where he sitting, he threw an occasional glance towards the Mustang. It was in full view, however he did not see the Rover pull up some metres behind.

Crane looked at Daniella and delved into a pocket and produced a set of keys for the Mustang, 'Follow me up in the Rover and once we are out of the town, I'll contact Gerard and he can get the French police to alert the authorities in Spain of Bradley's whereabouts.'

Bradley ordered another beer and just as he was taking his first sip he saw something from the corner of his eye that distracted him; the Mustang began to move. Slamming the glass down he rose up in a panic, stumbling across the bar. Turning heads watched curiously and shrugged shoulders as he pushed chairs out of the way, thrusting himself towards the door, but it was too late; Crane had driven the Mustang away. Anger and frustration rose in him. Immediately his eyes darted towards the Rover and he ran towards it. Daniella, sitting in the driver's seat, had put the car in gear, but her foot slipped on the clutch and the engine stalled. She was busy staring at the dashboard, watching her right hand as it turned the ignition key. She did not see Bradley run up towards her, not until he grabbed hold of the rear door handle, yanked back the door and threw himself inside. Daniella felt her breath drain away as the engine fired up and Bradley, scrambling in his pocket for the Glock, sank low in the rear seat and snarled, 'Get going then, you don't want to lose him do you? Oh, and don't do anything silly or this gun may go off.'

Daniella glanced nervously at Bradley through the rearview mirror as she followed the Mustang. It seemed to both her, and to Bradley, that Crane was totally oblivious to what had happened.

'How did he find me?' Bradley snapped.

Daniella hesitated, but before she could utter a word, Bradley continued matter-of-factly as though talking to himself, 'His car is obviously fitted with a tracking device; we checked it over, but couldn't find one, it must have been well hidden.'

After a few kilometres, Crane stopped the Mustang in a lay-by and waited for Daniella to catch up. Peering between the front seats, Bradley ordered her to pull the Rover in behind the Mustang. 'Stay in the car,' Bradley hissed, 'let him get out and come to you.'

Daniella sat still and remained quiet. She watched Crane as he leapt out of the Mustang and walk nonchantly towards the Rover with his hands in his pockets.

Crane glanced briefly at Daniella's terrified face – staring blankly at him through the windscreen – but his eyes were focused on the top of Bradley's barely discernible head tucked behind the driver's seat. It was no surprise to him, when Bradley showed his hand, revealing the semi-automatic resting on the back of Daniella's head, but Crane had been expecting this and in the same split second brought his right-pocketed hand up and shouted, 'You shoot her and I'll make you suffer before I kill you.'

Bradley was not expecting this move. His mind raced as Crane pulled the jacket away with his free hand revealing the semi-automatic Glock. Daniella, although tense, felt a breath of relief pass through her but there was no chance of leaning over or falling to one side; her movements were restricted by the firm embrace of the seat belt.

All three remained inanimate for a few seconds, until Bradley called out, 'Consider this; give me the Mustang and the tracker and nobody gets hurt.'

Crane thought for a moment before agreeing, 'Okay, but I need to get the tracker out of the Mustang.'

'Then be quick about it. Step well back from the car while we get out,' Bradley cautioned, adding, 'we don't want any accidents do we?'

With the gun still aimed at Bradley, Crane backed off towards the Mustang, a few metres away, opened the passenger door and held the tracking device high in the air, 'Here,' he called out.

'Put it on the boot lid,' Bradley snarled, 'and step away from the car.'

Crane moved back, but kept his gun trained on his adversary.

Bradley gripped Daniella's arm with one hand and held the gun trained on the back of her head with the other hand, as they walked towards the Mustang.

'Open the door,' he commanded and Daniella reached forward opening the door to its full extent.

'She comes with me,' Bradley called out to Crane.

'No way!' Crane replied steely, his grip on the handgun unwavering as he levelled the Glock at Bradley.

Bradley let go of Daniella's arm, but still held the gun to

her head, as he swung himself into the car behind the steering wheel. For a brief instant Daniella saw Bradley's gun hand waver as he groped for the ignition. Seizing the opportunity, in that split second, she threw herself out of the way onto a grassy verge, with all the force that she could muster. At the same time, the engine fired up and Bradley crashed it into gear, ramming his foot down hard. The Mustang sped off leaving the driver's door to slam shut from the momentum.

Crane lowered his gun and, with some concern he rushed up to Daniella, 'You okay?'

She got up, brushing herself down with her hands, 'I am now,' and with a smile of relief said, 'what next?'

'We tail him.' Crane produced the tracker from his jacket pocket as they walked towards the Rover and climbed in.

'I thought you handed it to him.'

'I did, but I had a spare; it was duff. I saw him get into the back of the Rover. I'll follow at a distance from now on and when there's a chance of a hotel... '

'Promises, promises, you're just trying to cheer me up.'

\*

Bradley was disappointed that he had not been able to nail Crane, but was elated once again at the thought of retrieving the Mustang and his ego came in to play big-time, *"Nobody gets the better of me!"* He decided to put some distance between his encounter with Crane and drove for seventy-odd kilometres heading towards Motril, eventually nestling in amongst the traffic in and around the town. He continued to keep a lookout for a hotel, with car parking facilities, where he could tuck the Mustang out of sight; well away from curious eyes.

*

Jack Crane kept a distance of two kilometres from his adversary, but edged much closer when he entered Motril, a large commercial town near to the coast. Daniella, held the tracker like a mobile phone, continually looking at the tiny screen when she announced, 'He's stopped and the signal is fading, are the batteries okay?'

'They're brand new. Maybe he's entered an underground car park; that would weaken the signal. How far away is he?'

'Not far off; about one hundred metres.'

'Okay, let's find a place to park and we'll go on foot.'

Crane managed to park on the main road and, after feeding the meter, they looked around the immediate area. An underground car park was sited nearby which was an obvious choice to start with. However they had no success there. Widening the circle a little, they came across a hotel with a sign that indicated secure parking for guests. Crane looked at Daniella and remarked, 'Now that's a fair bet.'

Daniella shuddered at another possible encounter and said, 'Going from bitter past experience, do you think the police should check this one out?'

'The police could do it. The downside is that answering their questions could take up a lot of time and Bradley could be elsewhere, so I need to make sure he is in the hotel.'

Crane nodded towards the other side of the road and added, 'In the meantime, there's a nice little tapas bar across the road. It may be best if you wait for me there.'

Daniella readily agreed, pecked him on the cheek with her parting words of, 'Do be careful.'

Crane smiled and said quietly, 'I always am.'

Daniella crossed the road, entering the tapas bar and settled down with a coffee by the front window, facing the hotel.

Crane ran back to where he had parked the car and, delving into his holdall, pulled out a beanie hat which he put it on. Next he grabbed hold of his sunglasses and checked himself in the mirror. *"Reasonable,'* he thought, *'but not quite."* Digging further into his holdall he felt thankful he had stowed away some things that he had not used for quite a while; a moustache and a small tube of spirit glue. Within five minutes his disguise was complete and he strode boldly towards the El Mundo Hotel.

Crane, upon entering the main swing doors, rounded his shoulders to add to his makeshift disguise. Looking around, he found the foyer to be unattended, but chatter echoed through from an adjacent bar. He spotted the hotel register lying on top of the desk and quickly checked the latest entries; no English names were listed. His next move was to enter the bar. No one seemed to as notice he sauntered in and out. Then, back in the foyer, he looked over the information notice board which gave details, in four languages, of the location of its sixty rooms and, more importantly, the underground garage.

A lift was positioned next to the staircase and, looking around to make sure he was unobserved, Crane quickly leapt inside and descended to the basement garage. He stepped out and stood still by the lift for a few moments, whilst he adjusted his eyes to the dim lighting. Looking around, he was surprised to find that most of the parking area spaces were taken but, within seconds, he noticed with relief a red car in a corner. It was almost hidden between two pillars; there stood his cherished Mustang! Crane strode up to the car and producing his spare set of keys, unlocked the door, but as he began to open it, a gruff accented voice called out menacingly, '¡Quítate de ahí!'

Crane spun round to find a stocky well-built man standing several metres away.

'This is my… ' Crane began, but was immediately interrupted by the man advancing threateningly with another gruff order, this time in English, 'Get out of here!'

It went against the grain but Crane decided that it was best to comply, so he threw his hands up into the air and, shaking his head, said, 'Okay, okay, I'm going!'

The man's fierce eyes followed Crane as he walked towards the lift but, when stepping inside the open doors, Crane found he could not resist giving the man a cheerful wave goodbye.

Back in the tapas bar Daniella gazed through the window at Crane as he crossed the road with a huge grin on his face. She greeted him with, 'You've found it then?'

'Yeah, now I can sit back, get the ball rolling and call the… ' He stopped short of saying police. His eyes widened when the Mustang suddenly roared out of the hotel's underground car park, joining a stream of traffic and then disappearing from view.

*

Bradley had been comfortably settled in an armchair in his hotel room, sipping a large brandy, when the garage attendant phoned through and told him that someone had tried to get into his Mustang. 'What does he look like?'

Apart from the beanie hat, sunglasses and moustache, the English accent and build would fit Crane. The information spooked Bradley so he decided to leave – fast! As he approached the exit of the garage, he paused and looked up and down the street. He could see no sign of Crane's old Rover, so he pulled out and blended in with the constant stream of traffic. His mind settled down on getting out of Motril and he concluded that, if it was Crane back at the hotel wearing a disguise, then it figured that he must still have a tracking device. He guessed that the tracker may be old and must have been hidden well inside the chassis, in any event he concluded that it would have a limited range.

He kept a constant eye on the mirror for the Rover as he drove the car back on to the E15 coast road, but could see no sign of it. He drove on to the dual carriageway where the Mustang was able to perform at a constant speed. With it came the reassurance of outdistancing Crane.

Maybe the intruder in the garage was not Crane; just someone being curious, or even a potential thief. He considered that perhaps he was being over cautious, but then, that was how he had survived, over the years, since his escape from Broadmoor.

*

It took Crane twenty minutes to get the Rover out of the public underground car park and back onto the road but, all the time, the Mustang was gaining ground. Stuck in a stream of traffic, Daniella, looking intently at the tiny tracker screen, said, 'He's fifteen kilometres away; fifteen was its range right?'

'In miles, not kilometres; there's a button on the side to change over.'

Daniella pressed a button, converting the distance and read out, 'Nine miles away and going to... ten.'

By the time Crane reached the E15 dual carriageway, the tracker was near its limit of fifteen miles, but now, at the edge of Almunecar, an ancient coastal town, he picked up the dual carriageway and, with the help of the Rover's twin-turbos, he gradually began to narrow the gap.

The signal disappeared completely as they travelled through a series of tunnels but, when it reappeared, they realised that they were closing the gap. However, after the fifth tunnel as they drove out of Granada Province into Malaga Province, the screen did not reappear and the tracker remained silent.

'Battery's good; green light is still on,' Daniella commented, 'maybe the Mustang is in a tunnel.'

'Maybe,' Crane echoed grimly.

\*

Bradley turned off the motorway at the coastal town of Nerja and shortly after doing so, noticed a wide stretch of water – which had accumulated from recent a downpour – trickling into the Rio Chillar. He had an idea. Still obsessed by the thought of a transmitter hidden somewhere in the chassis, he drove down a slight incline to investigate further. When he was satisfied that he would not get bogged down, he eased the Mustang into the water until it was up to the bottom of the door sills in the hope that whatever was hidden in the chassis, water would flood through the hollow structure and cause a short circuit, permanently damaging the device. He was right, however, it not only knocked out the transmitter, but also fused the source of its power: the ignition switch.

Bradley's self-satisfied feeling deflated. He began to feel hot around the collar when the realisation dawned upon him that the device had been wired directly into the ignition. In disbelief, he turned the key several times, without response. He checked the glove box for spare fuses; there were none. He got out of the car and cursed as the water filled his shoes and ran up his legs. He waded round to the front, opened the bonnet and searched. He saw nothing that resembled a fuse box.

With dripping wet feet he got back into the car and looked under the dashboard until at last he saw a small, black kick panel near the steering column. He removed the burnt out fuse and replaced it with the one that operates the headlamps. However, as soon as he tried to start the car, the fuse blew again. The only chance to stop this from happening would be to disconnect the wire that ran under the car, but the problem was, which one? He could easily use up the other high amp fuses in trying.

Bradley now realised that the best way out would be to get the car out of the water. He remembered a garage that he had passed, no more than a kilometre away; perhaps they could pull him out with a tow truck. He checked his watch. It was late afternoon, and so grabbing his large black holdall, he walked along the edge of the watercourse and onto the road.

*

Crane looked at the mileage counter on the speedometer. 'How far behind were we when the tracker stopped?'

'Twelve miles.'

Crane thought for a moment and said, 'Okay, let's stay on this road and see what happens twelve miles from now.'

Crane immediately eased up on the accelerator when Daniella said, 'The Nerja exit is the nearest to our twelve miles,' and Crane turned off the road with an, 'Okay, we've nothing to lose.'

As they approached the town, he caught sight of the stretch of water running into a river that had attracted Bradley. Just as they passed by, Daniella called out excitedly, 'Hey, there's a red car with a black top in the water.'

Crane slammed on the brakes, reversed a few metres and, leaning across Daniella, said, 'That's it! My car. I wonder what it's doing down there?'

Crane pocketed the Glock handgun and left Daniella inside the parked Rover. Alert to any possible danger, he walked cautiously down the shallow gradient pausing now and then, listening intently. Filled with suspicion, he moved forward. His eyes were like hawks as they darted to and fro. When at last he became satisfied that he was alone, he waded up to the Mustang and peered inside. He could see the fuse cover resting on the passenger seat and, after a moment's thought, guessed just what Bradley may have been up to. He figured that Bradley had realised his idea had backfired so had scampered off to get help.

He sprinted back to the Rover. In the distance, he could

see an illuminated service station sign that towered into the sky and surmised that Bradley was probably there right now. He decided it best to keep well out of the way and u-turned the Rover, taking it further away and completely out of sight.

*

Bradley felt that he was in luck. With the help of another customer – acting as translator – together with a fist full of euros, the mechanic agreed to drop everything and tow the Mustang out of the water. Bradley climbed into a large pick-up truck and directed the mechanic the short distance down the road.

*

Hidden behind a large spread of bushes, Crane looked on as the vehicle, under Bradley's watchful eye, was brought back onto the road and towed away in the direction of the service station. When they were out of sight, Crane hurried back to the Rover and headed after them. Daniella said, 'Now that he is immobile, do you think it's time to bring in the police?'

Crane's eyes were fixed on the distant tow truck and as it turned into the garage, nodded and said, 'I think so.'

*

Bradley watched as two men uncoupled the tow rope and pushed the Mustang into one of the workshops. When they closed the doors, he stayed outside looking through the glass panels as a blow heater was directed underneath the vehicle.

With a hand firmly grasping the holdall, Bradley paced up and down the forecourt when suddenly he stopped and stared in disbelief as the Rover, that he had been so desperate to avoid, cruised past the service station. This time panic set in; he felt trapped. His eyes, wide with foreboding, fell upon the open door of the tow truck; a set of keys dangled enticingly from the ignition. For the first time in weeks, thoughts of the Mustang were abandoned. In an instant he was behind the wheel of the tow truck, firing up the engine and crashing it into gear, tore away from the forecourt in the opposite direction.

One of the men in the workshop saw what happened, nudged his companion and immediately phoned the police. Bradley surmised that this would happen and resolved to abandon the truck as soon as practical and concentrate in putting some distance between himself and Crane.

*

When he caught sight of Bradley standing on the garage forecourt, Crane was unsure whether his enemy had spotted him in the Rover and so slowed down, keeping an eye on the rear-view mirror. However, there was no doubt that he had been seen, when he saw the tow truck charge out of the service station and dash off in the opposite direction. Crane became entangled in traffic as he circumnavigated the nearby roundabout before he was able to follow in pursuit.

It seemed only minutes, but minutes can be vital. Crane saw the tow truck parked in a lay-by a few kilometres further down the road. A police car stood adjacent to it; the truck had obviously been abandoned. Crane drove around the area for some time in a vain hope of catching sight of Bradley, but without success. It was getting late and there would be no chance of finding him in the dark, so Crane suggested they find a hotel for the night.

The following morning, Crane paid a visit to the service station and with the help of an interpreter from the hotel, he showed the mechanic his registration documents and explained the situation. He also arranged for the car to be shipped back to England together with its original number plates. With that out of the way, Crane and Daniella began to relax as they drove to Bilbao and took the overnight ferry back to Portsmouth. Within a little over two hours of the ferry docking, they were turning into Palmers Rise and right back into trouble.

# CHAPTER TWENTY NINE

Crane stopped the car at the end of his lane and got out. Daniella looked at him quizzically and he said, 'I'm just going to check the rear entrance of the cottage to make sure everything is okay,' and he disappeared into the bushes. Crane was well used to this trail, which he had created some time ago. He walked quickly and stealthily through trees and scrubland until he had a clear view of the rear of his cottage. His prudence had paid off. He seethed when he saw a burly-looking stranger, a brute of a man, leaning back lazily on one of the patio chairs; it was though he owned the place. Crane remained quietly in position and watched for a few moments, in case others were around; there were none. The stranger, totally oblivious to Crane's presence, was smoking a cigarette and swigging beer from a can until, eventually he drained the can and carelessly tossed it to one side, to join a collection of other empties on the lawn. He was about to open another can when Crane crept up behind and said quietly in his ear, 'I do hope you're going to pick up those empties before you leave.'

Immediately the startled man turned his head and tried to rise but Crane anticipated this and gripping his shoulders, pulled him back hard. The man lost his balance and fell backwards in the chair onto the patio. Crane kicked the chair out of the way, leaving him splayed out like a huge turtle on its back and placed a booted foot across his neck. 'You just keep very still,' Crane hissed, 'or I'll break your windpipe!'

Not daring to move, the stranger looked up at Crane as he snarled angrily, 'Where's Bradley?'

'He's gone out to get something to eat,' gasped the big man, still getting over the shock of being trapped.

'Anyone else around besides you?'

'No, just me and him.'

Crane was concerned that Daniella had been left alone in the car at the end of the lane. He considered how best to secure Bradley's new henchman before he went back for her.

\*

Daniella felt tired and fidgety after the long journey. It was warm weather and, with the car's engine switched off, the air conditioning was inactive. She flipped the sun visor down. Looking in the mirror, she was not impressed by its reflection. A pair of weary eyes stared back and she dabbed them with a moist tissue. They suddenly widened with fear when a car turned into the lane and screeched to a halt behind. It was Bradley.

In a panic to leave, Daniella's hand scrambled at the door lock, but Bradley was too quick. By the time she got out of the Rover, he was up close. He snatched at her wrist, gripping it tight. In his other hand, he held a long-bladed knife which he waved around threateningly in front of her. 'Where's Crane?' he snapped.

Before she could utter a word, he nodded towards the bushes and said with a sickly grin, 'Taken his secret path, eh? We'd better join him then.'

He held the knife on Daniella's back as he pushed and shoved her along the lane towards the cottage.

'Anyone home?' Bradley called out cockily as they moved towards the rear of the cottage.

Crane still had his foot resting on the burly stranger's neck. On hearing the familiar voice, he suddenly increased the pressure and the man lost consciousness. He turned and saw Bradley standing behind Daniella, holding the knife against her neck. Bradley looked impassively down at his henchman and said calmly to Crane, 'Here we are again. Where's the Mustang?'

It was the last thing Crane expected him to say. He regarded him for a moment. He had the look of a spoilt child; a very dangerous spoilt child and Crane, not for the first time, realised that he was dealing with someone who was unhinged; mentally unstable.

'Where you left it; in Spain.'

Bradley's eyes glared hatefully, 'Don't lie to me; it left there three days ago. Lie to me again and I'll draw this knife across her throat. Now where is it?'

Crane tried to play for time and said, 'Let her go and I'll tell you.'

'I'll think about that when I'm seated in that Mustang.'

'Okay, it's on its way; the last I heard it had just crossed the French border.'

'And when exactly will it arrive here? And don't bullshit me!'

'Subject to channel crossing, it's should arrive early this evening.'

'That's better.'

Bradley's henchman stirred and rubbing his neck got to

343

his feet. Bradley flicked a glance in his direction and said casually, as though the man had just appeared on the scene, 'Ah you're with us, Bruno; it seems as though you've already met Crane.'

Bruno seethed as his head cleared and as his eyes began to focus on the trio, they settled on Crane. He balled his fists and began to move towards Crane, but Bradley had anticipated this move and said, 'Later, Bruno, later. Fetch me one of the guns from the kitchen table and while you're about it you'd better pocket one of them.'

Without taking his scowling eyes off Crane, Bruno grunted an assent and did as he was told, then disappeared through the patio door. Within seconds he was handing Bradley a 9mm Sig Sauer Model 224 semi-automatic. Bradley took the weapon and tucked the knife into a sheaf, that was hanging from his belt and he said, 'That's better.'

He regarded the weapon briefly, looked up and commented, 'One of the handguns that the SAS favour I believe.'

Crane responded with, 'Is that a fact?'

Bradley looked Crane square in the face and said deliberately, 'Yes, it is!'

Without taking his eyes off Crane and Daniella, Bradley called Bruno over and said, 'There are two cars at the end of the lane, mine and theirs. Bring them up this end.'

With Bruno gone to do his bidding, Bradley waved the gun towards the patio table and said, 'Both of you, sit yourselves down.'

Crane wishing to keep the conversation going said, 'I'm curious. Tell me, how did you get away from Nerja?'

Bradley could not help looking smug as he replied, 'Taxi.

I saw it parked in the lay-by. I pulled up right behind it, paid him double the fare and he took me, no questions asked, straight to Malaga Airport. Surely you must realise by now that nobody gets the better of me; not even you!'

This was the first time that Crane was face to face for a tête-à-tête with Bradley. He realised that this was a fanatical egotist; a man who must have his own way at all costs. A man he knew to be an opportunistic, evil, cold-blooded killer, kidnapper and thief, but Crane was content to let Bradley enthuse about himself. With Bruno out of the way for a few moments, Crane hoped to catch Bradley off-guard, but the madman's ice-blue, piercing eyes, remained unblinking. They were firmly fixed on Crane's face, together with the gun held in a rock-steady hand.

*

It was a clear blue sky on a late September afternoon and the whole area was basking in warm sunshine. For the first time in months, Penny felt relaxed and happy as she turned her red Mini Cooper into Palmers Rise. Her forthcoming marriage to Girard was high on her agenda and she began delivering invitations to a small group of people she hoped would be able to attend. She was surprised when pulling up outside *Bramble View*, Crane's cottage, to find three cars parked outside. As she rattled on the letterbox, Andrew clambered out of the back seat of the Mini and stood by her side. Penny's second surprise came in the form of the burly frame of Bruno, who stood in the door frame with a facial expression like a tight shoe. 'Is Jack around?' she enquired hesitantly.

Without a word of reply, Bruno nodded his head and motioned her to come in. Penny, with Andrew clutching her hand, glanced around uncertainly before stepping inside and inching past the well-built doorman. At the end of the narrow hall she entered the lounge and seeing the patio doors wide open walked towards them. Stepping outside, she froze and a look of horror spread across her face when she saw Bradley.

'Well, well, what a nice surprise,' the unsmiling Bradley said. 'I was going to get around to you next, but as you are here it saves me the bother.'

Penny was too shocked to answer. Instead she turned her head towards Crane and Daniella, who were seated at the garden table and gave them a pleading look.

Bradley gestured with the gun and said, 'You can join them.'

Penny pulled out an empty chair and sat down. Andrew shuffled up close beside her, looked quickly around and then, looked down and kept his eyes focused on his feet.

Bruno made an appearance from the patio doors. He was sucking beer noisily from a can. Traces of the liquid ran down either side of his mouth, dribbling down his chin and onto his chest. This seemed to irk Bradley who commented, 'The object of drinking is to aim for your main orifice without spilling any of it.'

Bruno was unruffled as he came out from behind the can for air, belched and replied, 'Practice makes perfect.'

Bradley's eyes hardened, but he let the subject drop.

Daniella stood up, glared at Bradley and said firmly, 'I need to use the toilet.'

'Okay, I'm sure you know where it is and no funny

business; Bruno will be keeping an eye on you,' and looking at Bruno said, 'won't you, Bruno?'

A grunted reply escaped from Bruno's mouth as he upended the beer can and poured the remainder of its contents down his throat. As he followed Daniella inside, he crushed the empty can in his fist and tossed it over his shoulder to join the pile of empties on the grass. When they returned to the patio, Bradley's ears suddenly picked up the sound of an approaching vehicle and, looking at Bruno, said, 'I'm just going to see if that's my delivery. Keep your eye on this lot – if Crane gets up shoot him.'

The big lout nodded, removed the handgun from his pocket and grunted a, 'Yeah.'

After Bradley had left, Crane said to Bruno, 'Ever shot anyone before?'

'What's it to you?'

'Just curious; you're ex-army, right?'

'What if I am?'

With Bradley out of the way, Crane was trying to grasp some kind of rapport with the reluctant Bruno and continued, 'I guess you might know some of the places that I've been to.'

'I don't think so.'

'Iraq, Afghanistan, for example.'

'You been there?'

'Yeah.'

Bruno was beginning to open up, 'When?'

'Right from the start, how about you?'

'Didn't do Iraq, but a couple of tours in Afghanistan; lost two good mates there.'

The sound of the transporter departing briefly interrupted the conversation and Crane continued, 'How did you meet Bradley?'

'Through someone I knew who did a bit of thieving for him. He asked me if I was interested in some easy money. I gave the fella my mobile number ages ago, but didn't hear anything until this bloke, Bradley Kemp, contacted me the other day.'

'That someone wasn't Ryan by any chance, was it?'

He looked at Crane askance and breathed out a quizzical, 'Yeah... do you know him?'

'Sort of. Bradley owed him money, but he received a long-bladed knife, pinning him to the seat of his car, in lieu.'

Bruno leant against the wall of the building; he was all attentive now, 'How do you know all this?'

'It was me who found him and called the emergency services. He is probably still in Southend Hospital. And he wasn't the first.'

Bruno looked at Crane in disbelief. He glanced at Daniella who nodded in confirmation of the statement. Crane went on to tell Bruno how he first became involved with Bradley and about Davy Porter who was not as lucky as Ryan and died from a fatal knife wound.

Bruno suddenly realised that the transporter had departed some twenty minutes ago and Bradley had not reappeared. He felt disappointed. He wanted Bradley to appear and refute all that Crane had just told him. In his mind he had already spent the money that had been offered for his services. A chirping noise resounded from his jacket pocket, interrupting his thoughts. His free hand dipped in and sought out the mobile; the call was from Bradley.

'Sorry, Bruno, I had to leave in a hurry; paperwork and all that.' The voice sounded relaxed and friendly. 'Put a bullet in Crane and the women; they deserve it and I'll settle up with you this evening, okay?'

'How much?' Bruno asked.

'Five grand each; that's fifteen grand. Just leave their bodies where they fall and fifteen grand cash is yours.'

'Fifteen grand?'

'Cash!'

'Where do I meet you?'

'Tonight, say eleven o'clock, at the seafront car park, next to the Aquarium. You know the one – opposite the Kursaal.'

'I know where it is; you'll have the cash with you?'

There was laughter in Bradley's voice as he said, 'Of course I will.' He paused for a second and added, 'By the way, you'd better take some photos as proof of their demise.'

Bruno's eyes were fixed on the seated trio as he spoke with Bradley.

'No problem, consider it done then. See you there.'

# CHAPTER THIRTY

Bradley was pleased with himself. People always did what he told them to do and he was confident that Bruno would follow his instructions and would rid him of Crane and the two women. In his mind, he felt secure with the knowledge, that he had again regained possession, of the iconic Mustang, for the last time. He had spent the last two nights at a hotel in Westcliff-on-Sea. On his instructions, the transporter driver, followed his car to the hotel. He was gleefully contented as he confidently instructed the driver to offload the Mustang into the hotel car park.

\*

Bruno pocketed the mobile phone, walked over to Crane and said, 'Whereabouts was Ryan when Bradley knifed him?'

Crane paused for a moment before he replied, 'Ryan drove his car into the parking area on the seafront, next to the aquarium. Bradley owed him money and Ryan had gone there expecting to collect. I saw him get into the passenger seat of Bradley's BMW but it was only seconds before Bradley got out and drove off in Ryan's Mondeo.'

Bruno looked sceptical, 'How can you be sure it was Bradley?'

'I was there with Daniella.'

Bruno threw a glance at her and she nodded in agreement.

'Anyway,' Crane continued, 'he survived, thanks to Daniella here; she's a doctor. Ryan was lucky but he is still in Southend Hospital.'

Bruno was quiet for a moment before saying, 'I'm supposed to be meeting Bradley this evening, at that very same car park, after getting rid of you lot.'

Daniella and Penny glanced at each other and shifted uneasily in their chairs. Crane looked at him as he continued, 'He wants me to take photos to prove that I've done his dirty deed. I'm not into cold-blooded murder. I only got involved because Bradley said he wanted protection.'

Bruno checked his watch; it was six pm. He put the handgun in his jacket pocket and said, 'Got any ketchup?'

Sounding somewhat relieved, Daniella called out, 'Top of the cupboard – next to the sink.'

Bruno set to work. He dabbed the ketchup on all of them, to make it look as though they had been shot in the head. Young Andrew looked on with curiosity and of course he had to be included too. Bruno took several pictures with his mobile phone, all from various angles. They all agreed that the images looked impressive enough to fool anybody.

When the photoshoot had finished, Daniella and Penny, with their hearts still thumping, leant back in easy chairs quaffing double measures of Scotch whisky. After Bruno had finished collecting up the empty beer cans, Crane handed him a protective vest, 'Here you'd better wear this, it may come in handy.'

Bruno cast a glance at the item, but scoffed at the idea, 'Thanks, but I have the advantage of knowing what to expect.'

Crane's words took on a serious tone as he said, 'He's a very dangerous man to play with; cunning and unpredictable and he can also think fast on his feet. If he smells a rat and even if he doesn't, well you just be careful, that's all. I'll be watching from a safe distance in the hope that I can find out where he left my car.'

*

Bruno drove into the car park just before the appointed hour. Bradley was already there, waiting, like a spider at the corner of his web. Upon seeing Bruno's car enter, he flashed his headlamps twice and Bruno pulled up alongside a dark-coloured Range Rover. Before he had time to switch off the engine, Bruno felt a cool rush of air swirl around the car as the rear door swung wide open. Like a wraith, Bradley slithered inside and positioned himself directly behind Bruno, who sat in the driver's seat. Bruno instantly recalled with trepidation what he had been told and he began to feel uncomfortable with Bradley sitting behind. A shiver ran down the big man's spine and he wished he had taken Crane's advice and worn the protective vest.

Bruno stared into the rear-view mirror; Bradley's face appeared ethereal in the reflected lighting of the car park. He sat on the edge of the rear seat with a small neat holdall perched across his lap. Bruno killed the engine. Bradley leant forward and rested an arm on the top of Bruno's seat. A calm, hushed voice said, 'Photos.'

Bruno's hand fumbled in his jacket pocket and produced the mobile phone. After selecting the picture mode, he turned in his seat and held it aloft in the palm of his hand. Bradley took the mobile and scrutinised the pictures. After a moment, Bradley said softly, 'The child; the little boy – you killed him too?'

Bruno's voice faltered slightly as he replied, 'Well, it err, seemed like the thing to do.'

Bradley was quiet for a moment. In the silence that followed, Bruno felt apprehensive and tense as he recalled Crane's warning. His hand slowly fingered its way towards his jacket pocket. His ears were fine-tuned to the papery sound of money leaving a holdall, or the unsheathing of a knife. Suddenly his ears picked up the short, sharp, ripping sound of a zip fastener, as Bradley opened his holdall and uttered a prolonged, 'Hmmm… '

With Bradley's razor sharp long knife in mind, Bruno half turned and edged forward in his seat. The heel of his right hand brushed against the butt of his gun. It was ready for action. There was no need to pull the slide back. All he had to do was flip the safety off and thumb back the hammer; a noiseless one-handed job. But he was too late. Two bullets ripped noiselessly through the back of his seat, from a suppressed handgun, and Bruno slumped forward.

Bradley's shadowy figure slipped wraithlike out of Bruno's car then sidled back into the Range Rover parked alongside. He tossed the holdall on the front passenger seat then his hand groped towards the dashboard for the keys, which he had left dangling in the ignition. They were not there. Puzzled, he dived both hands simultaneously into his jacket pockets. They were empty. He was about to lean over to one side to check a trouser pocket, when a voice from behind made the hairs on the back of his neck stand on end. 'Looking for these?'

Crane sat in the back seat rattling the small bunch of keys. Bradley's hand darted towards the holdall, but froze when the menacing voice said, 'Move another inch and I'll blow your head clean off of your shoulders. Now sit up straight.'

Bradley straightened up and said defiantly, 'What now?'

'What have you done to Bruno?'

'Put a bullet in the lying bastard; he showed me pictures of you – dead!'

'Well, I don't share your disappointment.'

Crane pulled out his mobile and called Daniella, 'Bruno's in his car with a bullet in the back; go and see what you can do for him and get an ambulance.'

In the dim light, Bradley's eyes were sharply focused on Crane using his mobile. It was an opportune moment. Without hesitation, he snatched his bag and bolted out of the door ignoring Crane's shouts of, 'Stop or I'll shoot!'

He need not have worried, Crane didn't even have a gun, but then Bradley did not know that, as he dodged and weaved his way across the car park towards the edge of the beach. Without hesitation, Crane scrambled out of the rear door. He gave chase, running into a myriad of shadows. He came to a halt, staring ahead looking and listening for signs of movement. He did not have long to wait. A sudden flash, followed by a ricochet, reminded him that he was standing near a lamp post and could easily be seen. Two more flashes followed. He ran in the direction, where he had seen the flash from the gun and then halted once more. He fell to the ground as two more flashes appeared. He now regretted not searching for Bruno's hand gun, before giving chase, but had he done that, he might have lost Bradley's trail altogether. Keeping low, Crane moved nearer to the latest flash, noting that five bullets had been spent; he guessed that the gun had a ten round magazine – five shots to go, unless Bradley had a spare clip.

Crane kept low, staying in a crouching position, listening. A light inshore breeze rustled past his ears, making it difficult for him to any detect movement. A brief lull was interrupted by a sudden raucous sound of the emergency services as they were driving into the car park. Then all was quiet until the sound of feet, scurrying across the sand, propelled him to move forward. The sound stopped and so did Crane. He had a feeling he was being lured. Crane realised it was futile to make sense of a chase in the dark and silently cursed himself for ignoring his own advice, that of the bullet proof vest which he had offered earlier to the unfortunate Bruno.

Crane put himself in Bradley's position. He surmised that Bradley probably realised, by now, that he was being followed by someone who was unarmed and who would lie in wait and attack from the rear. His lack of a protective vest, would make Bradley's task much easier.

Disappointed, Crane thought it prudent to return to the car park. As he neared, the ambulance crew were stretchering Bruno on board and Chief Inspector Harris was talking to Daniella. Their conversation was interrupted by the sound of Crane's leather shoes slapping hurriedly across the tarmac and they turned in his direction as he jogged towards them.

'Major Crane,' the Inspector began.

'It's 'Mr' now, Inspector – there's an armed man in the

shadows along the edge of the foreshore. I haven't got time to explain now but… '

'Are you getting involved in police matters, Mr Crane?'

Crane realised he needed to be tactful and replied, 'No, of course not, it's the man who stole my car. He also shot the guy in the Peugeot. I think a chopper would be useful and…'

'One is already on its way, Mr Crane. I believe you can leave things to us from now on.'

'It's not quite that simple. I know what he looks like and with due respect Chief Inspector, you don't!'

CI Harris gave a long, hard accusing look at Crane and said, 'You're not armed – are you?'

Crane smiled and said, 'Not this time. Are you offering?'

There was a touch of exasperation in Harris's voice as he said, 'Now, Major, erm, Mr Crane… '

Crane interrupted with, 'Look, this is who you are dealing with. He's just shot a man here in this car park. He killed a man in Felixstowe. He knifed a man who now lies seriously injured in Southend Hospital. He's wanted for murder in France, where he killed an English woman and buried her. He killed two gendarmes and seriously injured another. He did this in order to free a man on bail who himself was awaiting trial for kidnapping, and, as for the French police, they don't know what he looks like either.'

Harris's eyes narrowed as he said, 'Kidnapping? Do you know anything about the young girl, Samantha, who was freed by someone called Jack… ' he paused for a few seconds and added with a smile, 'it was you, wasn't it, Jack Crane?'

'You know my background and I'd rather you kept quiet about that.'

Harris nodded solemnly and said, 'That changes

everything. I'm throwing the rule book away for now and I'll accept any help that you can give us.'

Their conversation was drowned by the arrival of a police helicopter. Straight away its searchlights and infrared cameras began scouring the area.

*

Crane's theory was right. Bradley had found an ideal niche in which to conceal himself, where he could await his pursuer to pass by and then finish him off once and for all. He waited patiently in his hiding place, but to no avail.

The approaching helicopter, all noise and swirling lights, hovered close by. Bradley was irritated by the intense beams sweeping and poking its bright lights into dark recesses. The machine churned up the shadows around the coastline, ripping out the darkness in its wake but, for Bradley, the up side was that he could clearly see there was no sign of Crane. He figured he would be better off edging his way towards the brightly lit road, amongst the noise and clamour of the amusement arcades. He dodged in and out of the shadows, stealthily hastening his way along the seafront until he came to the pier. He swiftly crossed the road to mingle with an eager chatting crowd, some of whom had their arms raised and were looking skywards, pointing and poking towards the aircraft as it hovered opposite.

It was a Saturday evening and, as usual, there were many people milling around the busy seaside town. This made it very easy for Bradley to get lost amongst the crowd.

Crane turned to Harris and said, 'It's a long-shot, but if I wander along the other side of the road, perhaps you can get the chopper to throw the lights in that area.'

Harris seemed resigned to Crane taking charge and said, 'I suppose it's worth a try.'

Harris gave Crane a fixed-frequency mobile and said, 'Look, don't take any chances and keep in touch.'

'Thanks.'

And on a cautionary note Harris added, 'By the way, that thing is signed for, so don't lose it.'

As Crane started to move off, Daniella quickly sidled up and said, 'Bruno's dead, bullet in his heart. Do take care.'

Crane nodded solemnly as Daniella threw her arms around him and whispered in his ear as she embraced him, 'You may need this.' He felt something drop into his jacket pocket; it was Bruno's handgun. She had removed it from Bruno's clenched fist before the emergency services had turned up. Daniella stood for a moment, watching intently, as Crane strode off and disappeared into the throng, lining the pavements. She was reluctant to go back to the cottage and elected to stay in the company of Harris until she heard from Crane.

Crane tried to brush aside the thought that his next move was something of a lost cause but he felt that he had to try it. One thing was for certain, he knew Bradley's vehicle remained in the car park which meant the criminal would be on foot. Crane walked hurriedly along the pavement. Coloured lights flashed, shimmered and winked as he passed through the Saturday night crowds of people, many of whom were still grouped together in a fixed stare, standing and looking upwards, wondering what was going on. He kept his head down, but his eyes were looking up, scanning as many faces as possible as he traversed the pathway for half a mile, from the Kursaal to the Palace Hotel, but he had seen nothing of his adversary. It was here that his nostrils caught something that stirred his gastric juices. It was the smell of fish and chips, wafting enticingly through the evening air. Crane could not resist throwing a hungry glance through the open door of the late night premises and in doing so, he stopped in his tracks. He witnessed Bradley, standing in line as bold as brass, waiting to be served.

Crane dodged back into the shadows. He knew there would be gunplay if he were spotted and people could get hurt. He reached for the mobile given to him by Harris but, for the safety of all concerned, he thought it best to play down the situation and said briefly into the phone, 'I'm on to him,' and, without waiting for a reply, he switched off the device.

Within minutes, Bradley left the shop with his fingers delving, greedily into the wrapping, totally unaware that Crane was on his trail and following at a distance. To the casual observer, Bradley would not have attracted a second glance as he casually ambled up Pier Hill towards the High Street. By this time, he had finished eating and tidily popped the spent wrappings into a wastepaper bin.

Meanwhile Harris had given the helicopter pilot instructions to stand down and return to base in Chelmsford. Upon hearing the chatter of the rotors above, Bradley looked up and a surge of triumph swept through him as he caught a glimpse of the machine passing high overhead, illuminated only by its tell-tale aviation lights. Now and again, he would pause and turn round. If by any chance he saw Crane, he would have been looking at a stooped old man ambling along with an exaggerated way of walking, at a safe distance.

Ever cautious, Bradley looked behind before turning off the High Street into a side road. Crane, not far behind, blended well into the background, weaving in and out of small groups of people who were laughing and chattering boisterously. Others paused outside the stores, doing occasional window shopping. The side road attracted fewer people and Crane altered his gait in the hope that this would allay any suspicions, that Bradley may have about being followed.

Bradley felt more exposed away from the crowds as he strode between rows of tall buildings and shops in Alexander Street and he began to quicken his pace towards the Westcliff area. Crane also speeded up. It was his guess that, wherever Bradley was staying, the Mustang would be nearby. It was Crane's intention to discover this before calling in the police but he had to make sure.

Crane was trailing behind Bradley at about seventy-five metres when, in the dim street lights, he saw a woman suddenly appear from one of the houses. After a few paces a man appeared to join her and they walked side by side for a while until suddenly they both disappeared from view. Crane took little notice of this; his mind was focused on the man who was ahead of them – Bradley.

A few cars continued to pass by, illuminating the road ahead, but one particular vehicle began to slow down and Bradley, clearly in view of the car's headlamps, raised his arm – it was a cab. Crane swore under his breath. The vehicle was too far away for him to identify and he immediately quickened his pace. He hoped, at the very least, to see where it would turn off. It was too late. The cab pulled away smartly and faded into a light ground mist at the end of the lengthy road. It could have gone anywhere. He slowed his pace when he came near to the spot, a smooth grassy area, where he had seen the couple together. They had vanished but suddenly he heard stifled breathing. Pausing, he stepped back a few paces. In the dim street lights he could see the couple again. They were still on the ground but it appeared to Crane that the woman's arms were being held behind her back.

The man, his face in the shadows, leant forward and looked up towards Crane and grunted irritably, 'What do you want?'

'Nothing, I just wondered if everything was alright.'

'Yeah, why shouldn't it be?' And shaking the woman, he said, 'Tell him it's alright, dear.'

The woman winced slightly as she said, 'Yeah, yeah, it's alright.'

But in the dim light Crane saw abject fear in her eyes and he knew that she was not alright and was saying this under duress.

Crane stood for a moment pondering his next move, however a prompt for him to act, was provided by the man as he replied irritably, 'There! You've got your answer, now fuck off!'

The woman remained quiet but her eyes were watery and silently pleading, *"Please don't leave me."*

Crane remained still and said, 'You got a mobile?' Because you'll need to call an ambulance.'

The man's face emerged from the shadow again, 'What? What the fuck for?'

'Because nobody talks to me like that, especially a little shit head like you.'

The provocation worked. The man let go of the woman, sprang to his feet and with clenched fists moved quickly towards Crane saying, 'You're the one that's gonna need an ambulance.'

Crane side-stepped the lunge and, grabbing hold of the assailant's arm, swung him around violently then kneed him in the groin. As the attacker began to double up, Crane, still gripping his arm, forced him back upright again and brought the bully's elbow down heavily across his knee. 'Now you can call the ambulance. You need to get your arm re-set.'

The young woman struggled up. She was shaking nervously as she edged past the groaning man lying on the ground. She mumbled stifled thanks to Crane and said uncertainly, 'Please, can I walk to the end of the road with you?'

'Yes of course. You got far to go?'

'Not really, about fifteen minutes or so.'

'Okay, you look a bit shaken up, I'll see you back.'

'That's so kind of you, I hope I'm not putting you out.'

Crane was resigned to having lost Bradley and replied gently, 'No, not at all.'

'I've never seen that man before in my life. I only just left my friend's house when he seemed to appear from nowhere.'

Crane was frustrated at losing Bradley, but it was not her fault and he felt it appropriate to accompany her to where she lived. Within fifteen minutes, the woman seemed to be regaining her confidence and became quite talkative, until she stopped momentarily outside a large building. Crane looked up at the green fluorescent sign above the entrance; "Kent View Hotel". 'This is where I work and live,' she said. 'It's handy having a job with accommodation. You meet all kinds of people. A man came in earlier today; he had a beautiful American car that he kept going to look at.'

Most of her chattiness had passed over Crane's head, but now she had his full undivided attention.

'American car? What sort, erm, make?'

'I don't know; it was one of those with the top that comes down; a convertible, that's it. I saw it in the car park late this afternoon; a lovely red colour.'

Crane felt a surge of elation and said, 'Any idea of the man's name?'

'No, I wasn't on reception then.'

Not wishing to probe further, Crane checked his watch and said, 'Well I must go. Take care.'

The young woman thanked him profusely once more, before she traipsed up a set of broad paved steps and then disappeared through the hotel's plush main entrance.

Within seconds, Crane darted round to the Kent View Hotel car park. It was dimly lit, but there was no mistaking what he saw. Tucked away in a dark shadowy corner, was his Mustang. He walked over and stood in front of the car, transfixed for a moment and not believing his luck. It was all the confirmation that he needed and he could now inform Harris of Bradley's whereabouts. Reaching in his pocket, he pulled out the police mobile and switched it on, but when he heard a ground floor sash window being raised, he promptly put the instrument back into his pocket. Quickly and silently he shrank into the shadows of an overhanging tree. Apart from the gentle rattle of leaves, all was quiet for a brief moment. He stood listening, like a wild animal that has just sensed danger. Suddenly, his ears picked up the sound of footfalls treading on the car park's loose gravel surface. They were heading towards the Mustang.

In spite of the poor lighting, the outline was unmistakable. Bradley was carrying a holdall and there was what appeared to be a handgun, dangling from his other hand. It seemed as though he was about to do a moonlight flit. Crane eased the handgun from his jacket pocket and waited until he heard the audible metallic click of the car door being unlocked. Moving from the shadows he pointed the weapon at Bradley, 'That's as far as you go.'

Bradley found it difficult to hide his surprise and hesitated before he replied, 'Well, well, quite the resourceful adversary, aren't you, Crane?'

Crane stepped towards him, but without hesitation, Bradley threw the holdall violently towards Crane's gun and it clattered noisily to the ground. In the same instant, Bradley whipped up the silenced handgun and fired two rounds in quick succession towards Crane's vague outline. Crane was just as fast and, by then, he had scooped up the holdall then hurled it back with all his strength. Bradley's two bullets thudded harmlessly into the airborne bag, but the spent ammo did nothing to stop the bag from disarming Bradley as it crashed into him.

Both men were no more than four metres apart as they scrabbled on the ground, looking for their weapons, but to no avail. Their guns were swallowed up by the shadows.

Instinct took over Bradley. Like a greyhound he leapt up and ran towards the car park exit. Crane followed in hot pursuit. As he ran, Bradley unsheathed the long knife that was hanging from his belt. Within seconds he turned the corner of the building and unseen, flattened his body against the wall in a crouching position. He held the knife in a vice like grip, ready to lunge upwards into Crane's stomach as he passed. Crane turned the corner slightly wide and almost ran onto the blade. As he dodged out of the way, the knife's razor-sharp edge sliced through his trousers and slashed the top of his thigh, sending him careering sideways. Still gripping the knife Bradley leapt up and ran off, satisfied that he had at least done some damage, enabling him to put more distance between them.

Crane felt a warm trickle of blood running down his leg, but it only strengthened his resolve of getting Bradley once and for all. The clouds began to lift, revealing a bright vanilla moon. The moon outlined the retreating figure of Bradley, as he darted along the road at a high point overlooking the Thames Estuary. He disappeared behind a tall building; the Cliffs Pavilion, a local theatre. Crane followed and approached the Pavilion on the opposite side. He paused at the rear of the edifice and listened. A noise told him that Bradley was descending on the opposite side. Crane began to ease himself down the steep slope, but after a few steps he lost his footing on the dew-sodden surface and slid noiselessly down the grassy bank. He sat for a moment, eyes straining in the poor light. A pearly grey mist hugged the ground and the wet grass began to soak through his trousers. He got up carefully in time to see the outline of Bradley, some twenty-five metres opposite, carefully picking his way through the undergrowth of the incline.

Crane, ignoring the discomfort in his leg, made his way painfully to the road at the bottom of the slope. A crack of dawn, aided by a full moon, in a cloudless sky acted like a beacon. He stepped onto the pavement just in time to see Bradley, on the opposite side of the dual carriageway, clamber over the barrier and out of sight onto the beach.

By now the wound on Crane's leg was beginning to feel sore and throbbed as he hobbled across the road in pursuit, but as he approached the barrier, instead of leaping over, he peered cautiously over the top. He saw Bradley leaning against the wall, puffing and panting, gulping in lungfuls of air. It was getting lighter by the minute and Bradley's sinister-looking figure was no longer an outline. He looked up and caught sight of Crane, 'Nobody gets the better of me,' he spat breathlessly.

Crane was little better off. Blood from the wound on his leg had saturated his right trouser leg and he was beginning to feel weak. He straightened up and, in an effort to close the wound, he pulled the belt off from around his waist and strapped it tightly around the blood soaked thigh. He leaned on the barrier and looked out across the dawn-streaked Thames Estuary. He could see the tide coming in. He calculated that Bradley would have to get off the beach and back onto the pavement, within fifteen minutes or so, before the waves would start to lap around him. However, Bradley also realised this and decided to move nearer towards some steps. As he did so, he saw Crane binding his bloodied leg and grinned wolfishly as he clambered up onto the pavement. Crane's eyes followed Bradley's stealthy movements. Bradley mistook Crane's look of anticipation as a look of fear.

Crane was standing quite still. Confidence streamed through Bradley's body when he recognised a distinct advantage and moved predator-like towards Crane, as a jackal would advance upon a wounded animal. With eyes glowering hatred, he inched towards the immobile Crane. Slowly at first, in a semi-crouched position and then, when Crane didn't move, he quickened his pace until suddenly he charged forward like a madman. With his arm outstretched, holding the knife like a sword, he screamed out loud like a banshee, 'Nobody gets the better of me!'

In the distance blue flashing lights competed with the oncoming dawn and high-pitched sirens shattered the tranquillity of the shoreline. Approaching from above, the flutter of helicopter rotors added to the cacophony of noise, but neither man seemed aware of this.

Crane knew he was in no fit state to waste energy. Timing was all important. When Bradley's deadly blade was within inches, Crane turned, like a bullfighter, swivelling on his good leg. Crane felt Bradley's foul, hot panting breath as he swept past, blind with rage and stabbing viciously at the air with his razor-sharp knife. But within four strides, Bradley stopped dead and spun round. Without hesitation he made for his quarry once more, and like a panther in for the kill, leapt towards the immobile Crane. However, Crane's eyes had gauged every movement and his brain was fully alert to Bradley's incensed assault. In the last split second, Crane moved imperceptibly like a flash of light. His body twisted skilfully to one side as he flicked his foot out like a switch blade. Bradley tripped and faltered as he scraped past. Crane spun on his heel and pushed hard with both hands against Bradley's shoulders as he teetered forward, causing him to fall heavily to the ground. He lay there briefly before trying to get up. Accusing eyes stared up at Crane, but the fire had gone out of them as he gasped and cursed trying to get up. He lay flat on his back. His body quivered slightly as he tried to rise once more, but with a gasp, he slumped back down. He appeared to be stuck to the ground. From where he lay Bradley turned his head and looked around, as though trying to focus his eyes. His face, twisted in agony, was like a grotesque mask as he looked up scathingly at Crane.

Crane shuffled cautiously towards him and he could see that Bradley's hand no longer held the knife; only its hilt was visible through his open jacket. Bradley had impaled himself and now he groaned as he lay dying.

Crane stood for a while transfixed, staring down irreverently at the man behind so much evil, and he stayed until Bradley exhaled a final breath of air. Blue flashing lights suddenly appeared at the kerbside. Harris leapt out of a police car with Daniella following close behind. Harris strode hurriedly towards Crane and, when he noticed Crane's blood-drenched trouser leg, the officer barked orders into his mobile demanding an ambulance.

Harris stood with Crane as they looked down at the lifeless form of Bradley. Harris broke the silence with, 'Is he... dead?'

Through a sigh of exhaustion Crane replied, 'As mutton,' and he dipped a hand into his pocket and produced the police mobile. Harris palmed it and said, 'Good job you had it switched on. It took us a while to trace you.'

Daniella rushed up to Crane's side put an arm around his waist and with a sigh, breathed out an, 'It's over.'

*

A few stitches later, Crane was back in his cottage with Daniella and his cherished Mustang. Within a week, Crane and Daniella attended Penny and Girard's wedding, held at St Peters Church in Ashingdon. The Frenchman looked very much at home as he posed with his beautiful wife and little Andrew in tow, for photographs to be taken in front of the small unimposing building set on a hill overlooking the River Crouch. Just like King Canute and his Vikings, who built the little church in the far distant past, Girard was very pleased with his conquest and was sure they would lead an interesting life in the vicinity for many years to come.

After the wedding, Crane took Daniella to Southend Airport for her flight home to Romania. 'I can't say my stay with you has been uninteresting, but please, next time… '

Crane grinned hugely as he looked at her attractive smiling face and interrupted with, 'There's going to be a next time?'

'Oh yes, you'd better believe it! Next time I'm planning to find work in your country. I could end up being your local doctor and maybe have you all to myself.'

'You're not put off with all this erm… ?'

'No! Only the next time we meet and it will be very soon, perhaps things will be a little less, erm… less life threatening? Is that the correct expression?'

# AUTHOR'S NOTE

During my years as a motorhome dealer, I had six vehicles stolen. After each theft I tightened the security until there were no further thefts. Nowadays keys are all important, but if someone is determined to steal a vehicle, they will. Trackers are an excellent device in helping to recover stolen vehicles, but are expensive and the time in reporting the theft is crucial. If you are away and you are unaware that your vehicle has been taken, it would leave the thieves plenty of time to locate and remove the tracker.

There is only one device I know of that would inhibit theft; lockable tyre deflators. A minimum of two would be sufficient. They are inexpensive and once locked in position, they will deflate a tyre in less than half a mile. No thief would want to bother changing a wheel – let alone two or more – on a hot vehicle.

I actually came across such a Rover 620 as mentioned in the story; I took it in part exchange. When I sold it, my regrets were allowing a prospective buyer to take the wheel. I did not realise how he would drive and had to remind him to 'take it easy'. The dents from my feet may still be in the carpet – if not the floor-pan. Secondly, I should have kept a copy of the glossy motoring magazine article referring to this awesome beast.